Praise for
THE SECOND OPINION

"A heart-pounding medical thriller...satisfying, expertly paced [with] enough suspense to keep readers happily turning the pages." —*Boston Globe*

"The novel is not merely a thriller but also an exploration of its central character's unique gifts and her determination to communicate with her comatose father despite overwhelming odds. Another winner from a consistently fine writer." —*Booklist*

"A splendid novel." —*Gl... ...ail* (Canada)

"An exciting ... ...is full of surprises and captures the intense atmosphere of the White House, how the medical system works, and how the 25th Amendment could be brought into play. I thoroughly enjoyed it." —President Bill Clinton

"An incredibly realistic, frightening thriller that is every White House doctor's nightmare."

—Dr. E. Connie Mariano,
White House Physician 1992–2001

MORE...

"Endlessly entertaining…the roller-coaster ride of a plot builds to an undeniably shocking conclusion."
—*Publishers Weekly*

"If medical thrillers are what you're after, Palmer delivers."
—*Booklist*

THE FIFTH VIAL

"An ingenious medical thriller, suspenseful and cleverly plotted." —Kathy Reichs, author of *Break No Bones*

"A terrifying vision of the Hippocratic Oath gone very wrong."
—*Entertainment Weekly*

"Palmer taps a real medical issue for storytelling thrills."
—*Boston* magazine

"A tale set at the very edge of our medical knowledge. I loved it!"
—Tess Gerritsen

"Palmer is adept at tapping into people's natural fear of disease, doctors, and hospitals and converting that fear into unnerving suspense."
—*Booklist*

"In his entertaining twelfth medical suspense novel…Palmer, himself an M.D., does a good job of informing the reader on an important ethical issue."
—*Publishers Weekly*

Also by
MICHAEL PALMER

THE
SECOND
OPINION

MICHAEL PALMER

St. Martin's Paperbacks

This is a work of fiction. All of the characters, organizations, and events
portrayed in this novel are either products of the author's imagination or
are used fictitiously.

THE SECOND OPINION

Copyright © 2009 by Michael Palmer.
Excerpt from *The Last Surgeon* copyright © 2009 by Michael Palmer.

Cover photograph © Brownstock Inc./Alamy

For information address St. Martin's Press, 175 Fifth Avenue, New York,
NY 10010.

Library of Congress Catalog Card Number: 2008040693

ISBN: 978-0-312-93776-8

Printed in the United States of America

St. Martin's Press hardcover edition / February 2009
St. Martin's Paperbacks edition / January 2010

St. Martin's Paperbacks are published by St. Martin's Press, 175 Fifth
Avenue, New York, NY 10010.

10 9 8 7 6 5 4 3 2 1

To Jane-Elisabeth Jakuc,
for more than three decades a worker of miracles
for special-needs children, and to her hench-veggies,
Steve Lyne, Kathy Faria, Chesley Wendth,
Judy Seligman, Cara Morine, Jake and Dan O'Hara,
Elsa Abele, and all the rest of the staff,
past and present, of the magical Corwin-Russell
School at Broccoli Hall

ACKNOWLEDGMENTS

My deepest thanks to everyone at St. Martin's Press, especially my brilliant editor, Jen Enderlin, and Matthew Shear, Matthew Baldacci, and Sally Richardson.

Thanks, too, to everyone at the Jane Rotrosen Agency—especially Jane, Meg, Don, Michael, and Peggy. Thirty years, and I never once even considered changing agencies.

In addition, my deepest gratitude to Dr. Steve Defossez and his staff at the Beverly Hospital Imaging Center; Kate Bowditch of the Charles River Watershed Association; Daniel, Matt, Susan, Donna, Ethan, Chef Bill, Kate, Howard, Sensei Howard, and Robin, for the ideas and readings; Luke, for the inspiration; Stanley, for the phone calls, the carrots, and the sticks; hlkt, for the puzzling initials and the example of how good a doctor can be; Bill Wilson, Dr. Bob Smith, and their friends, who have taught me all the tricks of the trade.

And special thanks to Trish Psarreas, writer, philosopher, and enthusiastic lover of all things Greek. Seven stars to you.

PROLOGUE

"I'm afraid I have some bad news."

Hayley Long, just two weeks past her fifty-first birthday, heard her physician's words as if they were being spoken through a long steel tube.

I'm afraid I have some bad news. . . .

She wondered fleetingly how many thousands of people heard the same thing from their doctor every day? How many patients every hour, maybe every minute, rode those words screeching through a sudden right-angle turn in their lives.

I'm afraid . . .

Stephen Bibby, a graduate of Emory Med, had been her physician since a bout of pneumonia twenty or so years ago. He was a man Hayley respected, if for no other reason than that Bibby knew his limitations and never hesitated to make a phone call and arrange a specialist referral for a second opinion.

Hayley felt a wave of nausea sweep over her, and thought for a moment she was going to have to excuse herself to go and get sick even before she found out precisely what she was up against. She made a largely unsuccessful attempt at a calming breath, and tried to maintain an even gaze.

"It's cancer?"

Hayley heard the word in her own voice, but couldn't believe she had actually uttered it. Her thoughts wouldn't stay still.

Cancer . . . How could that be? . . . Oh, God, no.

Her initial symptom had been nothing more than an annoying sequence of belly pain and gas. She almost hadn't even bothered to mention them to her executive assistant. He was the one who had talked her into calling Bibby. It was his fault.

The MRI Bibby had requested was of her abdomen.

Cancer.

The dizziness and nausea intensified.

David didn't handle illness at all well, in himself or others, but at some point she would have to tell him. Not yet, though. Not until all the data were in. He was off skippering his boat in a round-the-world race—his lifetime dream. He had lost his first wife to a brain aneurysm, and had waited more than ten years before marrying again.

Now this.

She had to tell him soon, but not yet.

Bibby, a Southern gentleman in his early sixties, looked toward the door as if hoping that another doctor would march into the office and take over.

"I asked, is it cancer?"

Biting at his lip, the physician nodded.

"Operable?" she asked.

Come on, Stephen! Help me out here!

"I . . . I don't know. It looks to have started in your pancreas. That's the organ which—"

"I know what the pancreas is. I hear Jimmy Carter talking about pancreatic cancer every time I turn on the damn TV. Has it spread?"

"It's . . . it *appears* to be in some places in your liver."

Bibby turned on his computer with a click of his mouse and rotated it so Hayley could see. A child could have picked out the cancer in her MRI—an obscene white mass, dead center in her belly. *Dead center.* How ironic that her mind's default for something in the middle would have been those words.

Please let this be a dream. Please let it be a fucking dream.

Hayley rubbed at her eyes as if trying to paw away the disbelief. She had everything she could ever have wanted—marriage to a wonderful, caring man; stepchildren who treated her like their birth mother; more money and influence than most people could even dream of; and a perspective on life that made everything make sense.

Now this.

Pancreatic cancer . . . Inoperable . . . God, don't let it be, Hayley Long thought desperately. *Let it be a dream. . . . Let it be nothing but a bad dream.*

Petros Sperelakis's awareness returned gradually and spasmodically. The pain came first—a dull throbbing in his groin and burning sensation in his low back. He tried to move, to shift his position, but his body did not respond.

Please, I don't think I can move. Someone please help me. I'm Sperelakis, Dr. Petros Sperelakis. I can't see and I can't move.

"Connie, why don't you take a break. I'll be here for another hour."

"Okay, thanks. Listen, Vernice, he could use some range-of-motion work on his wrists and ankles."

Connie? Vernice? I can hear you. I can hear you. Are you Beaumont nurses? It's me, Dr. Sperelakis. What do you mean, range of motion? Am I paralyzed? What happened to me? An accident? A stroke? A tumor? Why can't I see? Why can't I speak?

The man many considered to be among the premier diagnostic physicians in the world struggled to make sense of his own symptoms. He knew he was having difficulty holding on to a thought, and that fact frightened him more than almost anything.

Why am I in such pain? Can someone please tell me what happened? What happened to me? I can feel that, Vernice. I can feel you moving my ankle. Oh, my God. . . .

ONE

Multiple contusions and abrasions . . . Fractured pelvis . . . Nondisplaced fracture, proximal humerus . . . Pulmonary contusion and laceration secondary to posterior displaced fractures of right seventh, eighth, and ninth ribs . . .

With the grim litany ticking through her thoughts, Thea Sperelakis approached Cubicle 4 in the medical ICU of the Beaumont Clinic.

Transverse linear skull fracture . . . Extensive mid–brain stem hemorrhage . . . Level I coma . . .

Thea hesitated, envisioning what her father would look like and knowing that, as an internal medicine specialist herself, her projection would not be far from on the mark. According to her brother Niko, police estimated that the vehicle that struck their father at five thirty in the early morning eight days ago, then drove away, had to have been traveling seventy, at least. It was a miracle he had survived the impact, which threw him more than twenty-five feet. But then, for as long as Thea could remember, Petros Sperelakis was, to his children, the Lion—aloof, powerful, and brilliant, often to the point of majesty.

The Lion.

The absence of skid marks suggested that the driver never saw his victim. Make that his *or her* victim, Thea edited, intent on enforcing that sort of accuracy, even in her thoughts. The police still had no clues and no witnesses.

Alcohol, she guessed. According to an article by Eileen Posnick in a seven-year-old issue of the *American Journal of Drug and Alcohol Abuse,* alcohol was involved in more than 90 percent of hit-and-run accidents where the drivers were eventually apprehended.

Behind her, Niko stepped out from the group that included his twin, Selene, plus a trio of Beaumont Clinic dignitaries, and took Thea's arm. He was swarthy and broad-shouldered, with their father's strong nose and piercing dark eyes, but with features that were somewhat softer. At forty, he was already an associate professor of cardiac surgery at Harvard—a wunderkind, with several significant contributions to the field. Selene, exotic, elegant, and totally self-assured, was no less accomplished as a hand surgeon.

"You okay, Thea?" Niko asked softly.

As she had been taught to do, Thea searched her feelings before responding. Her father, bigger than life itself, was in a deep coma from which there was a 0.01 percent chance he would recover even minimal function—at least according to the retrospective study of traumatic midbrain hemorrhages published by Harkinson et al. in the *American Archives of Neurology,* volume 117, page 158. One in ten thousand, not counting the ribs and other fractures.

Poor Dad.

"I'm okay," she replied.

"Want to go in alone?"

Why would I want to do that? she wondered, shaking her head. Would their father be any less comatose if she saw him by herself?

She shrugged that it made no difference, but sensed she could have come up with a more acceptable response.

"Suit yourself," Niko said in a tone that was quite familiar to her.

Thea knew her brother cared about her—Selene, too. She also knew that the twins had always thought she was odd, though certainly not as odd as their oldest sibling, Dimitri. But their attitude, as emphasized over and over by Thea's longtime therapist and mentor, Dr. Paige Carpenter, was their problem.

One in ten thousand . . . Poor Dad.

Thea ran her fingers through her short chestnut hair, took a single deep breath, and stepped through the doorway.

As anticipated, there were no surprises. Legendary Petros Sperelakis, medical director of the Sperelakis Institute for Diagnostic Medicine, lay motionless—the central figure in a tableau of medical machines. Across the room, his private duty nurse (Haitian, Thea guessed) rose and introduced herself as Vernice.

"I have heard a great deal about you, Dr. Thea," she said. "I hope your flight was an easy one."

"I just read," Thea said, taking the husky woman's smooth, ample hand.

I just read.

It was, Thea knew, the most resounding of understatements. During the twenty-hour series of flights and layovers from the Democratic Republic of the Congo to Boston, she had read *Don Quixote,* the second edition of Deadman's *A Manual of Acupuncture* (for the second time), and Darwin's *Voyage of the* Beagle—more than sixteen hundred pages in all. She would have made the trip home sooner, but she was on a mission moving from refugee camp to camp in the bush with a team of nutritionists, and simply couldn't be reached.

"There's been no change," Vernice said.

"I'd be most surprised if there were. He has taken a severe beating—especially to his head."

Thea approached the bedside, instinctively checking the monitors and intravenous infusions. Petros lay quite peacefully, connected via a tracheotomy tube to a state-of-the-art ventilator. The various Medecins Sans Frontières (Doctors Without Borders) hospitals to which Thea had been assigned over the past five years had been reasonably well equipped, but nothing like this place.

The Beaumont, as nearly everyone referred to the institution, was a sprawling campus, the size of a small university, consisting of what had once been Boston Metropolitan Hospital, now augmented by two dozen more buildings, varying widely in architectural style. The buildings were linked by tree-lined sidewalks above, and an intricate maze of tunnels below, some with moving walkways and others with tarnished tile walls, leading in places to stairways that went down for two or three damp stories, and dating back to Metro's earliest days in the mid-nineteenth century.

Oxygen saturation . . . arterial blood pressure . . .
cerebrospinal fluid pressure . . . central venous pressure . . . urine output . . . chest tube drainage . . . cardiac rhythm and ECG pattern . . .

Thea took in the complex data and processed them
as if they were a grade-school primer. Steady. Everything was nice and steady. At the moment, the fierce
battle for the life of Petros Sperelakis was being fought
at a cellular and even subcellular level. And his youn-
gest offspring, cursed by him when she made the decision to avoid academic medicine and "give her services
away" to third-world countries, pictured the micro-
scopic conflict clearly in her mind's eye.

At best it would probably be weeks before the man
regained any consciousness. Along the way, his system
would have to negotiate a minefield of infections, blood
clots, kidney stones, embolisms, cerebral swelling,
chemical imbalance, intestinal obstructions, and cardiac
events. But in this setting, with this equipment, he would
at least have a fighting chance. Still, from what Thea
knew of her father, if it were his choice, it was doubtful
he would try very hard to steer clear of the mines.

She took the man's hand and held it for a time. It had
been only eight days since the accident, but his muscle
mass was already beginning to waste away. In addition
to the trach, he had a gastric feeding tube in place, two
IVs, a urinary catheter, which was draining briskly into
a collection bag, and a BOLT pressure manometer that
passed through his skull and into the spinal fluid-
containing ventricle of his brain. His eyelids were
paper-taped down to protect his corneas from drying

out, and splints on his wrists and ankles were strapped
in place to prevent joint contractures, against the remote
possibility of a return of function.

Petros Sperelakis—an icon brought down by a driver
who was either in an alcoholic blackout or was aware
enough to try and get away before anyone showed up.
Never had Thea's father looked even remotely vulnerable to her. Now, he looked frail and pathetically in-
fantile.

Thea sensed that she was expected to stay at the
bedside a bit longer, and she planned to be there as
much as possible in the days to come. But she had slept
little if any on the planes, and the exhaustion of the
flights was beginning to take hold. Fifteen minutes, she
decided. Fifteen more minutes would be enough to stay
at the bedside whether the others thought so or not.

Niko had invited her to stay at his house, but three
kids under ten, much as she loved them, provided more
commotion than she could handle.

Selene and her partner, a banker or businesswoman
of some kind, lived in a designer high-rise condo by
the harbor.

The obvious choice was the spacious Wellesley home
in which she and the others had grown up, and where
Petros still lived with the ghost of their mother and
with Dimitri who, many years before, had moved into
the carriage house along with his computers, his monitors, his shortwave radio, his telescope, his machinery,
his library of manga, graphic novels, and Dungeons
and Dragons manuals, and his vast collection of Coca-
Cola and Star Wars memorabilia.

It would be good to see her brother again for many reasons, not the least of which was that of all those in her family, he was the one she related to the most— something of a mirror of what she might have been like had she not had the benefit of early diagnosis, intervention, and extensive behavior modification therapy.

From her early childhood, Thea had memories of the family talking about Dimitri's aloofness and strange behaviors—his lack of friends, offbeat humor, and often-inappropriate statements. Physical age, twelve years ahead of her. Emotional age, inconsistent and unpredictable.

"Dimitri, this is Robert, your new piano teacher."

"Oh, hello. When's the last time you went to the dentist?"

She would never know the bulk of what the family said to one another about her, but she also knew that the choices she had made, with Dr. Carpenter's help, were the right ones for her, and ultimately, for her patients. Keeping her life as uncomplicated as possible, she had learned, was not only a pathway to happiness, it was her roadmap to survival. If there was any single word that did *not* apply to Petros Sperelakis, it was uncomplicated.

Born and raised in Athens until his late teens, Petros was strictly Old Country in his attitudes and philosophy—a brilliant physician as dedicated to his calling and his patients as he was hard on his family. Verbal chastisement and high expectations were his weapons, as well as his only means of expressing love. His wife, Eleni, had rebelled against him in one way and one way only, by continuing to smoke cigarettes despite his vehement edicts that she stop. The lung cancer that took her did nothing to soften Petros, and virtually every mention of her by him was followed by the impotent plea: "If she had only listened to me . . . If only she had listened."

Thea reached between the tubes and brushed some damp, gray hair from her father's brow. The sadness she was feeling at seeing him in such a state was, she knew, as much learned as it was deep-seated and visceral. But she also knew that it was still as real an emotion as those of her two "neurotypical" siblings.

From the beginning, Petros could never understand her shyness, or the severe reactions she had to certain noises—especially vacuum cleaners and hair dryers—as well as to certain foods, and different textures of clothing. When she was twelve, pressured by Eleni that she was seeming more and more like Dimitri in her lack of friends and her pathological obsessions, especially with books of all kinds, Petros consented to allow his wife to bring her to Dr. Carpenter. It was Carpenter who subsequently suggested that Thea was exhibiting many of the symptoms associated with the condition called Asperger syndrome.

The decision to allow his younger daughter to undergo neuropsychiatric testing and therapy did not come easily to Petros. In the lexicon of his life, there was no such word as *can't* and no such concept as psychotherapy. If he had any weakness at all as a diagnostician, it was in the area of psychosomatic illness and the mind-body connection.

"I think he's comfortable," Vernice ventured from across the bed.

"I'm sure he is," Thea replied, managing with some difficulty to swallow her belief that if Petros was feeling anything, then he was certainly not comfortable, and if he was feeling nothing at all, then trying to equate that void with comfort was a stretch.

"Your brother Dimitri said that if your father was in as deep a coma as he appears to be, it was a futile exercise to wonder if he was comfortable or not."

"Sometimes, Dimitri says things just for the shock effect," Thea replied, smiling inwardly at the number of times and situations in which her eccentric sibling had done just that. Vernice had gotten off relatively easily.

"Well," the nurse said, "at least we have the comfort of knowing that Dr. S. is being taken care of in the greatest hospital in the world."

"Yes," Thea said, wondering where Vernice, and *Newsweek,* and the countless others who believed as she did about the Beaumont, could have gotten such quantification about something so unquantifiable.

At virtually the same instant, in the Susan and Clyde Terry Cancer Center, on the far side of the broad campus of the so-called greatest hospital in the world, the treatment nurse was doing her job, injecting a cutting-edge experimental drug into the central IV port of a burly man named Jeffrey Fagone.

Fagone, a trucking magnate from western Pennsylvania, had his rapid accumulation of wealth interrupted by an unusual variant of the blood cancer known as Waldenstrom's macroglobulinemia. His presenting symptom had been lower-back pain. The referral by his primary care doctor had been to the expert in the disease at the Beaumont, where Fagone went yearly for his five-day spa pampering and executive medical checkup. Now, he was part of a cutting-edge treatment protocol—the sort of protocol that the doctors at the Beaumont were renowned for establishing.

Fagone flew up to the Terry Center weekly on his Gulfstream G500 corporate jet. Now he was about to receive the third in a series of ten treatments. The first two had been absolutely uneventful.

This injection, however, would be different.

The vial from which the medication was drawn had been skillfully switched during its journey from the research pharmacy to the cancer center. The new vial, with the same ID number as the old one, now contained enough concentrated bee venom to turn Fagone's bee sting allergy, duly noted in his medical record, into an anaphylactic reaction—a fearsome medical emergency, equivalent to the Fourth of July fireworks on the Charles River Esplanade.

The eruption did not take long to begin. The first few molecules of the venom instantly began mobilizing mast cells from all over Fagone's body. The cells released huge amounts of histamine and other sensitivity chemicals. More venom, more mast cells, more histamine. In less than a minute, Fagone's tongue, cardinal red, had swollen to the size of a golf ball, and his lips to violet sausages. The muscles in the walls of his bronchial tubes went into vicious spasm. Seconds after that, his larynx, also in spasm, closed off altogether. His entire body became scarlet, and his fingers became nothing more than nubs protruding from softball-sized hands.

The team in the Terry unit acted quickly, bringing out a stretcher and hoisting the two-hundred-and-seventy-pound former teamster onto it, then wheeling him to an area that could be screened off from other patients.

But they were paddling against a medical tsunami.

The IV port was available, but the oncologist covering the unit, a young woman less than half Fagone's size, was not skilled in dealing with emergencies of this magnitude. By the time she got the right medications into the man, Fagone's blood pressure had been zero for nearly three minutes. By the time she gave up trying to force an endotracheal breathing tube past the massively swollen, distorted vocal cords, and began clumsily performing her first emergency tracheotomy while waiting for the ENT surgeon to answer his page, there had been no effective respirations for four minutes. She had just sliced a scalpel across her patient's massive throat when his heart stopped. The blood flowing from the gaping laceration was gentian.

When the oncologist, frustrated and utterly demoralized, called off the resuscitation at the ten-minute mark, a useful airway had still not been established.

Jeffrey Fagone, who years before had survived two assassination attempts during his rise to wealth and power in the Teamsters Union, had no chance of surviving this one.

Unlike the other attempts, however, there was no suspicion of anything sinister at work here. Fagone had been done in by a lethal allergic reaction to Waldenstrom's macroglobulinemia experimental drug #BW1745. No one present that day thought otherwise. There would be no analysis of the contents of the vial, and the perfunctory autopsy performed the next morning would disclose nothing out of the ordinary.

The treatment protocol for #BW1745 would be suspended indefinitely, but within just a few months, the principal investigator, supported by a hefty grant from one of the pharmaceutical giants, would roll out another experimental drug to meet the demand of referrals from all over the world.

The Susan and Clyde Terry Cancer Center closed for cleanup and staff support for an hour after the tragic event, but there were patients to treat, many of whom had come from even greater distances than Jeffrey Fagone.

Soon, like the surface of a pond disturbed by a jumping fish, the ripples had subsided, and the world's greatest hospital had gone back to being the world's greatest hospital.

TWO

For another ten minutes, Thea stared down at her father, mentally cataloguing his injuries. It didn't take a Petros Sperelakis to discern that given the sort of excellent medical care practiced at the Beaumont, none of them was immediately life-threatening, except the hemorrhage in his midbrain. On the plus side of the ledger, she believed that at almost seventy, the man was in remarkable shape thanks to a disciplined diet, exercise, the right genetics, and the preservative effects of a daily shot glass or two of seven-star Metaxa.

Thea's eyes were X-ray probes, seeing through Petros's skull and visualizing the intricate folds and contours of his magnificent brain. According to Niko, the hemorrhage had occurred in the center of the middle portion of the brain stem, a tight bundle of nerves connecting the gray matter and the spinal cord and known technically as the mesencephalon. It had been a while since Thea had read a neuroanatomy textbook, several of them, in fact. But it had not been so long that she had forgotten very much. In fact, forgetting material she had read was something that essentially did not happen.

In just a few seconds, she connected with a vast amount of information concerning midbrain anatomy and function. Her mind's eye saw the information as integrations of a number of texts, but if she had to, she knew that she would be able to quote the actual passages virtually verbatim, with few or no mistakes, along with the page numbers on which they appeared.

There were curses connected with having the form of autism called Asperger syndrome, but her obsession with the details of what she saw, and her mastery over the printed word, had always been blessings—refuges in the often-confusing world of the neurotypicals. She flashed on Dimitri, never officially diagnosed, but undoubtedly afflicted with abnormal neurology that was similar to hers. The "autism spectrum" was the label du jour for a series of conditions. Somewhere in the middle of the spectrum was the offshoot first described by Austrian pediatrician Hans Asperger in 1944.

Asperger syndrome.

For her immeasurably brilliant brother, the gray matter once destined for learning such things as nonverbal communication, social grace, small talk, interpersonal pragmatics, group dynamics, and executive function had largely been usurped by an understanding at his mind's deepest levels of electronics and computer science. The groupings of neurons responsible for fine motor control and hand-eye coordination had yielded in large measure to the remarkable ability to focus for long periods of time on those things that interested him.

It didn't matter that he and Thea were probably different in as many ways as they were similar. If not the same, their diagnoses were certainly kissing cousins, layered on their unique personalities. Thea forced her focus from her brother back to their father. The injury to Petros's brain stem was indeed a frightening one.

The cerebral lobes and cerebellar hemispheres were the parts of the brain largely responsible for thinking, balance, and movement. Outgoing efferent nerve fibers from them coursed through the midbrain on their way to activate the muscles of the body. At the same time, incoming afferent fibers were skirting the central midbrain, carrying sensory information such as pain, light touch, and position up to the cerebrum and cerebellum for processing.

The hemorrhage in Petros's midbrain, as described by Niko, had probably effectively sliced across the efferent bundles like a blade, killing neurons and disconnecting the upper nervous system from the lower— thought from movement, intellect from physical ability, reason from function. The result: paralysis involving literally every muscle in the body.

Behind her, she sensed Niko and Selene, and the team from Beaumont standing patiently by the doorway. Dr. Sharon Karsten, a onetime endocrinologist, had been the president of the sprawling medical center for nearly as long as Thea could remember. Under her guidance, the hospital had enhanced its worldwide reputation as one of the places to go for second opinions, knotty diagnostic conundrums, and top-notch surgical specialists.

One of her most successful brainchildren was Medicon, Inc.—highly paid, highly trained physicians who were scattered around the globe, networking and advising doctors to the wealthy, the influential, and the powerful. One product they were offering, in addition to their knowledge and experience, was the hospital's renowned five-day Executive Health Evaluation—a hundred thousand dollars' worth of the most sophisticated medical testing and specialist evaluation available anywhere. EHE was based in the luxurious Beaumont Inn and Spa, located on the grounds of the hospital.

With Karsten was Dr. Scott Hartnett, tall, handsome, and intellectual, the director of development for the Beaumont, and still a part-time practicing internal medicine physician at the Sperelakis Institute. Thea remembered her father once saying that if the government could generate money for the country the way Scott Hartnett could for the Beaumont, there would be no national debt.

And finally, there was chief of nursing, Amy Musgrave, five feet tall, if that, introduced to Thea as the glue that held the entire Beaumont system together—a system that now included three satellite hospitals in Boston, and expanding facilities in Washington, D.C., and Charlotte. Thea had never met Musgrave, but immediately took to her straightforward manner and powerful dedication to her nurses.

It was Musgrave who first stepped to Petros's bedside.

"Is there anything further you can think of that we should be doing, Doctor?"

Thea shook her head. "It seems he's getting remarkable care," she said.

"Your father was—*is*—a wonderful man. My nurses love him. He treats them as equals, and most of the time, at least, he seems to understand that the true measure of any medical facility is the minute-to-minute, hour-to-hour, day-to-day nursing care its patients receive. The more nurses, the better the care. It's as simple an equation as that."

"I totally agree," Thea said, wondering if Musgrave expected her to be more effusive.

"In fact, Vernice is one of several nurses who are volunteering time to work with him."

"Thank you," Thea said.

Musgrave continued without a pause. "We have the highest nurse-to-patient ratio, and we're at or near the top of every listing of the best hospitals. I don't think that's a coincidence."

Together, she and Musgrave returned to the others, and were ushered down the hall to a small sitting area, where the three hospital officials asked the three siblings to wait for a short while, and then walked off together. The moment they were gone, the twins each pulled out their cell phones, checked their messages, and made calls—three or four apiece. Thea smiled inwardly at the notion of when she had last made a cell phone call. It might have been two years—the last time she was back in Boston. It might have even been five, dating back to her first posting with Doctors Without Borders.

"Well, what do you think?" Niko asked, after completing the last of his calls.

"About Dad?"

"Yes, of course about Dad."

Again the slightly annoyed edge that Thea had become used to over the years. Selene closed her phone and set it in her purse. Dressed in a striking beige designer pants suit, without a wisp of her sorrel hair out of place, her nails perfectly manicured, she might well have been taken for a bank president or movie studio head, or even a model, before anyone came close to guessing orthopedic surgeon. However, no one would ever even mention Selene's ostentatious style once they watched her reattach a severed finger or two, or create a functional replacement thumb—her true specialties.

Brother and sisters were in a small sitting area at the end of the sixth-floor corridor. Beside them, seven-foot windows overlooked a man-made pond with several fountains spraying gracefully. A flock of Canada geese pecked its way around the perfect emerald lawn.

"It doesn't look good," Thea said. "From the description of the MRI you gave me, according to Therrian et al. in the textbook *Traumatic Brainstem Injuries,* he has a sixteen percent chance of making it four months."

"Not seventeen percent?"

"You know, it's okay *not* to make fun of me, Niko."

From her earliest memory, Thea couldn't stand being teased.

"Hey, I'm sorry. I really am."

"Okay, because I've never been very good at distinguishing good-natured from mean-spirited teasing. I just could never understand why someone would tease me to make me feel that I was one of the gang. And as far as me teasing someone else, when I try, it usually leads to unbelievably disastrous consequences."

"I don't know if I'll ever get used to your . . . your, what would you call it, gift? Condition?"

"You don't have to call it anything, Niko. It's simply who I am, just like you have great coordination and a rock-steady hand, I couldn't hit a pitch if the thrower was using a beach ball, and I have to print so that people can read what I've written."

"Sorry," Niko muttered again.

"He doesn't mean anything hurtful, honey," Selene added. "You know that."

"They had Dad here in less than an hour after the accident," Thea said. "Do you think they could have operated?"

"I spoke to Joe Rizzo, the neurosurgeon, and he said not a chance given where this hemorrhage is located."

Thea shrugged and stared out the window, absently wondering if Dimitri had been told that she was flying in and had simply decided there would be too much commotion and he would see her back at the house.

"At least it was quick," Selene said.

"It's not over," Thea countered, "at least not yet. This is mostly a ventral pontine hemorrhage. With the technology and rehab hospitals we have today, one reference I can recall reported five-year survival rates as high as fifteen percent."

"At Dad's age and in that condition?" Selene sounded incredulous.

Thea shrugged impotently. "Sorry."

"He wouldn't want to live like this."

Nobody would want to live like this, Thea thought. *But how far back can he come? That is the question.*

She found herself integrating everything she knew of the man and his condition. Critical? Yes. Grave? Absolutely. But hopeless?

Thea tried wishing that Petros Sperelakis would

simply stop breathing. No, he had to make it. He had to survive this. There remained unfinished business between them. The man had never, in all her memory, told her that he loved her, nor had she taken the initiative and told him. At the very least, she needed that exchange to happen between them before the end.

It was a mistake not to have told him before now. She had done so well in all of those role-playing therapy games. It was a mistake to have held back in real life—to believe they had time to work things out. She needed him to make it.

Then, she found herself wondering what the Lion himself would wish for.

THREE

"What If You Knew the Exact Day and Time You Were Going to Die?"

The irony of that thought wasn't lost on Rev. Gideon Bohannan. The phrase was the title of his most beloved and requested sermon, and his personal favorite as well.

What if you knew the exact day and time you were going to die? The exact moment, my friends. What would you choose to do differently? Who would you tell that you loved them? To whom would you say you were sorry? How would you make your peace with the Lord?

Oh, but that was one hell of a sermon.

The words ran through his mind like a stock exchange ticker as he fished behind the shoes on his closet shelf and brought out the .38 Smith and Wesson revolver he had virtually forgotten was there—until last Wednesday, that is. The bullets were in a small envelope beside the gun. There were six of them, but Bohannan expected to use only two—three at the most.

It was Friday. Caroline and the children had gone off to her mother's for the weekend. The thought of not seeing her ever again wasn't all that hard to take, but he surely would miss the girls. They would understand. The note he had left for them would see to that.

Feeling surreal, distant from himself, Bohannan drew the huge motorized drapes spanning the south wall of their home—the wall that overlooked the interior of the vast All Praise the Lord Sanctuary. Far below, the 7,500 seats of the sanctuary, beneath an enormous geodesic dome, stretched off in perfect symmetry. The design had been his, and the remarkable golden dome a dream of his from the day he'd visited the Royal Bank of Canada building in Toronto, with its 27,000 gold reflective-glass windows. This was his vision, his golden sanctuary.

In just an hour the whole goddamn thing would belong to Glenn Lovering—the prick. *Lovering.* Even the thought of not existing anymore wasn't as difficult to take as that one.

If Bohannan felt there was even a 1 percent chance he could survive the scandal of being diagnosed with AIDS, let alone the exposure of his homosexual affair, he would try to stick it out—if for no other reason than to keep his slimy assistant pastor from taking over his hundred-million-a-year baby. But there wasn't a 1 percent chance. There was no chance. Bohannan's hardline conservative stance had seen to that.

The public had forgiven Swaggart and Bakker and any number of sinning evangelicals, but there would be no warmth in their hearts for Gideon Bohannan. And even if there were, the doctors at the Beaumont Clinic gave him a chance at remission from the virus, but virtually no chance at recovery.

Word would get out. He had managed to keep his affair with Race DuPre under wraps, but now Race had let him down by sleeping around. Word would get out and after being booted out of his church and his home, Gideon Bohannan would progressively sicken and die, shriveling away alone and disgraced.

Bohannan slipped the revolver into the pocket of his sports coat.

What if you knew . . . ?

The midday desert heat was already bearing down, and Bohannan, twenty-five pounds overweight, was sweating by the time he reached the garage and his Mercedes. Race would beg, Bohannan was thinking, but it wouldn't do any good. Maybe while he was pleading for his life, the bastard would share who it was who had passed the virus on to *him*—who had gotten DuPre so hot that he threw caution to the wind and had unprotected sex.

Stupid . . . just stupid.

DuPre, a bass player with a jazz combo that played the club scene throughout the area, had been a wonderful lover and friend.

Parked in the driveway of the man's modest ranch-style house at 10 Briarcliff Road, Rev. Gideon Bohannan was in a near fugue state as he flipped open the cylinder of his gun and checked that he had loaded it properly. Then he slipped it back in his pocket and used a key to enter the back door, just as he had done for over five years.

What if you knew the exact day and time you were going to die?

As expected, Race denied cheating—and convincingly so.

Even after seeing the lab reports and the repeat lab reports from the hospital in New England, he denied cheating. Bohannan felt himself weakening.

"Even if you have it, we'll still be together," DuPre said. "People do it all the time. They're just careful. I love you, Bo. I really do. We can beat this. Together we can beat this."

Bohannan lowered his gun. Visions of Swaggart, Bakker, and others filled his thoughts. Maybe they *could* get through this.

The kitchen door opened and closed. There were footsteps across the tiled floor. Before Bohannan could react, there was a man in the room—jet-black hair; olive skin; cold, dark eyes. He wore thin black gloves. The pistol he held looked as if it had never left his hand.

"The gun," he barked. "Set it on the table, there. Now!"

Startled and bewildered, Bohannan did as he was ordered.

The intruder hefted it for a moment, and then, without another word, shot Race DuPre in the center of the throat. In a second, he grabbed Bohannan with one hand around the back of the neck, his grip so powerful that the man dropped immediately and soundlessly to his knees. The first shot went through Bohannan's head, temple-to-temple. The second one, with the now-deceased minister's hand around the gun, hit precisely between DuPre's brows.

A minute and twenty seconds after he picked the back door lock at 10 Briarcliff Road, Gerald Prevoir walked out again. Five minutes after that, he picked up a Diet Coke and grilled chicken sandwich, no mayo, at a McDonald's drive-through on the highway. He was eating at the far end of the parking lot when he called his employer.

"I had to be of some assistance to the good reverend," he said, between bites, "but in the end, he performed admirably. They both did. Give my best to Reverend Lovering, and congratulate him on his new position."

FOUR

Identifying feelings and then responding to them appropriately was an area Thea and Dr. Carpenter had worked on for years, along with a group of other teens and twenties with recently diagnosed Asperger's. Most of those with the condition had been born without the social and emotional filters that kept most neurotypicals from being labeled odd or inappropriate.

Those absent neurological pathways had to be created and then practiced repeatedly, just as if the Aspie, as many of them called themselves, had suffered a stroke and were learning how to walk all over again—only in their cases, the "stroke" had probably happened to their developing brain before they were born or as the result of some environmental insult during the early years.

Karsten, Hartnett, and Musgrave approached, looking solemn but purposeful.

"There's a conference room at the end of the hall," Karsten said. "Would you three mind if we talked there?"

The six walked back down the hallway and into a small but elegant room paneled in dark wood, walnut, Thea guessed, although she knew next to nothing of the subject. The table in the center, same wood, had ice water and glasses set out for them.

"Well," Karsten said to Thea after they had settled in, "what do you think about what you saw back there?"

"It looks as if our father is getting excellent care."

"Oh, he is," Hartnett said. "I promise you he is. As you might surmise, when a person as eminent as Petros has something as disastrous as this accident, it's like a three-ring circus of specialists, nurses, and technicians of various kinds. As his primary care physician, I have taken on the role of ringmaster, along with our best physician assistant. Petros never actually had a private physician until this hospitalization. In fact, it was a running joke here that his doctor was the man reflecting back at him from his computer screen. That's where he seemed to spend most of his time—reviewing patients' records."

"The Beaumont has one of the most comprehensive and secure record systems in the country, Thea," Niko said.

"Correction," Karsten added, "in the world."

"I'm not surprised," Thea replied. "It's the law now, yes?"

"Exactly," said the CEO. "We've had an elaborate electronic medical records system in effect here for years. We call it Thor, because of its unbridled power. Now we feel that it's as near to perfection as such a system could be. Security built on individual patient control numbers, and achieved through a triple combination of password, thumbprint, and for some areas, retinal scan. It's really quite remarkable, as well as fail-safe. I suspect you know it, but your brother Dimitri was among those responsible for its creation and subsequent perfection. He participated on one of our research and development teams."

"Dimitri participated on a team?"

Thea was incredulous, and at the same time sensed she needed to slow down and measure her words.

"Surprising, huh?" Niko said. "And he did a hell of a job, too. Dad has insisted that he pay rent for the carriage house, so when he had to, Dimitri looked for programming work. Apparently he answered an ad here and spent more than a year working for the hospital."

"That's terrific. I don't think I ever heard about it."

"Ol' Dimitri may be a tad on the offbeat side, but when it comes to computers, there's absolutely no one like him."

"I agree with you there," Thea said. "An IQ of a hundred and eighty can get you far in this world."

Still, *far* didn't describe the distance her brother had come if he spent more than a year cooperating with others on a research and development team. She recalled him not emerging from his lair in the carriage house for days on end, during which he allowed no visitors except for the pizza delivery man, and at times, his little sister Thea. The job meant so little to him, and the rest of the family for that matter, that no one had even bothered to mention it when she last visited Boston two years ago.

"We think our electronic medical records system is the gold standard," Karsten said, "and the governments of a number of states, plus the federal government, are discovering that is true. Before too long, Thor or some variant might well be required of every hospital and health-care facility in the country. With the patents Beaumont holds, the system your brother helped invent could bring in billions."

"That sounds wonderful," Thea said. "I'm afraid we at Doctors Without Borders haven't quite reached that level of sophistication. But then again, without managed care, HIPAA laws, and all those malpractice suits, it's quite possible we won't have to."

An uncomfortable silence followed during which it seemed as if a poll was being taken to see who should be speaking up. Thea looked from her brother and sister to the others, and wondered if she might have said something wrong. Finally, Sharon Karsten cleared her throat and adjusted her half-glasses.

"Um . . . Thea," she began, "I don't think it would be overstating things to say that we here at the institute are most impressed with the sort of physician you have become. Your father spoke very highly of you, and your brother and sister made it clear that we could search forever and not find anyone more capable of filling our needs."

My father spoke highly of me? Thea was so blindsided by the notion that she almost missed the words that followed.

"Capable of filling your needs?" Thea asked when she realized what had been said.

The last thing in the world she wanted to do here was fill anybody's needs.

"Your father served as a physician and advisor to patients and doctors from around the globe," Karsten said. "He cared for royalty as well as for the poor and disenfranchised, whose care is paid for by foundations he has helped develop."

"Yes?"

Thea felt sick at what she sensed was coming next. She looked over at the twins, but in concert they averted their eyes.

"Well," Karsten continued, "we would need approval from our board, but I suspect that will be no problem. Put simply, we want you to stay here at the Beaumont and take over your father's practice."

Hartnett straightened up and took the baton.

"I can and will handle Petros's administrative responsibilities as medical director of the institute until you feel up to assuming them," he said. "And if by some . . . what I mean is if your father's condition should improve to the point where—"

Thea was on her feet, glaring at her brother. She felt as panicked as if she had just been asked to spend the rest of her life in a broom closet.

"This is your doing, Niko!" she snapped. "You and Selene told them I didn't really have a job and would be happy to take over here. Why would you do that?"

"We didn't do anything, we merely—"

"Well, I *do* have a job. I have a job and friends and a life I enjoy, just like you normal people do! I'll stay here as long as I feel Father needs me, but you know that I have my reasons for working where I do."

Without waiting for a response, Thea whirled and marched down the hallway and back into the ICU.

Embarrassed, the three hospital officials muttered apologies and left the conference room.

The twins stayed behind.

Petros knew now. He had brain damage. He had profound damage and he could not move or speak. The pain in his back and pelvis was unremitting and unbearable, but he was helpless to do anything about it. One of the nurses had said something about an accident, but then he must have faded out again before he could hear any more. An accident? If he had had an accident of some sort, with damage to his brain—his midbrain, probably—he had absolutely no memory of it. Was he driving? Walking? In someone else's car?

Thea was here. I heard her voice. She must be back from Africa. It's been so long. When she first left, she was so terribly angry at me. She thought I didn't care. That wasn't true. Why couldn't I make her understand how much I wanted for her? Dimitri had been a complete waste, and the twins were technicians—bright enough, but technicians all the same.

Help me! For God's sake help me. I have to speak to my Thea. I have to help her understand that I only want what's best for her. I have to help her see what she's done to me by leaving the way she did and how she can make it right.

FIVE

Handling stress had never come easily to Thea, especially in the area of athletics, where she had little ability, and also during interviews, which usually played into her insecurities and difficulty with language nuances. Before beginning treatment, when confronted with a pressured situation, she would usually become restless, defensive, and combative, and before long might melt down in a fit of anger. With the help of Dr. Carpenter, and an improvisation therapy group geared to being in tense situations, she practiced being interviewed until she could maintain her composure. Eventually, she was able to get a sense of whether her answers to the interviewer were appropriate or not, but even now, she often wasn't certain.

The twins knew that she had gone to work for Doctors Without Borders to avoid the pressure-cooker medicine and politics of a major academic medical center. Yet without consulting her, they had encouraged the powers at the Beaumont Clinic to offer her the practice and position that had belonged to their father, and to spring that offer on her when she was totally unprepared.

Had they meant to put her in a situation where she

would humiliate herself as she had just done? Did they want to ensure that the hospital bosses knew that regardless of her intellect, Thea Sperelakis was most assuredly not her father's daughter? If so, they had most assuredly succeeded.

Thea entered the unit and stood on the other side of the glass sliders, breathing deeply, but unable to keep herself from trembling. She had come a long way in dealing with stressful situations, but obviously not far enough. Her difficulty handling pressure should have led her to a specialty like pathology or radiology or public health. But she loved people and wanted to feel she was directly helping them, much as she had watched her father do from her earliest awareness. In addition, her intellect and powers of deductive reasoning made her a natural for diagnostic medicine. To her, having to deal with an occasional true emergency was worth the trade-off to be an internist, and most of the time, especially if she had enough warning to ready herself for the situation, she could manage most emergencies quite well.

She had largely composed herself and started back toward Petros's high-tech, glassed-in cubicle, when the sliders opened again and Niko entered, followed by Selene. Through the glass Thea could see CEO Karsten and nursing supervisor Musgrave standing quietly by the waiting area in the corridor outside. Scott Hartnett was probably off someplace, she mused, implementing a switch to someone other than a Sperelakis to head up the institute.

"Thea, wait," Niko said.

Thea continued to the bedside, at once embarrassed and still somewhat angry.

"You didn't have to do that, Niko—certainly not just a few hours after I got here."

"We didn't say anything," Selene said, "except to agree with what Hartnett and the others had heard from Father, that you were a very brilliant doctor."

"The name Sperelakis is worth millions in referrals," Niko added. "They asked us if we thought you'd agree to take over Petros's practice, and all we could tell them was to ask you, but that you were a great doctor. We had no idea they'd charge in and bring it up right after you've stepped off the plane."

"You know I'd never succeed in this setting, Niko."

"I'm not so sure," Selene said. "You've managed to succeed in almost anything you've ever done. Please don't be angry with us, baby. We've got enough to deal with right here."

Thea looked over through the forest of tubes. Petros, his raccoon eyes and battered face making him a grotesquerie of the powerful man who had ruled their home, was lying peacefully on his back, being attended to by a tall, young unit nurse named Tracy. Vernice, the nurse who had volunteered to help with his bed care, was gone.

His splinted hands were restrained to the sides of the bed against the remote chance that he might suddenly wake up and pull out his arterial line or IVs or his tracheotomy tube. The top bedsheet had been pulled aside, exposing him and revealing his penis and urinary catheter. One indignity piled on the next.

High on the wall, the monitor protruded on a mobile arm, displaying various parameters as continuous tracings and numbers in different colors. Blood pressure and mean arterial pressure were red; heart rate yellow. Central venous pressure, indicating the volume of blood returning to the heart, was blue. Oxygen saturation, core body temperature, respiratory rate, and spinal fluid pressure were being continuously recorded as well. Many times over her years in medicine, Thea had seen overwhelmed, impotent, often bored visitors to patients in the ICU staring up at the monitor screen as if it were televising some sort of sporting event.

Almost subconsciously, she herself scanned the screen, making a mental note of the various tracings. Details, always details. Three of the tracings resonated to a mild extent—a drop of five in the mean blood pressure, the appearance of occasional extra heartbeats (one or two every minute), and also what seemed like a slight change in certain portions of the individual heartbeat tracings. The observations were not enough to trigger any alarms, and also not the sort of thing neurotypicals were likely to pick up on. They were just . . . there.

"Okay," she said to the twins. "I'm sorry to have gone off at you like that. You're right. We do have our hands full."

The extra beats were of little concern to her, and in many instances, at a rate of only one or two a minute, were the result of stress, mucus in a bronchial tube, or even a stimulant such as caffeine. In fact, Petros was on some IV theophylline, a bronchial tube dilator for wheezing that often stimulated heart muscle irritability. But Thea felt certain that the subtle changes in what was known as the PQRST complexes of Petros's cardiogram were new from when she first arrived in the unit.

". . . starting with the health care proxy Father left," Selene was saying.

The news startled Thea's focus away from the monitor.

"He left a proxy?" she asked, surprised that no one had mentioned it before now. "What does it say? Who did he appoint to administer it?"

"Actually," Selene replied, sweeping a wisp of errant hair back into place, "it doesn't say much. It turns over all decisions regarding his treatment to the four of us."

"The four of us?" Now Thea was incredulous. "Did he leave a living will?"

Selene shook her head.

"None that anyone's been able to find. His secretary had the proxy in a file with our names on it. We have the power to decide if heroic measures should be instituted or continued, but only if we four are in agreement."

"Including Dimitri?"

"Including Dimitri."

Selene's expression and tone made it clear what she thought about including their oldest sibling.

"Petros Sperelakis, the master of control," Thea said.

"Right to the grave," Niko added. "There's a copy of the proxy in his record. We've already signed off on it."

"Did Dimitri sign?"

"Not yet. I don't think he's even been here more than once. The proxy doesn't really say anything other than we four must concur on any action."

"In that case I'll be happy to sign."

"But you're not certain what you want to do about instituting heroic measures?"

"Niko, look at him. We've already instituted heroic measures."

Out of the corner of her eye, Thea saw an increase in the frequency of the VPBs (ventricular premature beats) from one or two a minute to four or five. Something was irritating the electrically charged cardiac muscle, possibly the theophylline, she was thinking, although a number of other possibilities began marching through her mind. She glanced about for the intensivist—the specialist in critical care medicine—but he didn't seem to be in the ICU.

"I see what you mean," Niko was saying, "but that still doesn't answer the question of what to do if—"

"Tracy," Thea cut in, "what's up with these extra beats?"

"I just saw them, too, Thea," the nurse said.

"His pressure's dropped as well."

"He's been having some VPBs all day, but this is more. I've been here with him all afternoon. I can page the intensivist. He's at dinner."

"I think it's okay if he's not going to be too long, but do what you're comfortable with."

"What's happening?" Selene asked.

"There are some very small changes in his monitor— widening of the QRS complexes and also some subtle changes in the QT interval and the PR interval."

"You are too much."

"I'm not sure I agree with you about the changes, sis," Niko said.

"Well, Niko, you're the cardiac surgeon, but I have the tendency to notice such things. Something could be off with his electrolytes, maybe his calcium. He's on theophylline, which can contribute to that, and also a diuretic that can do the same thing. Is he on any kind of antacids?"

"He's been getting ranitidine IV," Tracy said. "Dr. Kessel likes to use it in patients on steroids."

Thea felt a tension materialize in her throat. Something was definitely wrong.

"Well, I think you should order a full twelve-lead EKG," she said to the nurse. "Also, I would stop the theophylline for the time being and send off a tube to the lab for electrolytes—sodium, potassium, CO_2, and chloride—as well as for free or ionized calcium, whatever they call the test here; just not total calcium."

"Right away," the nurse said. "I am going to page Dr. Kessel. It's a hike from the cafeteria to here."

"Fine. Selene, perhaps it's worth paging Dr. Hartnett as well. He's Dad's primary care doctor."

"What do you think is going on?" Niko asked.

"I don't know, but something's different than it was earlier today. I'm almost certain of it."

"Whatever it is, don't you think we should just let it happen?"

"What?" Thea was incredulous.

"Look at him, Thea. He's a vegetable. Existing like this is nothing he ever would have wanted."

"Then why didn't he say so? He took the time to write a proxy. He could have written a living will."

"Honey, he was always so busy and so distracted," Selene said. "He probably meant to and just never got around to it. We need to just let him go. We've all encountered enough patients with severe head injuries to know where this is going. This isn't the man who was our father, Thea. It never will be again. Why torture him?"

"It's too soon," Thea said.

The twins glared at her.

"If he could speak," Selene said, an edge to her voice, "he'd scream at us to just let him go. This may be the chance to do it."

"You know the man, sis," Niko said, "and you know where this is headed. Be reasonable."

"Niko, I *don't* know where this is headed. I agree that the odds favor a poor outcome, but we only have one father and he only has one life. Is there any reason we can't see this through for a little while longer?"

"Let me think," Niko said. "For starters, he could be in terrible pain. We have no way of knowing that. For seconds, a great life is grinding to a halt in total humiliation. Catheters and bed baths for a man known around the world for his brilliance and caring. For thirds, the worst thing that could happen is something truly terrible. We could succeed in keeping him alive. One of the greatest medical minds of our times reduced to being lashed to a chair in the hall, soiling himself, drooling on himself, incapable of speaking, and unable even to hold his head up straight. It would be a hell of a lot easier for everyone if we just choose to throw our lot in with benign neglect—with choosing *not* to intervene. That way we don't have to plug in the morphine drip and take an active hand in his end."

"It's only been eight days. There's something going on here, Niko. Right now. Whatever it is could very possibly be reversible. We need to try and figure out what that is and treat it. We don't have enough information to make the decisions you're asking us to make."

"Thea, we understand where you're coming from," Selene said, "but we've been here with him every day. You haven't."

"That's exactly the point, Selene. I just got here. I need more time with him before we . . . before we let him go. Can't you understand? Niko, look. Look at his neck veins. I think they're becoming distended. Do you think the chest trauma could have caused bleeding around his heart?"

"Tamponade?" Niko said, with no more than a glance at their father's neck veins. Distension of them was one of the first signs that blood or other fluid was accumulating and causing life-threatening pressure to build up between the pericardial membrane and the heart muscle itself. "After eight days? Doubtful. Almost impossible. Besides, I don't think there's any distension at all."

"But look," Thea said. "His blood pressure's dropped and his venous pressure has gone up and he's having those extra beats. It could be tamponade."

"Or too much calcium or too little potassium or a

drug reaction or an internal hemorrhage, or just an old man's old heart giving up. Thea, be reasonable."

At that instant, with no increased warning whatsoever, one of the errant premature beats fired off precisely on the ascending portion of the following T-wave, and Petros Sperelakis's heart stopped.

SIX

Thea felt herself go cold.

Her father's heart was in ventricular fibrillation. The powerful cardiac muscle was quivering impotently within his lion's chest like so many strands of spaghetti, unable to generate a heartbeat in any organized fashion. The colored monitor readings overhead were recording the disaster.

Pulse 0 . . . Mean arterial pressure 0 . . .

Selene had run off to page Scott Hartnett. The ICU intensivist was heading across campus from the cafeteria.

The biological clock of brain death had begun ticking the instant Petros's heart had stopped.

Thea's own heart felt like an expanding balloon, her stomach a pit of molten acid.

Calcium . . . potassium . . . Perhaps it was an abnormality of one or the other of those, she thought desperately. Or maybe some drug toxicity. Or maybe tamponade.

"Tracy," she heard her voice say with no great authority, "please call a Code Blue."

To one side of the cubicle, Niko stood, his arms folded, his face stone.

"Code Blue Medical ICU . . . Code Blue Medical

ICU . . . ," the overhead page operator's voice droned from speakers outside the unit. "Code Blue Medical ICU."

Tracy raced in with the crash cart and immediately reached up and hit the button that started the red sweep-second hand on the code clock set high on the wall over the door. The time started at zero, but Thea knew fifteen seconds or more had already elapsed. Every one of those seconds diminished the likelihood of a successful resuscitation and increased the evolving brain damage. The point of no return in any cardiac arrest was felt to be four minutes. No blood pressure beyond four minutes, unless deep body cooling had occurred from exposure or drowning, and brain damage would be irreversible. The only way to extend the four minutes was through effective CPR.

Seconds later, the hospital CEO and nursing supervisor were there, along with one of the other ICU nurses. Amy Musgrave took up the Code Blue clipboard that was hanging by the door and began recording the event.

"I've got this, Susie," she said to the nurse. "You help Tracy. Where's the intensivist?"

"On his way from the caf."

The first technician arrived pushing her EKG, and began hooking Petros to the leads of his machine. Inhalation was next, then the evening nursing supervisor, who saw Musgrave handling what would have been her role had the chief not been there, and backed out of the rapidly filling cubicle.

Thea glanced at the door, her mind unwilling to

grasp that this was her show. The code clock was nearing thirty seconds. She was off to a terrible start.

Do something! her mind screamed. *This is your father. Do something!*

She had taken, and of course passed with top marks, any number of advanced cardiac life-support courses. She had instant total recall of the step-by-step problem-solving algorithms related to cardiac arrest.

Rhythm: ventricular tachycardia . . . Institute basic life support including chest thump . . . Give amiodarone 300 mg IV and prepare to defibrillate at 200 joules . . .

All she needed to do was compensate for the wave of anxiety that seemed to be smothering her. Over her years of training, she had participated in a number of codes, but almost always, she had deferred control to one of the other docs. In Africa, more than a few of her patients had died, but a cardiac resuscitation was seldom successful when nothing could be done about the underlying condition that had caused it. And with the populations she was caring for, there was no shortage of lethal underlying conditions.

Suddenly, she was at the bedside, delivering a sharp blow to Petros's sternum with the side of her fist, and beginning chest compressions over the same spot.

"Niko, you outweigh me by seventy-five pounds," she said over her shoulder. "You should be doing this, not me."

There was no response from her brother.

"Oh, Niko," she groaned.

A burly resident entered the cubicle.

"What do you need?" he asked

"Some good, strong compressions," Thea said, stifling the white-hot burn she was feeling toward her brother.

The resident moved in and began what Thea felt was adequate pumping, rhythmically squeezing Petros's heart between the underside of his breastbone and his spine. She set two fingers on her father's groin and felt a soft-but-definite jet of blood with each compression. Not great, but good enough provided it did not take too long to reverse the fibrillation.

The code clock swept past forty seconds.

"Two hundred joules," Tracy said.

"Amiodarone in," the other nurse reported.

Thea took the paddles of the defibrillator, placed one to the left of Petros's sternum and the other lower and farther to the left. Then she glanced back at her brother, who hadn't moved.

"Two hundred joules! Everybody clear!" she called out.

The muffled pop of electricity jerked Petros's restrained arms upward. Then just as quickly, they dropped back to the bed.

"Sinus rhythm," Musgrave called out excitedly. "Nice going, Doctor."

"I've got a pulse," Thea said.

The normal rhythm lasted only twenty or thirty seconds before deteriorating, once again, to ventricular fibrillation.

"Resume compressions, please," Thea said to the resident. "One milligram of epinephrine IV, please, Tracy. Prepare to shock at three hundred."

"Three hundred," the ICU nurse said, setting the defibrillator.

"Three hundred," Thea said, now totally immersed in the resuscitation and in replaying the algorithms in her mind. "Ready, clear!"

Again the odd pop; again the marionette-like jerk of Petros's arms; again the short-lived appearance of a normal rhythm before the reversion to fibrillation.

Thea felt the tension building once again. The sweeping second hand on the code clock passed two and a half minutes. On the bed, Petros lay rather serenely, his eyelids taped down, the ventilator supplying oxygenated, humidified air with a steady, repetitive whoosh. They would continue until there was no effective heartbeat and no hope of getting one, but unless something was done to deal with whatever was keeping the normal rhythm from rapidly deteriorating, the conclusion of this affair was foregone.

"Resume compressions, please. Could someone send for the ultrasound tech and bring me the kit for doing a pericardial tap?" Thea asked.

She wondered if her voice sounded as strained to everyone else as it did to her. She also wondered what people thought of Petros Sperelakis's cardiac-surgeon son, who remained a statue outside the crowd around the bedside.

I can't let him go like this, she was thinking. *I have to find the answer.*

Thea pressed her fingers into her father's groin once more. The pulse being generated by the resident was significantly less forceful.

Where was the intensivist?

"Are you getting tired?" she asked the resident.

"A little."

Niko, what are you doing? Help us!

"Just give me one more good minute," she said.

"You've got it."

The compressions intensified and the resulting pulse became sharper. Three and a quarter minutes.

"Pericardiocentesis tray is ready, Doctor. Gloves are right here. Six and a half okay?"

"Perfect."

Don't die like this, Dad. . . . Don't die like this.

Was it worth waiting for the ultrasound to demonstrate that there was or wasn't fluid pressing in around the heart? Absolutely not. Even with adequate CPR, there was ongoing brain cell death by the second. The pericardial tap had to be done now. The problem was that except for working on a cadaver in medical school, she had never done one. The anatomy presented no problem, but the technique might.

In her mind, Thea opened the instruction pages she had once studied in a syllabus on procedures and techniques. Then she gloved and put the special cardiac needle together. Did she go up under the sternum, or down between the ribs? Did it make any difference? Under, she decided. The syllabus she had memorized ten years ago said *under*.

Where's Ultrasound, dammit?

Her mouth dry, but her focus sharp, Thea snapped an alligator clip to the near end of the long cardiac needle, and attached one of the EKG leads to it. When the tip of the needle hit the heart muscle, there might be a noticeable change in the fibrillation tracing. Then she could withdraw the needle just a little and be in the space between the pericardial membrane and the heart muscle. Otherwise, the best she could hope for was getting fluid before hitting the heart. It all seemed perfectly logical—at least on paper it did.

"All right, let's try shocking him one more time at three hundred and sixty," she said, with surprising determination and force, "then we'll go for the tap."

This time the shock produced no return at all to a normal rhythm—only a change in the ventricular tachycardia from a rough, sawtooth-like pattern to a form of V-tach where the irregular spikes were smaller. Petros's heart was giving out. Thea ignored the fear and anxiety that continued clawing at her, and prepared to perform a pericardiocentesis for the first time on a living patient, driving a thick four-inch needle up under the tip of her father's breastbone and into his heart, hoping to avoid piercing the left lobe of his liver along the way.

"You need to have the catheter ready, sis," Niko said suddenly.

"I have it right here. You want to do this or not?"

"It isn't going to make any difference."

"Then you have nothing to worry about, Niko."

"That jungle certainly toughened you up."

"This day has toughened me up more than all those years in the jungle ever did. Yes or no?"

Niko worked his way through the bedside crowd and confidently pulled on a pair of latex gloves.

"You were doing well, Thea," he said.

Thea glanced up at the code clock. Four minutes.

"Keep pumping until Dr. Sperelakis asks you to stop," she told the resident. "So far, you and you alone have saved this patient with your excellent CPR."

In the hands of a skilled cardiac surgeon, the pericardiocentesis took just seconds. The return of a striking amount of blood-tinged serum from beneath the pericardial membrane was diagnostic.

"Well, I'll be," Niko said. "You got me, sis. You got me good. Resume pumping, Tim, until I get this catheter sewn in place to keep the drainage going. . . . Great. Now, let's try once more at three hundred and sixty joules. Ready . . . and . . . clear!"

SEVEN

Wagner's "Ride of the Valkyries" exploded through four suspended mega-speakers the moment Thea opened the door and stepped into the subdued light of the carriage house. The structure, large enough for half a dozen carriages at least, featured dark paneling, post-and-beam construction, and an expansive loft. Throughout her childhood, Thea had usually been frightened to enter the place, perhaps responding to the sensory defensiveness that had influenced so much of her life—in the case of the carriage house, an aversion to the dim lighting and dark corners, as well as to the broad staircase leading up to the unknown gloom of the loft.

Later, as it became more and more the domain of her older brother, she allowed him to coax her inside for mock dragon battles and role-playing games. In her best school years, Thea still had few close friends, just a couple of them of her gender. Dimitri did better in that regard, often hosting the "Nerd Squad"—a gang of boys and an occasional girl who closed themselves in the carriage house, playing countless hours of computer games and intricate role-playing adventures such as Dungeons and Dragons. By the time Thea reached her mid-teens, many of her brother's Nerd Squad had graduated from MIT or Harvard or other top colleges, usually in computer technology, engineering, or some obscure area of science. Dimitri, however, possibly the brightest of the bunch, had graduated from no place, but instead, after a brief try at a local college, had receded deeper and deeper into the isolation and recesses of the carriage house.

"Dimitri, shut that off! Shut that off or I'm leaving!"

The powerful music, famous in part as the accompaniment of helicopter bombing runs in the movie *Apocalypse Now,* continued unabated. Thea pressed her palms against her ears. She had gained some control over her reaction to loud noises and other elements of her sensory defensiveness, but certainly nothing like total mastery. Smiling in spite of herself at how little time it had taken for her brother to reestablish his outlandishness, she stood by the ornately carved oak door and called out one more time.

After what had just transpired in the hospital, between her and her buttoned-down siblings, it was impossible not to measure them against Dimitri, who had always been something of a hero to her.

"Dimit—"

The music stopped mid-note. Dimitri materialized at the head of the stairs, then slid down the banister, vaulting over the end cap with practiced ease to land just two feet away from her.

"Dimitri, you child."

They embraced briefly and awkwardly. Even after many hours of social role-playing improv games during various group sessions, Thea was still more reserved than many when it came to hugging—although much less so with her patients than with her friends and family.

Two of the three boyfriends she had had in her life were neuroatypicals, and weren't excessively touchy. The third, Rick, neurotypical and her first true lover, told her over and over that she was the smartest, sexiest, most beautiful woman he had ever known. They stayed together for more than six months in college, sharing what Thea felt was an appropriately passionate love life. Then, with little warning, Rick drifted on to a woman who was, in his words, less physically inhibited. As she did with most of the emotionally charged situations in her life, Thea intellectualized his decision, and after seeing him together with his new girl, Thea decided he was right. She was still the most beautiful woman he had ever met.

"Welcome home, little sister."

"Thanks. You look good."

In fact, despite his perpetual dark stubble, he did. Thea remembered dense shadows under his eyes and persistent blinking, from stress or fatigue, or meds if he was taking any. Now there was less tension. In fact, there was almost a calmness to him. He looked more than ever like Petros—certainly more than Niko did—dark, swarthy, and classically Greek, with a spare physique that featured none of the soft prosperity that Niko's did.

His loft looked like the communications center for a portion of NASA. There were five monitors, two of them large flat screens. Both displayed video games in progress. In front of several of them were game consoles—Xbox, PS2, Wii, and a couple that Thea suspected her brother might have built himself. In addition, there were oscilloscopes and screens related to several other computers. To one side of the space, in front of shelves of Star Wars models, memorabilia, and games, was a broad worktable, strewn with ongoing projects and partially dissected hard drives. The area spoke to her of isolation and solitude, and would have saddened her greatly except for the word at the hospital that, some years before, Dimitri had actually participated on a team working on the development of a complex system of electronic medical records.

"So," Dimitri said, "how's the man?"

"He died, but I resuscitated him," Thea said matter-of-factly.

It was much easier for her to speak with her older brother than with either of the twins. With them she was constantly monitoring herself to gauge whether she was being too blunt or insulting, or whether she was overlooking some social nuance. She didn't always pick up gaffes before they happened, but she knew she was still, and always would be, a work in progress.

"Uh-oh. How did that sit with you-know-who and you-know-who-two?"

"How does it sit with you?"

Dimitri propped his bare feet on the counter beneath the monitor screens.

"You're the doctor. Is he ever going to wake up, Doctor?"

"I don't believe so, but I really can't predict at this point."

"And what will he be like if he does? Animal, mineral, or vegetable?"

"Sometimes people make it pretty far back from these sorts of things."

"Sounds like another way of saying vegetable. I've been in to see him once. Sure didn't look to me like he's coming back."

"So you think I should have just let him go back there? No resuscitation?"

"I think you're a doctor. You gotta do what you gotta do. But I also know that the twins are doctors, too. And I know they've been waiting for you to come home so we all can sign a paper telling the doctors at the hospital not to do what you just did."

"You were going to sign that?"

"Actually, I told Niko and Selene that if you signed, I'd sign. Us against them, just like the old days."

Thea tilted her chair back and set her feet up next to her brother's.

"It's not time yet."

"There's a lot of money at stake, I would guess. That's got to be of interest to the Twinkies."

"They're both surgeons, Dimitri. They have plenty of money."

"Suit yourself. You want to see this great new Mario game? I have a friend online who is just the ultimate artist. I think he's from Japan someplace. He can take any video game, like *Super Mario World,* and make it X-rated. Just imagine what the princess is doing in that other castle? See, I help him with the technical end. He chips in the artwork. The guy's a genius. You should see what he did with *Pac-Man*. Ms. Pac-Man can't keep her snapper off him."

Thea grinned. The abrupt subject change was Dimitri's way of saying that talk about their father and the twins had gone on as long as he could handle. For Dimitri, as for her, in fact, life was all about keeping stress down to a manageable level. Chaos, uncertainty, unexpected changes, difficult social situations, and confusing topics were some of the enemies. The difference between the two of them was that she initially had their mother and now Dr. Carpenter as advocates and guides, and Dimitri had never really had anyone.

As far as Thea knew, her brother's diagnosis had never been established, although she suspected that whatever had placed him squarely among the neuroatypicals fell somewhere on the autism spectrum, quite possibly some variant of Asperger syndrome or Asperger's combined with some other condition.

"Another time, Dimitri. I'm going to head back to the hospital. I'm sort of reverse jet-lagged right now."

"If you see the lights on up here, I'm up. Just ignore my alarm system and come on in."

She wondered as she stood to leave what, if any, impact the death of their father would have on him. She glanced over at his sleeping area: a rumpled double bed, armoire, hot plate, and apartment-sized refrigerator. Over the time she was here, she resolved to spend more time with him, possibly outside of his lair, and to get more of a sense of his survival skills. He didn't seem particularly miserable at this juncture of his life, but he didn't seem especially joyful either.

"Okay, maybe I'll see you later or in the morning," she said. "I might just stay in the family room at the hospital tonight."

"It might not have been an accident," Dimitri replied, continuing to shoot at an advancing horde of demons, each one of whom exploded in green blood when hit.

"What?"

"The man's accident. It might not have been one. Someone might have hit him on purpose."

"Why would you say that?"

Dimitri remained focused on the demons.

"I don't think everyone every place loved him. Not that often, but sometimes, the man would ask me to come with him on his morning walk. He always went the same route. After he was hit, I drove out to the spot with Niko. It was on a curve right by a three-foot-high stone wall. There was blood and hair on the wall where the man hit it, and he ended up well behind it."

"A woman walking her dog noticed him, yes?"

"That's what we were told."

"Go on."

"Got 'em!" he exclaimed, gesturing to the screen. "Did you see that shot, lady? Two at once."

It was hard at moments like this for Thea to believe that her brother might be among the most intelligent beings on the planet, but she had been told by her mother and the twins of testing done by the college he briefly attended, indicating that it was, by some measurements, the case.

"Dimitri, get to the point," she insisted, an edge of exasperation in her voice.

With no introduction, Dimitri jumped to his feet, marched two screens over, and activated the computer that was there. Instantly an animation appeared showing the road and a stick-figure man walking beside it. The curve was there, and the stone wall, shown in nearly perfect proportions and three-dimensional perspective. Then, in slow motion, the figure became airborne, striking the wall with his head and then flipping over it.

"To knock him in this direction, the car would have to have been coming like this."

Dimitri pressed a key and the stick figure returned to its original position. Then a green four-door automobile moved into the picture, coming from the right, and struck the figure, sending it tumbling once again, slamming against, then over, the stone wall. Thea saw the point immediately.

"Niko said there were no skid marks and no tire tracks in the dirt," she said. "The driver of the car would have had to hit Dad, then make a really sharp left in order to keep from going across that stretch of ground and hitting the wall himself."

"Exactly. If he was drunk, he wouldn't have been able to do it. If he were sober, he would have had a hundred and twenty feet to see the man before he hit him."

"Was it dark?"

"Not according to the police."

"Have you shown anyone this?"

"I told Niko and Selene that I had made it, but they really didn't seem all that interested. The truth is, they're not all that interested in anything I do."

Dimitri again immersed himself in killing demons. Thea knew he had retreated into the emotional safety of his video games, and for the moment, at least, he was announcing that all consideration of their father's near-fatal accident was over.

For Thea, however, that was not the case. She wandered out of the carriage house and back to Petros's Volvo, immersed in the possibility that the hit-and-run disaster might *not* have been an accident. It was chilling to think that someone could have purposely done such a thing to their father, but at the same time, her finely honed analytical sense was already at work probing the overriding question—why?

"Papa, what is that? The house is shaking. Papa, what's happening? Is this another earthquake?"

Nine-year-old Petros and his father, Konstantine, were in the living room of their modest house on a dusty hillside in the town of Lixouri, prefecture of Kefalonia—an island in the Ionian Sea west of mainland Greece. Konstantine Sperelakis was a teacher of Greek history and literature, and it was said of him that he knew what he knew. It was his absolute belief that Kefalonia, not Ithaca, was the birthplace of Odysseus, and he never passed up the chance to present the evidence to anyone who would listen.

There had been tremors and small earthquakes before—Konstantine had explained that Kefalonia lay on one of the great faults of the world—but something about these tremors was different. In spite of himself, because he knew his father's strict rules, Petros began to cry.

The year of the earthquake—the worst in many decades—was 1949. Sixty years later, lying helpless on his back in the intensive care unit of the Beaumont Clinic in Boston, Petros was reliving that horrible day piece by piece: the sounds, the sights, even the smells. Horrible . . . fateful. For a brief time, images of the earthquake faded, yielding to the sounds and sensations of another disaster—this one right here in the hospital, and not long ago.

"Clear!"

Thea's voice. Had he arrested? Yes, he had arrested and he was dying . . . No, he must have been dead. He couldn't focus his thoughts well, but he remembered enough to know he had been resuscitated—just as he remembered the death of his family.

"One milligram of epinephrine IV, please, Tracy. Prepare to shock at three hundred. . . ."

Thea . . .

The tremors were coming closer together. Pieces of the ceiling were beginning to fall.

"Petros, I slapped you because this is no time for hysteria. If I told you once, I told you a thousand times, no crying! Now go find your mother and your sister and get them out from under this roof before I have to slap you again."

"Papa, the floor! I can't stand up! Papa, help! . . ."

EIGHT

Night—post-midnight morning, really—had always been Thea's favorite time in the hospital. During her residency she had often signed up for extra duty as the night float, relieving the other residents from 10 P.M. to 8 A.M. so they could get caught up on their paperwork and their sleep.

It was nearly 3 A.M. when she wandered through the glassed-in causeway that connected the venerable Clark Pavilion, where the reconstructed medical ICU was housed, to the third floor of the ultramodern Sperelakis Institute for Diagnostic Medicine. The situation with the founder of the institute was gratifyingly stable. After Niko removed a significant amount of bloody fluid from Petros's pericardial sac, he was electrically converted from ventricular fibrillation to a normal rhythm on the first try, and there he had remained, with his blood pressure gradually returning to effective levels.

Thea ambled past the closed and open doors of the Beaumont Clinic in-patients, taking in the night sounds of labored breathing, coughing, and restless shifting in bed. Regardless of the politics and the personality clashes and the empire building, this was a special place.

She had done a month of study here during med school, following her father and his retinue of house officers and students from room to room, listening to him cajoling the young doctors to be their best, employing a wit and patience he seldom used at home. Later, during her residency, she had come back for two more rotations.

Her thoughts this night kept drifting back to her brother Dimitri's computer-graphic depiction of Petros's accident. Could someone really have tried to kill the nearly seventy-year-old icon—a man who had done so much for so many over the years? Of course, she acknowledged, no matter how brilliant a physician was, there were bound to be disgruntled patients and their families. In addition, her experience with hospital politics exposed her to the passionate mesh of allies and enemies that characterized every medical staff, with each specialty protecting its turf, its OR time . . . and its income.

It was hard to believe that Selene and Niko refused to pay any attention to Dimitri's theory. If the physics behind it were correct, the depiction of the alleged accident was compelling. And knowing her brother's massive intellect, regardless of how eccentric he might be, it was difficult not to at least consider what he had to say.

From the third floor, Thea took the stairs up to traverse the fourth, then the fifth. Not surprisingly, every room was occupied. She was on the sixth floor when a sudden, mountainous wave of fatigue washed over her. No surprise. After spending time with Dimitri, she really should have stayed home. But she was still wired from the resuscitation and the clash with the twins, to say nothing of the long flight to Boston, the lack of any food in the house, and the spirit of Petros and her own often painful past, which seemed to pervade every corner of the creaky old place.

Trying to drive the ten miles back to Wellesley now was out of the question. There would be a tree trunk or telephone pole waiting at every corner. Barely able to lift her feet from the floor, Thea made her way back to the ICU. Four hours later, she awoke stiff and sore on the couch in the family room, remembering only that she had stopped in for a final check on her father before lying down. Someone, one of the nurses most likely, had thrown a blanket over her.

After another quick visit to the unit, she washed her face and brushed her teeth in the restroom, and headed across campus to the cafeteria. The Lion's vital signs were stable, and the drainage from the fine plastic catheter Niko had left in the pericardial space was minimal. Saving the man's life wasn't what the twins had wanted, but in truth, thanks to logic and following process, it had been quite simple.

"The hard part is figuring out what to do," Petros was often quoted as saying when trying to convince medical students to choose internal medicine over surgery. "The easy part is doing it."

It just wasn't the man's time yet, Thea thought now, recalling any number of medical "pearls" from her father. The twins' arguments notwithstanding, it just wasn't time.

The cafeteria was on the far side of the hospital campus. Thea took the brightly lit basement-level tunnels, following solid blue guide lines artfully tiled on the walls, along with at least a dozen other colors coded for various laboratories and clinical buildings. Signs posted at every tunnel intersection made it almost impossible to get lost. Whoever had designed the system was thoughtful—and clearly well funded.

Over the past decade or so, the Beaumont had grown from being a decent-sized medical center to being one of the largest, most influential hospitals in the country, on par with the Mayo, and well beyond Boston's revered White Memorial. Every specialty was represented by giants in their field. The nursing service had won countless awards and was viewed in the press as the paradigm of what such services could and should be, as well as the ultimate plum job for any aspiring nurse. Where once there had been a floor of operating suites, now there were several buildings, with every one of the ORs booked solid—often long into the night. Thea had read online not long ago that the endowment of the Beaumont was in the tens of billions and growing— this at a time when 25 percent of hospitals were reported to be losing money.

Several of the offshoots of the Beaumont tunnels had no color coding, only signs that read RESTRICTED ACCESS—AUTHORIZED PERSONNEL ONLY. During her rotation at the hospital, the medical students and new residents had been taken on a tour that included some of these areas. At the end of the unlabeled tunnels were gates blocking off stairs down to the subbasement, and in many spots a sub-subbasement as well. At the deeper levels, the walls went from bright tile to time-blackened brick. In spots, moss had overgrown the cement grout. Bare incandescent lights battled to a draw with the darkness, and a number of metal doors along the corridors were corroded and barred.

In such a litigious society, Thea was surprised that the old tunnels hadn't been permanently sealed off in some way. Then she and the others were shown a number of facilities down there still in use: a primate lab and storage area, a similar room for smaller animals, a laundry annex in full operation, and a backup furnace space with equipment that was still functioning but appeared to date back into the nineteenth century. Eventually, they were given a tour of the laundry room annex by a Hispanic woman who looked as if she hadn't seen daylight in years.

It was nearing eight when Thea entered the bustling cafeteria. The vast space was compartmentalized by creative carpentry and lighting, as well as different food groups and ethnicity, giving the area a remarkably cozy, homey feel. Still, at this time of the day, there was little that could be done about the crowds. The central bank of cashiers had queues six or seven deep.

Thea put together a tray of fresh fruit and yogurt, plus a croissant and black coffee with a single ice cube, a throwback to her days as a resident when there was never time to wait for coffee to cool down. Then she found a seat in one of a pod of small tables for two and settled down gratefully, her mind pierced by the double-horned questions of how much validity there was to Dimitri's theory about the hit-and-run accident, and how he would do when Petros was gone.

There was no doubt that the twins would want to sell the Wellesley house as soon as possible. The family home, several acres in one of the most desirable of the west suburbs, needed some serious refurbishing, but several years ago she had heard Selene quote a value of five million. Was there any way they would consider separating the carriage house off and selling just the main house? She had no idea what Petros's will said about the house and the executors of his estate, or in fact, if a will even existed, but she felt certain that if she took Dimitri's side in any carriage house negotiations, the lawyers for the twins would have a field day. Then she reminded herself that the death of the owner of the house was still far from foregone.

Thea had just pulled the tip off her croissant when a boy caught her eye. He was eleven or so, with a rebellious look to him. A shock of dark hair protruded from beneath a baseball cap, which was pulled twenty degrees or so off center. His black T-shirt advertised the cities of some sort of band tour on the back, and his baggy jeans were pulled low—very low. He was approaching the queue of one of the cashiers, carrying a tray piled with pastries, several bananas, a plate of scrambled eggs, fried potatoes, and three cartons of chocolate milk. Thea had no idea what it was about the boy that attracted her attention, but she knew from the moment she first saw him that he had no intention of paying for his meal.

The literal approach to life characterizing many

people's Asperger syndrome allowed little room or tolerance for lying or other forms of dishonesty. In an earlier time, Thea would have been so disturbed by a person treating the rules with such disregard that she would have become severely agitated until she could point out the thief to someone. But after sessions on the subject with Dr. Carpenter, and her experiences in poverty-swept countries, she had mellowed considerably.

She followed the youth with her gaze, looking to see if, perhaps, he was there with an adult, but he was no more than ten yards away from her, and clearly looking for an empty table. She viewed him as underprivileged and quite possibly underfed. The mighty Beaumont Clinic with all its billions could certainly absorb the loss. Still, a largely dormant part of her wanted to confront him or report him to—

Off to the right, she spotted a blue-uniformed security guard, a tall man with close-cropped brown hair, striding purposefully toward the table where the thief had settled down. Thea's breakfast remained untouched as she watched the drama unfold. The approaching guard was even bigger than she had first thought— six-three, she guessed, with a broad chest that suggested he was or had once been an athlete. She couldn't see the man's expression, but knowing how seldom most security guards actually got to thwart crime, she suspected it was ravenous.

The man encountered his prey just as the boy was opening the first of his cartons of chocolate milk. Thea expected to see a paw clamp onto the youth's neck, lifting him to his feet as easily as if a bear were pulling up a carrot. Instead, the man knelt down, setting his arm across the back of the boy's chair and speaking softly into his ear. The youth, staring straight ahead, shook his head vehemently. Again, a whisper from the guard. This time the boy shrugged and nodded, resigned to having been caught.

Ah, the pinch, Thea thought. *Banned from the Beaumont for life!*

But there was no pinch. Instead, the solidly built man withdrew his wallet from his hip pocket, extracted some bills, and handed them to the boy. Then, without looking back, the guard went to the coffee bar and poured himself a cup. Thea kept her eyes on the boy, certain that he was going to pocket the money and bolt. Instead, he carried his tray to one of the lines, patiently waited his turn, and paid for his breakfast.

If there were others who had observed the drama, Thea did not notice them. She watched until the boy had returned to his table and begun to attack his meal. It wasn't until she had turned her attention back to her own breakfast that she realized the hero of the piece had sat down at the table next to hers.

NINE

Thea knew she was staring over at the security guard, but didn't see anything particularly embarrassing about doing so. He had absolutely beautiful kind blue eyes, which seemed to be smiling even when he wasn't. From this close, his broad shoulders looked capable of pushing a mountain.

"G'morning," he said, glancing over, his voice as gentle as his eyes.

"Good morning to you. . . . That was quite a nice thing you did with that boy."

"Huh? Oh, thanks. It seemed like what was called for. He's been in here a few times before. I figured he needed the little bit of food he took each time and I just let it go, but this time he went a little overboard."

"There's a lot of taking things where I work, but the children don't have much, so it's understandable."

"And where's that?"

"Where's what?"

"Where you work."

Thea knew she was having trouble concentrating, and wondered if it was due to being so tired, the underlying ADD that coexisted with her Asperger's, or something else—something about the man.

"Oh, the Democratic Republic of the Congo," she replied as if she were saying, *Oh, just down the street.*

"I see."

The guard didn't look as if he totally believed her. He took a sip of coffee, peered into his cup, and appeared to be ready to end their conversation right there.

"I saw everything that happened. You were very kind. I don't have any children. . . . Well, I'm not even married. . . . But there are a lot of children where I work."

"In the Congo."

"The Democratic Republic of the Congo. Yes, exactly. It's in Africa."

"I know."

"It used to be called Zaire."

"I guess I knew that, too."

Thea sensed she might be annoying the man, but she didn't want the conversation between them to end.

"Do you have children?" she asked.

"Um . . . yes . . . one . . . a son."

"But he doesn't live with you?"

The question triggered Thea's Aspie alarm, but too late.

"No," he said. "No, he doesn't. How did you—?"

"Oh, I don't know. Just something about the way you answered."

"Oh."

There was a protracted silence during which Thea sensed that anything she chose to say at this point would be the wrong thing. It would have been nice to have Dr. Carpenter around to confirm that, and to cue her as to what to say next.

"So why do you think he keeps coming to the hospital?" she suddenly heard her voice asking.

"Who?"

"The boy. The boy you just helped."

The big man sighed and turned toward her as if he really didn't want to. In just the few seconds that followed, Thea took in a great number of things about him: the thin scar through his right brow, the fine, early crow's-feet at the corners of his wonderful eyes, the absence of a wedding ring, a rubber bracelet with the word DARFUR on it on his right wrist, and the name tag that read OFFICER DANIEL COTTON, SECURITY. There was also a slight redness to his cheeks—a touch of rosacea, she diagnosed.

"He says his mother is a patient here."

"Have you checked?"

Daniel Cotton sighed and glanced down at his watch with a lack of subtlety that even Thea picked up on.

"The truth is, I haven't been on this job very long. Once I learn the ropes, maybe I'll have the chance to get involved with some of the people I bust."

"Were you a policeman?"

This time, Cotton turned completely toward her. Thea tried to get a fix on what his odd expression might mean, but it was a skill she had never been even close to mastering.

"I . . . was. How can you possibly have known?"

Thea felt relieved that their conversation wasn't going to end. She spoke as she often did, with no great planning, no editing, and no firm idea as to what was going to come out.

"Well, the word *bust* is used all the time by almost everyone, but it has fewer nonslang meanings than people might suspect. In fact, according to Kornetsky's *Origin of Words and Slang,* page twenty-two or twenty-three, I think, bust has only two acceptable definitions: a sculpture of a person's head, shoulders, and upper chest, and also, a woman's bosom. There are many other meanings of the word, but they are all slang, such as to smash or break; to cause to come to an end such as to bust up the union; to demote in rank; to punch, usually in the face or mouth; to become bankrupt or short of money; to be a failure or a flop; to lose at blackjack; and finally, two slang meanings used primarily by police, and meaning to place under arrest or to make a raid. Oh, yes, and there's also a somewhat vulgar use of the word, to bust one's ass, meaning to work very hard."

Cotton was wide-eyed.

"Do you rattle off things like that often?" he asked.

"Not really that often, but I could."

"My name's—"

"I know. Officer Daniel Cotton."

She pointed to his name tag.

There was a silence that Thea found vaguely uncomfortable until she realized that Cotton was waiting for her to give her name.

"I don't have the benefit of your name tag," he said before she could.

"Oh, I suppose that's because I don't have one. But if I did, and if it was accurate, it would say Doctor Alethea Sperelakis, like yours says Officer Daniel Cotton. Alethea means *truth* in Greek. Everyone has always called me Thea, though, just like everyone probably calls you Dan, or maybe Danny."

She sensed it was nervousness that was making her speak so rapidly and so much, and cut herself off.

"Dan is right. I was Danny until I started towering over my parents, then Dan. Sometimes Daniel. It really doesn't matter to me. So is that Sperelakis, as in—"

"Yes. He's my father."

"Are you the one who . . . who saved his life last night? They talked about his close call at report this morning."

"I suppose so. My brother Niko helped by doing the pericardiocentesis—that's sticking a needle into the space around someone's heart—but I guess I did most of it. At a resuscitation, it's important for everyone involved to know who's in charge. Last night that was me."

"You just say it like it is, huh?"

"Is there another way to say it?"

Dan looked at his watch again.

"Listen, Dr. Sperelakis—Thea—my break is over. I . . . um . . . I hope you don't think I'm being too forward, but I would enjoy getting together maybe for dinner or . . . or for coffee sometime after your father is . . . better."

"That's a nice way to put it, Officer Dan Cotton, but the truth is, unless there's a miracle, I don't think he's going to get better. My brother and sister don't think even a miracle would help him make it back to any decent quality of life. If they had their way, there would have been no resuscitation last night and he would already be dead."

"Aren't you something," Dan said, as much to himself, it seemed, as to her. "You just say it like it is."

"You already said that. The answer is yes."

"Yes what?"

"Yes, I would enjoy having dinner or coffee with you, but I think you should consider giving coffee up."

"Why?"

"That redness on your cheeks is a condition called rosacea. Women get it quite a bit more often than men, but men get it, too, and you've got it. It's not really curable, but there are some fairly effective treatments for it. Your case is very mild and may just get better if you stay away from hot liquids like coffee. And alcohol, too."

"That's it?"

"Well, actually, no. Most doctors who know about rosacea, and I'm one of those, feel that stress is causative as well. Merriman and Blalock published a paper in 2004—April, I think, in the *Journal of Dermatology*—where they applied a stress scale to rosacea patients and pretty well proved it. So, since you've got to be under stress from your change in jobs from the police force to here, that could be contributing to your outbreak. Maybe a nice dinner will be just what the doctor ordered, so to speak. Do you still want to go?"

"Of course I do."

Thea sensed from Dan's expression that she might

have said something wrong, but he still wanted to have dinner with her, so it couldn't have been that wrong.

"Great," she said.

"You seem very . . . serious."

"Lots of people think that at first because I don't really try and hide the fact that I know a lot of things. But the people I work with think I'm very funny. Smart but funny. My brother Dimitri tells me I'm one of the funniest people he's ever met. Speaking of Dimitri, there's a favor you could do for me."

Thea didn't come close to picking up on the astonishment in the man's eyes.

"Name it," he said. "I owe you for the medical consultation."

"This involves putting on your policeman's hat—I mean your *former* policeman's hat."

"Go on."

"Our father was the victim of a hit-and-run driver."

"I heard that."

"Well, my brother Dimitri is very bright—smarter than me. He has a theory that whoever hit Father did it on purpose. He's made some computer animations that seem to prove his point. But apparently no one, including our twin brother and sister, seems interested in what they show. Could you come by sometime soon and look at the animation and talk about Dimitri's theory with him?"

"If you want. I suppose I could do that."

Why would I ask you to do something unless I wanted you to do it? Thea wondered.

Just as quickly, she answered her own question. "If you want" was sort of a figure of speech—a polite confirmation that Dan Cotton respected her and would be happy to do what she asked.

Dr. Carpenter would be pleased.

TEN

"Please take off your clothes in that tent, sir, and throw them outside the door. Then put on the wet suit we have left for you. The suit should fit you, but snugly. Then, once we are certain you have no wires and no weapons, we'll be ready to go. It's not as if Mr. Rose doesn't trust you in particular, it's that he doesn't trust anyone."

"I understand," Gerald Prevoir said.

And he did.

Throughout his life, Prevoir had survived and supported himself by following directions to the letter. As a Marine in Afghanistan over most of a decade he had learned to kill and to enjoy it. Then he had dropped his honorable discharge, Purple Heart, and Bronze Star medal into the bottom drawer of his bureau and had signed on as a mercenary in Kazakhstan and later in central Africa.

It was five years ago that he came under his current employ. He was between jobs, spending time with his latest girlfriend at his beach house in the Keys, when he saw the ad in *Soldier of Fortune*.

WANTED: Jack-of-all-trades willing to get it and go, and experienced in same. Must be able to

follow directions to the letter, no questions asked.
Salary negotiable.

"Willing to get it and go," in *Soldier of Fortune*
terms, meant willing to kill. That had never been a deal
breaker for him, so he responded to the magazine box
number listed. He never met his employer, nor had
he to this day. An initial interview took place before a
camera in a motel room in Kittery, Maine, during which
he was questioned by a man—or woman—whose voice
was electronically distorted.

After he was hired, his instructions arrived via cell
phone or a CD sent to a post office box, and he responded the same way. The pay, deposited in Prevoir's
blind account in a Cayman Islands bank, was excellent,
and the work so far, with the exception of having to as-
sist the Reverend Gideon Bohannan, had been clean.

Hatred, envy, and greed. As long as there were hatred, envy, and greed, his employer had assured him,
there would be business.

They were on a totally deserted beach on Pamlico
Sound, North Carolina. Anchored a hundred yards
off the coast was Gregory Rose's yacht, *Zoe May*. This
would be Prevoir's second meeting with the shipping
magnate, who was reputed to have begun amassing his
considerable fortune from drug money, but had long
since turned his illegitimate enterprises over to others.
The previous meeting between them had taken place
almost three months ago.

With Rose's man watching, Prevoir undressed unhur-
riedly, and meticulously folded his black pants, sports

coat, and turtleneck, setting them on a towel outside the tent. Then he pulled on the short-sleeved, knee-length, eight-inch-thick wet suit and zipped it up the back. He was a muscular man, six feet even, more wiry than bulky, and without a bit of flab. He honed his body through two or three hours a day of aerobic exercise, Kenpo karate, and weightlifting when he was not on the road, and at least an hour a day when he was. At the interview in the Kittery Motel, he had done a hundred push-ups for the camera and could easily have done more.

Rose's man inspected Prevoir front and back, but didn't bother patting him down. There was no need. Then he led him down to a ten-foot inflatable Zodiac powered by an eight-horsepower Yamaha, and drove him out to the *Zoe May,* a sleek though not particularly pretentious Palmer-Johnson yacht, which Prevoir estimated at 120 feet—maybe six or seven million depending on the add-ons. Gregory Rose was waiting for him at a table on the second deck. He was a slightly built man, with small, feral eyes.

Rose ordered two bottles of Dos Equis. By the time they arrived, Prevoir felt quite confident that if necessary, he could use the bottle and his skills to dispatch his host and both his bodyguards. At the moment, however, there was no reason to believe he would have to.

"So, Mr. Prevoir," Rose said, "you said there have been developments with our little snipe."

"Very important developments," Prevoir said. "Namely, that she has cancer."

"Of the pancreas."

"Of the pancreas," Prevoir echoed, genuinely

impressed with the reach of the man's intelligence network. "Exactly."

"That is just so sad," Rose said, his narrow eyes dancing.

"I told you when we last met that was going to happen."

"Yes. Yes, you did."

"And I also told you that we were aware that through her stubbornness and unwillingness to commit to a merger of her Wildwood Enterprises and your Seven Palms resort chain, Ms. Hayley Long was in the process of costing you, what was it *Forbes* estimated, one hundred and fifty million dollars?"

"You shouldn't believe everything you read in magazines," Rose said, scowling. "Their estimate of what she is costing me is low."

"I'm sorry to hear that. If that indeed is the case, then we have strong grounds to believe what was written about the bad blood between you and the lovely Ms. Long, yes?"

There was a pregnant silence during which Rose finished his beer.

"Hayley Long is a bitch," he said with sudden vehemence, "a backstabbing bitch, who delights in causing others pain."

"You in particular, from all we have heard. Am I correct in believing that you have openly wished her ill?"

"If I wished for such a thing, then my prayers have been answered. Cancer is a bad business and cancer of the pancreas is one of the worst, most painful of all. Such a pity."

"Mr. Rose," Prevoir said, "please don't ask me how

we know, but we promise you that Hayley Long is going to receive chemotherapy for her cancer according to one of the latest experimental protocols, and is going to survive and be cancer-free. We guarantee it."

"What an odd thing to guarantee."

"But it's the truth. I promise you that."

"But how—?"

"I asked you not to question me on this matter."

"Now, I find that quite distressing. I was counting on a different outcome."

"Without her in the picture, your Seven Palms/Wildwood merger will probably go through. There are those in Long's company that support it."

"You people certainly have done your homework. How did you—?"

"It doesn't matter. The point is we know, and the point is we can provide a service in which you should be interested."

"Go on."

"I can promise you, Mr. Rose, that we have the power to see to it that Hayley Long does not recover from her cancer, and in fact, that she never leaves the hospital alive."

Gregory Rose considered the statement and its implications.

"Without any suspicion or possibility that I was involved?" he asked finally.

"None whatsoever. Patients die in hospitals all the time."

"Patients die in hospitals all the time." Rose ruminated on the words as he repeated them.

"Your payment instructions will be delivered to you via a DVD," Prevoir said. "Terms are half in advance, half when Hayley Long, sadly, succumbs to her disease."

"Half of how much?" Rose asked.

"Three million dollars. Not a penny more—ever."

Rose didn't blink at the amount.

"And what if I don't come up with the second half?" he asked.

Prevoir grinned coldly.

"Let's see," he said. "Your doctor's name is Lance Goldfarb, 313 Paradise Road, Key Biscayne. You are blood type B positive. You had your appendix out seven years ago. You have hemorrhoids. You also have genital herpes which you got from someone other than your wife. You are severely allergic to sulfa and are having persistent nightmares, mostly around a fear of snakes that goes back to your early childhood. I think there's enough material in there to ensure that we'd know what to do if you decided to hold out on us."

"I'll kill that son-of-a-bitch doctor," he said, through nearly clenched teeth. "I'll fucking kill him."

"Then you'd be killing an innocent man, who incidentally seems to be a pretty decent doctor. By the way, your mother's doctor is—"

"Enough! Tell me what to do."

"You'll get your instructions soon. Don't waste any time, though, Mr. Rose. Hayley Long's chemotherapy has already begun."

ELEVEN

It was midday when Thea awoke in her childhood bedroom in Wellesley—a room that spoke in many ways to her early difficulties with so-called executive function. Posters of rock stars, supermodels, and Star Wars characters covered most of the walls and some of the ceiling, taped on at odd angles.

The only framed items (courtesy of her mother) were Xeroxed achievement certificates from various summer camps and schools, and later, as Dr. Carpenter's one-on-one therapy and groups took hold, report cards showing all As. There were stuffed animals and a couple of dolls, but what there were the most of were books—shelves and shelves of books. There were also stacks of books along the baseboards, in the corners, and even under the bed: novels, biographies, textbooks, comic books, manga, how-to manuals, self-help.

For a time, she lay in bed, images in her mind ricocheting from her father and his near death, to the twins and their anger, to the oddly eager hospital triumvirate of Amy Musgrave, Sharon Karsten, and Scott Hartnett, to Dimitri's animation and unappreciated theory of attempted murder, and finally to her own need to spend some time with Dr. Carpenter before returning to the Congo.

But connecting the dots of her rambling thoughts were those involving Dan Cotton. Put simply, she liked the man—liked him a lot. The caring way in which he dealt with the young thief; the dismay in his expression when she rattled off more than anyone might ever want to know about the word *bust*; the sadness when he responded to her asking whether he was at one time a cop—he was at once interesting and perplexing, confident and vulnerable, and very, very cute.

Gentle Dan.

They hadn't settled on a specific day to get together again, but he had said he wanted it to happen, and she felt certain it would. Now, she began worrying if she should try and help him understand her Asperger's before she inadvertently said or did something that put him off. It wouldn't be the first time that had happened with a guy. Like many Aspies, when she spoke, she inadvertently used words that simply weren't part of everyday conversation, often sounding like a professor addressing a class, despite the fact that, even as a voracious reader, her usage of some of the words wasn't always accurate.

Men were attracted to her looks, but were often intimidated by her intelligence or put off by what they perceived was pomposity. Despite some early efforts in improv groups, she had never been able to mask that trait, even though some of her very intelligent neurotypical girlfriends easily and purposefully kept their vocabularies under wraps around men.

She rose, made the bed, and showered. Then she pulled on worn jeans and a turquoise blouse, checked herself front and back in the mirror she had first used as a child, and then lay down on the bedspread for a few more minutes of reflection, staring up at a twenty-year-old poster of KISS on the ceiling. She was, she acknowledged, intrigued with Dan Cotton's easy manner and rugged good looks—especially his eyes. However, if he turned out to be the sort who wouldn't give her the benefit of the doubt, who jumped to judgment, then she really didn't want him.

But she did.

Carrying a cup of coffee, Thea padded across the yard to the carriage house. She wanted to get Dimitri's approval to bring Dan Cotton by to discuss the possibility that their father had been hit deliberately. Of course, merely getting permission from her brother was no guarantee against some outrageous act, but she sensed Dan could handle just about anything, and asking Dimitri was at least a start. She also wanted to talk him into coming to the hospital with her. Steeled against another session with the "Ride of the Valkyries," she pressed her palms against her ears and eased open the heavy oak door.

The silence was breached by the theme from *Zorba the Greek,* playing through the high-tech speakers, but at quite a manageable volume.

"A few years ago," Dimitri said as they ascended the broad staircase, "I discovered a whole closet full of traditional costumes on the third floor. I guess the Lion must parade around in them when no one's home. Those zany Greeks."

"Dimitri, need I remind you that *you're* one of those zany Greeks?"

"Very funny. I think it's sweet the way Dad hangs on to tradition."

"Like the old Greek tradition of nitpicking your kids' egos to bits," Thea said.

"Okay, okay, he's not perfect."

"So, you want to come into the hospital with me?"

"I already went," Dimitri answered.

"That's like saying don't buy me a book for Christmas, I already have a book."

"You'll excuse me for being so logical, but if he's in a coma, what difference does it make if I'm there or not? Last time I went in, Aunt Mary was there stalking around the bed all hunched over, muttering about ridding the man of the evil eye."

"The *mati*," Thea said.

"She left one of those weird sets of eye beads."

"*Vaskania.*"

"I don't know how you learned this stuff. It's all Greek to me."

"Very funny, part two."

"Is old Mary really our aunt?" Dimitri asked.

"If she says she's our aunt, she's our aunt."

"How about all the other Aunt Marys?"

"They're our aunts, too. It doesn't matter whether the genetics are there or not."

"I think I'm going to pass on this one, sis. I've got some green meanies to destroy."

A child with an IQ of 180, trapped in an adult's

body. Thea looked at the screens and the costume, at the workbench and the unmade bed.

Could be worse, she thought. *Could be worse.*

"Okay, one other thing. You mentioned that Niko and Selene didn't take your theories about the accident very seriously."

"They don't take anything about me very seriously."

"I've met someone at the hospital—a security guard, but he used to be a policeman."

"Alcohol problem?"

"I . . . I don't know. But I don't think so."

"Did he shoot someone by mistake? Shoot someone on purpose? Rob the evidence room? Sleep with the commissioner's daughter? Give away Batman's identity?"

"Dimitri! This is someone who is willing to listen to you. Why are you challenging him when you don't even know him?"

"You like this guy?"

"I just met him."

"You like him. I'll be happy to tell your new friend what I know and what I think I know."

"That's big of you. I'll see how I feel about exposing him to you. Last chance to come along, cowboy."

"Be sure to say hello to Aunt Mary for me."

TWELVE

There was dedicated parking for Petros just outside the front doors of the Sperelakis Institute. Thea pulled his Volvo into the space wondering how her father must have felt at the moment of impact. It had to have happened too fast for him to think that he was about to take his last step, or that he had driven his car for the last time, or taken a nice, hot shower, or pondered a patient's perplexing diagnostic problem.

You never know, she thought sadly as she headed to the unit. *You just never know.*

Hospital CEO Sharon Karsten was standing in the deserted waiting area, talking on her cell phone. She motioned for Thea to wait before entering the unit, and quickly ended her call. Her fleeting expression looked strangely uncomfortable, giving Thea the impression that whoever was on the other end of the call was someone Thea knew.

"Hi, Thea," Karsten said. "They're working on him for a few more minutes. I was hoping I might bump into you before I had to run off for a meeting."

Karsten, wearing a tan linen suit, was a trim, aristocratic woman in her midfifties, who, thanks to her taste in clothes, her hairdresser, and carefully applied makeup, looked younger than Thea knew she was. There was a time when Petros had held Karsten up as a potential role model for Thea, claiming that the woman was one of the brightest endocrinologists in the city. Not long after that, Karsten was chosen commander in chief of the Beaumont Clinic. It was under her guidance that the medical center's steady growth had skyrocketed, and an era of massive acquisition and expansion had begun.

"How does he look to you?" Thea asked.

"The same as he has," Karsten replied, her distress apparent. "Some of the bruising is going away. I heard about what happened last night. It sounds like you were quite a hero."

"Niko is the one who did the pericardiocentesis."

"Only kicking and screaming. I know that he and your sister feel strongly that Petros is unsalvageable."

"They may be right."

"But you don't feel that way."

"It's not time to give up," she said for what seemed like the thousandth time.

"Thea, do you have any idea how much your father is worth?"

"Not really. I do know he was pretty conservative and responsible with his money."

Karsten glanced about to ensure no one had entered the waiting area.

"He's worth between fifteen and twenty million dollars—probably closer to twenty."

"My goodness," Thea said, realizing at the same instant that she had no real idea how much money twenty million dollars was, nor did she care.

"His will divides the money among the four of you, but not equally. Niko gets the largest portion because of his children. When—if—your father dies, Niko will go from being well-off to being quite rich. Your sister, with a high-paying, high-profile specialty, is already a millionaire, maybe several times over. Her inheritance will enable her to live the lifestyle she has chosen, but to live it at a level she and her partner have only dreamed of."

Thea mulled over the CEO's revelation about her father and her family, and wasn't impressed one way or the other. Her own pay from Doctors Without Borders would not have been enough to keep her afloat in a city like Boston, but it was fine for her needs in Africa. She wondered briefly if this was another attempt to get her to stay at the Beaumont, but she couldn't see how.

"Sharon, do you mind if I ask you how you've come to know so much about my father's financial . . ."

"I can see that you've answered your own question," Karsten said. "Your father and I have been involved with each other for five years or so. He was—is—a very wonderful man and a marvelous doctor, but he was also very private. That's why our relationship wasn't more . . . commonly known, and also why it's so hard for me to see him in there like that. He was—is—such a dignified person. Still, I don't want him to die, Thea. I don't want him to die no matter what your brother and sister say."

Thea was affected by the vehemence of the statement. She sensed some sort of commiseration was being asked for, but she didn't trust her words to come out right to a woman she knew only minimally, who had just admitted to a long-standing love affair with her father.

"I don't know what to say except that I think he's getting excellent care," she managed.

At that moment, the unit nurse opened the glass doors and nodded that they were done.

"I'd better get going," Karsten said after checking her watch. "I'm glad you're home, Thea. And don't worry about that business yesterday. Your father's name carries a great deal of weight with donors to this hospital as well as those sending referrals. As chief development officer, Scott was merely seizing on the opportunity to have that name continue at the Beaumont."

"I understand."

Thea waited until the CEO had vanished down the corridor to the elevators, and then entered the ICU. The battered Lion lay peacefully on his back, eyes taped shut, machines whirring. The bed linen, pulled up to his shoulders, was crisp and very white. On the bedside table, surrounded by swabs, rolls of tape, and ointments, someone had left an *eikona*—a small framed picture in gold leaf of the Virgin Mary holding baby Jesus. Double protection along with Aunt Mary's *vaskania*. Greeks were nothing if not superstitious and religious. God first, but protection against the *mati* never far away.

Instinctively, Thea checked the monitor numbers, and found them all within normal range. Then she let the bedrails down, bent over, and kissed her father on the forehead.

"I love you, Dad," she whispered, the first time she had said the words.

Then, as she had done once the day before, she removed the paper tape that secured his eyelids shut, and checked his pupils, which were mid-position as opposed to too constricted or dilated, and slightly reactive to light.

"I love you, Dad," she said again.

A second later, Petros Sperelakis's left eye moved.

THIRTEEN

Thea stared down at her father, her mind unwilling to accept fully what she had just seen.

The movement of Petros's left eye was a slight upward gaze of the globe, and with it a flick of his left upper lid. No movement whatsoever on the right.

"Dad, again," she urged. "Please try and move your eye again."

After what seemed an eternity, the Lion repeated the movement—no more complicated, but no less.

Limited focal movement clearly in response to a command. For Thea the news her father could move at all was mixed—dreadfully mixed.

Locked-in syndrome, possibly the most nightmarish medical condition imaginable in a person.

In normal neuroanatomy, the cerebral hemispheres and cerebellums of the brain received and processed information from sensory receptors in the body, and then sent a response message back down to the muscles. In locked-in syndrome, injury due to a hemorrhagic brain stem stroke or, rarely, brain stem trauma, effectively severed the pathways from the brain to the muscles of the body while leaving intact the incoming nerve fibers. Pain, yes . . . sensation, yes . . . consciousness, total . . . ability to move, none.

A fully functioning, fully alert mind locked within an absolutely motionless, unresponsive body.

Could there be anything more horrible than that?

Ordinarily, it would be completely impossible to tell if a comatose patient was, in fact, conscious and alert and immersed in locked-in syndrome. However, through a quirk of neuroanatomy, in a percentage of those with bleeding into a specific location of the pons region of the brain stem, one small set of muscles remained connected to the gray matter of the cerebral hemispheres: the muscles controlling a specific movement of one or sometimes both eyes.

Her heart pounding, Thea held her father's hand and asked him to repeat the movement of his left eye. Could this be anything other than locked-in syndrome? Perhaps, she began praying, it was the first step in a more generalized recovery.

"S'agapo, Mpampa." I love you, Daddy.

Again the movement—slight, but definite.

Thea cast about for someone to come in and validate what she was seeing, but neither her father's nurse nor the intensivist covering the unit were outside the room where she could see them, and Thea was reluctant to break the fragile connection with him.

For his part, the Lion looked unchanged, lying serenely supine, eyes closed, although it seemed to Thea as if he had been aged many years by the battering he had endured.

"Dad, can you open your eye? Can you open it just a little?"

Thea had not read a great deal about locked-in syndrome, although she planned on a long night in the hospital's extensive library as soon as this evolving situation had become stabilized. She had heard about the remarkable case of an editor of a French magazine who suffered a sudden brain stem hemorrhage while in his forties. As she recalled, he remained completely comatose with a tracheotomy and on a ventilator for some weeks, before awakening and discovering his gruesome condition. In his situation, communication was possible only through the elevation of his gaze. One eye? Both? Thea couldn't remember.

What she did remember was that the victim, through a scribe, developed the means to react as she was pointing to letters on an alphabet page. Together, painstakingly, they were able to record his story and his thoughts in a bittersweet memoir of a man's reaction to this most unimaginable of medical disasters. There was a book recording that memoir. Thea felt certain of it. And some time after that, there might actually have been a movie. As soon as possible, she vowed to read the man's memoir and to become an expert on the subject.

"Please, Dad. Just a little."

The eyelid creased, then opened just the tiniest crack, then closed again. Thea separated the lids upper from lower and pleaded again for a response. Slowly, but definitely, the iris and pupil rotated upward a millimeter or two. Thea had little doubt that the movement had been purposeful and in response to her urging.

"Dad, can you squeeze my hand?"

Nothing.

She parted the lids again.

"Look up if you can hear me. Look up."

Again, the eye rolled upward just enough for her to know for certain that the gesture was voluntary. Thea allowed herself to again focus on the possibility that this development might represent the first step on the path to neurological recovery. The elation was brief, giving way once again to the horrible sinking sensation that Petros was experiencing the pain and utter frustration that went with locked-in syndrome. One more confirmation that what she was witnessing wasn't merely in her head, and she would bring in the nurse or the intensivist and notify the twins and Dimitri, and maybe Sharon Karsten as well.

Was it possible Petros had been awake and alert when Niko and Selene were standing by the bedside, insisting that nothing be done to extend his life? How much of the discussion that preceded the resuscitation did he hear? How much of the closed-chest cardiac compressions did he feel?

"Dad," she said, "show me once more that you can hear me. Open your eye and look up at the ceiling. . . . Dad?"

Thea again spread his lids. For a full minute there was no movement of the eye—no movement whatsoever. Then Petros looked upward—a gaze more pronounced than any preceding it. Excitedly, Thea hurried for the nurse, Tracy Gibbons, who had helped her run the code. She didn't mention locked-in syndrome, but instead said that her father had shown signs that he was awake and responsive.

"Oh, my God, that's wonderful," the nurse exclaimed, hurrying with her to the bedside.

"Dad, I'm here with Tracy, your nurse. Can you open your eyes for her?"

No response.

"Dr. Sperelakis, it's me, Tracy. I'm so excited you're waking up!"

Thea waited for a minute, feeling increasingly edgy. She opened her father's lid as she had just successfully done. There was still no movement. She could feel the enthusiasm draining from the nurse beside her, and she imagined what the woman was thinking. Before them, Petros's eye stared unblinking at a point somewhere straight ahead.

"Dad?" she tried, testing her own conviction that movement of the eye had actually happened. "Please show Tracy and me that you can hear. Please move your eyes."

"Maybe he's just tired out," Tracy said in lieu, Thea knew, of saying, *Maybe you just want this so much and are so jet-lagged and so emotionally involved after last night's resuscitation that you are trying to will this to happen.*

"Maybe," Thea said.

"Well . . . I've got a little more charting to do. Just give a yell if he moves his eye again."

The nurse took two steps backwards, then turned and left the glass-enclosed room.

Thea stayed at the bedside, holding her father's hand and trying to sort out what could possibly have just transpired. Had she simply imagined the whole thing? No, she thought firmly. She didn't believe that at all. It wasn't like her. Petros had reacted to her and he had voluntarily moved. Could he have gotten worn out or slipped back into unconsciousness?

More likely, she acknowledged.

Perhaps it was worth bringing Sharon Karsten up to speak with him. It had been ten years since Eleni Sperelakis's sad death. Karsten said she and Petros had been together for five years. For a Greek woman to become involved after five years of widowhood was a bit against tradition, but as in almost everything Greek, men had more leeway. Karsten had made it sound as if their relationship was quite serious. Thea remembered that the woman was divorced and wondered now if her marriage had ended before or after their involvement.

The situation was not one Thea was put together to handle very easily. She had seen what she had seen. Her father had opened his eye, and that was that. Furthermore, he had done it at her request. Why was he unable or unwilling to repeat the gesture?

More analytical and puzzled than frustrated, she bent over the bed once more and implored her father.

"Dad, please. I know you can hear me. Open your eyes so I know. It's very important that I know you understand me. Show me you can hear me and I'll help you to learn what is happening."

Thirty seconds passed before Petros's left eye quivered and opened just a slit, then closed.

"Thank you, oh, thank you," she whispered.

She hurried to the nurse's station and returned with Tracy. Again, there was no response from the man. None at all. This time, Thea merely thanked the nurse and watched her leave. It was clear that the woman was trying to be polite, but it was equally clear that she didn't believe her deeply comatose patient had suddenly started responding to commands, only issued when he was alone with the daughter who was desperate for him to wake up. He was the invisible man, who was only invisible when there was no one around to see him.

Thea stepped back from the bed and peered down at her father's battered face. Petros was the one who imbued in her the notion that in diagnostic medicine there was always an explanation that fit the facts. A good physician's duty was to start with that assumption and to keep testing and examining until the wayward explanation became apparent.

In this case, the fact was that her father would signal to her and not the nurse. The most viable explanation, though there were certainly others, was that the only person he would respond to was her. The reason for that behavior would be another fact that needed explaining. But for now, what was clearly called for was another person Petros was likely to respond to—friend or family.

At that moment, as if on cue, Dr. Scott Hartnett knocked on the glass and entered the cubicle.

"I feel as if he might have just responded to me,"

Thea said after she and Petros's friend and internist had exchanged greetings.

"Responded?"

"I think he opened his left eye a bit and looked upward."

"Locked-in syndrome?"

"Hopefully not," she replied.

She felt pleased at having picked up on the possible effect that hearing the grim diagnosis might have on her father. Until recently, it was not the sort of thing that her Asperger syndrome would have allowed her to consider.

Hartnett, whom she had always felt was a kind and intuitive physician, nodded that he understood her concern, then turned to his patient.

"Petros, my friend," he said, his rich bass resonating throughout the cubicle, "it's Scott. Squeeze my hand if you can hear me. . . . Come on, old boy, you can do it. . . . All right, then, how about opening your eyes? Just look up. . . . Look up and I'll write off your donation to this year's development fund. . . . I don't know, Thea."

"Try lifting his left lid."

Hartnett gently did as she asked and repeated his request. The mid-position pupil stared blankly forward. Thea could only shake her head.

"I was so sure," she said, still certain of what she had seen, but unwilling to push matters any more.

Her experiment had a result. Now she had to process the significance of the finding.

Hartnett patted her on the shoulder.

"Sometimes we want these things so badly. . . ." His voice trailed off.

For a time, the two physicians stood silently by the bedrail.

"Have you spoken to the neurologist?" Thea asked finally.

"The neurologist, the neurosurgeon, the intensivist, the orthopod, the urologist because there was blood in his urine. Wait and see. That's all they have to tell us. Wait and see. Well, I'm going to make rounds. I may stop by again before I head home." He guided Thea out the door, and added, "The good news is that at least he doesn't appear to have locked-in syndrome."

Thea smiled wanly and accepted a paternal hug. Then she returned to the bedside and gazed down at her father. She could almost see the steely set of his jaw. He was awake. Awake and alert, but stubbornly unwilling to share that fact with anyone except her.

"Dad, it's just me," she said softly. "Nobody else is here. Now open your eyes. Open your eyes if you can hear me."

Twenty seconds went by before the Lion's upper and lower eyelids on the left separated a millimeter.

I knew it!

"You don't want anyone but me to know you're awake. Is that it?"

Thirty motionless seconds passed before, with what seemed like a consummate effort, Petros opened his eye once more.

FOURTEEN

One A.M.

Thea gave up trying to establish some sort of yes/no code with her father and left the ICU for another walkabout in the hospital. Petros seemed too slow and somnolent to endure a back-and-forth dialogue. His responses to her questions took thirty seconds or even a minute, and she couldn't be certain if they were actually connected to the question or not. She reminded herself that more often than not, the emergence from a coma was gradual—the reduction of brain swelling past a critical point or the slow restoration of normal neurochemistry. The Hollywood version of a sudden reappearance of consciousness, motor ability, and awareness was certainly reported in real life, but more often there was a period of fogginess and even transient recurrent coma.

She warned herself again and again to be patient, and to fight an increasing sense of loneliness and isolation. At the moment, she didn't feel comfortable sharing her thoughts and concerns with the twins, nor with Karsten, Hartnett, or even the energetic, dedicated nursing director, Amy Musgrave. Dimitri felt much more like an ally, but in their life together, he had hardly proven to be reliable. Perhaps Dan, she thought, as she headed through the glassed walkway into the Sperelakis Building.

Throughout the evening, Thea had remained in the ICU except for two breaks—one at eight to wander the wards, and one at eleven thirty through the tunnels to the cafeteria, largely in hopes that she might run into Dan if he happened to be working more than one shift.

Visitors to her father's bedside had included the twins, and later, briefly, Sharon Karsten and Scott Hartnett. Thea didn't mention the mounting evidence that Petros had locked-in syndrome, and Hartnett made no reference to their earlier attempts to get him to respond.

Selene and Niko arrived separately, but at almost the same time. It wasn't surprising that they seemed to function almost as one. They had, after all, been together since they were each a single cell. Nevertheless, Thea had always found their intense connection a little unsettling. Dimitri, as expected, was more vocal and direct about the twins, who both went to the Rivers School, then Harvard College, and finally Harvard Med. He referred to them, at various times, as Tweedledee and Tweedledum, the Dynamic Duo, the Twinkies, and the Twofers.

The fifteen or twenty minutes that the twins were in the ICU with Thea were subdued and somewhat strained. It was as if they felt that she had closed the window for putting the matter of Petros Sperelakis forever to rest, and now they were all in it for the long haul. Thea found herself wondering how much they knew of what Karsten had told her about the size and apportionment of Petros's estate.

"Good evening."

Completely lost in thought, Thea had nearly passed the doorway of Room 412 when the occupant startled her. The woman was reading in a chair placed just inside the door. An IV was running into her left forearm, draining both saline and, piggybacked through a large-bore needle into the rubber infusion port, a drug that had a yellowish cast. She was forty-five or fifty, Thea guessed, and nothing—not her tortoiseshell glasses or the black fabric elastic holding back her auburn hair, not her plain, quilted robe or the lack of any makeup— could hide the fact that she was a strikingly attractive woman. Her eyes, even through her glasses, were bright and intelligent.

Beyond where the woman sat, Thea could see books piled on the bedside table and also on the mantel of the faux fireplace that decorated every room in the institute. Laid on the throw across her lap was the book she was reading at the moment—Gabriel García Márquez's intense romance, *Love in the Time of Cholera*.

"I loved that book," Thea said, not bothering to mention that she had read it twice in the same week. "It was one of the first intellectual romances I had read, and it opened the door to my reading many more."

"Which is more important, being in love or—"

"Suffering for love," Thea excitedly joined in.

The woman with the IV beamed. "Yes, exactly. Personally, I believe that every day you can make it through without suffering is another day you made it through without suffering."

"My brother Dimitri used to have a poster of a blubbery man sitting on top of a beer keg. Underneath the photo was printed: 'No pain, no pain.'"

"Exactly."

Thea added the woman's laugh to things she liked about her.

"So where are you right now in the story?" Thea asked.

"Well, Juventus is dead after falling off the porch. Fermina hates Florentino, but I think she's going to end up with him. Don't tell me, though."

"I promise."

"It looked like you were lost in thought. Sorry if I interrupted. You passed by here late last night, then again earlier this evening. I started feeling like we were becoming friends, so I thought I'd say hello. My name's Hayley. Hayley Long."

"Pleased to meet you, Hayley," Thea replied precisely as she had done in countless exercises in pragmatics group. "I'm Thea Sperelakis."

"Petros's daughter?"

"One of them, yes."

"I'm so sorry for what's happened to your father. He was supposed to be my doctor before his accident. Now I have Dr. Hartnett, he's the internist, and Dr. Thibideau, she's my cancer specialist."

Dr. Carpenter had spent many hours working with Thea on trying to see through spoken words and into the tone and manner in which they were spoken—one of the most difficult tasks for any Aspie. Hayley Long, Thea felt, had said the word *cancer* with strength and dignity.

"I don't know her well," Thea said, "but I have heard that Dr. Thibideau is a wonderful doctor."

Unfortunately, she was thinking, Thibideau's area of expertise was cancer of the pancreas—an extremely knotty medical problem because by the time symptoms developed, most often pain, the disease was usually far advanced. In all likelihood, the yellowish medication draining into the IV was part of some sort of experimental FDA protocol.

"You want to know what I like the most about her?" Hayley said. "She actually looks at me when she talks to me, and not at her computer screen—at least not every second. My doctor in Atlanta, Dr. Bibby, is a sweet and caring guy. There was a time when he would actually interact with me when I came to see him, but all of a sudden, things changed. His group practice went to all-electronic records."

"HIPAA," Thea said. "Health Insurance Portability and Accountability Act. It spells out the form a doctor's records and office notes must take."

"That's right. I forgot that you're a doctor, too. Dr. Hartnett told me that all of Dr. Sperelakis's children were doctors."

"Almost all."

"Well, needless to say, even with a doctor like Lydia Thibideau, I'm scared out of my wits over all this—especially when the drug I'm getting is so experimental.

I chose it over the standard treatment because the survival figures for those drugs are so dismal, and the side effects are so debilitating. I could have gotten both the standard treatment and the new drug, but my husband David and I both felt that was more than I could handle."

"I'm so sorry you have to go through this, but that's the way these protocols work."

"I understand. Dr. Hartnett tells me your father is still in a coma. I'm sorry to hear that."

"His coma may be improving."

"I hope so. Say, I know it's late—make that early—but if it's like the past few nights, the sleeping pill they gave me isn't going to work, and you seem pretty wide awake. Do you feel like hanging out here for a little while?"

Thea's knee-jerk reaction was to say no and retreat into her concerns about her father. But there was something about this woman—something wise and genuine.

"I suppose I could do that for just a little while," she said.

The two women talked about Proust and the Brontës. They discussed Asperger syndrome and alternative therapies for cancer. They laughed about men and families. They analyzed locked-in syndrome and what Thea's next move should be and the challenges faced by women operating in the world of high finance. They shared stories of Atlanta and the Congo, of being brought up in privilege and in poverty, of what it was like to have a child die in one's arms, and how much a billion dollars was.

Thea awoke in her chair at five, vaguely remembering nodding off. Hayley Long was wide awake and reading.

"With the Damocles sword of cancer hanging over my head, losing time to sleep doesn't seem like a wise choice," Hayley said. "Reading does."

"So does friendship," Thea said. "Thanks for not waking me. I needed the nap."

She brought two cups of coffee in from the small kitchen down the hall, and they drank largely in silence, each enjoying the connection that had formed between them. Finally, with an uncharacteristically warm embrace, and the promise to come back soon, Thea headed back to the ICU, determined to find a way to probe the secrets locked in her father's brain.

She was also determined to leave no fact undiscovered in understanding Hayley Long's inoperable pancreatic cancer.

FIFTEEN

When he joined the Boston police force, Dan Cotton knew there was the possibility that at some point he would have to kill, but no one ever said it would be a kid. No one ever said it would be a fourteen-year-old eighth-grader with caring parents and no criminal record. No one ever said he would kill a boy just a few years older than his own son.

The boards and a community hearing had met and cleared him. His partner, who was reaching for his own gun when Dan fired, had testified that Dan had no choice; that lives were in danger; that Patrick Suggs had tired of being beaten and bullied by a gang and had simply snapped, stealing a gun from an uncle, shooting one of the bullies in the face and one in the leg, and turning the gun on two others.

Dan and his partner were giving a gun safety presentation in the school auditorium when the shooting began outside. Wrong place, wrong time, unless you happened to have been one of the dropout punks whose life was saved.

Dan went to bed with the memory every night. He woke up with it every morning. He thought about it during his weekends and Wednesday dinners with Josh.

He had tried therapy and meds, yoga and self-help books, a desk job, and finally, resignation. It was a painful way to discover that he wasn't cut out to kill, but it was the hand he had been dealt, and with each passing day, the memories had seemed to be getting less vivid.

The job as a security guard at Beaumont was a comedown for a man who had a degree in criminology from Northeastern, and who finished high in his class at the police academy, but for the time being, Dan was relieved to have it—routine, low stress, a chance to interact with people, decent pay, reasonable benefits, and some responsibility. For now, he was where he was supposed to be. And yesterday, he had met still another perk of working in the prestigious Beaumont Clinic—Thea Sperelakis.

Dan was thinking about her as he clocked in at the security checkpoint on the first floor of the Blaylock Building, and headed across to the Clark Pavilion, which housed, among other facilities, the medical ICU. It had been four years since his divorce, three since the shooting. Over that time, he had dated a few women—several that friends had fixed him up with, two that he could remember meeting on his own. None of the relationships had lasted very long, three months at the most, but he had recently been feeling that his recovery from the killing had progressed enough to be more optimistic about his ability not to be constantly morose.

Thea Sperelakis was quirky and smart, with a peacefulness in her face and a lithe figure, both of which he found totally appealing. He had no desire to play policeman regarding her father's accident, but if that's what it took to get to know her better, that's how it would be.

Dan was lost enough in thoughts of the woman that he almost walked right past an orderly with a swarthy complexion, thick, black-framed glasses, and a dark mustache, pushing a cart of linens toward the entrance to the unit. But several months before, a man wearing hospital scrubs and apparently looking like he knew what he was about had strolled boldly into a patient's private room in the early-morning hours and chloroformed her. Then he duct-taped her mouth closed and her wrists to the bed, cut her gown off, allowed her to wake up, and molested her. When he was done, she reported, he kissed her on each breast and calmly left the hospital.

Since then, word had gone out to the security force that all those in hospital uniforms were to have their ID badges checked, and further, that paid "intruders" would be walking through the wards to check on the implementation of the policy. In addition, all visitors after 9 P.M. would be required to pick up temporary badges at the security desk by the main entrance. Failure to check a badge would be grounds for immediate termination.

"Excuse me, my friend," Dan said, looking more, he would realize after the fact, at the badge than at the man, "but as you've probably heard, every hospital employee who passes any of us security types needs to have his ID checked. Okay if I take a look?"

What happened next was a painful blur.

Clutching something wrapped in a sheet, the orderly shoved his cart aside and kicked Dan viciously in the groin, dropping him to his knees. A second kick, perfectly aimed and delivered with dizzying force, caught him underneath the chin, snapping his teeth together like a castanet, and sending him sprawling backward, his head slamming against the linoleum floor. Moments later, dazed and in excruciating pain from the first kick, Dan vomited all over the front of his starched blue uniform and onto the floor.

By the time he was able to fumble out his badly soiled radio and make a distress call, his assailant was long gone. The security camera trained on the door to the ICU recorded most of the assault and the reappearance of Dan's breakfast, but little of the face of the man with the steel-toed shoes.

SIXTEEN

"I'm sorry if I'm hurting you."

"No, it's all right. It's all right. Go ahead and look. I'll open my mouth wider."

The Eisenstein ER at the Beaumont Clinic was, like every aspect of the huge hospital that interfaced with the public, state of the art. Constructed as three circular treatment areas built around a central monitoring/nurses' station, the facility had separate medical and surgical pods, each with satellite nurses' stations, as well as a set of waiting rooms, each with a triage nurse office. The influence of Nursing Director Amy Musgrave was apparent everywhere in the busy ER, including the long waiting list of top-notch RNs anxious to work there.

Hunched over the stretcher in Surgical 8, Thea examined the gash inside of Dan's mouth with Pramjit Thakur, the ER chief.

"It should be stitched," Thakur said in a clipped Indian accent. "Usually no, this one, yes. Don't you think, Dr. Sperelakis?"

"I don't need stitches," Dan insisted.

"So," Thea said, "you're a doctor now? That hole inside your cheek is going to heal just like what it is—a hole. You'll be sticking your tongue in it so much that before long the tip will poke out right here."

"How do you know?"

"Are you trying to pick a fight with me now? Be careful if you do, because like my mother taught me, I use my words, not my fists. Now, let Dr. Thakur do what he knows how to do. After that, assuming your X-rays are negative, you can go home."

"I don't want to go home. What I want to do is to get my hands on the guy who did this to me."

"The unit nurse who saw what happened told me you were very brave," Thea said.

"What she meant was that I was very slow."

"Unless you still have objections, Officer Cotton," Thakur said, "I am going to get set up to suture your mouth."

"Okay, okay."

Thea patted him on the shoulder.

"That's better."

After leaving Hayley Long's room, she had wandered over to the cafeteria to see if by chance Dan might be there. Her plan for the day was to research locked-in syndrome, and to speak with Scott Hartnett about getting access to Hayley's medical records, which were held tightly by Thor, the Beaumont's superfast, virtually impenetrable electronic records system. In between, she had critical business to attend to with her father—the business of creating a code of some sort so the two of them could communicate. And when they had that code, the first thing she needed to know was why Petros was refusing to allow anyone except for her to know that he was awake and alert.

It was in the cafeteria that she heard a pair of nurses talking about the attack outside the medical ICU. When one of them referred to the tall, good-looking security guard, Thea rushed to the ER.

"I can't believe the bastard got away," Dan scowled.

"It doesn't exactly sound like it was a fair fight."

"Some security guard I am. I was right there face-to-face with him and I could hardly tell you anything about what he looked like. Glasses and a mustache, that's what I remember, but the more I think about it, the more I suspect they may have been fake."

"What do you think he was doing?"

"I don't know what he wanted, but I'm almost positive he was trying to get into the ICU. In fact, I'm sure of it. He had some sort of package or something wrapped in a sheet on top of his cart. He grabbed it before he kicked me, and had it under his arm when he kicked me the second time. Damn, but I feel stupid."

Thea didn't hear Dan's last few words. Her muscles had tightened, chilled as if she had stepped into a deep freeze. An unpleasant buzzing filled her head. All ten beds in the ICU were occupied, yet somehow she knew that the bogus orderly was after her father. If Dimitri was right, and somebody was trying to kill the man with their car, then this would be a second attempt. But why?

She was the only one who knew that Petros was awake and alert.

What would make anyone take such a chance?

The answer hit like a wrecking ball.

Thea bent down over the stretcher.

"Listen, big Dan," she whispered, "I'll explain later, but I've got to get up to the unit. I think whoever did this to you may have been after my father."

"What?"

"Let the doctor sew up that gash. I'll explain later." She hastily wrote two numbers on a sheet of paper she tore from a pad on the desk. "My home number and my father's cell. Call me when you get out of here. I'll explain then."

Without waiting for a response, she raced from the room.

SEVENTEEN

Despite the fact that it had been less than an hour since she left the ICU, and that there had been two Boston policemen there taking statements, Thea felt relief when she saw the place was relatively quiet. A security guard, posted at a small table by the front doors, logged her in, checking the ID badge the twins had arranged for her when she first arrived.

"Anything on the attacker?" she asked the guard, a petite, officious blonde, who looked as if she would have been torn in half by the blows Dan absorbed.

"Nothing that I've heard," the woman responded. "Two detectives are downstairs in the security office right now reviewing the videos from that camera over there, and from others around the hospital. The whole place has been put on Code White, which limits visitors' hours and insists on visitor sign-in and badges."

"Goodness."

"Someone said it might be the same pervert who molested that woman on Bladd Five, but I don't know what sort of business he thought he could get done in an all-glass ICU. Not exactly fertile grounds for a molester."

"I agree," Thea said, sensing strongly that a laugh of

some sort was called for, and complying with one that sounded totally unnatural to her.

Bladd   Five ... Blaylock   Three ... the   Clark Pavilion ... the Eisenstein ER ...

It seemed as if every conference room, auditorium, and building, and even many of the patient rooms in the Beaumont, were named for a donor. Thea entered the Rebecca and James Kinchley Intensive Care Unit, wondering in passing how much of a donation it had taken from the Kinchleys to have their names connected to it. A million? More? Much more? She had so little feel for amounts of money that it was impossible to guess.

Raising those funds was, she knew, the primary responsibility of Dr. Scott Hartnett. Now, Hartnett and Nurse Tracy Gibbons were on a very short list of those who knew that Thea believed her father might be awake and alert, and in the terrible grip of locked-in syndrome. Of course, she realized as she entered his room, either of them could have said something about it to anyone else, including the twins, Sharon Karsten, Amy Musgrave, and almost anyone else. So maybe the list wasn't so short at that. From now on, until matters were resolved, she would be more careful to whom she spoke.

Meanwhile, she and her father had business to work out.

Thea approached the bed. Petros, eyes taped shut, looked as he always had: motionless, serene, being monitored in every way, fed intravenously, and breathed for through a ventilator. It was horrifying and hard to believe that he could hear every sound, feel every touch, and absorb every ache, but almost certainly he could. Thea took his hand in hers and glanced about to ensure that no one was taking any particular interest in them. His nurse passed by once, glanced in, but didn't stop. Thea carefully removed the paper tape and instilled a drop of lubricant in each eye to protect the Lion's corneas.

"Dad, it's me, Thea. Can you blink or look up?"

This time Petros's response seemed marginally more brisk than it had been—a definite upward flick of his left globe accompanied by a wisp of movement of the lid. Now for the difficult part. She had considered trying the obvious, one blink for yes and two for no, but Petros seemed so slow that she felt certain his answers would end up being ambiguous and confusing.

"Dad, I love you and I need to communicate with you. I know it's hard, but I beg you to try. I've been thinking about what might be easiest for us. . . . I will ask you questions. If the answer is yes, move your eye. If it is no, do nothing until I have counted to ten. Does that make sense to you?"

Thea held her breath, then began to count softly. She was at six when her father's lid moved.

"Thank you. I know this is hard. I know you're having trouble concentrating, but just do your best. With time things might get better." She realized almost immediately that the rather hopeless statement wasn't something a neurotypical would say, and corrected herself immediately. "No, Dad. Things *will* get better. Now, let's try a question. Are you purposely not letting anyone except me know that you are awake and alert? One . . . two . . . three . . ."

This time, Petros's response came at eight. Thea warned herself to be patient. She remembered being told that the French editor with locked-in syndrome was able to watch and focus as his assistant pointed through the alphabet a letter at a time until hitting on the proper one. Thousands and thousands of repetitions. That wasn't going to happen here—at least not yet.

Her father was awake, but he was still foggy. She imagined the debris and neuronal swelling still present in his brain, doing battle against the incredibly complex and precise processes of thought, memory, reasoning, movement, emotions, and so many others. She would have to formulate her questions to make them as clear and unambiguous as possible.

"Do you believe that the driver of the car did this on purpose?"

Seven.

Thea felt ill. Her father believed, as did her brother, that someone had purposely tried to kill him. Now, it appeared, a second attempt had been made on his life. What next?

A woman from housekeeping knocked on the glass and was beckoned in by her. Five minutes passed as the woman, who looked too old for her job, straightened the room, ran a mop over the floor, and left. Finally, Thea was ready for another question.

"Dad, do you know who did this to you?"

Again the count began. This time there was no movement through ten. Was the answer no, or was he too worn out to respond? Had he drifted off into coma again? As she had suspected, the system she had devised was an awkward one at best. If Dimitri and their father were correct, then the logical assumption was that Petros saw or learned something that would be damaging to whoever had twice tried to kill him.

"Can I keep going?" she asked after a minute had passed. "Can I try some more questions?"

Petros's response came at eight, a definite upward gaze, but Thea was at a loss as to where to go from here. There was no telling how much the man had left in him. What yes or no question was there left to ask him?

"Do you have something you want to tell me?" she asked finally.

The positive response came at four. She believed that she could actually sense her father was excited.

His nurse tapped on the glass and let herself into the cubicle. The woman had passed by and peered in several times before finally knocking. Thea wondered what the woman was thinking about her, about what she might be doing hunched over among the machines and tubes, speaking to a man who had been in an irretrievable coma for almost two weeks.

"Everything all right?" the nurse asked.

"Fine. I just want to be certain my father gets stimulation. You never know what's getting in and what isn't."

"Yes, of course," the woman said, her tone patronizing. "Perhaps we could put a pair of earphones on him—play some nice music."

"Medical journals would be better," Thea replied.

"He likes to keep up. Any new information about the man who tried to get in here?"

"Nothing yet. We think he might be the ex-husband of the woman in three. Apparently she's taken a restraining order out against him. That's my guess."

Not mine, Thea was thinking. By the time the nurse had completed her work and left the cubicle, close to an hour and a half had elapsed since Thea's arrival. Dan had probably been sutured and sent home. Despite the stressful circumstances, she felt her feelings for the man growing. He was at once vulnerable, frustrated, embarrassed, and angry. Thea knew that if she could read such abstract emotions in any person, they must be quite genuine and ill-disguised. Dan Cotton was much more comfortable playing the tough than he was the guy kneeling by the boy in the cafeteria, but his macho veneer was thin.

The image of him scowling on the ER stretcher made her smile. If he contacted her, and she thought he would, she would try and set up a meeting with Dimitri. It would be amusing to watch the two of them trying to figure one another out. Before that, though, she wanted to see if the library had the book dictated a letter at a time by the French magazine editor, as well as any other information on his life.

She also desperately wanted to get a look at Hayley Long's hospital record without having Scott Hartnett or Hayley's oncologist feel that she was in any way checking up on them. Hayley was a remarkable, remarkable woman, and anything she could do to help her through the ordeal of her cancer and treatment, she would do.

Thea turned her attention back to her father, desperately searching for a way to get at whatever it was that he wanted to tell her. Her back was beginning to ache from bending over, and she felt as if the muscles around her jaws were going into spasm from having been clenched too tightly. Finally, stimulated by the image of the editor picking his way through the alphabet again and again, she put her lips close to Petros's ear.

"Can you hear me okay? . . . Dad, can you hear me?"

It seemed like a consummate effort, but Petros looked upward a millimeter or so. With time, it was possible that the function and strength around his eye might improve, but Thea felt there was no time to wait. As far as she was concerned, there had just been a second attempt on his life, this one quite possibly brought on by her claim to Tracy Gibbons, and also to Scott Hartnett, that she had seen evidence he was awake.

Petros knew something—something deathly important. The problem she faced was getting at precisely what it was. If she understood things so far, he didn't know who had done this to him, but perhaps he wanted to tell her why.

"Dad, I want you to think of one word—one word that will point me in the direction you want me to go. Then I'm going to go through the alphabet starting with A. As soon as you hear the right letter, move your eye. I'll go slowly. I'll count to ten between each letter. Do you understand? One . . . two . . . three . . . four . . . five . . ."

At five there was movement. Thea added another drop of lubricant to each eye from the small vial on the bedside table.

"Here we go. *A* . . . One . . . two . . ."

As a schoolgirl, Thea had once been diagnosed as having another condition other than Asperger syndrome—ADHD, attention deficit hyperactivity disorder. It turned out that she didn't have an attention deficit at all—only a lack of focus and patience for things that didn't interest her. She learned to embroider before she was ten, and to knit at a time when, in many of her classrooms, she spent entire days staring out the window or pacing back and forth across the back of the room. And of course, she could read for hours on end without even changing position.

Now, a letter at a time, ten seconds per letter, she was totally immersed in the connection with the man who had never once told her that he loved her and that he was proud of who and what she had become.

At *K* Petros blinked.

"Yes, Dad, yes," Thea whispered excitedly. "Stay with me. Let's try the next letter."

She sensed even before her father confirmed it that the letter was going to be an *A*. *K-A*. . . . A name of some sort, she thought. Or a place. *It's going to be a person's name or some sort of place.*

The *L* came hard, Petros signaling at the last possible instant. The next letter, an *I,* was the same way. *K-A-L-I*. Thea waited for several minutes before taxing her father again. When she did, he seemed to have regained a bit of energy. *S* . . . *H* . . . *A* . . .

"Dad, listen to me," she said excitedly. "Is it Kalishar? Is it the owner of all those department stores? Blink if that's who it is. One . . . two . . ."

Almost gratefully, it seemed, the left lid closed, then opened, then closed again. Jack or John Kalishar, Thea couldn't remember which. Or perhaps the mogul used both. Kalishar's was the name he used for his world-wide chain of upscale department stores and products.

Kalishar's.

"One more question. Just one and we're done for now. John Kalishar—was or is he a patient here? One . . . two . . . come on, Dad, come on . . . three . . . four . . ."

Petros's globe turned upward ever so slightly. Each response had been like Sisyphus at his rock. But this time, at least for the moment, the Lion was done, and Thea knew what her next move had to be.

She sank back in the Danish modern visitor's chair and called Sharon Karsten. It took just seconds after Thea was announced to the hospital CEO before the woman was on the line.

"Thea, hi. Is everything all right?"

"No change in my father, if that's what you mean. At least not that I can see. But I've had a change of heart."

"A change of heart?"

"Yes. How soon can you get me staff privileges to take over my father's practice?"

"You mean that? . . . Why . . . why, that's wonderful."

"How soon?" Thea asked again.

"Well, I do have some clout around here. Let me talk to Herb Lesley, the head of credentialing. Since a number of us have known you since you were a child, and since you rotated through here and know a lot of the staff, I suppose we could move the process through quite rapidly and at least get you some sort of temporary credentials."

"Like by tomorrow?"

"Possibly. Possibly by then."

"Excellent."

"May I ask why the change of heart?"

"Of course. I believe my father is going to be around for a long while, and I want to be here with him."

"Have you told the twins yet?"

"Not yet, but I will."

"I'm sure they will be very pleased."

"Yes. I agree. Oh, one more thing."

"Anything, Thea."

"How soon can I get oriented to your electronic medical records system—Thor, yes?"

There was a prolonged pause.

"Yes, it's Thor," the CEO said. "I . . . I can't take any action in that direction until the credentials committee has its say. This place is positively paranoid when it comes to its medical records."

The hesitation and tone of Karsten's response made Thea wish she hadn't brought the subject up.

"That's fine," she said. "Whatever you say."

EIGHTEEN

The Stuart Drummond Memorial Medical Library oc-cupied three refurbished stories of the Coldwater Build-ing, one of the oldest on the campus. On her way to the expansive research center, Thea called Niko to report the ICU intruder and to formulate a strategy for pro-tecting their father. Given her decision not to mention Petros's locked-in syndrome, she knew convincing her cynical brother to do anything of the sort would not be easy. It wasn't.

"Tell me again why you think this man was after Petros?" Niko asked.

"Dimitri is convinced that the hit-and-run was no accident."

Niko groaned.

"You mean that animation of his? The damn thing looks like some sort of cave drawing."

"The way he presented it made sense to me. Niko, call him anything you want, but don't call him dumb."

"Oh, please. Nothing about Dimitri should make sense to anyone. He's one of those cases where he would have been better off without so much intelligence. Thea, I believe that you are grasping at straws. Petros was hit by a drunk driver or someone reaching for their cell phone, and has sustained massive, irreversible brain damage and a prognosis that is worse than hopeless. At the moment of impact he crossed the bridge of no return."

"That's cruel."

"No, it's not, it's realistic. Thea, Scott Hartnett told me you tried to demonstrate to him that Dad was awake and alert."

So much for limiting those who knew about that to Hartnett and Tracy Gibbons, Thea thought. It wouldn't be the first time she had been entangled in a hospital grapevine. It seemed as if she had spent half of her residency there. One tells two, two tell four. Rumor at the speed of sound. Word of her behavior at her father's bedside, based on hopelessly naïve wishes, was making its way across the vast hospital like ripples on a pond.

"That was a mistake," she said.

"Now we're getting somewhere."

"So I take it you don't think he needs a guard."

"What he needs is benign neglect."

"Are you coming by the ICU later today?"

"Petey has a soccer game. I missed the last two."

"I hope I get to see him play."

"We'll have you over for dinner next week on an evening when he's playing. I'll speak to Marie."

"That would be great."

"Thea, I know you think I'm being harsh about this, but we've both been doctors long enough to appreciate that Dad's situation is as hopeless as it is degrading. Deep down inside you must know that I'm right."

Deep down inside I know that you're not, Thea barely kept herself from saying.

A number of the oak tables, carrels, and computer stations of the Drummond Library were occupied. Thea and the reference librarian, a lanky, bespectacled brunette named Rachel, were pleased to find a copy of Jean-Dominique Bauby's powerful memoir of his locked-in syndrome, *The Diving Bell and the Butterfly.*

Thea took only forty minutes to read the 132 pages. It wasn't easy for her to comprehend why the once-powerful magazine editor would have chosen to write such a positive, life-affirming book when his condition was so abysmal and painful, but she dutifully took notes, and promised herself that she would spend more time thinking about what Bauby was trying to tell the world. Perhaps it was something she and Hayley could talk about.

She next moved to an available computer for more in-depth research and note-taking on the syndrome that only she and her father knew was holding his body hostage. According to Petros's longtime lover, Niko stood to inherit millions. Did Niko himself know that? If so, he would certainly have reason over and above his philosophical and medical beliefs to want the tragedy in the ICU to be over quickly.

As she worked, Thea's thoughts mulled over and over the questions raised by the Lion's refusal—not reluctance, *refusal*—to share with anyone else the fact that his mind was keen and totally alert to what was transpiring around him. Was it a manifestation of his well-established need to be in control? Was it fear? Pure petulance? It didn't really matter, she decided. At that moment, as helpless as he was, Petros was in control—unless, of course, someone other than Thea believed he had locked-in syndrome and was capable of communication. In that case he was not only *not* in control, he was in serious danger.

An hour of work on the Internet brought a mix of encouraging and frightening news. Locked-in syndrome, LIS, whether caused by hemorrhage, clot, or trauma, was rare, but common enough to have a number of outcome studies reported in the literature. One such study published in the *British Medical Journal,* hard for Thea to believe, alluded to an 80 percent ten-year survival. Another estimated the four-month mortality of LIS at 60 percent.

Most striking in one of the articles was the fact that most long-term survivors with locked-in syndrome chose to return home in hopes that the interaction with loved ones would enhance their desire to live. Improved communications technology such as infrared eye movement sensors and computer voice prosthetics, coupled with a plain old alphabet board, had actually made it possible for a lawyer with LIS to return to his profession.

With time, Thea vowed, she would begin to educate her father in what she was learning about his condition. Only then, only when they knew everything there was to know about LIS, along with the amount of neurological function the Lion was going to regain, would it be fair to sign any health proxies.

The afternoon light had begun to thin by the time Thea set aside her notes on LIS and turned her attention to the next item on her list—billionaire businessman Jack Kalishar.

First the basics, she wrote on her yellow legal pad. *John (Jack) Joseph Kalishar, age 57 . . . Occupation: businessman. President and CEO of K-Group, corporate raider. Born: Indianapolis, IN. Current residence: Boca Raton, FL. Married, two children—24 (m-Mark), 22 (f-Marcy). Estimated worth: 1.7 billion . . . Pilot, speedboat ocean racer . . . art collector.*

His photos—there were dozens on Google Image—were of a lean, tanned man with an aquiline nose and narrow, dark eyes. His looks weren't that appealing to Thea, although she suspected that many women would find him attractive. Why would he be so important that of all the words, of all the names her father could have chosen, he had picked *Kalishar*?

Why????

Thea scribbled down the word and ornamented it with flowers, then continued clawing through item after item on the Internet searching for a clue—any clue.

Why?

When the clue finally appeared, it almost passed her by. It was in a *Wall Street Journal* article on philanthropic giving in which Jack Kalishar's name was mentioned exactly once.

Reginald Pickard's World Vaccine program
is just one of a number of health-related

philanthropies established by this group of
businessmen. Following his close call with
cancer, Jack Kalishar of Kalishar Invest-
ments has formed the Breath of Life Foundation to fill needs in the areas of medical
research, medical student education, and the
upgrading of health care facilities.

Cancer, Thea wrote after copying down the segment
verbatim.

What kind of cancer?

Was K treated here?

Connection to Dad?

Another hour added little except for the address and
a phone number for the Breath of Life Foundation. The
information about Kalishar's cancer she could get from
his medical record. She was gathering her notes together with plans to visit Hayley Long, when her father's cell phone began to vibrate. Thea hurried to an
empty glassed-in carrel to one side of the main floor,
built along with two others for cell phone use or for answering pages.

"Hello, this is Thea Sperelakis," she said, precisely
as she had done until it came naturally in role-playing
pragmatics improv class.

"Thea, it's Sharon Karsten here."

Perfect timing, Thea thought.

"Yes, how are you?"

"A little perturbed, and I guess a little embarrassed,
too. Thea, there are some members of the credentialing committee who resent my efforts to circumvent

what has been established as standard procedure. Out of respect for your father they are willing to cut some corners, but they are steadfast against giving you unrestricted privileges without the usual check of your references and employment history. The application forms will be in your new mailbox in the mail room outside the library. The best I've been able to do is to get you provisional staff privileges that will require Dr. Hartnett to sign off on all your patient notes."

"Including admission notes?"

"We have hospitalists who will do that for you if you decide to write any admission notes in addition to theirs. I'm talking about office patients and notes you write as a consultant."

"That doesn't make a lot of sense. Neither does just accepting the hospitalist's admission note when it's *my* patient. I'll write my own admission history and physical if that's okay, but I'll be happy to have one of the hospitalists or Scott sign off on anything, even though it seems like I'll just be making more work for them."

"He's grateful to have you. He has been handling referrals to your father from around the country, and indeed around the world. We have a force of physicians out there recruiting patients to be sent to our most renowned specialists, including the great Petros Sperelakis."

Thea remembered Hayley speaking about the doctor, sort of a salesman, who had convinced her physician in Atlanta to begin sending her to the executive health program at the Beaumont, and subsequently to Petros and to Lydia Thibideau.

"Well, I'll do whatever I have to," she said.

"Excellent. Scott will be so relieved to turn Petros's appointment book over to you. Most of the referrals in there are quite ill, but there are many chronic problems as well."

Thea felt edgy. Just a few days ago they were begging her to step in and take over her father's practice. Now that she had agreed to do so, they weren't ready to give her unrestricted staff privileges.

"What about medical records?" she asked. "Will I have access to them?"

"Actually, Scott will retrieve them electronically and forward them to you. The credentials committee has been adamant about protecting our system and our patients' records from anyone without full staff privileges."

"So, there's no way I can just read through any of my father's patients' records—see how he did things?"

"Why would you be wanting to do that?" the CEO asked.

Danger!

Suddenly Thea felt out of her element. Karsten's query had been made in an offhand way, but there were layers beneath it, Thea could tell that much. This was the sort of complex business that had driven her away from hospital politics and intrigues in the first place.

"I . . . I've been reading some patient notes Dad has on file in his office, and I just wanted to learn about them in more detail. That's all."

The lie took just a few seconds to materialize, and it probably could have come out smoother, Thea supposed. But considering that she couldn't remember the last time she had told one, she had conjured it up quickly and told it quite well. Still, lying bothered her. No guile. That was how Dr. Carpenter had described Aspies to her—people incapable of telling a decent lie. Now, after just a short time back in civilization, one had simply rolled out.

Welcome home.

There was little left to the conversation with Karsten. Thea rang off and sat on the edge of the small desk, trying to make sense of why they had begged her to come on board the medical staff, and then were suddenly making it difficult for her to do so. Scott Hartnett, from all she could tell, was a fine doctor and a good person. Still, the last thing she wanted was for anyone to be looking over her shoulder. If Dimitri's and Daniel's suspicions were right, someone had twice tried to kill her father. If restricted staff privileges were the best she could get from the credentials committee, she would find a way to work around them.

The strength of her intellect was in logic and concreteness. This situation was, to this point at least, neither logical nor concrete. Bewildered, she returned to the computer station and was packing her notes when the tall reference librarian, Rachel, approached.

"Dr. Sperelakis," the woman said, "I haven't got very much for you on John or Jack Kalishar, but I did find this article in the *Beaumont Bugle*. That's our bimonthly newsletter here at the clinic. The article's on microfiche and it's almost exactly three years old. Here, I printed it out for you."

Thea took the single sheet and settled into the

high-tech computer chair. Basically, the short article, with a photo of Kalishar posing with six or seven hospital dignitaries, was about the businessman/ philanthropist's attendance at a black-tie dinner honoring the hospital's researcher of the year, Dr. Lydia Thibideau. The name registered instantly—Hayley Long's oncologist, the world-renowned specialist on cancer of the pancreas. Thea focused back on the photo. Thibideau, shorter by half a foot than Kalishar, stood directly to his right. She was a stocky, jowly woman with a determined, bulldog look. Directly to Kalishar's left, looking positively dashing in his tuxedo, was the Lion himself.

Why would Kalishar be attending such a dinner?

Thea read the caption beneath the photograph, which identified each dignitary by degree or academic title.

Petros Sperelakis, Davis and Edwina Hart Professor of Medicine, Director, Sperelakis Institute for Diagnostic Medicine . . . Jack Kalishar, benefactor, the Lydia Thibideau Gastroenterology Research Center . . .

Thea checked her notes once more, and next to where she had questioned what kind of cancer Jack Kalishar might have survived, she wrote *pancreatic*. It wasn't that surprising that Kalishar had the same cancer as Hayley Long, or that he had been treated by the same oncologist. Lydia Thibideau was famous and undoubtedly had patient referrals from all over the world. What was surprising and interesting was that Kalishar was still alive.

Cancer of the pancreas was one of the most common of cancers, and one of the most lethal. The pri-

mary reason for such a high mortality was the lack of
alerting symptoms until it was too late—until spread to
distant organs had occurred.

Thea used the Internet to refresh her memory about
the disease, although there really was no need. Her vast
mental library held both primary journal articles, and
secondary articles from textbooks:

- Major known associated cause: advancing age
  (majority of cases over sixty years old)

- Five-year survival: 4 percent

- Most effective treatment for disease localized to a
  limited segment of the pancreas: surgery, radiation, and chemotherapy in combination

- Average survival in this aggressively treated
  group: seventeen months

Was Jack Kalishar's pancreatic cancer an adenocarcinoma, the most common type, or was it one of the
more obscure types such as an insulinoma, arising
from any one of a number of different kinds of pancreatic hormonal cells? Kalishar was, against long odds, a
five-year survivor of an extremely deadly disease. Had
he been operated on? Was he part of an experimental
drug protocol, like Hayley?

Suddenly, there were so many questions, each one
of them easily answerable if she could somehow gain
access to his medical record, locked electronically in a

cybersafe named Thor, which was, at least for the time being, inaccessible to her without disclosing her interest to Hartnett.

Thea flipped through her notes and slid them into her briefcase.

With some thought, she would find a way. And that way, almost certainly, would involve some lying—a skill at which she had never been even the least bit adept. She flashed back on an exchange with her mother when she was a young girl—one the two of them would laugh about over the years as Thea's lack of guile became apparent.

"Thea, did you brush your teeth?" Eleni had asked one evening before bed.

"Yes," came her firm response.

"Thea, I asked if you had brushed your teeth."

"No."

NINETEEN

No matter how hard he tried, Dan couldn't keep his tongue away from the stitches inside his mouth. He thought about just giving in and tearing them apart to create the permanent hole Thea had warned him about. He felt angry and embarrassed, frustrated and impotent. He had taken martial arts at the police academy and been among the most capable in his class, yet his reaction time outside the ICU had been as slow as syrup.

Since his decision to leave the force, he knew he had been living through a smoldering depression. It wasn't hard to understand. He had shot and killed a fourteen-year-old. Now, just as it felt as if his self-esteem might finally be on the rise, he had allowed himself to be beaten to the floor in the hallway of the hospital, kicked in the groin and then in the face, and his only response to the attack had been to throw up on himself.

He sat there on the bench in the locker room, staring down at the plastic bag that contained his rancid uniform. They had told him to go home, but that was the furthest thing from his mind. He needed to find the man who had done this to him. It was a matter of pride, but he knew it was something else as well. He needed Thea's respect. There was something about her, a gentleness and innocence, that appealed to him greatly. She had thanked him for saving her father's life, if in fact that was what he had done, and even held his hand as he was waiting to be evaluated in the ER. But when she asked him what the assailant looked like, and all he could say was that the man had a tan, a mustache, and black-rimmed glasses, her disappointment was nearly palpable.

Why hadn't he paid better attention? Why hadn't he been sharper? This job wasn't much, but it was a stepping stone back toward life—back toward at least a modicum of self-respect, maybe even back to the force. Josh was a great kid and had been totally understanding about his taking the security guard job. What would he think when another disparaging story about his dad hit the papers?

Dan knew he was probably projecting too much—he had a tendency to do that. Still, he had been badly humiliated by a man and he wanted payback. That the man might have been after Thea's father just made the matter that much more acute. He had already lost several hours, but there were still things he could do. Failing at those, there was Thea's brother and his theories. If the bogus orderly was after Petros, it stood to reason he might be connected with the hit-and-run as well.

The security office was in the basement of the Sherwood Building. Dan dropped his uniform off at the laundry and then followed the yellow line through the broad main tunnel. The officer manning the twelve central video consoles, an ample, cheerful woman named Jessica, was an acquaintance if not a friend. Her concern for his injuries was genuine.

"Police gone?" Dan asked after assuring her that his pride had taken a far bigger hit than his body.

"A while ago."

"They take any tapes?"

"We made a copy of the one from video eight that included the ICU, but we have the original."

"Can I see it?"

"You sure you want to?"

"I can handle it."

"It's bundled with video from every other camera on every floor in the building. A minute per site."

"I know. What about the rest of the tapes? The guy had to get in and out of the hospital somehow."

"At that hour, do you know how much foot traffic there is, and how many entrances? We made copies of them, too, but it may take weeks for anyone to do a decent job of reviewing them."

Jessica motioned him to the small supervisor's office, pushed some buttons on her panel, and electronically sent the video to the screen where Dan was sitting.

He found the attack and began watching it over and over again. Unfortunately, the position of the camera made him the star and included an Oscar-worthy full-face shot as he took one for the team and sank to his knees. There was very little of the assailant besides his back, except for two shots. Dan froze them each half a dozen times. By the sixth pass, he was convinced of several things. The man was a pro—a martial arts expert with incredibly quick feet and textbook balance. He had placed a thin towel over the bar on the cart to keep from leaving fingerprints. He had enough of a

contact within the hospital to be able to obtain a false
ID badge, although it was not one that would have
stood up to close scrutiny. The instant it was clear he
wasn't going to make it into the ICU, he acted defini-
tively, put his adversary down, and walked rapidly but
calmly away, exiting the way he had come, toward the
Sperelakis Institute.

A pro.

Another conclusion was that both the glasses and
the mustache were fake. Dan felt almost sure of it now.
They were just too obvious—a diversion, like an eye
patch or a cast. A hundred out of a hundred witnesses
would have remembered the mustache, but none the
shape of the man's face or the color of his eyes.

Finally, there was the bundle on top of the steel cart.
A weapon of some sort? A change of clothes? Something medical? Whatever it was, the killer—Dan had
no doubt that the murder of a patient or nurse was the
man's intent—took pains to carry it away with him. If
the police had thought things through as he had, they
would be checking the hospital-wide videos for the man
and the bundle.

Unable to watch himself get pummeled one more
time, Dan tilted back in the supervisor's chair and
looked away. He had majored in criminology at Northeastern, and always knew he would someday be a police detective. His high grades in every related course
reflected that goal. One of those subjects was forensic
logic—a trip inside the mind of a criminal. For a time,
Dan focused on the man as he had been programmed

to do by the crusty, but brilliant, criminologist who taught the course.

It may seem at times as if there are an infinite number of scenarios by which a criminal could have committed his crime and escaped, but in truth there is only one—the real one.

On one wall of the office was a large whiteboard map of the entire Beaumont Clinic campus, with the tunnels shown as lightly dotted lines. First Dan chose the entrance that might follow the most logical movements of his assailant: through the Sperelakis Institute, then up to the third floor and across the walkway to the ICU. It was certainly the shortest route from the outside to the unit, but there was a security desk in the lobby, which was manned until the hospital entrances were shut down at the end of visitors' hours. That meant the killer would have had to enter, sign in, and then find a place to change, most likely in a restroom stall. Possible, but risky—and riskier still heading out, especially if there was trouble. No, Dan thought. The man had probably taken the crowded main entrance on Collins Avenue, changed in a restroom, then made his way someplace to where a steel cart was . . . was what? Waiting for him?

"Hey, Jess," he said through the open office door. "Where do you think the guy got the cart?"

"The what?"

"The cart he was pushing."

"I don't know. I think the ones that aren't on one of the floors are all in the basement—"

"—of the Bladd Building."

Dan finished the sentence with her, then turned back to the map. Assuming the killer knew where the carts were kept, and assuming he had come into the main entrance of the hospital, and assuming he had changed into orderly's whites, he would have chosen one of two men's rooms in which to do so, probably the smaller, less trafficked. In fact, Dan decided, with the trash cans screened from view in a recessed alcove in the wall, he might well have bundled his street clothes in a plastic bag of some sort and placed the bag into the trash for retrieval when he was finished.

Even though he had nearly been caught, the killer wouldn't have panicked. He would have walked quickly back to the men's room, retrieved his clothes, changed, maybe left his orderly's outfit in the same trash can, and calmly exited through the main doors, possibly carrying with him whatever was wrapped in the towel. The real question was, if in fact the glasses and mustache were fake, what he had chosen to do with them. He had made an error by not knowing that the security force was checking all employee IDs. Could he possibly have made another?

Dan used a washable marker to circle the men's room he had chosen. If he was wrong about that one, he would try another. If the janitorial staff had emptied the trash cans, there was nothing he could do. If they hadn't, he could probably get them to hold off.

"Found everything you need?" Jessica asked as he headed out of the office.

"I'll let you know," Dan replied.

He paused for a moment by the door to run his tongue across the stitches in his cheek.

On his way through the tunnel to the main entrance of the hospital, Dan called janitorial and made sure there would be no emptying of any restroom trash cans for at least an hour. Then he took a small cutoff that dead-ended in the expansive central supply center of the hospital, open twenty-four hours. Across from the counter was a large storage area containing stretchers, wheelchairs, rolling oxygen holders, several ventilators, tray tables, and a dozen or so steel carts.

There might have been a security camera inside the supply room where the surgical instruments, procedure kits, and countless other kinds of equipment were sterilized and stored, but there were none covering the hallway or storage area. It would have been no problem for the killer to walk into the space, ensure that whoever was working across the hall wasn't watching, and simply walk off with a steel cart. Of course, such an action presumed knowledge of the hospital, but Dan already felt certain that directly or from someone else, the man had that.

He returned to the main tunnel and headed toward the front entrance. Foot traffic was heavy, accompanied by electronic cars, beeping their warning as they towed huge hampers of laundry or bins of trash. As always, Dan was amazed at how many people and how much equipment were involved in caring for the sick.

He tried to imagine the complexity of running such a place as this, but simply couldn't get his mind around the notion.

Aware for the first time of the dull, unpleasant ache in his groin, he mounted the stairs to the main lobby. The bastard who kicked him had done so with surgical precision—a direct hit.

Someday, Dan thought. *Someday . . .*

The men's room he had reasoned out was off the broad corridor from the Sederstrom Family Lobby toward the first of many banks of elevators. It was, as he had surmised from the whiteboard map, small—two urinals, one stall. And it was deserted. The trash can, set in the wall and accessible through a swinging metal panel, was a large steel bin, three feet high and two square, lined with an industrial-strength plastic bag, and perhaps built from the same primordial slab of steel as the rolling cart. The bag was full.

Feeling somewhat foolish, Dan pulled the container out onto the tile floor, considered rummaging through it blindly, then suddenly dropped it noisily onto its side, grabbed a small ledge on the bottom, and emptied it out. Crumpled paper towels, the equivalent of a modest-sized tree, spilled out onto the tiled floor. Along with the towels were the contents of any number of men's pockets: two sections of the *Herald,* an empty pint of Jack Daniel's, a pair of boxer shorts no longer wearable for obvious reasons, and a thin paperback western. Nothing else. Dan's enthusiasm drained. The killer's movements seemed so logical when he thought them through in the security office. He had been wrong. The other men's room candidate he had considered was past the bank of elevators at the base of the Bladd Building. Going that way would have exposed the killer to the main hospital thoroughfare rather than the less-traveled tunnel, but it was possible. Certainly it was worth a try.

Wishing he had thought to bring a pair of gloves, he was about to push the mound of trash back toward the bin with his uniform shoe, when instinct made him peer into the plastic bag. It hadn't completely emptied. He tipped it nearly upside down, and a white orderly's uniform tumbled out, along with something wrapped in a paper towel.

Dan bent down and gingerly picked up the small bundle. Even before he exposed the contents, he knew what was there. Visualizing the killer stuffing his uniform and the package down to the bottom of the bin, he laid the paper towel on the sink, opened it up, and stared down at a pair of black-rimmed glasses and a thick, bogus mustache.

His pulse hammering, he rewrapped the package and slipped it into his Windbreaker pocket.

"You should have taken this stuff with you, pal," he muttered, already thinking of the woman at the state crime lab he could get to check his find for fingerprints. "If you touched something here even once, I've got you."

TWENTY

The Lydia Thibideau Gastroenterology Research Center occupied the entire fifth floor of the Cannon Building—a modern glass and steel structure built in tribute, the bronze plaque by the elevators read, to the skill and compassion of the physicians and nurses of the Beaumont Clinic. After checking to ensure that there would be restricted visitors and a guard on duty outside the ICU for at least until morning, Thea followed the directions the GI chief had given her and swiped her hospital security card to stop the elevator at Cannon 5. As Thibideau had promised, the main door to the center was unlocked, and the waiting area was now deserted.

Getting the card had taken most of a day. After numerous forms and a detailed interview with the head of hospital security, Thea had been granted Beta clearance, which she was told would get her into most common areas, her father's office and small laboratory, plus the hematology/blood chemistry lab, and the radiology suite. She was never given the explanation as to why those particular facilities were chosen, but Niko had, at some point, let slip that his clearance level was Delta. In fact, in order to access Petros's modest office, it was necessary not only to swipe her ID card, but to enter a password into the ten-digit keypad by his door. Not at all surprisingly, Petros's code, printed on a wallet-sized card given to Thea by the security head, was 2-8-4-3-6-7: ATHENS.

Security codes . . . ID cards . . . sign-ins . . . guards . . . electronic medical records . . . staggering malpractice insurance premiums . . . malpractice attorneys recruiting clients through television ads . . . other TV ads directed at having patients badger their doctors for various prescription medications . . . managed care companies dictating how much time a physician can devote to each patient.

The practice of medicine had evolved into something Alice would have encountered had she gotten ill on her trip through the looking glass.

Thea pictured the bustling jungle hospital near Katanga, DRC, where she had worked for almost two years now after transferring from a similarly vibrant facility in the Guidan Roumdji district of Niger. Sick and malnourished patients; skilled, devoted caregivers; miracle after miracle. It was an equation, a simple, straightforward system she could understand. Her income of around twenty thousand dollars a year couldn't stand up to the hundreds of thousands Niko and Selene each made, but she was actually saving a reasonable portion of her salary.

Now she was trying to track down why, with only a single word available to him, her father had chosen the name of a man who had survived a brutal cancer, fatal to all but the very fortunate.

During her rotation through the Beaumont, Thea

had met Lydia Thibideau once, and had attended several of her lectures. The woman never seemed particularly warm or open, but like many of the super-specialists at medical centers like this one, she was undeniably brilliant. As instructed, Thea took a seat in the empty waiting room. Twelve-hour workdays were the norm at her hospital, but she seldom felt stressed or too exhausted to go on. Now, though, she was feeling the strain of her father's devastating condition and the tension of dealing with the twins. Most of all, she was struggling with the terrible secret her father had imposed on her by allowing no one else to know that he was awake and alert.

In spite of herself, Thea's eyes closed. Her thoughts became disconnected fragments, many of them centering around Dan Cotton. In just the short time they had known each other, he had behaved nobly with the teen in the cafeteria and bravely with the assailant by the ICU. His rugged good looks were totally appealing to her, and although she was seldom consumed by sexual fantasies of a man, various images of them embracing and kissing and undressing each other began materializing. For a time, Dan galloped through her thoughts in full armor, carrying a lance and a shield. Moments later, he was lying next to her in the deep, rich grass of a meadow, slowly undoing the buttons of her blouse, unhooking her bra, touching her. . . .

How could this be? her mind asked over and over again. *How could this be? . . . How—*

"How do you do, Dr. Sperelakis?"

Thea's eyes snapped open, but took a few moments to focus. Imposing Lydia Thibideau, wearing a knee-length white lab coat, was standing less than five feet away, her arms folded tightly across her ample chest in a position, Thea sensed, that was typical of her. She had aged some since the photo in the *Bugle,* and perhaps gained some weight, but her stern expression was the same. Her hair, styled short, was more red than brown, and she wore no jewelry except for a plain gold band, partially buried at the base of her marriage finger.

"Oh, I think I fell asleep," Thea said, not feeling the least embarrassed.

"So it appears."

In improv class, Thea would have stood up, extended her hand, and asked, "How do you do?"—a phrase she never completely understood. Now, although there was nothing in the professor's manner that encouraged her, she did so anyway.

"How do you do. I'm Thea," she said, rising as the last wisp of her fantasy vanished.

"I . . . knew that," Thibideau replied, her hand like a trout. "I want to tell you how very sorry I am about your father. He was—*is*—a dear man and a dear friend."

There was an all-too-familiar cadence to the woman's speech, and Thea stopped herself at the last second from asking if she, too, had Asperger's.

"He seems stable right now," she said instead.

"Excellent. You said you wanted to speak to me about one of my patients. Shall we go into my office?"

"I would like that," Thea replied.

The fifth floor was a spacious, gleaming laboratory behind a glass wall on one side of a corridor, and across from that, a conference room with ceiling-to-floor bookcases, original artwork, and a wall-sized white-board, as well as several examining rooms and a corner office overlooking an elegant duck pond, complete with two fountains. Aspie or not, whatever Lydia Thibideau had done in her professional life, she had done it right.

Thea flashed on the corner of a vast tent that she called her office, and barely suppressed a grin. Thibideau did not offer her anything, but simply motioned her to a chair next to the desk.

"I wish to warn you in advance, Dr. Sperelakis, that it is my policy not to share information about any of my patients, even to another doctor, without a signed release. And even then I may choose not to."

"HIPAA, I know. Well, do the best you can."

On something of a roll, Thea had thought through the lie she was about to tell, and even imagined the words she was going to use to tell it. Still, despite her previous success at it, manipulating and restructuring the facts felt foreign and uncomfortable.

"I've agreed to take over my father's practice until he is able to resume work himself."

"Well, that's . . . very gracious of you. Weren't you practicing in the jungle somewhere?"

"The Congo, yes. I expect to go back there someday. Well, last night and today I've been going through some of my father's papers, and I came across a sheet with a name, a date, a diagnosis, and your name on it."

"Can I see it?"

"See what?"

"The paper—the sheet of paper you found."

"Oh . . . I . . . don't have it with me. I didn't stop back at the office after I called you."

Thibideau rolled her eyes.

"What was the name?"

"The name was Kalishar. I wondered if he's the Kalishar from the department store."

"And the diagnosis?"

"Pancreatic cancer."

Thibideau sighed.

"Dr. Sperelakis," she said wearily, "I don't know you beyond having your father tell me in the past that you broke his heart by going away to the jungle as you did. I'm sorry, but I don't think you're being completely forthcoming with me. Now, exactly what is going on here?"

Thea felt the grip of panic. What was Thibideau talking about? Clearly, she had seen through the lie, but there was no way Thea could share any information about Petros's locked-in syndrome. What was she supposed to do now?

"I . . . I just need to know about Jack Kalishar," she stammered.

"And you expect me to answer you without knowing why?"

Thea felt frozen, unable to respond. Twisting the truth had seemed so easy the last time she did it.

"I've been spending time late at night talking with Hayley Long," she suddenly heard herself saying. "We've been talking about . . . about her diagnosis."

"I know."

"You do?"

"Doctor, she's my patient. I don't know the medical customs in the jungle, but here in Boston we talk to our patients."

Thea felt herself unraveling.

"I'm sorry," she managed.

"Your visits have greatly buoyed Ms. Long's spirits. Now, I can't tell you much about Mr. Kalishar beyond that, as you surmised, he is my patient."

"Then he's still alive?"

"That fact is constantly reported in the *Wall Street Journal*. Yes, he's still very much alive and in excellent health, I might add. We do manage to save some patients, you know."

"I know," Thea said, "but the review article by Lawrence and Kelleher in the 2004 issue of the *American Journal of Gastroenterology* reports some pretty low survival rates."

"So, you've been doing your homework."

"My homework?"

Again, a queer look.

"Yes, research. You've been doing research on pancreatic cancer."

"Oh. Yes, I've done a little. But the Kelleher article I read some time ago—right when it came out, as I recall."

"I'm impressed you would remember such a thing."

"Don't be. I remember lots of things I read. Most, in fact. The survival numbers weren't very encouraging back then. I don't think they've changed all that much since then. Can you tell me what Mr. Kalishar was treated with?"

Thibideau mulled the question for a time, then said, "It was a developmental drug we labeled SU890. We developed it right here in our lab—well, in the lab that preceded this one."

"Is that what Hayley is getting now?"

"No. Ms. Long is on a new investigational drug, SU990, the next generation of the drug Mr. Kalishar got. I believe he got some other chemotherapy as well."

"But you said that Mr. Kalishar was completely disease-free after five years."

Once more, Thibideau hesitated in replying.

"He is," she said finally, "but others . . . weren't as fortunate. There were some deaths. We . . . had to stop the study and withdraw the drug."

"And go back to the drawing board."

"Not all the way back."

"I suppose with pancreatic cancer being such a lethal condition, the FDA has given you some breaks in that regard."

"Tell me, Doctor, are you always so . . . direct?"

Thea nodded modestly. "People have said that about me, yes. Some of them think it's refreshing. Some of them think that I'm a bit of a jerk."

"My Lord. Is there anything else you'd like to know?"

"Have you treated enough patients with this new generation of drug to have an idea how it's doing?"

"The results to this point are rather promising. Dr. Sperelakis—Thea—I'm sorry I said what I did about you breaking your father's heart."

"I know that I did. But Dr. Carpenter—Paige

Carpenter, she's my therapist—helped me learn that sometimes a person has to do what they have to do."

"Yes. . . . Well, I wish you luck in your new practice. If you are just a fraction as talented as your father, you are sure to be a success."

"I can't be as good as he is. I can only be as good as I can be."

"Dr. Carpenter, too?"

"Why, yes. Good guess."

"You are a very unusual woman, Dr. Sperelakis."

"Unusual. I think I like being that."

"If there's anything further I can do for you, you may at least ask."

"Well," Thea said, "there is one thing."

"Yes?"

"I'd like to bring an acupuncturist by to see Hayley."

"A what?"

"A revered acupuncture instructor from the school I used to study at. I was hoping he might give us some idea as to how Hayley is responding to her treatment."

The little warmth that had been radiating from Lydia Thibideau vanished.

"Doctor, are you trying to undercut me in some way?"

"No, no. All I wanted to do was help."

"Well, you're not helping me. I have no truck with acupuncture or herbalism or reflexology or chiropractic or any of those other quacks. You seem to have inherited not only your father's intelligence, but his penchant for getting in people's way."

Thea was stunned.

"Wh-what's that supposed to mean?" she managed.

"It means that if your acupuncturist so much as touches my patient with a needle, I will have you brought before the executive committee so fast it will make your head spin."

TWENTY-ONE

The more Thea thought about her session with Lydia Thibideau, the less sense it made. One moment she was saying how much she respected Petros, another she was disrespectfully calling him a meddler. What did that mean?

As she walked through the tunnels to grab some dinner at the cafeteria before heading to Hayley's room, she tried sorting out what she had learned regarding Jack Kalishar. The man, because of his metastatic pancreatic cancer, had been referred by her father to Thibideau, one of the foremost specialists in that disease in the world. She had designated him for inclusion in a clinical trial, one of a number of such trials she was continuously running on various chemotherapeutic agents, developed in her lab or in conjunction with one of the big drug houses. In Kalishar's case, it was a drug named SU890.

The investigational drug accomplished something that was almost impossible to believe. It cured Kalishar—cured him of a cancer with an average five-year survival of 4 percent. Cured him of a cancer where the survival from the most aggressive treatment—

surgery, radiation, and chemo in combination—in the most localized disease, averaged seventeen months.

Seventeen months in a best-case scenario.

Jack Kalishar was a miracle, and SU890 was the maker of the miracle.

There was just one problem. Other patients receiving the miracle drug had died. Exactly how many, what percent of those in the SU890 treatment group, Thibideau would not say.

Thea wondered how many deaths it would take to offset a miracle like Jack Kalishar.

Four-percent five-year survival. That was the starting point. Extending that statistic to eight percent, or ten, or even fifteen would be miraculous in its own right, but a cure . . .

What about Hayley? Did SU990 have any track record yet? Had she and her husband made the right decision in choosing to forgo treatment with the other established anticancer drugs to concentrate on this one?

Four percent survival. Not a heck of a lot to hope for.

Thibideau had been hardly forthcoming about her research. At times in their brief conversation she seemed unpleasantly patronizing. Then there was the attack on Petros. Thea tried to understand why, but got nowhere. Was it just the woman's personality? Was she unusually paranoid about her data, or was this simply the way world-renowned scientists acted? It would seem that Petros Sperelakis's physician-daughter might have deserved more respect. Perhaps the gastroenterologist had learned about her Asperger's from Petros or one of the twins. Perhaps, in addition to her loathing for all those alternative healers, she just couldn't take seriously someone who'd worked in Africa.

It was half past seven and Thea was famished. Once she got settled in with a salad and whatever pasta they were serving, she would call Dan to see how he was doing, and if he might be free tomorrow to spend some time with Dimitri. She also wanted at least to leave a message for Professor Julian Fang at the Eastern Massachusetts School of Acupuncture to see if he could stop by at the hospital to evaluate Hayley. Just no needles—isn't that what Thibideau had said?

A year after her graduation from medical school, weighed down by the stress of too many patients and not nearly enough sleep, Thea had taken a basic acupuncture course taught by Fang, and had embraced both the philosophy and the man. She took another course in which she clearly demonstrated an aptitude for alternative medicine, and then, later in the year, used most of her vacation to go on a retreat with Fang and some of his most promising students.

For some time after that, Thea gave serious consideration to switching from Western to Eastern medicine. Fang had spent several hours discussing change with her—not the specific change she was considering, but the nature of change in general, and the difficulty she often had around flexibility and dealing with the unexpected. Ultimately, although it would have meant another student for his school, and a favorite of his at that, Fang recommended that she wait until her training was over before considering such a radical alteration of her life.

Eventually, Thea decided on a commitment to Doctors Without Borders. But she continued her study of acupuncture and herbal medicine, as well as her contact with Julian Fang.

Dan answered her call and sounded excited to hear from her, but he was locked in a game of chess with his son while they waited for the boy's mother to pick him up.

"I can call you back right after I get beaten," he said. "Make that get beaten *again*. Between Josh and the orderly with the fancy fast feet, I'm on quite a roll today."

Thea imagined a comfortable den with thick leather furniture, and put Dan Cotton in a huge chocolate-colored leather easy chair. There were pictures of sports heroes on the wall, and trophies on the mantel for baseball and football and . . . and weight lifting.

"That was a sneak attack in the hospital," she said, "just like Pearl Harbor."

"Well, I don't intend to go through a world war and an atomic blast before I get even."

"I'll help."

"I'm counting on that."

"Dan, listen. I know you have to get back to Josh, but I just want you to know that I'm really sorry you got hurt and I really want to see you again as soon as possible."

"I don't know how long it will take me to get used to being around someone who actually says what they mean. Let me try. Alethea Sperelakis, I really want to see you again, too. Let's talk later."

"Let's talk later, Dan Cotton."

Thea slipped her father's cell phone into her pocket and did some people-watching as she ate. She also continued to try and sort out the meaning and significance of her strange, tightly controlled exchange with Lydia Thibideau. Was there any sense in trying to set up another meeting to get any more information from the woman? Doubtful. Was there anyone else she could speak to about Jack Kalishar and the other patients who had been treated with SU890? At the moment, there was only one she could think of—her father. But unless he brightened considerably in terms of his processing speed and ability to respond to the sort of code that enabled Jean-Dominique Bauby to dictate his memoirs, it was going to be next to impossible. For now, the key to moving forward had to rest not with the man himself, but with the man's office, and his cluttered study at home.

Across the expansive cafeteria, a security guard wandered along the sandwich counter making his choice. He was quite a bit shorter than Dan, though, and didn't look nearly as handsome in his uniform. In seconds, the trigger of seeing the man had her fantasizing again about making love with Dan—this time in the den she had conjured up for him, and even more passionately than what she had envisioned in Thibideau's waiting room.

Sitting there in the still busy cafeteria, eyes half-closed, she wondered if anyone else in the crowded place was having a fantasy as rich and as enjoyable as was hers.

Aspies were defined in part by their concreteness and lack of latitude in their thinking. Yet many of them were involved in role-playing games that required the ability to transport themselves into alternative worlds, and to live in those wild, unpredictable worlds for hours on end. It was an ability that actually separated many with Asperger syndrome from the majority of neurotypicals. Did this ability carry over into other aspects of their fantasy life? Were their virtual sex lives richer, more passionate, and more quickly engaged than those of the typicals, even as their realities were more tightly bound?

Thea made a mental note to ask Dan. It would be as much fun to see his expression at the question as to hear his answer.

Before leaving for the ICU, she left a message for Julian Fang asking if he would be available to render an opinion about the extent and potential for treatment of Hayley's cancer. Thea had never responded sanguinely to being pushed or told what to do. Her many clashes over the years with her father attested to that. If the acupuncturist put even a single needle into Hayley. That's what she had said, almost word for word. Fortunately, Thibideau had said nothing of checking Hayley's acupuncture pulses—a skill at which Julian was profoundly adept.

Wondering if she might run into either of the twins, Thea set her tray on the conveyor belt and headed for the unit. If there were no visitors and no volunteer nurses in Petros's cubicle, she might try another question for him—one carefully formulated to determine where she would be most likely to hit paydirt in her search for more information about Jack Kalishar. Hopefully the Lion would have brightened enough to be ready for some yes-or-no exchange.

The woman at the security desk in front of the unit had been replaced by a husky man with tattoos on the backs of both hands, whose name tag read OFFICER WILLIAM SAUNDERS. He dutifully checked her ID badge and watched as she signed in.

"Leave something behind?" he asked.

Distracted, she barely heard the question.

"Huh?" she replied. "Oh, no. No, I didn't leave anything."

What an odd question, she was thinking as the glass doors glided apart and she strode into the unit, anxious to see who might be visiting. She was actually inside her father's cubicle before she realized that the figure in his bed, partially obscured by machines and tubes, being tended to by a nurse she had never seen with Petros, was an elderly woman.

TWENTY-TWO

"The step-down unit? How can you possibly transfer him there?"

"We . . . needed the bed—two beds, in fact—and your father was first on the list."

The intensivist on duty, a doughy, baby-faced doc named Spiegel, withered before Thea's eruption.

"What list?" she demanded.

"Every day we make a list of who can be transferred out of here. Then we clear the name with their PCP. As soon as we need beds, we start at the top of the list. Because of the numbers at the Beaumont, the average patient stay here is not very long. Sometimes it's measured in hours. Your father's been here for many days."

"But he had a pericardial drain in place."

"It wasn't draining anything, so we pulled it. Same with the intracranial ventricular drain. I'm sorry, Dr. Sperelakis, but as I said, we're getting new patients all the time. We've got to keep them moving."

"Who authorized this?"

"Well, the truth is no one has to authorize any transfer from the unit except the intensivist on duty, which, at the moment, is me. But because of who your father is, I consulted with Dr. Niko, who put in the drain, and also with Dr. Hartnett, his PCP. They both approved moving Dr. Sperelakis to the step-down unit on Eaton One."

"I can't believe this."

"The patient that took his place is very unstable. Go and see for yourself."

"I can't believe this," Thea said again. "Do you know that just this morning someone tried to kill him?"

"Kill him?"

"The fight in the hall between a man dressed as an orderly and the security guard—that was about my father."

"I wasn't told that."

"Well, it's true. . . . Listen, Dr. Spiegel. I'm sorry to snap at you. I know you just did what you thought was right. I just wish you had contacted me before moving him."

"I spoke with Scott and your brother, and your sister is down there with him right now. He really is quite stable. Besides, anything we can monitor here, they can monitor on Eaton One."

"But with less staffing than you have here."

Thea apologized again and took the stairs back down to the tunnel. The Eaton Building, home to the cardiac cath lab and most of the powerful cardiology service, was so new that Thea had never been in it. Everything surrounding Petros in the step-down unit was as gleaming and sophisticated as in the ICU. The nursing coverage, Thea's benchmark for just how good a hospital was, seemed reasonably comprehensive.

In every way the Beaumont's worldwide reputation

for excellence seemed well earned, except that something within its walls was wrong—very wrong—and the man connected to a ventilator and monitor screen in Step-Down 6 almost certainly knew what it was.

Reflexively, Thea scanned the numbers as she entered the private room. Nothing worrisome.

"Hey there, sis," Selene said. "One small step-down for a man, one giant leap for old Petros."

"Do you think he's stable enough for this move?"

"What do I know? I'm only a dentist. At least according to what Dad believes about us hand surgeons, I am."

Thea wanted to warn her to watch what she said, that in fact their father was in no coma whatsoever. But she had given her word, and even if she shouted the truth from the rooftops, Petros would give no sign that supported her. Still, even without any indication, someone believed her enough to have tried to silence him forever. Now, thanks to this transfer, he was again in danger.

Like everything else in the Beaumont, the fourteen-bed step-down unit was large and bustling and well staffed. But despite the excellent coverage, the nurses could not be expected to police SD 6 anything approaching 100 percent of the time. It wasn't a simple matter to kill someone on a ventilator and cardiac monitor, with nurses around who were skilled in resuscitation, but it could be done. One possibility was something as simple as a four-minute replacement of the oxygen driving the ventilator with something like nitrous oxide from a small, portable tank.

"Do you think we should get someone in here around the clock?" Thea asked.

Selene, wearing a perfectly tailored gray linen suit that might have come straight from a Paris design house, and enough gold bangles on each wrist to sink a lifeboat, looked at her queerly.

"The volunteer nurses that were helping out in the unit just sat around most of the time reading magazines."

"I was thinking more in terms of security people, like off-duty policemen."

"Do you have any idea how much that would cost?"

"No, but I have Dad's bankbook. Believe me, he can handle it."

"Pardon me for asking, but what is this all about? That cartoon Dimitri has put together of the accident?"

"That and the incident with the bogus orderly."

"You think they're connected?" Selene sounded incredulous.

"I do, actually," Thea said, carefully measuring her words so as not to upset Petros, who she felt certain was listening. She also found herself wondering if whoever had sent the killer up to the ICU could have had anything to do with ordering or authorizing the transfer.

"Oh, honey, I know how badly you want to believe Dad is coming out of this," Selene said, "but logic and medical science say he isn't. He had an accident, his brain was damaged, he's in a deep coma, he's not going to wake up, and sooner or later, more likely sooner, pneumonia or heart failure is going to take him. And if he had a say in the matter, I believe Dad would insist on it."

"I don't think we should be talking about his condition at the bedside like this, just in case."

"Whatever you say, baby."

"I do have something I wanted to ask you about."

"Shoot."

"Do you know anything about Jack Kalishar?"

"The department store guy?"

"Yes. He was a patient of Dad's."

"I didn't even know that. Dad took the confidentiality of his patients pretty seriously, just like he took everything else in life, except maybe parenting."

Thea winced, but did not repeat her warning to keep remarks about him away from his bedside. She knew that she was asking about the billionaire as much to communicate with their father as with Selene.

"I've become friendly with a patient at the institute named Hayley Long," she said. "She has metastatic pancreatic CA. Jack Kalishar was treated here for the same thing, and according to Dr. Thibideau, is fine after five years."

"I want *that* treatment."

"Exactly. Selene, I assume you've heard that I've told Karsten I would take over Dad's practice for now."

"She called and told me. You know that the two of them are an item, Dad and her, right?"

Please don't say anything nasty about her.

"Yes, she let me in on the secret. She's gotten me temporary privileges, but I don't have access yet to his patients' medical records. I have to go through Scott

Hartnett for anything like that, at least until my staff privileges are expanded. I want to see Hayley's records and Kalishar's, too. Is there any way you can save me the hassle of going through Scott and just send them over to Dad's office?"

"Wish I could, but it isn't possible. Each patient has a number that restricts who on the staff has access to their electronic records. If your friend Hayley adds my code number to her records, I suppose I can get her chart over to Dad. I have no idea what his code is. Mine has like eight numbers and two letters in it. If I ever got caught giving it out, I'd be suspended."

"Does Hayley have access to her own records?"

"Within a few months I think she will. Google and Microsoft are ahead of us in that regard."

"Well, not to worry. I won't ever ask you to do anything compromising. First I'm going to check through Dad's desk and see if I can find his code. Then I'll let you and Hayley know if I need help with her record."

"Just be careful."

"What's that supposed to mean?"

"With this Thor system, things work both ways. Any request for information gets recorded someplace and transmitted to records security."

"Brave new world," Thea said.

"More like Kafka. For all I know there's a security team watching over that security team."

Selene patted Petros on the cheek, her bangles clinking.

"Well, I've got to go, old shoe," she said. "I would think the least you could do was to wake up. You're not acting very grateful to this woman here for saving your life." She turned to Thea. "Take care, Princess Buttercup. Welcome to the staff of the Beaumont."

Without waiting for a reply, Selene was gone. Thea ached for what their father was listening to, especially when the twins were at the bedside together. It was probably just as well that Dimitri wasn't among the man's regular daily visitors. She moistened a washcloth and mopped, then dried his forehead. Then she looked about, untaped his eyes, added some lubricant, and bent low by his ear.

"Dad, did you hear all of that?" she asked. "I need to get your records code so I can see exactly what was done with Jack Kalishar. Dr. Thibideau hasn't been very helpful. All she really told me is that he's still alive. Move your eye if you understand what I said."

Thea gently moved his lids apart. Petros's pupils were mid-position—perhaps a bit smaller than usual.

"Dad, look up. . . ."

He couldn't be sleeping, not after the conversation that had just gone on with Selene.

"Dad, please. Look up if you can hear me. . . ."

There was no movement at all.

"Dad . . . ?"

Nothing. Thea pulled back and stared down at the man. He wasn't hearing her. Not at all. She felt certain of it. There was no hint whatsoever that he was aware but locked-in. He wasn't aware at all. At this moment, Petros was as unconscious as everyone else believed he was.

TWENTY-THREE

"You all right? You don't look so good."

It was the patient with virtually incurable pancreatic cancer who was asking the question of the doctor.

"I was just going to say the same thing to you," Thea replied.

"You'll get your chance," Hayley said. "In fact, I'm feeling bloated and a little uncomfortable up here in my stomach. I interpret every little ache, every little gas bubble as being another little cancer cell biting the dust. But you go first."

Thea reviewed the developments surrounding her father and Jack Kalishar, the bizarre visit with Lydia Thibideau, and also the oddly truncated staff privileges conferred on her by Sharon Karsten and the credentials committee. Hayley, who had been reading Joyce Carol Oates in her usual spot near the doorway, had set her book aside and listened intently.

"So I think this Kalishar business might turn out to be a hopeful sign for you," Thea said, unable to speak the name without wondering once again why her father had chosen it, of all the helpful words he could have given her. "He was treated by the same physician in the same hospital as you, and he's a five-year survivor with no evidence of residual or recurrent disease."

Hayley sighed.

"Doc, I got where I am today by being able to read people—many of them extremely oblique and difficult in that regard. You, my dear woman, are neither. It's great that you're trying to be upbeat and cheerful around me, but we'll get a lot farther a lot faster if you just take the things that are bothering you one at a time."

"Sorry. I'll try."

"Do we know if Kalishar and I are part of the same study?"

"Actually, we know that you're not. According to Thibideau, the drug you're getting is an improvement over the one he got."

"Bad side effects?"

"Enough to modify the original drug. But Thibideau says this new version is showing great promise. You sleeping any better?"

Hayley took her hand.

"I'll assume that the wonderful, unselfish, caring physician in you wants to reach out to me," she said, "and to do what you can to make me feel better. We'll get to me later. I promise. Now, number one on the list of things that are weighing on you is . . ."

Thea sighed and stared down at their hands. Over the years, she had improved a thousand percent in the art of making direct eye contact when speaking with someone, but the improvement still left her well below the average neurotypical in that regard. Hayley either didn't notice the tendency, or more likely, chose not to comment on it.

"Well, number one is my father," Thea said finally. "I told you he was communicating with me, but refused to communicate with my brother Niko or my sister Selene. She's—"

"Niko's twin. I have this terrible shortcoming in that I pay attention to what people say to me—especially people I care about. What about Dimitri?"

"I don't know. He hasn't been here very much. I think Petros has chosen me and only me. Unfortunately, I didn't realize that at first, and told one of the nurses and Dr. Hartnett that he was awake and had communicated with me."

"But they didn't believe you when he didn't respond to them."

"Exactly."

"Go on, please. I'll try not to interrupt. Interrupting is another one of my shortcomings."

"Well, even though they might not have believed he had regained consciousness, one or both of them said something about it to other people. Now I have no idea who knows my father might be awake, and who doesn't. Not long after I failed to demonstrate Petros's ability to communicate, a man disguised as an orderly almost got into the ICU. I think he was trying to kill him."

"But you're not certain of that."

Thea shook her head.

"Earlier today, without my knowledge or opportunity to object, Petros was transferred from the ICU to the step-down unit. A little while ago, I was alone with him and tried to communicate. He's been very slow at give-and-take, but I thought he might be improving. This time, he didn't respond. Not at all."

"Has he slipped back into a coma?"

"I don't know. They took the pressure monitor out of his head, so there's no easy way to tell if there's a new blockage."

"If the chief of the institute is treated that way, what can *I* expect?"

"You're doing fine, and from all I can tell, you're getting great care. You know, it's possible my father is just being petulant. Thinking he was in a coma, Selene said some pretty harsh things about him at the bedside. If he heard her, maybe he just stopped talking."

"Or maybe she knew he was awake. . . . I'm sorry, sweetheart. That was the cynical broad from the land of Trust No One speaking."

"That may be better than the land of Trust Everyone, where I come from. Now, tell me what's going on with you."

"In a minute. First, tell me a little more about Jack Kalishar."

"Do you know him?"

"No, but I know people who do. We billionaires are a pretty close bunch, you know, bound by the spirit of competition, plus an unbreakable creed of dislike, envy, and mistrust. Oops, there I go again. The wicked witch of the Southeast."

"I think you're wonderful."

"Kalishar."

"Okay. From what I can tell, my father believes that

the hit-and-run that nearly killed him was no accident. I have the sense that he knew something he shouldn't know, or saw something he shouldn't have seen, and then maybe he told the wrong person about it. After he allowed me in on the secret that he had regained consciousness and had the ability to communicate, I convinced him to summon all his energy and let me walk him through the alphabet searching for one word—just one word—to help me understand what might be going on."

"And he gave you *Kalishar*. I like the clothes they carry in his stores. The Kalishar's Department Store chain is just the tip of his empire, though. The man's got his thumb in more pies than Little Jack Horner."

"Any of it dishonest?" Thea asked, a hopeful note in her voice. "Something that my father might have learned about him?"

"Not that I've heard. People like us don't get to where we are without stepping on a toe or two or reinterpreting a law here or there. Dr. Thibideau wasn't very helpful?"

"Typically, I just couldn't tell if she was holding back from me, but she certainly wasn't forthcoming either. You and I have talked about HIPAA. She only told me things she was certain I already knew or could find out by reading the papers."

"Tell me something, Thea. While you were there, did Thibideau refer to anything in a yellow file folder?"

Thea shook her head.

"No," she said. "There was nothing about that."

"Well, they exist—at least for me one exists, and I'm

pretty sure I caught sight of a lot more of them. They're in a walnut or oak file cabinet behind her desk."

"Four drawers tall. I saw it," Thea said, closing her eyes to bring the image of Thibideau's office into shaper focus. "Brass handles and a little statue of . . . of a ballerina on top."

"Aren't you something."

"I remember thinking that Dr. Thibideau was one of the least ballerina-like women I have ever met. I almost asked her about it."

"Probably just as well that you battled that particular impulse back, kiddo. Your Asperger's therapist would be proud."

Thea managed a thin smile.

"So Dr. Thibideau was using a folder and not an electronic record?"

"Actually, she had her computer going, too, but mostly she paid attention to me and referred to the yellow folder."

"So, do you think she has a folder for Jack Kalishar?"

"I wouldn't be surprised."

"Maybe I could talk to her about that."

Hayley smiled at her patiently.

"If she didn't pull Kalishar's file out when you were there in her office, do you think she'd do it just because you went back there and asked?"

"Just a thought."

"And a very excellent thought, too. . . . But I might have a better one."

"What?"

"Flowers."

"But what would giving her flowers accomplish?"

Hayley laughed out loud.

"Not those kind of flowers, Dr. Thea. *Sean* Flowers. He works for me."

Thea didn't understand why Hayley had found that miscommunication so funny.

"How can this Flowers help us with Dr. Thibideau?" she asked.

Hayley sighed and cast about as if searching for guidance in picking her words.

"There are times in various aspects of my business enterprises," she began, "where a rival company might have hidden away information that would help our company make important decisions."

Thea looked at her blankly.

"Such as?"

"Such as whether that company plans to release a product that we have only recently begun to research at the cost of tens of millions of dollars. It would be worth a great deal to us to have that information. Sometimes, the secret to getting it is Sean Flowers."

"I think I'm beginning to understand."

"Good. Sean is an expert at getting ahold of information. Other companies have their version of Sean also."

"You mean like industrial spies."

"Well, I suppose that's one way to put it."

"Is there another?"

There was admiration in Hayley's expression.

"No," she said. "No, I don't suppose there is."

"So you want to have this Mr. Sean Flowers of yours break into Dr. Thibideau's office."

"He does have that ability. Yes."

"And he would know what he was looking for?"

"Well, Thea, that depends on precisely what we want. It may be that you would have to go in there with him and review the charts right there."

"I wonder how many of them there are."

"Altogether? Hundreds, I would bet. I mean, pancreatic cancer is one of the most common, and she is one of the most referred-to experts in the field. The cases come rolling in to her. You think you could learn stuff from studying charts other than mine and Jack Kalishar's?"

"Quite possibly. I wish I knew exactly what I'd be looking for."

"I think when you see it, you'll know. Somewhere in that locked-in brain of his, I think your father feels the same way."

"Maybe. Maybe so."

"Okay, then," Hayley said, "we're on?"

Thea thought for a few moments, then shook her head.

"I don't think so," she said. "Earlier today, I told the president of the hospital a lie about why I wanted staff privileges here. I don't remember the last time I lied to someone like that. Then, just a little while later, I lied to her again. It wasn't as hard the second time."

"I promise you, Thea, companies do this sort of thing all the time, even companies like ours that have a reputation for high standards and ethical practices. The last thing I want is for you to think badly of me and the way I do business, but getting this information seemed important to you, and in case you forgot, it might turn out to be sort of important to me as well."

"You have a point there."

"So are we a go?"

Thea considered the question again.

"There are a lot of aspects of my Asperger syndrome that I wish I didn't have," she said finally, "but on the other hand, there are a lot of aspects I like having. It's hard to explain."

"I think I understand."

"Then you understand why at this point at least, I don't feel comfortable breaking into Dr. Thibideau's office."

Hayley stared down at her hands as she picked at a cuticle.

"We'll see if we can find another way," she said at last. "Now, when are you bringing this acupuncturist of yours over to see me?"

"Tomorrow evening. Not a word to Dr. Thibideau if you can help it."

"Not a word."

"Do you think that omission is a form of lying?"

"I think you're a really terrific person, Thea. That's what I think."

"Professor Fang and I will be here right after dinner, I think."

"I'll be right here. And don't worry, darling, I'm not the least bit disappointed in you for choosing not to involve Sean Flowers in this."

"Actually," Thea said, "I hadn't even considered that you would be."

TWENTY-FOUR

Before heading out to Wellesley, Thea took the tunnels back to the step-down unit. Visitors' hours were over, and the hospital, like a beast with a thousand hearts, was stretching and yawning, settling into the night. The SDU seemed quiet, but Thea was disturbed that there were no security people on watch, and no private-duty nurses tending to her father.

He looked peaceful enough, lying there by his ventilator, but Thea couldn't help but wonder if the two of them had communicated for the last time.

"Dad?" she whispered. "Dad, it's me."

The monitor overhead continued to record a pattern of stability, which it then transmitted to the nurses' station. Thea removed the paper tape from Petros's eyes and inserted the lubricating drops. Melancholy had rarely been an emotion that was a part of her, but she had talked about the feeling from time to time with her neurotypical friends. At the moment, there was a heaviness in her chest and a fullness in her throat that felt foreign and strange, and that she suspected might represent melancholy.

So much was confusing to her. So little of what was swirling about her father made sense.

"Dad, it's Thea. Move your eyes if you can hear me. Just look up." The Lion's dark eyes stared ahead, fixed on a spot somewhere on the ceiling. "Dad, what's going on? Please tell me what's happening?"

It was only then that she recalled the slight change in his pupils. They were smaller than they had been—not quite the pinpoint pupils of a narcotics overdose or certain brain stem disasters, but headed in that direction. She made a mental note to call the finding to the nurse's attention, and to review his meds and the reports on his hourly neuro checks, which would include pupil size and reactivity.

The unpleasant fullness in her chest intensified.

Melancholy.

Maybe she shouldn't have been so quick to turn down Hayley's offer of help from Sean Flowers. Her father's tenuous, spiderweb connection with the world seemed to have snapped. Was this the natural progression of his brain injury? If not, who did this to him? Who was responsible? What did Jack Kalishar have to do with anything? What was she willing to do, what principles was she willing to sacrifice to get to the bottom of things?

"Please. If you can hear me, Dad, let me know. Move your eyes."

Thea blinked back a sudden rush of tears. Things might have been better if Niko had never been able to reach her in the Congo. This was going to be a nightmare. No, no. It was a nightmare already.

Replacing the paper tape, Thea bent forward and kissed her father on the forehead. He wasn't going to wake up again. She felt it in the deepest part of her. If this was melancholy she was experiencing, she wanted no part of it. She stopped by the nurses' station and was allowed to review her father's medications. None of them could have caused his pupillary constriction. Perhaps it was time for another MRI, or at least a recheck by the neurologist.

What difference does it make? Thea found herself thinking as she cut through the deserted lobby of the Sperelakis Institute and out into the parking lot where she had left Petros's Volvo.

What difference does any of it make?

The lighting in the lot wasn't the best, but there were still a number of cars. It would be good to spend a little time with Dimitri, who had left her a note that he would be up late as usual.

Thea fumbled through her purse for her keys and opened the lock with the remote. At the instant she was about to open the driver's side door, she became aware of movement behind her, but there was no time to react. A plastic bag was pulled over her head and a drawstring at its mouth was tightened around her neck. At the same instant, she was slammed against the Volvo, a man's full weight pressing against her from behind.

Driven by a rush of adrenaline, she clawed at the bag and at her attacker, but she had no leverage. The cord securing the heavy plastic seemed made for that purpose. In fact, she realized as she struggled, the cord was knotted or held with a clamp, and both of the man's gloved hands were free. She wasn't being strangled, but there was little space in the bag—no more than a couple of minutes' worth of air, she guessed. The choking sensation and the smothering black plastic were terrifying.

Thea tried with only minimal success to force herself not to panic, and to analyze her situation.

For fully half a minute, she was totally helpless, pressed against the car, her hands held tightly at her sides, the hardness of the man's groin jammed into the small of her back. If he was going to rape her, he certainly didn't seem frantic about getting on with it. If he was intent on killing her, her larynx would already have been crushed, or her neck snapped. If he wanted her to slowly asphyxiate to death, he was well on his way to succeeding.

Was there anything she could do to stop him?

"Please, no!" she screamed, but the sound was lost in the bag. "No!"

She kicked backward, but her one connection with his shin was feeble.

The erection expanding against her low back might be a target, but how could she get at it? The air was beginning to feel heavy. She had to slow down. Breathe slower. *Think . . . Think.*

Not letting up the pressure holding her face and chest against the car, the attacker pushed her down to her knees.

If he tried forcing her to give him oral sex, she thought immediately, he was going to be in for a most pleasant surprise—for about one second. Then the *real* surprise would come.

Still holding her fast on her knees, he knelt, setting one of his knees between hers. Then, still holding her arms against her sides, he leaned close to her ear and spoke, his voice a menacing, harsh whisper.

"Okay. Listen and listen good. I could kill you right here and right now. I can kill you anytime I want to. You have been meddling in things that are none of your business. Continue to do it, and you're dead. And while you're dying, you'll wish I had used this bag. I promise you that. Now, just lay off anything to do with the man in the hospital, and go back to where you came from."

"But—"

"Shut up! Lie down on your face! . . . Okay. Now, if I so much as see you twitch in the next minute, I'm going to come back here and stamp on your neck. Is that clear? Just nod if it is. Okay. And if I learn you've spoken to the police about this conversation— and I assure you I will—that's it. I'll find you, and I'll kill you."

Thea, her pulse hammering at the viciousness of the man's words and tone, felt his pressure on her body let up, then vanish. Soft footsteps moved slowly away, then there was silence. She lay there, prone on the pavement, for as long as she could comfortably breathe. Finally, she reached behind her neck and slid open the clasp that had been holding the narrow drawstring in place, and pulled the bag off her head.

It was another two minutes before she risked pushing up to her knees. There was no sight of the man, but there wouldn't be even if he were watching her. She felt badly shaken at having been so close to such a person, to such unabated evil, and she felt confused at what was behind his demand.

Almost certainly he had been hired by someone to frighten her. But by whom? How did whoever it was expect her to respond? Did they think she would just pack up, leave her father, and fly back to the Congo? Were they warning her to stop trying to find out what had happened to him, or were they demanding that she stop being so aggressive and just let him die?

The questions swirling about in her mind far outnumbered their answers.

For a time she sat in the car in the dimly lit parking lot, nearly hyperventilating as she tried to get her feelings in some order.

One thing at a time. . . . Breathe in. . . . Breathe out. . . . One thing at a time.

Thea heard the words as if Dr. Carpenter were sitting there speaking them.

Breathe in. . . . Breathe out. . . . When you're becoming overwhelmed, just make a list. Make a list and do one thing at a time.

She withdrew a pen and a small spiral-bound pad from her bag.

Musgrave.

Dan.

Hayley.

Police.

She studied the short list for a minute. Then she looked down at the plastic bag on the passenger's seat and crossed off *Police*. If Dan wanted her to go to them, she would go. But first he had to be made to understand the evil—the absolute, quintessential evil emanating from the man; evil that had led him to actually become sexually aroused at the thought of hurting or killing her.

She flipped to a page in her pad with two dozen or so phone numbers written on it. Her first call, despite the hour, was to Amy Musgrave, the director of nursing. The woman had said, "Call anytime," she reasoned, and this was certainly anytime.

"Amy, it's Thea, Thea Sperelakis."

"Is everything all right?"

"Yes . . . Well, no . . . Well, I don't know. Amy, I want to hire special-duty nurses to stay with my father."

"I heard they transferred him to the SDU."

"I would have fought it if they told me before they did it."

"It's always a tough call—especially with a patient as important as your father. But the importance of the patient isn't a factor we usually take into consideration."

"It seems like it's too late to do anything about it now."

"Unless his condition suddenly deteriorates, I would agree. You want a special just for nights?"

"Twenty-four hours a day."

"That can get very expensive very quickly, and we have excellent coverage during the—"

"Twenty-four hours starting now. We can afford it."

"I'll see what I can do. Do Selene and Niko know you're doing this?"

"They will tomorrow."

The shakes had stopped, and much of her confusion had begun to abate. A few more breaths and she called Dan.

"Hi, it's me," she said.

"Hi there, me."

"Were you sleeping?"

"Do you want the socially expected answer or the Thea answer?"

"What does that mean?"

"It means yes, I was sleeping."

"Some bad things have been happening. I feel like I need to tell you about them."

"Go ahead."

"In person. Can you come out to Wellesley?"

"Now?"

"Now."

"I'm looking for my other sock right this second."

"I've been thinking about you a lot."

"That's great. That's really great, because I've been thinking a lot about you, too."

"Thanks. I don't want to shock you or scare you, but I'm probably going to want to make love to you."

For ten seconds, fifteen, there was silence.

"I just found my other sock," Dan said.

The third call on her list was the most difficult. The hospital switchboard was closed, but Hayley's business card, wedged in the small notebook, had her cell phone number on it.

"Hayley, I've changed my mind," Thea said.

"About what?"

"About Sean Flowers."

"But why?"

"I'll tell you in the morning. For now just know that people are pushing against me, and I've decided to push back."

TWENTY-FIVE

Thea drove out on Route 9 toward Wellesley, barely aware of the traffic moving alongside her. Only one thing seemed clear to her at this point: If the assault on her was a warning, it was also, in essence, a confession that the near-fatal hit-and-run was not accidental. Dimitri had been right from the beginning, and the twins had been wrong not to listen to him.

Now they needed to work together if they were to identify the motive and the person behind the first attempt on Petros's life, as well as the attempt in the hospital. It seemed likely that the man in the parking lot and the orderly in the hospital were the same. Who had hired him?

Thea also needed help understanding how much immediate danger she was in, and also Petros. It wasn't that simple to get away with killing a patient who was on constant monitoring, assisted ventilation, and close observation. Of course, even with the sort of excellent CPR that most ICU nurses were trained to perform, there was always a bullet, a garrote, or drugs that, if given intravenously and in a large enough dosage, could stop a heart irretrievably.

The killer would have to be ready to escape from

Petros's bedside during the commotion of the cardiac arrest. In fact, Thea felt certain that was precisely what Dan's bogus orderly had intended to do. In the ICU, most visitors were logged in or at least noted. In the SDU, that was not always the case, but the special-duty nurses she had just ordered would close that loophole.

Lost in thoughts about murder in an SDU and Dan coming out to Wellesley, Thea had to lean on the brakes and screech into the turn to avoid missing the road home. Their house, a sprawling Tudor dating to the late nineteenth century, was set back from the street on several wooded acres. During her childhood, Thea remembered, their home always seemed warm and busy. But since the death of her mother, most of the rooms were never used, and the place had grown cold and lifeless. The constant presence of her brother in the carriage house, and their father's sixteen-hour workdays, only added to its strangeness.

Thea left the Volvo to one side of the drive where Dan would be able to see it, and turned on some lights. Then she crossed the back lawn to the carriage house. Many lights were on there, but the doors were locked. She walked around to the back, where Dimitri kept his sports car—an Audi, she thought she remembered. The small gravel parking area was deserted. Odd.

Before she asked Dan to come out to the house, she had called Dimitri to tell him she would be stopping by when she got home, and would bring Dan over to hear Dimitri's theory about the disaster. He hadn't mentioned having any plans, but when they were last together he had in passing spoken of a girlfriend. When Thea asked for some details about her, he quickly changed the subject without even giving the woman's name. Perhaps he was off somewhere with her. The notion made her smile. Her brother was always such a loner, much as she had once been. It would be great to learn that he had someone, and to get to know the female who could become close to him despite his eccentricities.

She finished circumnavigating the carriage house, peering in the windows as she passed. Then she returned to the main house and brewed some decaf. Dan had been drinking coffee when they first met—that was one thing she knew about him. Actually, through her affinity for details and her ability to listen and retain, she had gleaned quite a bit about the man: about his caring and gentleness and determination, his pride and intelligence, and the tragedies and other events that had shaped his life.

They hadn't known each other long, but with all that had been going on in her life, he had already become something of a rock for her. Did she mean anything yet to him? How much had he noticed that she was different from most of the women he had been with?

Dr. Carpenter had made it clear that there was no sense in trying to be someone that she wasn't just to attract a man, and the truth was, Thea didn't feel capable of being someone she wasn't anyhow. But it would be sad to drive the man away when they were just getting to know each other. If it happened, he wouldn't be the first. One man had said he was breaking up with her because she wasn't aggressive enough. Another had said he felt she was too outspoken and aggressive. It had never made sense.

Over the years, as she had come to understand more and more of what it meant to have Asperger's, she had found ways to deal with her family issues and her career. She had learned what it meant to be a friend, and had discovered that it was something she was good at, so long as she spent as much time listening as she did talking. She had largely mastered the art of small talk, both face-to-face and on the phone, and had gained the skills necessary to conduct the simple business of her daily life. Defensiveness to fabrics and sounds had become less of an issue, as had playing certain sports, which she enjoyed even though her poor motor planning skills often caused the ball to arrive before she even knew it was coming.

But there were two areas where she didn't feel she had learned much of anything—men and sex.

"Join the club, honey," a nurse friend at the field hospital had told her when she expressed her disconcerting confusion. "Join the club."

Now, in just a few minutes, a man she found immensely attractive and was growing to care about was due to come over. Had she already messed things up by telling him how much she wanted him? Would he consider her too assertive?

Thea checked the time—almost ten thirty. She looked down at her clothes—a loose-fitting pair of chinos, a broad leather belt cinching her waist, and a bright plaid blouse she had bought at a bazaar in Kisangani. Did she have time to change? Did she have anything to change into? What would he like?

Men.

She hurried upstairs to her bedroom and looked at herself in the mirror behind the door. *Not so bad.* Most people thought she was pretty and often said so, and in truth, she thought so, too. She ran a brush through her hair and then put on a swatch of pale pink lipstick that seemed serviceable despite having been on a corner of her desk for at least two years.

Finally, she slipped off her blouse and bra, dropped them over a chair, and returned to the mirror, arching her back so that her breasts seemed more prominent. *Not so bad,* she thought again, appraising them. Decent shape. Decent size. Much bigger and that might be all he would be looking at. Not that that would be so horrible. Men were just into women's chests—especially when culturally breasts were treated as forbidden fruit, unlike they were in much of rural Africa. She was wondering if the other bra she had brought from the DRC would make her look any larger, when she heard him call out from downstairs.

"Thea? It's me. The bell's not working."

Startled, she made one last check of her lipstick, then bolted from the bedroom. Halfway to the stairs, she glanced down at her bare breasts and realized her oversight. Smiling, she decided simply to go with the plaid blouse. She hurried back to her bedroom, plucked it off the chair, and buttoned it as she went down the stairs.

"Hey, there," Dan said as she bounded down the staircase. "You look great."

"So do you."

And he did. Thea realized that except for the hospital scrubs they had given him in the ER, she had not seen him out of his uniform. Tonight he was wearing sneakers, tightish jeans, and a black long-sleeved tee that stretched across his chest in a most appealing way. His eyes, still the best of many good features, crinkled at the corners when he smiled.

"You okay?"

"Sure, I'm fine."

"But when you called you said—"

"Oh, you mean the man who attacked me in the hospital parking lot."

"The what?"

"The man. He pulled a plastic bag over my head and said he'd kill me if I didn't back off and stop messing in business that was none of my affair. He kept referring to himself as 'us' and 'we,' so I think he's working for someone. I also think he might have been the orderly who kicked you. Maybe we should go into the living room. Do you want some water?"

"Water would be perfect. Did he hurt you?"

"He wanted to. I could tell. But I think whoever hired him to scare me told him not to hurt me."

"Jesus. Thea, this is serious stuff."

"I suppose. It sure felt serious."

"Given what happened to you, you seem so calm."

"Seeing you is like a paradox—a mysterious paradox. I get excited in one way and calm in another. You know what I mean?"

"I . . . think so."

He followed her to the kitchen, then to the living room, and sat down next to her on the couch. The large room, heavily furnished, had once been the center of their family life. Now she wondered when the last time was that someone had actually sat down in it. There was a slight mustiness to the air, but the Oriental rug and sofas looked recently vacuumed, probably by Bernice, the devoted cleaning lady, who had been with the family for as long as Thea could remember.

Anxious to achieve just the right ambience, Thea leaned over and turned on a table lamp. Then she assessed the result, got up, and switched on a sconce over the broad marble mantel. Then she turned off the sconce and lit a standing lamp across the room. She was headed back to the sconce when Dan patted the sofa cushion next to him.

"The lighting's fine, Thea. Everything's fine. Now, come and tell me about the man."

Thea turned off the standing lamp, kicked off her sandals, and sank down onto the couch next to him, with one leg folded beneath her, close enough so that their shoulders and legs were touching. As she recounted the details of the attack, Dan listened intently, and placed a hand reassuringly on her knee. It was the first time she had noticed how beautiful and sexy his fingers were.

She recounted the information as quickly as possible, afraid that she was losing her focus. Experiencing a sudden, vague lightheadedness, she ruled out dehydration by silently estimating her fluid intake over the last twenty-four hours, which was unremarkable. Could the sensation be an effect of Dan's hand on her knee?

"If you never saw his face and he wore gloves, I don't know what good it can do to involve the police unless maybe they can come up with a rapist or someone who used a bag like this guy did."

"I couldn't think of anything helpful I could tell them."

"Why don't you let me bring the plastic bag into the crime lab and see if they can find anything on it. Then we can decide about the police."

"Sounds like a plan. So tell me, do you miss being on the force? What made you quit?"

Even to Thea, the transition seemed awkward. She managed to edit herself enough to stop, but she sensed damage might have already been done.

If you've wrecked this, Sperelakis, I'll never speak to you again! she shouted at herself.

Dan rescued her.

"Is that what you want to talk about?" he asked. "Why I left the force?"

"People often talk before they, well, you know. I just thought that might be an interesting subject."

He brought her hand to his lips and held it there.

"You are a piece of work, Doctor," he said before setting her hand down. "An absolute piece of work. Okay, you ask, you get. But I warn you, it's not a very pleasant tale."

For half an hour they talked about the terrible sequence of events that led up to and followed the shooting of fourteen-year-old Patrick Suggs in the front yard of the Montrose Middle School. As she listened, Thea ached for the man. His sensitivity was what had drawn her to him in the first place. Now, it seemed, that deep gentleness and caring were destroying much of the promise of his life.

"Isn't there a position in the police force where you wouldn't have to carry a gun or . . . or shoot anyone?" she asked.

"Nothing I'd really care to do. For as long as I can remember, the only thing I ever wanted to do was to be a cop. The fallout of the shooting is that I was unemployed and unemployable. Then I stumbled on the ad for a security guard here. So far, so good."

"So far, so good," she echoed, her eyes nearly filled.

His scent was intoxicating. It didn't matter if it was cologne, aftershave, or shampoo, or his own unique chemistry. She felt herself getting excited just breathing him in. Dan slid his hand from her knee up along her inner thigh.

"Mmmmm," she murmured. "There's more that I want to learn about you, but I can't wait any longer to kiss you."

"Good idea," he said.

He held her face gently between his hands, bringing his own face so close that their breaths became one. Her eyes closed, she felt him briefly kiss each eyelid, then the tip of her nose before setting his lips upon hers. Her lips parted as his tongue moved between them.

Kissing Dan was not what she had expected. It was better. It would have been perfect if she hadn't suddenly found her mind listing all of the muscles involved in their kiss. Although such a thought was absolutely typical for her, she fought back the urge to laugh and share it with him.

"Until you know a man, and know him well," Dr. Carpenter had once told her, *"don't ever laugh during sex no matter how happy or giddy you might be feeling. Regardless of the saintliness of the fellow you're with, he's sure to misunderstand and take it as a personal affront to his manliness."*

With their lips still touching, his hand slid from her neck and brushed across the front of her blouse, pausing over each erect nipple.

"I . . . um . . . forgot my bra upstairs," she said, wondering if an explanation was even called for.

"Hey, no problem. You're just sparing me the humiliation of wrestling with the clasp."

He removed his black T-shirt before unbuttoning her blouse and letting it slip from her shoulders. His hands caressed her breasts and glided over her hips, resting on the curves of her behind.

"I really love doing this with you," she whispered, unbuttoning, then unzipping his jeans.

Tighty whities. Where had she first heard that term, she wondered now. It had to have come from Dimitri. When he was a teen, he was always parading around in his underwear.

"So, Thea—the question of the day," Dan said. "Do you prefer men in boxers or briefs?"

"Well, I'm not sure. I believe I need a closer inspection before I can give you an answer."

"Inspect away," Dan said.

Thea placed her palm over the fly of his briefs.

"Briefs," she declared. "Based on this scientific assessment, I definitely prefer briefs over boxers. However, there may be an element of bias due to the . . . um . . . due to the experimental subject's impressive underlying . . . attributes."

"Well, then, to avoid any unnecessary bias, it's probably best if I ditch the underwear altogether."

She ran her fingertips across his lips, then reached up and flicked off the table lamp. They made love on the rug, in the moonlight washing through the century-old living room windows. Later, much later, Thea was nestled in the curve of Dan's body, pleasantly exhausted, when they heard the crunch of tires heading past them toward the carriage house.

"It's Dimitri," she said. "I don't trust him not to show up here."

Dan gathered up their clothes and Thea, giggling, helped him sort them out.

"Hey, Doc," he said after they had dressed, "don't be any more frightened about that guy in the parking lot than you have to be. I won't let anything happen to you. Not now, not ever."

TWENTY-SIX

The day was gray, but balmy, with a warm breeze raising tiny sand devils on the beach. Dan pulled the rented Avalon to a stop before a small, gray-stained clapboard cottage on a narrow seaside street, then stepped out into the late afternoon sun and cleared his head with some deep breaths of salt air. There was a dark blue Nissan Sentra in the drive.

His friend, June Tilly, had come through big time at the crime lab—not only a match for the single print taken from the glasses, but a twelve-year-old military photo as well, and a name: Gerald Prevoir. There was no way to be absolutely certain that the man in the grainy snapshot was the orderly who had assaulted him outside the ICU, but Dan believed it enough to take a personal day off from work in order to fly from Boston to Philadelphia, and drive down the coast to South Carlisle, Delaware, the last known address of the man, who had received a Marine Bronze Star with valor device for action in Afghanistan.

There was no hall of records in South Carlisle, but 57 Salt Spray Lane was listed in the registry of deeds in Dover, and had been owned by a business called Hessian Homes of Miami for nearly ten years. No surprise.

Dan had gotten several breaks already. It was unlikely that finding the man who attacked him would be smooth sailing all the way.

If the trip to Delaware brought him no closer, he would consider the risk of having Thea file an official report claiming assault and battery, and use his friends on the force to expand the search for Gerald Prevoir. He also had a bit of savings he was willing to use for a private detective. If needed, he knew he could ask Thea for help.

A day had passed since his evening with her. She had been an exciting, passionate, and joyous lover, open and enthusiastic, lithe and as sexy as she was unselfconscious. There would be no fake orgasms from this woman. No fake anything, for that matter.

They would have spent the night together, but Dimitri was waiting up for them. In addition, the attack on Thea, and the threats, most definitely upped the ante of their situation. She was in danger, as was her father.

In his own way, Dimitri Sperelakis was as unique as his sister. He was mercurial in his personality and in his attention span, camped in front of his bank of computer screens, moving from video games to complex, well-supported theories of attempted murder, to YouTube clips of his favorite illusionists, the Pendragons, performing their remarkable Metamorphosis. It was almost as if he needed the constant motion to stay focused. Even his voice seemed modulated. One moment he sounded like a child, the next like a nuclear physicist.

After reviewing his animation and theories regarding Petros's hit-and-run, Dimitri had scrambled into the backseat of Petros's Volvo as Thea drove them to the scene of the accident. Having viewed Dimitri's cartoon at least as many times as the Pendragons' inconceivably rapid transformation from men to women, Dan had little difficulty understanding why Thea's brother had come to believe the accident was premeditated and purposeful. The angle at which the car had to be coming, the flight of Petros's body, and the lack of skid marks led to no other conclusion.

Dan had expected Thea's brother to be something of a smart aleck. Instead, he was delightfully self-deprecating and offbeat, and certainly not afraid of verbally stepping on Dan's toes or Thea's. It remained to be seen if he was reliable, but no matter what, his intelligence could prove an important asset.

"Hey, big fella, you sure are a tall one."

An elderly woman in a shabby faded blue housedress looked up at Dan from a foot or so beneath him. Her face was badly sun-damaged and deeply etched, and what teeth she had were in poor repair. Gnarled mats of silver hair protruded from beneath a paisley bandana tied in place behind her head. Her breath carried an odd, fishy odor.

"Six-foot-four," Dan said. "Name's Dan."

"I have a cousin named Dan, or maybe it's Daniel. I can never remember."

Dan had little hope that the old woman was going to be of any help, but he nevertheless took the time to establish that her name was Noreen, that she had lived across the street for more than twenty-five years, and that she knew most of the people who lived in the neighborhood, but not the people who lived in number 57 Salt Spray Lane and were, as she put it, "foreigners from another country."

"They're renters," she added. "A nice young couple who don't have much interest in chatting with an old woman like me. I know it's hard to believe, but I wasn't always this old. I was once the runner-up for Miss Dover."

"That's terrific, Noreen." Dan brought out the photo of Gerald Prevoir. "Actually, I'm looking for a man who once might have lived in that house."

He passed the photo over and watched the woman's expression as she examined it. There was not a flicker of recognition.

"You a policeman?" she asked.

"Nope. Just a man looking for a man. That man."

"His name Dan?"

"No, no. That's *my* name."

Dan wrote his full name and phone number on a sheet from his notepad and passed it over.

"And you're a policeman, you say?"

Dan smiled patiently.

"Thanks for your help, Noreen. I think I'll go and talk to the people who live in that house."

"Probably just the woman will be there. I've only seen the man once or twice. Not nearly as big and tall as you. Six feet tall, you said, right?"

Noreen seemed to be getting more addled as their time together went on. Dan slipped the photo out from between her fingers, thanked her, and headed up the front walk of the cottage. Noreen shrugged and backed across the street to lean on a telephone pole and watch.

The pretty young woman who answered the door of 57 Salt Spray Lane spoke only Russian—at least that was Dan's guess. Her name was Ludmilla, and she conversed with him through the three-inch space allowed by a brass chain, which she showed no inclination to undo. She managed to overcome her mistrust, lack of understanding, and fear just enough to look at the photo of Prevoir and vehemently shake her head. Then she smiled nervously and gently shut the door.

The entire encounter took less time than it had taken the flight attendant on US Airways to give safety instructions. When Dan turned back to the street, Noreen was gone. The round-trip flights, the rental, the loss of one of his two personal days at work—hardly an even trade. Still, it had been worth the try.

Dan decided to use the two hours he had left to canvass the neighborhood with Prevoir's photo. He knew he would draw blanks, and in that regard wasn't disappointed.

For a time, he sat on a rocky jetty, flipping stones into the ocean, and trying to think of something, anything, he could do next. His resources were limited, and between Josh and the job, there was no way he could muster the time to push on with his search. But Gerald Prevoir was a man who had not only beaten and humiliated him and, in all likelihood, had tried to kill Thea's father, but had also assaulted and threatened her. The goal of nailing such a beast would keep him going for as long as it took.

The best he could come up with after half an hour of thought was a name—Albert Mendez. Mendez was a low-rent private eye from Manhattan whom Dan had met at a forensics course at NYU. He was something of an operator, and a bit taken with himself, but he was also quite sharp, streetwise, and amusing to be around. He had, it seemed, watched every *CSI* show ever made, and it was his grand plan to use the course as a stepping stone to getting an investigator's job in a medical examiner's office.

"The forensic guys get all the chicks," he had said more than once.

Mendez had mentioned that his office was in Greenwich Village, and directory assistance had a PI with his name listed on Houston Street. The woman who answered Dan's call—a service, he guessed—had a dense New York accent and was almost certainly chewing gum as she talked. Dan left her his name and cell number, and a little prompt in case Mendez had forgotten him.

Five miles from the Philadelphia airport, the detective called, and by the time Dan pulled into the rental car return, a fee—a *reduced* fee, Mendez assured him—had been agreed upon.

"Send me what you got and that retainer, and I'll find the dude," Mendez said. "You have the ol' Mendez guarantee. Good thing you got ahold of me when you did, pal. I got something big pending that's gonna get me out of this racket and into the office of the Chief Medical Examiner of New York City himself."

Dan promised to send a check along with the details of what he had learned, and turned his attention to trying to find a decent Philly cheesesteak before catching the flight back to Boston.

Down the street from 57 Salt Spray Lane, Noreen Ecklestone had fetched a scrap of paper from a metal file box filled with such scraps. This particular scrap had the name *Gerald* written on it in pencil, and below the name, a phone number. An answering machine picked up after the third ring.

"Leave a message," was all it said.

"Hello, Mr. Gerald," she said. "This is Noreen from Sea Spray Lane. You asked me to call if anyone came snooping around asking about fifty-seven. Well, a real tall man was just here showing a photo of someone named Prever or Peever or something like that. His name was Dan, Dan Cotton, and his number is 617-426-9444. I hope you'll send me that reward you promised."

She set the receiver down, put her bandana aside, and opened a can of sardines from a shelf full of similar cans, representing most of the food she kept in the cottage.

TWENTY-SEVEN

There was an hour before Thea was scheduled to meet Julian Fang. The man had been an acupuncturist for more than sixty years, and had skills in the area of diagnosis that were regarded among those in his profession as uncanny and unequaled. If anyone could evaluate the success or failure of Hayley's therapy, it was he. So far, she had a few, nonspecific symptoms from her treatment with SU990, but nothing at all debilitating, and she certainly looked like a woman who was handling a devastating disease as well as possible.

Thea had time to visit the step-down unit. She sensed the moment she entered her father's room that he was still unresponsive and unaware. He was propped forty-five degrees onto his side by pillows, a position designed to relieve pressure on critical points such as his heels and sacrum. Those places where pressure was a concern were carefully protected.

Thea checked several of the critical areas where a skin breakdown could sometimes lead to death as surely as a blood clot or cardiac catastrophe. Perfect. All of them perfect. No redness, no cracks, no discoloration. For all of her responsibilities as director of the most renowned service in the world, Amy Musgrave was still the quintessential nurse. Every one of the hundreds of nurses on her staff seemed to know and respect the importance of attention to detail in achieving optimum patient care.

"Anything, Marlene?" Thea asked the private-duty nurse sent over from the agency.

"No change," the woman, a young grandmother with years at the Beaumont, replied. "I've washed him down and given him a massage. He's not moving anything."

Thea excused the nurse and did an exam searching for any encouraging neurological sign. His pupils remained mid-position with minimal, if any, reaction to light. Despite his locked-in syndrome, he had been able to respond to her, albeit sluggishly. Now there was no movement at all. Several times, Thea begged him to move his eye. Nothing.

Questions about the persisting change in his condition were quickly sorted out as to their possible significance and how well they fit what she was observing. Over his long life in medicine, that had been the clinical technique of the man lying there before her and, largely because of him, it was her way as well.

Was this the natural evolution of his trauma? Had brain swelling suddenly become an issue even though there had been none for days? Could he possibly be having a reaction to one of his medications? Was there any way someone could be administering a paralytic, curare-like drug such as succinylcholine or pancuronium? Of all the questions, this last one seemed the most disconcerting—and in some ways the most possible.

Thea sent for the special-duty nurse.

"Do you have the list of visitors I asked you to keep?"

"Right here, Thea."

She produced a notebook and handed it over. Twelve men and women had visited including the neurologist, the twins, two of their Aunt Marys, and the group Thea had begun thinking of as the big three—Amy Musgrave, Sharon Karsten (twice), and Scott Hartnett (three times). There were no unexpected names on the list except possibly for Hayley Long, who had been wheeled down by an aide and had stayed in the stepdown unit from three o'clock until ten minutes of four. Hayley's visit came as no surprise at all to Thea. During their nightly talks it had become clear what a genuinely caring person she was.

"Keep your eyes open whenever he has a visitor, Marlene. I especially want to be sure that no one is giving him any medications."

"Medications?"

"I can't explain . . . well, actually, I *can* explain, but I don't want to. Please, Marlene, just keep your eyes sharp for anything unusual and call me on my cell if you see anything at all that doesn't seem right."

Thea stopped at the nurses' station and read the neurologist's note, which stated that he saw no change, but would have an ultrasound and MRI done tomorrow. He also suggested that as soon as the orthopedist felt Petros's shattered pelvis could handle it, transfer to a rehab facility should be considered.

The recommendation stung, but Thea knew that

sooner or later, a rehab or nursing home was where he was headed—provided he survived.

The day, spent reviewing some of her father's patients, and scheduling some for office visits, had been an exhausting one. She was buoyed by thoughts of Dan Cotton. He was special. Handsome, yes. Funny, yes. Devoted to his son, most certainly. But *special* was the overriding word she could think of.

The deep sadness that stayed with him, and would likely remain with him to some degree or another for the rest of his life, had her feeling desperate to ease his pain. By the time he had finished his version of the poignant and horrifying story, she knew that she was falling in love with him. Their unforgettable love-making had only sealed the deal.

When Thea arrived at the largely deserted main lobby of the Beaumont, Julian Fang was waiting on one of the benches. He was as unimposing in his manner as he was in his dress, this time a pair of dark slacks, a white long-sleeved dress shirt, and a neatly knotted dark blue tie. He was no more than five-seven, and almost painfully thin. But there was an aura about him, a serenity, that made Thea and many others feel more at peace in his presence regardless of their problems at the moment.

For more than two years of her residency, Thea spent her free weekends and much of her spare evening time studying under Fang. By the time she passed her boards in internal medicine, she was seriously considering switching permanently to Eastern medicine. Ultimately, though, bowing to her father's insistence, she elected to stay an internist. The next time the two of them clashed over a life choice issue, Thea would follow her heart and sign up with Doctors Without Borders, but she never lost her fascination with acupuncture or her contact with Master Fang, as he had always been known.

"Master Fang, thank you so much for coming," Thea said, taking the man's aging hand in hers.

"Thea, it is a pleasure to see you again," he replied in a dense accent, but grammatically perfect English.

"You'll enjoy meeting this woman. She is a very unique person."

"The most generous donation she has made to our school suggests that, although it was totally unnecessary."

"I've told her some of the diagnoses I have seen you make during your examinations of patients, and she wanted to express her gratitude that you would come and see her. Believe me, whatever she gave the school, she can afford."

Thea nodded to the security guard as they passed. To her right, the master also smiled and nodded. His silver hair was cut to the nubs, and he was clearly making an effort to keep his posture rigidly erect. Thea had heard the rumor that Fang had ten children, but she had never confirmed it by asking.

"So," he said as they moved along the broad corridor toward the Sperelakis Institute, "you said this Ms. Long has cancer."

"Of the pancreas, yes. I have recently seen her MRI for the first time. It seems quite advanced."

"But she is on treatment?"

"She is part of a protocol where she is receiving a new experimental drug. I believe the drug has been quite effective in some patients, lethal in others."

"But you do not wish me to treat her?"

Thea flashed back on the vehemence with which Lydia Thibideau swore to have Hayley removed from the study if she learned that any treatment was done on her. Then she flashed on a number of cases she had observed in which Fang the Master had cured the seemingly incurable.

"We'll see," she said.

Hayley had gotten dressed up for her visitor with a fresh set of pajamas beneath a white terry-cloth robe. Her room had gradually made the transition from a library to a business office, although the collection of books that had initially attracted Thea to her was, if anything, even larger and more varied. Hayley, on her cell phone, motioned that she would only be a minute.

"Go ahead and tell her she's done a wonderful job for us," she was saying. "She can take as much time as she needs to have her baby and get settled in as a first-time mommy. If it's six months, it's six months. Full salary for the first three; half for the next three provided she does some work at home. Gotta go. Ciao, Tommy."

Thea knew that one of her possible weaknesses as a physician, resulting from her Asperger's, was a detachment—an analytical, clinical approach to patients—that some had viewed as a lack of empathy. At this moment, though, there was no flatness in her feelings, no lack of emotion. At this moment, as happened each time she entered Hayley Long's room, she experienced an ache in her heart at the notion that such a woman should be as sick as she was. No, not sick, Thea heard her mind say, *dying*.

Introductions were made and gratitude from both sides expressed. Then the legend in acupuncture and the legend in business sat down together to talk.

"Dr. Thea has asked me to evaluate the state of your cancer," Fang said. "This I will be happy to do. If you know anything about how we acupuncturists diagnose, please tell me."

"Assume I know nothing," Hayley replied.

"Very well. If you have trouble understanding me through my accent, please ask me to speak more slowly."

"Thank you."

Hayley's glance at Thea said that she was already impressed. Years ago, Master Fang had given the introductory lecture on acupuncture to Thea's small class. She wondered now how many had heard that fascinating talk over the years . . . no, over the decades. Tonight, she felt certain, would be an abbreviated version.

"There is a force flowing through our bodies," Fang began, "a life force that we call *Qi*, spelled *Q-I*, but pronounced *chee*. When *Qi* is hindered or imbalanced or blocked, diseased states result, whether mental, physical, or emotional. When we use our needles, they are to unblock or redirect the flow of one's *Qi*. Like Western medicine, one of the tools we use to formulate a treatment plan is a physical examination. One of the most important aspects of our physical examination is the tongue. Another is an evaluation of the pulses at the wrist."

"Like the one right here?" Hayley asked, pointing to the correct spot.

"Precisely," Fang replied, "but instead of one pulse, we take measure of twelve—three superficial and three deep on each wrist. Each pulse has a different significance, and we use descriptions for them such as slow, sunken, choppy, floating, and slippery depending on how they feel to us."

"Are you going to treat me tonight?"

Fang looked at Thea, who shook her head.

"You and I will have to decide that later or tomorrow, Hayley," she said. "For now, our friend is only here to give us some idea of how you are progressing relative to your condition and treatment."

"In that case, Professor Fang, I'm ready."

Fang went to wash his hands.

"You okay?" Thea whispered.

"He's very cute."

"I know."

"Are things going well with your friend Dan?"

"He's been away all day, but pretty well, yes."

Hayley smiled conspiratorially.

"That's wonderful to hear. You deserve it."

"He's very . . . special."

"I can tell. Well, Sean Flowers is now in town doing a little reconnoitering. If you're still up for it, he'll be ready to get you into Dr. Thibideau's office tomorrow night."

"I'll be ready," she replied intensely.

"Remind me to stay on your good side."

"So," Fang said, returning to Hayley, and motioning her to the bed, "let us see what we shall see."

The examination took longer than Thea had expected based on seeing Fang work in the past. In fact, she realized, the master went over Hayley once, and then again, checking her eyes, her tongue, her abdomen, and at length the twelve pulses at her wrists. When he finished, he hesitated, and then asked Thea if she would like his conclusions given to her alone or to the two of them together.

Thea silently polled Hayley, who had returned to her chair.

"We're in this together," Thea said. "You look concerned. I'm sorry to see that."

"Cancer of the pancreas, you said, yes?"

"That's right, yes. A five-centimeter central mass in the head of the pancreas, with spread to the liver."

"And also to some abdominal lymph nodes," Hayley added.

Fang rubbed his brow, then his chin.

"Well," he said, "the news I have for you is good. Quite good, in fact."

"That's wonderful," Hayley said. "The treatment is shrinking the cancer?"

"It is doing better than that," Fang replied. "From all I can tell, your cancer is gone."

"What do you mean, gone?"

"Just that. My examination reveals no cancer whatsoever in your body—no disease or illness of any kind, in fact. Your *Qi* is quite powerful and healthy."

There was no way any cancer treatment could have cured Hayley of so much cancer in such a short time.

Thea stared over at the master in utter disbelief.

"Are you sure?" was all she could think of to say.

TWENTY-EIGHT

"Doc, over here!"

The man's gravelly whisper, from the shadows to her right, nearly stopped Thea's heart.

"Sean?"

Still she couldn't see him.

"Here, to your right, by the corner of the building."

Thea took a few seconds to allow her vision to adjust and then moved toward him. She was dressed in black, as was he, and as instructed, wore a black watch cap pulled low and a pair of black cloth gloves. She guessed him at thirty, but it was only an estimate because his narrow face was covered in black greasepaint. In seconds, he had covered hers as well. His touch wasn't very gentle.

Thea had been well prepared for the industrial spy by Hayley, who made it clear that, as much as it grated against her morality, anyone with a serious interest in manufacturing, technology, and industry who didn't take pains to keep current with what their competition was up to wasn't in the competition for long. Thea was embarrassed at how easily she embraced the notion, but she also knew that much of her attitude sprang from her admiration of the woman who gave the orders.

"Black face paint, black clothes," she said. "This is serious."

In fact, Hayley had already told her, based on the reports Flowers had relayed to her, that it was going to be.

"Sean has been all over the hospital campus, and through as much of the Cannon Building as he dared," Hayley had told her. "He's studied blueprints, heating-duct diagrams, maps of the tunnel system, and even the sewers. Earlier today, he actually chanced going into Dr. Thibideau's office, allegedly to find out how to make an appointment. There are security problems everywhere, but he thinks he has figured out a way to get you in."

"Terrific. I'm ready. Hayley, I'm very excited with what Master Fang found in his examination of you, but I'm also very confused and bewildered."

"He's for real, though, right? He seemed so sure of himself, but I'd hate to get my hopes up on this one."

"What can I say? Just as he speaks a different language and comes from a society with different customs, he practices diagnosis and healing in a way that is foreign and unfamiliar to most Westerners."

"But you've seen enough to trust him."

"I've seen enough to believe in what he does, but I was brought up around a brilliant Western physician and I studied physiology and anatomy and the scientific method as taught by more Western physicians. There was no discussion of *Qi* in our classes. No acupuncture points. No deep wrist pulses."

"This ain't easy, sister. *Qi* is no easy concept for a poor little ol' farm girl like me."

"I know. But I will tell you that most of the time, we Western doctors carefully avoid any head-on collisions with the power of the mind-body connection because we have all seen enough to respect it. Patients recovering nicely from an illness tell us they are going to die, and then later that night they do. Autopsy negative. People who have no right to survive their illness spend days on end in prayer with their loved ones, and suddenly they're better. We've all experienced such things."

"If you were me?"

"I would keep doing what you're doing. We've got some tests that will validate what Master Fang found. We'll get them run as quickly as possible."

"Perfect."

"If I found myself seriously ill, I would try to take advantage of both Eastern and Western treatments. Western, so-called allopathic, doctors often get quite pompous about how far we've come and how much we know about the mechanism of disease, but I promise you there is much more we don't understand than what we do. I am going to go through with whatever your Sean Flowers has planned because I need to know about Jack Kalishar. I need to know why my father connects the man with what happened to him. At the same time, I intend to learn about your cancer as well and about as many other of Dr. Thibideau's experimental patients as I possibly can."

"And you know there may be trouble along the way."

"I know."

"I have told Sean to take care of you at all costs, but that's the most I can do."

"I understand."

"There's one more thing. Sean tells me that this whole business could be much easier if you would involve your friend, the security guard."

"No, Hayley." Thea was firm. "I would call the whole thing off before I'd involve him. I'm certain about that. He's had some really tough things happen to him. I don't want to add to it by having him lose his job because of me. Flowers and I are going to find a way into that office ourselves, or we're simply not going to do it."

"Well said. I'm with you a hundred percent."

"Great."

"In that case, I only have one other question for you."

"Shoot."

"You have any fear of heights?"

TWENTY-NINE

The night was largely overcast, and above the clouds was a new moon. Thea and Sean Flowers were pressed against the ancient Veteran's Memorial Building on the southeast corner of the massive Beaumont Clinic campus. Veteran's was essentially a dormitory housing students, house staff, and visiting faculty members. Thea herself had stayed there for a time during her specialty rotations through the clinic.

Flowers, whom Thea decided was older than her initial impression, was a man of few words, who carried a cat-like edginess, constantly scanning the area around them. It was after eleven, and the walkways crisscrossing between buildings were largely deserted. Thea felt keyed up and more than a little apprehensive. She had been reluctant to ask Hayley what she had meant by asking if she was afraid of heights. If her friend had wanted her to know, Thea reasoned, she certainly would have said something.

Thea's response to the question, which was, "A little, I guess," was not completely accurate. As a child, she'd had a major meltdown on a chairlift, and for whatever the cause, she had gotten sick on her first ride on a Ferris wheel. She had never again been on either one.

More recently, when she looked down from a balcony railing, she inevitably got a queasy feeling, but she had assumed that more or less everybody did.

"Here," Flowers said, handing her a black canvas military backpack, identical to the one he was wearing. "Adjust the straps if you need to. Is it too heavy?"

In fact, the knapsack did have a fair amount of heft.

"I work in the African jungle," she said. "It may not look it, but I'm pretty strong . . . and tough."

"That's good to hear. You might need both."

Thea looked at the man and tried to gauge how serious he was, but the only visible cue, the whites of his eyes, gave her nothing.

"What's in here?" she asked.

"Not much. Some rope, a decent-sized pocketknife, a notebook, a couple of pens, a two-way radio set to the same frequency as mine, the sort of camera you might need if you don't want to stay in the lab to read, a pair of top-of-the-line night vision goggles, pocket flashlight, larger flashlight. I'm not sure we're going to be able to turn the lights on up there."

Up there.

The words fanned her curiosity.

"Sean," she said, "when Hayley told me you had found a way into the office, she asked me if I was afraid of heights. What's that all about?"

"She didn't tell you?"

"The truth is, I didn't ask. I guess I had decided I would be going through with this no matter what."

"Well, the office you want is on the fifth floor of the Cannon Building."

"I know. I've been there."

"Well, then, you might know that after five o'clock, the elevators don't stop on that floor without a key card. One way around that would be to freeze the elevator on the fourth floor, go up through the emergency hatch, and take a pry bar to the door on the fifth. But I wasn't sure you could handle all that, plus there's more security around the door into the office."

"So what did you decide?"

"I decided we're going up the outside of the building and through the window."

"Through the window? I was up there. They don't open."

"That did present a problem," Flowers said. "So I turned my attention to the outside."

"It's sheer glass."

For the first time, Thea detected a faint smile.

"Sheer glass is always a challenge." Flowers checked the time. "Let's roll. Stay against the building, and don't cross a walk until I say it's okay. You know what an aerial bucket is? It's also called a boom truck bucket."

"The kind they use for pruning trees?"

"Or electrical work. Exactly."

"I know what they look like."

"Well, in just a couple of minutes you're going to feel what one is like to ride on. Think you can handle that?"

Thea immediately envisioned herself riding up Loon Mountain on her first—and last—chairlift ride.

"I can handle it," she said. "But what about the window?"

"That's my job," Flowers replied, patting his backpack.

The other thousand or so questions Thea had went unanswered. They turned onto the walkway that went between the Cannon Building and another modern building that seemed to have popped up in just the two years since Thea had last been at the clinic. There was a sawhorse at the entrance to the passageway, on which was nailed a sign that read CLOSED.

A finger to his lips, Flowers led her around the sawhorse, checking behind and ahead of them continuously. There were no trees or electrical wires along the concrete walk, but there was a truck—an aerial boom truck—parked to the Cannon Building side, but taking up three-quarters of the passage. Thea scanned five stories up from the ground and sensed a churning in her gut. She leaned close to Flowers's ear.

"Where did you get the truck?"

"I moved it from the other side of campus where they were doing some tree work," he whispered back, seeming too proud of his ingenuity to keep silent. "In this world, all you ever have to do is look like you know what you're doing, and nobody ever stops to question you unless they happen to be the person who's supposed to be doing it. If that happens, it's just plain lousy luck. I waited until the crew had left for the day, hot-wired the truck, put the 'closed' signs on the back, and drove it around to here simple as you please."

Thea flashed on Dan possibly saving her father's life by taking the time to check the average-looking orderly's ID—an act he could just as easily have let pass. He must have been a terrific policeman.

"Have you ever worked one of these?" she asked.

"It's just a few buttons and levers. I can do buttons and levers."

Thea glanced at the small bucket, then upward again, and felt an involuntary chill.

"No, seriously," she said.

"Okay, I tried it out."

"And?"

"No sweat. Except that we have to keep the truck running in order to make the boom work. It's a little on the noisy side, but at this hour I don't think anyone's in any of these labs. And even if they are, I doubt they'd think the truck was anything other than what it seems."

"You enjoy doing this sort of thing?"

"When it all works, I do. In fact, sometimes I enjoy it even when it doesn't work. I guess I'm just not cut out for *Do you want fries with that, ma'am?* Well, ready to go?"

He motioned to the bucket, then slipped into the cab of the flatbed truck and turned on the engine. Her heart pounding, Thea scrambled up next to the folded boom on the flatbed, then climbed into the bucket. Moments later, Flowers was standing beside her.

"Is there a weight limit?" she asked, battling back another wave of queasiness.

"I'm sure we're not close to it. But there is one thing. With the boom fully extended, the bucket doesn't quite reach the fifth floor."

The wave grew large enough to surf on.

"That sounds like it could be a bit of a problem," she said.

"I laugh at such problems. Seriously, don't be worried. Once I've taken care of the window, you'll have to stand up here on the edge of the bucket to get through. It should be easy."

"You want fries with that?" Thea asked.

The rumbling engine noise reverberated between the walls of the two buildings as Flowers pushed a lever forward and the bucket glided up one floor, then another, with just enough bounce and sway to mentally propel Thea back to the chairlift on Loon Mountain.

"Just don't look down," Flowers said.

"I'll try not to."

Thea wasn't sure until she heard her voice that she would be able to speak.

"There's some sort of file cabinet inside, yes?"

"Yes," she managed. "I know right where it is."

"I'll come in after you, then I'll open the cabinet in a way that won't leave any scratches and return to the truck so I can turn the engine off. You take care of business as quickly as you can, then call me on the radio and I'll bring the bucket up."

"Got it."

They jounced up another floor. Inside the third-story window, Thea could make out the glassware and other equipment of a lab. Over her years with Doctors Without Borders she had been in many odd and often dangerous situations. But this . . . She risked a look at the specter who had taken control of her life. Even through the black greasepaint she could sense his exhilaration. A pull on the lever, and they advanced past the fourth-story windows up toward the fifth. Then, with a final bounce, they stopped. One of the huge plate-glass windows of Thibideau's laboratory was still a foot or so above the top of the bucket.

Don't look down.

There was no obvious way through the windows until Flowers opened his backpack and extracted a pair of heavy-duty disc-like clamps. With simian movement, he hopped up onto the top edge of the bucket, set the clamps on the window pane and, using some sort of implement taken from his pocket, quickly drew a rainbow arc, two feet high, beginning and ending at the sill. The next cut was across the sill itself. The whole maneuver, end-to-end, took less than a minute. Then, with a few well-placed taps from a cloth-covered mallet, the thick semicircle of glass came free.

Amazing, Thea thought, as Flowers lowered the glass to the floor inside and slithered face-first through the opening. According to Hayley, this sort of thing went on all over, every day, with an equally inventive industry devoted to preventing it. People got caught, people got arrested, people got away with whatever they were after, people kept trying. *Absolutely amazing.*

"Psst! Quick, through here. Don't look down."

The bucket was swaying with each movement. Once again, Thea began to feel ill.

Don't look down. . . . Don't look down. . . .

Chewing on her lower lip, she pulled herself up onto the edge of the bucket, bracing herself against what remained of the window. She passed her knapsack inside, put her hands on the sill, and dove, more than slithered, through the new opening. Her landing, assisted by Flowers, would have won few points from the judges, although the medical team standing by would have been pleased that he had moved the glass plate aside, and that none of her bones were broken.

Seconds later, they were standing in front of the locked door to Lydia Thibideau's office, and seconds after that, thanks to some sort of strange-looking tool Flowers carried on his belt, they were inside. The lock on the file cabinet was no more of a challenge.

"That what you're after?" Flowers asked, gesturing to a drawer completely full of perhaps a hundred yellow files. The drawer just below held an equal number.

Even before she slid one out, Thea knew that, as Hayley had promised, she was dealing with the dinosaurs of American medical care—paper printouts and actual X-ray photographs.

Nonelectronic medical records.

THIRTY

Thea crouched beneath the conference table on the plush Oriental rug in Lydia Thibideau's office, listening to the pounding of her own heart. Beside her were the two flashlights, the camera, the notebook, the two-way radio, and twenty-five or so patient records including Hayley's and Jack Kalishar's.

There were, by Thea's estimate, five hundred files altogether in the four drawers of Thibideau's cabinet, all of them, it seemed, patients with cancer of the pancreas, none of them, from what she could tell, any less recent than six years ago. They were arranged in alphabetical order, not by date. The patients' records dating back from six years were probably in cartons in some storage area. Given the mortality of pancreatic malignancy, few of them, if any, were likely to be alive today.

Earlier in the day, spurred by Julian Fang's remarkable pronouncement, Thea had researched the prevalence and lethalness of various types of cancers. The results relative to cancer of the pancreas were not encouraging. In the past year, 215,000 new cases of lung cancer had been reported in this country, and 160,000 patients were estimated to have died from the condition over the same period—74 percent. Bad disease. On the more sanguine side, the number of deaths from thyroid cancer (1,590) was 4 percent of the number of new cases diagnosed (37,300), down from 6 percent the year before. Conclusion: The number of thyroid cancer survivors was growing steadily.

The number of new cases each year of pancreatic cancer was almost identical to thyroid (37,700), but there had been 34,200 reported deaths (90 percent) over the same period, and 90 percent the year before. More data were needed to form any definitive conclusions, but the results implied that there had been little progress in the treatment of the disease.

Jack Kalishar had cancer of the pancreas. Of that there could be no doubt. From what Thea had learned of Hayley's disease, Kalishar's was quite a bit less far advanced at the time of diagnosis six years ago, but cancer of the pancreas was still cancer of the pancreas, and 90 percent was still 90 percent. Kalishar had been a healthy, robust man with a negative medical history, followed yearly in the Executive Health Evaluation program of the Beaumont. His MRI was difficult to read without using the four fluorescent view boxes fixed to a wall in Thibideau's office, so Thea decided to chance standing up and turning the box on for just a few seconds at a time.

Her father had made the diagnosis on Kalishar based on the MRI taken during a routine executive physical. The subsequent needle biopsy was reported as showing adenocarcinoma—the most common form of the cancer. It was Petros who had made the referral to Thibideau. It was she who had entered Kalishar in the treatment protocol evaluating the then-new drug SU890. There were a few documents related to the study— mostly permissions signed by Kalishar validating that he was aware of the experimental nature of his treatment and knew the risks, but most of the paperwork was either in storage someplace or simply on the Internet.

There were no slides showing the pathology, and no further notes of interest, except one. It was a three-year-old thank-you to Kalishar from Director of Development Scott Hartnett—a straightforward and businesslike acknowledgement of a donation to the Beaumont Clinic in general and to the establishment of the Lydia Thibideau Gastroenterology Research Center in particular. The amount of the donation was not mentioned, but written on the side of the note in a feminine hand— perhaps Thibideau's, Thea thought—was the figure *$200,000,000.* Two hundred million dollars!

Thea checked the time and knew that she had to move faster, and in a more organized fashion. Sean Flowers had put a limit on her investigation of one hour. Longer, and they would be risking discovery even more than they already were. She decided to check records, starting with Hayley's, for half an hour, and then to begin taking photographs of anything that looked interesting. She realized now that she should have been better prepared, but it was too late for that.

Hayley Long's chart told of an MRI done in Atlanta for vague abdominal pain and showing pancreatic cancer just ten months after a similar MRI, done at the Beaumont, was normal. Crawling out from under the table, Thea snapped the two films side by side onto the view box. The initial film done as part of the Executive Health Evaluation program was normal—absolutely negative except for faint white calcium deposits in three abdominal lymph nodes, probably the result of some long-ago infection. The finding was so minuscule and unimportant that the radiologist who had read the film either had missed it altogether or hadn't bothered to mention it in his report. But Thea's life was all about details.

She was studying the extensive cancer in Hayley's more recent film, and wondering how Julian Fang could possibly say that such a cancer had been cured after less than two weeks of treatment, when her eyes were drawn back to the original film. The calcified nodes in that one were not present in the more recent MRI. Thea stepped back, then moved in close. There were a few even more minuscule differences in the two films—the shape of a vertebral wing here, the density of a rib cartilage there. Both subjects were women of about the same age, but they were not the same woman. Thea felt virtually certain of it.

Stunned, she sank down onto the rug, staring up at the films as if they were saucers from Mars, trying to make sense of what she was seeing, to sort out what she should do next. Five minutes passed. When she finally stood up, the approach she had been missing was clear to her.

She took the notebook and drew the rough outline of a pancreas on a dozen consecutive pages. Then she replaced all the records except Hayley's and Kalishar's, randomly chose patients from each of the four drawers in the filing cabinet, and went directly to the MRIs of each, quickly mapping their cancers. Half an hour later she had recorded twenty-five patients and had found nothing. With the twenty-sixth, she struck gold.

The patient's name was Samuel Blackman, a fifty-four-year-old computer wizard who had parlayed a software invention into a fortune. The pattern of the cancer in his MRI was an identical match for the cancer in another of Lydia Thibideau's patients, this one named Warren Grigsby. The two men, wildly successful, had both been patients of the Beaumont executive health program. Both were diagnosed with pancreatic cancer, only four years apart. The difference was that Grigsby never left the hospital alive. On his tenth day of treatment with the same drug as Hayley was receiving, SU990, he suffered a cardiac arrest and essentially died before the Code Blue team could be mobilized.

Blackman was a completely different story. Like Jack Kalishar, he had survived his devastating diagnosis, and like Kalishar he had the copy of a letter of gratitude from Scott Hartnett in his record. Again, there was no mention in Hartnett's letter of the amount donated other than to call it "gracious," but this time there was no note of the amount from Thibideau either.

What did it all mean? What had happened to Grigsby? At that moment, the questions defied answers. But Thea strongly suspected that if she had enough time and mapped enough charts, somewhere in there was at least one, and maybe even more than one cancer identically matching the cancer in Hayley's MRI.

The betting now was that Julian Fang's diagnosis

was true. Hayley Long was cancer-free. But the reason for her fantastic cure was probably not her treatment or her genes or her powerful constitution or her *Qi*. The reason, in all likelihood, was that she had never had cancer in the first place.

But how could that be?

At that instant, Thea was startled by the two-way radio.

"Thea, get out, get out!" Flowers cried. "They're here. They may not know where you are yet. Use the stairs! Use the stairs! Over!"

Thea raced through the lab to the window and, staying low, peered down. Three uniformed security people were closing in on the truck. Flowers had already climbed down from the cab. She watched as he hesitated, taking in the situation. Then he bolted down the walkway in the opposite direction from the guards. The three of them yelled something at him and took off in pursuit, but Flowers had a significant head start, and from what Thea knew, none of the hospital security force carried guns.

THIRTY-ONE

Thea often described herself as a plodder, not a thoroughbred. Faced with a medical crisis, her reaction time and decision-making were usually reasonable enough, but seldom extraordinary and never flashy. She almost always was able to move along at the pace demanded by the situation, but she was at her best when there was time to think such situations through. On the other hand, she was seldom prone to the mistakes of haste.

Now, with the urgent radio call from Sean Flowers, she was experiencing an emotion that was quite foreign to her. Panic. First, she was on her knees, stuffing all of her supplies into the knapsack. Then she was sweeping all the charts together like oversized playing cards, slipping X-rays back into their folders as fast as she could, and then trying, with little success, to replace the charts in the filing cabinet in alphabetical order. Twice she dropped records, mixing up the contents. Finally, she simply jammed the remaining charts into the drawer, paying no attention to where they had come from. Moments later, she inadvertently knocked a clamshell full of paper clips and coins off the corner of Thibideau's desk. In scrambling to pick them up, she slammed her head so hard that she had to stop and check for blood.

The stairs! Get to the stairs!

Thea surveyed Thibideau's office and could see nothing out of place. Of course, Flowers had cut away half of one of the windows in the laboratory—a reasonably strong clue that someone had been inside. Her mouth was desert dry. Her heart and her thoughts refused to slow.

What would happen if they caught her? . . . Surely she would be kicked off the staff even before she had begun. . . . When word got out, would she have put herself in even more danger from whoever had attacked her? . . . What about Petros? . . . If she got caught, would he become a more urgent target? . . .

Hayley!

Thea was on her way out of Thibideau's inner office when she remembered that she had decided to take Hayley's MRIs with her. In her rush to straighten out the charts, she had put the films back. Did she have time to look? . . . Had they caught Flowers? . . . What was the penalty for breaking and entering? . . . She could never be locked up. Never! . . . She would leave the country first—forever. . . . Would they even let her back in Doctors Without Borders if she was running from this kind of trouble? . . . She had been living such a mellow, uncomplicated existence. . . . How did this happen?

Thea braced against the file cabinet and willed herself to settle down.

Where did I put Hayley's record? Breathe in . . .

breathe out. . . . Easy does it. . . . Easy . . . Come on!
You know how to do this. . . . Get ahold of yourself. . . .

After a minute or two she was able to focus enough to make a decent guess. The record was one of those she had put back in some degree of alphabetical order in the second drawer down.

Yes!

She snatched the two films from Hayley's file. Each one was about nine inches by twelve. Carrying them loosely rolled in one hand, she rushed down the glassed-in corridor separating the clinical area from the laboratory. She had entered the tastefully appointed waiting room, where not that long ago she had enjoyed such vivid fantasies of Dan, when she heard men's voices from just outside the door.

"Is this the floor where the window is out?"

"That's what Kim said. Fifth floor, Dr. Thibideau's office and lab."

"She going to call the police?"

"I think she already did."

Thea stumbled backward into the hallway, casting about from one side to the other for someplace to hide. The exam rooms were small, and the conference rooms and Thibideau's office offered nothing. It had to be the laboratory—a large area, covering two-thirds of the entire floor, busy with the workbenches, glassware, and complex electronic equipment of basic science research. She could duck behind a counter and wait for the right moment to bolt—or perhaps sneak—down the hallway and through the waiting area to the stairs. She had never been a very fast runner, but the notion of what was in store should she get caught was flooding her body with adrenaline.

Keeping low, she entered the research center and prowled from one row of workstations to the next, searching for one that looked more inconspicuous than the others.

One that looked more inconspicuous than the others... Thea almost laughed out loud at the absurd notion. She heard the voices enter the office and ducked down where she was, as far toward the rear of the lab as possible. Somehow, there had to be a moment when she could move forward along the cluttered workbenches back toward the waiting room.

The voices grew louder. Three people, maybe four, including one woman. Thea knew that surprise was the only element in her favor. She crawled ten feet in the direction of the waiting room. There was no choice but to make a dash for the staircase—at least to try—and soon. Realistically, though, she knew there was still too great a distance to the door and the stairs.

She glanced down at her knapsack and the two MRIs. It was going to be even more difficult trying to make it out of the lab carrying them. Perhaps her best chance was to leave them behind inside one of the cabinets, and to come back for them later on. Even if she got caught and was arrested, the twins would help her get a good lawyer, and she would get out of jail before too long. It wasn't as if she had hurt or killed anyone. If nobody needed anything from the cabinet she chose, there was no telling how long the knapsack and films might stay there undisturbed.

The voices were getting louder, and Thea felt certain at least one person had entered the lab area. Slowly, fearing the hinges were going to squeal, she eased open the door beneath the slate-covered workbench next to her. There was no sound, the movement of the door was quite smooth, and in fact, she realized, the construction smelled new. But even more interesting to Thea was that the cabinet was empty—completely empty. In fact, peering in she could see that the space next to it was empty, too.

There was some electronic equipment on top of the workbench, but it looked as if no scientist had been assigned to this area. If that were so, not only could the knapsack remain there undiscovered, but with a little maneuvering, perhaps she could as well. There wasn't much space—if she were five-ten instead of five-seven, or overweight, there might not have been enough room, but the option felt smarter than trying to run.

"Someone go through the lab and try to find the window where they got in."

There was no more time. Terrified of scraping against the wood, or inadvertently kicking the door, Thea set the knapsack aside and eased herself feetfirst into the cabinet and onto her right side. Her knees could bend just a little. When she tried extending her legs, her feet just touched some glassware. The faint clink it made, given the circumstances, sounded like a church bell.

With a band of tension tightening around her chest, she drew her knees up an inch or two and pulled the knapsack and films into the curvature formed by her belly. Then she reached her fingers around the cabinet door and closed it soundlessly. The moment before her hiding place was plunged into utter darkness, she thought she saw that one of the films wasn't completely inside. There was no way she could be sure if part of it was sticking out, and no way she could move off her arm to pull it in farther.

Her position was terribly uncomfortable, especially her right elbow, which was pinned beneath her, and the bony medial condyles of her knees, which were pressing against each other, left on right. The knapsack made it extremely difficult to change position.

Outside the cabinet she heard the shuffling of feet as someone walked slowly down her row. Suddenly, directly beside where she was lying, the shuffling stopped. Something solid, a nightstick, she imagined, was laid on the countertop above her. Half a minute passed before Hayley's MRI film lying beneath her began to move as it was pulled out under the door.

She pressed her arched back tightly against the rear wall of the cabinet. Moments later, the door swung open, flooding the space with fluorescent light. She caught a glimpse of a dark blue uniform just before a powerful flashlight beam struck her in the eyes. The nearly blinding light stayed locked in place as the security guard knelt down behind it, peering in at her.

"Thea?" Dan Cotton said. "What the—?"

THIRTY-TWO

With security people and police throughout the lab, there was no way Dan could chance bringing Thea out of the cabinet. He promised to be back for her as soon as it was safe, then softly eased the door closed.

Thea lay in the cramped blackness for another three hours. The terrible throbbing in her arm gave way to a stinging numbness, and finally to no sensation at all. Twice her legs cramped up so ferociously that she had to risk opening the door just to stretch out. Each time she could hear voices not that far away, and each time she pulled her legs back before she was ready.

She knew Dan would do whatever he could to protect her, but she also knew that in terms of seniority, he was low man on the pole, and in no position to give orders. There was no choice but to battle the increasing pain in any way she could and to give her mind work to do. For a time she tried meditating—something she had never done with much success or enjoyment in the past, and didn't succeed at now. For a while she sang silently—native Congolese songs mostly. And for a time she tried to reason out the significance to what she had found in Lydia Thibideau's office.

She was in the midst of those thoughts when Thibideau's voice suddenly intruded from not far away.

"How did they handle the glass like that, Detective Putnam?"

"Glass cutter, suction devices. Not so difficult if you know what you're doing. Whoever did it were professionals, and bold ones at that. It was pure chance that one of the security people, who happens to be a former cop, was working a double shift and remembered the bucket truck parked at another location after working hours."

"Professional thieves? I . . . I just don't understand."

"You have no idea what they might have been after?"

"We have a number of anticancer agents under investigation or in development. It's possible one of the pharmaceutical companies is involved in some way. If even one of these treatments is approved for general use, there could be a great deal of money involved."

"Industrial spies are everywhere, especially in the drug industry. Could someone be after something in your patient records?"

"I can't think of what, and at first glance I didn't see any sign they were tampered with. But just in case, I've got maintenance here right now moving my files to a secured area until we get to the bottom of this."

The voices faded away. How ironic that Dan was probably the one who blew the whistle on her and Flowers. She probably should have told him what they were planning, but the truth was, she really didn't want to compromise him in any way. Now, if he could somehow get her out of there with Hayley's films before her arms and legs permanently stopped functioning, she would have what she needed, and Dan would be something of a hero for thwarting the robbery. Thea waited as long as she could stand, and finally eased open the cabinet door just long enough to move one leg a few inches. Her arm seemed beyond saving, but continuous flexing of her fingers suggested she wasn't giving her body enough credit.

She returned to the darkness. The lab was again completely silent. Had the police left? What plan did Dan have for getting her out? How big of a chance was he going to have to take? Should she just ignore his orders and try to get off the fifth floor and out of the building?

Their conversation in Wellesley had made it clear Dan wasn't ready to reapply for the police force yet, and might not be ready ever. The job here was important to him for a number of reasons, including making his child-support payments. If she were in any way responsible for him getting fired, she would have trouble ever forgiving herself.

Another long stretch of time passed during which she heard nothing but her own breathing and an occasional involuntary groan of discomfort from deep in her throat. For a while, she tried to focus on Hayley, and what she should tell her. Someone, somehow, had created an MRI with her name on it, taken at a private radiology center in Atlanta, and showing her to have a lethal cancer. How could that be? Was Thibideau responsible—drumming up business, perhaps? Was some doctor or other employee at North Central Georgia Imaging being paid off to switch films? Or had there simply been a terrible, terrible mistake in labeling or filing?

The unanswerable questions kept piling on top of one another.

There was just too much for her brain to get around. She needed to get out and she needed to talk with someone who knew medicine, and who understood the deviousness of people, and the lengths to which some were willing to go in order to . . . to what? The perfect person to help her was lying in a dense coma just a few buildings away. But in all likelihood, he was there because he had learned the very same things that she was in the process of discovering.

Strained near to coming apart, Thea closed her eyes tightly and began humming a Congolese lullaby—her favorite of all the music she had learned during her years in Africa. Her mind followed the tune to the village nearest her hospital—a simple, vibrant place where beautiful people woke up each day to profound poverty, illness, and uncertainty, yet still managed to smile . . . and to sing.

> *My little black dove*
> *Curled up in your nest of love,*
> *The moon is a charm*
> *To keep you from harm*
> *Asleep at my breast. . . .*

Humming, a coping strategy dating to her earliest days of therapy, when ferocious meltdowns were nearly a daily occurrence, brought her an almost immediate calm. Her breathing slowed, and the tightness in the muscles of her face abated. She had drifted off to sleep when the door to the cabinet was eased open. This time, a flashlight was shone not in her eyes, but up into the regal face of a man in his thirties. The concern in his expression was genuine. He was extremely handsome, with features and coloring that reminded her of a Congolese surgeon she had worked with a year or so ago. From what Thea could tell from where she lay, he was wearing the gray uniform of hospital maintenance.

"Dr. Sperelakis, I presume," he whispered. His voice was a rich bass.

"You presume right."

"My name is Lockwood. Dennis Lockwood. I'm a friend of Dan Cotton's. I'm also a cop." He flipped his wallet open and shined the light on his badge. "I'm going to get you out of here."

"That's okay with me."

"Can you move?"

Thea tried and was surprised at how easily her arms and legs responded.

"Here I come," she said, setting her knapsack and the MRIs onto the floor and squirming out after them.

There were no overheads on in the lab, but the walls of windows let in a good deal of light from outside streetlamps.

"It's just the two of us," Lockwood said, continuing to whisper as he helped her to her knees, "but I don't know for how long. Stay low just in case someone shows up or looks in from across the alley. Here, I brought you a limo."

He reached behind him and pulled over a large canvas laundry cart. Thea tumbled gracelessly over the edge and dropped onto some blankets on the bottom.

"Did you work with Dan on the force?" she asked. "Is that why you're here?"

"No. He saved my life. *That's* why I'm here. If he told me to roll on hot coals, I would seriously consider doing it."

"I don't think he would, though," Thea said.

"No," Lockwood said curiously, "I don't suppose he would. . . . Okay, Doc. Hunch down and pull those blankets over you. We're going to meet Dan outside."

Thea did as she was asked, and used a corner of one blanket to wipe the greasepaint from her face. It was a miracle that she was about to get away unscathed from what had been an absolutely horrible idea. And even more miraculous, she was coming away with serious, credible evidence as to what might have caused someone to try to kill her father. All she needed now was to figure out how best to use what she had gathered, what it actually meant, and what to advise Hayley to do.

Dennis Lockwood wheeled Thea out of the building without incident. When he finally told her it was safe to stand, they were in a secluded grove in the far southwest corner of the campus. Dan was waiting, and held her firmly against his broad chest.

"Thank you for rescuing me," she said to Lockwood.

"Anytime."

"I hope not."

"Pardon?"

"I hope you don't have to rescue me again."

"We need to get going," Dan said, making no attempt to explain Thea to his friend. "Lock will take you to your car. I don't want you to get caught now after all we've gone through, and I think the BPD are still nosing around."

"Did they catch Sean?"

"That's your cat burglar partner?"

"It's a long story, but yes."

"Well, he seems to have outrun the law. I think I could have had him, but my boss wanted the glory of making—"

"—the bust."

Thea joined him saying the words, and they both grinned.

"It's another long story," Dan said to Lockwood. "Thanks for doing this, my friend."

"You call, I come. You and me are still a long way from being even. We're saving your place at work, you know."

"I know, Lock. I know."

Thea could feel the sadness in his voice.

THIRTY-THREE

Through the faintest gray of early morning, Thea rode with Dennis Lockwood to the Sperelakis Institute parking lot on the exact opposite side of the Beaumont campus. It had taken Thea some time and thought to decide to park there and not in one of the high-rise garages on the other side of the campus. But in the end, she was determined not to have her actions dictated by the animal who had assaulted her.

"Do you think Dan did the right thing?" she asked Lockwood.

"Right thing?"

"Quitting the force the way he did after he was forced to shoot that boy."

"I've never killed a kid, killed anyone for that matter, so I really couldn't say."

"I have."

"You have what?"

"Killed a kid. Sometimes, in my business, when patients are really, really sick, we have to make choices and make them quickly. Sometimes the choices we make don't work. Sometimes they actually make a bad situation worse. Sometimes . . ."

Her voice trailed away.

"I understand," Lockwood said. "And I suppose you could say Dan should have rolled with the punch of what he had to do. But I was there. I saw how crazed that poor kid was after being picked on and bullied the way he had been. He didn't know up from Thursday. From what we learned later, he never did anything wrong except for trying to be himself. That got him chased and beaten up again and again. Some of the gang who did it didn't even go to his school. Some were several years older."

"That's so ugly and so sad."

"Dan yelled at him to drop his gun or he would shoot. That's when the kid whirled with the gun pointed right at my chest from like twenty feet away. His eyes were glazed over. There's no way he saw me as a person."

"Dan had no choice. Just like if he was a doctor. You do your best and then live with the consequences."

"I suppose that's one way of looking at it," the policeman said coolly.

Thea sensed that her statement didn't sit well with Lockwood—hard to believe since it made perfect sense to her. She sensed as well that there was something missing in her response—something else she should be saying.

"Is there anything I could do or say to help Dan out now?"

The moment she heard her words, she pictured Dr. Carpenter smiling at her and nodding from across her desk.

You're getting it, Thea. You're getting it.

Lockwood shrugged, but his expression said clearly that her question met *his* approval as well.

"Just be there, I guess," he said. "Be there and be patient. Don't try and force him into any decisions before he's ready."

Thea hugged Lockwood, thanked him again, then asked him to wait until she had locked herself into her car. She drove out of the parking lot behind him, and headed up Route 9 toward Wellesley, wondering if Dan was thinking she might be the woman he had been waiting for—if, in fact, he had been waiting for a woman at all.

It was after five when she pulled into the drive. The lights in the carriage house were on as usual, although she knew they were no guarantee Dimitri was awake. After she showered and changed, it might be worth asking his opinion as to how she should approach Hayley with the news of her MRIs, and also any speculation as to what the disturbing findings might mean. His contribution to any situation was always hit or miss, but his unquestioned genius often allowed him to think outside any box.

Perhaps she could even talk him into accompanying her to the barbecue Niko and his wife were having that evening in honor of her return. Niko promised that a full complement of Aunt Marys would be there, and it would be the first time all four of Petros's children had been together in years.

She set the knapsack and films on the kitchen table and showered upstairs. Toweling off in front of the bathroom mirror, she couldn't help but notice the change in her appearance since her departure from Africa. True, she had been up all night, and in difficult circumstances, but she couldn't begin to count the nights she had stayed up with a sick or dying patient. There was a pallor to her skin and a hollowness surrounding her eyes that were stark departures from what she had grown used to in the healthy, oxygen-rich air and uncomplicated work environment of the jungle.

It was, she knew, nothing more or less than stress or strain, whatever the difference was between the two. She was Valentine Michael Smith in Robert Heinlein's *Stranger in a Strange Land,* marooned on Mars, raised by Martians since infancy, and now returning to Earth. The book had been one of her absolute favorites from the first time she read it. If challenged, she could probably recite much of it by heart. Now, in some ways, she was Mike Smith. She could only hope her story had a less violent ending than did his.

She threw her cat burglar clothes into the hamper, and put on khakis, a tank top, and a lightweight, frayed flannel shirt that dated back to high school. Even her body seemed less muscular than it had been, similar to Mike Smith's initial weakness caused by a reaction to the atmosphere of Earth.

"You can do this," she said, vowing that, at least, she would begin jogging every day. "You can do this."

Her bed began beckoning, but she sensed if she lay down now, that would be it for the day, and she had things to do. The shower, fresh clothes, and the resolve to get more exercise had a buoying effect, and the moment she stepped out of her bedroom, she felt energized—ready for the day, and excited to examine the spoils of her raid on Lydia Thibideau's fortress.

Singing the sweet lullaby out loud, she danced down the back stairs to the kitchen, put a pot of water on for tea, picked up Hayley's films, and held them up to the window.

Then her heart stopped.

One of the films was the negative MRI that had been taken of Hayley almost a year ago at the Beaumont Executive Health Center. The other one was of a man named Fitzgibbon, with wildly metastatic pancreatic cancer, taken three years ago. In her haste to gather the films and records together, and to replace them in Thibideau's file cabinet, she had grabbed the wrong MRI.

In an instant, Thea's upbeat mood was gone, replaced by the exhaustion she had so successfully held at bay, and by a cavernous melancholy.

All that effort.

All that pain.

All that risk.

"Dammit! . . . Dammit! . . . Dammit to hell!"

Making no attempt to stem a flood of tears, Thea slumped forward, her face pressed against her arm, sobbing mercilessly.

"Hey, what gives? Something happen with your squeeze?"

Dimitri, barefoot in jeans and a T-shirt that read SAVE A TREE; EAT A BEAVER, sank down on the seat across from her.

"N-no," she stammered around sobs. "He's v-very sweet."

"You need a towel or some Kleenex or something?"

"N-no. I'm allowed to c-cry, you know. It's not such a b-bad thing."

"Hey, I know. I did it once myself. But I stopped when Mom finally backed the car off my foot. Go ahead. Let it flow. Then you can tell your old bro who's gone and done you wrong."

The teapot began to whistle, and by the time Thea had filled a tea ball with some black chai and let it steep, she had regained a modest amount of composure.

"You want some of this?" she asked.

"Yaargh! Never drink tea before the sun's above the yardarms, matey. Yaargh!"

Dimitri was clearly tuned in to how upset she was, and as genuinely anxious to help as he was capable of being. Thea liked him like this, although she couldn't actually remember when she had last seen him so. She set her tea down and took him step by step from her initial meeting with Hayley Long to the negative exam by acupuncturist Julian Fang, to her decision, after being assaulted in the parking lot, to allow Sean Flowers to get her into Lydia Thibideau's office, and finally to her disastrous error while replacing Thibideau's patients' records and X-rays.

Her story was choppy because she had decided to omit her communication with their father, and his giving her the name of Jack Kalishar. If her brother picked up on that, he gave no indication. Instead, probably overwhelmed by the situation, he shifted restlessly in his seat, jiggled his leg constantly, and tore several paper napkins into tiny bits. She asked for any theories he could come up with as to why Thibideau might have padded her caseload of cancers, but he had no interest in speculating. Only when she tried to show him the two MRIs did his interest seem piqued. He immediately took one of the films, the one of Edward Fitzgibbon, and held it up to the window with one hand.

"This his cancer?" he asked, correctly indicating the largest portion of the tumor.

"It is."

"And this is his liver, and here's his spleen, right? Destroys old red blood cells, pools new red blood cells, helps build the immunity strength of the body through the reticuloendothelial system. . . ."

Thea sat quietly while Dimitri correctly identified virtually every structure in the MRI, and even provided a tidbit or two about each one.

"Hey, I'm impressed," she said when he had run out of organs.

"I couldn't get into med school like the rest of you Sperelakis kids. Hell, I couldn't get out of community college. So a while back I decided to teach myself medicine. It was like toe-tally bor-ring." He said the words with a Valley girl accent and gesture.

"Well, I'm impressed just the same, Dimitri. I should have had you take my boards for me."

"Or better still, Niko. He barely passed his."

"How do you know?"

"I hacked into the National Medical Board's computer, just for fun. I could have made him flunk, but I didn't."

Thea giggled at the notion.

"Good thing. He's become a very good surgeon."

"If you say so."

"What I say is thanks for cheering me up a little."

"Glad to be of service. Say, tell me, do you happen to have a cell phone?"

"I've been using Petros's. It's in that knapsack. Why?"

"Because you've got it on vibrate and it's going off, that's why."

Only at that instant did Thea hear the faint buzz from among her burglar implements.

"You're like a mutant with that hearing of yours," she said, fishing out the phone and flipping it open. "Hello, this is Thea."

"Thea, it's Marlene in your father's room."

Thea went cold.

This was it. . . . She just knew it. . . . It was over.

"What happened to him?" she managed.

"Happened? Oh, nothing, really. No change. I'm sorry, Thea. I should have said that right away."

Thea exhaled.

"That's okay, Marlene. What's going on?"

She glanced over at Dimitri, who, completely lost in his own world, had poured half a shaker of salt onto the table and had begun dividing it into piles with a butter knife. She had once been told that no one at the busy neuropsychological evaluation service had ever seen anyone test as high for raw intelligence as he did.

"Well, you asked me to call if anything strange happened with any of Dr. Sperelakis's visitors," the nurse was saying.

"Yes."

"Well, something just did. I don't know what to make of it, but it involves Dr. Hartnett."

"Dr. Hartnett?"

Thea flashed on the thank-you note in Jack Kalishar's record from the director of development.

"He just left here," the woman said. "He comes in several times a day."

"I know. He's one of my father's closest friends, and he is also his primary care doctor."

"Well, he said he wanted to do a brief exam on Dr. Sperelakis, and for me to wait outside."

"Well," Dimitri said, standing up suddenly, and speaking as if Thea was not involved with a phone call. "It's time for me to get back to my *World of Warcraft* encounter. I'm up to level sixty-eight and rising. The baddest man on the planet. See you later, sis."

"See you . . . Sorry, Marlene. I was interrupted. He asked you to leave."

"Yes, exactly. Well, I went out of Dr. S.'s room, but I stayed near the door to the step-down unit."

"Go on."

"I couldn't see much because I was shielded by Dr. Hartnett's back, but I swear I saw him inject something into your father's central line."

THIRTY-FOUR

"What's the matter, Tony, are those fish chunks too scary for you?"

Hands on her hips, Stacy Sims stood on the Collins Avenue Pier, looking down at her lifelong friend with typical defiance. She was taller than Tony D'Allessio by several inches, and as light in hair, skin, and eyes as he was swarthy. Her hair was pulled back in a single heavy braid, and beneath her T-shirt were the first hints that her eleven-year-old body was beginning to change. Lying beside her on the sun-darkened wood, ready to drop into the water some thirteen feet below, was a baited hook at the business end of an ancient rod and reel that had once belonged to her grandfather.

"I'm doing it," Tony said, not at all happy with being teased by a girl—especially this one. "This stuff I got for my birthday is all new. It takes some getting used to."

"You could always use a plug. I have some good ones. They might not be as good as bait, but at least they're not slimy."

"I told you, I can do this. I want to catch halibut and they like live bait."

"What they really like is deep water. You'll never

catch any halibut fishing from here. A striper, maybe, but not any halibut."

"I meant striper."

"You sure hate to be wrong, Tony D'Allessio."

"Who doesn't?"

They were alone on the old pier, which was a popular spot for talking and for watching the ocean, but not such a great spot for catching fish.

"Stripers beware!" Tony cried out as he dropped the baited hook over the railing and into the water.

Moments later, Stacy had done the same. The sun peered out from behind a pure white cloud that looked like a crocodile, and flooded the pier with warm sunlight. At almost the same moment, Tony snapped his rod toward the clearing sky and let out a yelp.

"Got one! . . . A big one, too."

The new Penn bent in a rainbow arc. Stacy quickly reeled in her bait and set her rod aside.

"Go, Tony, go!" she cheered.

The youth wasn't the biggest kid in school, but he was wiry and strong and, in nearly everything he did, determined. He set the end of the rod against his stomach and stepped back from the railing, pulling with all his strength.

"It's coming!" he shouted, reeling in several turns, then several more. "It's coming!"

Stacy moved forward to the railing and looked over, expecting to see a giant striper, or even a shark.

What she saw instead was a dead body—a man, faceup, fully clothed, bobbing rhythmically on a slight chop. His arms were stretched to the side like Christ on the cross. There was a length of brown seaweed across his bloated, stone-gray face, and beneath the kelp she could just make out a protruding purple tongue. Tony's hook had gotten him in the center of his jacket. The line, through the eyes of Tony's new Penn rod to his new Penn reel, was still taut.

"Tony!" Stacy screamed.

"I almost have him!"

"Tony, you can stop!"

THIRTY-FIVE

Pancuronium.

The closer Thea got to the Beaumont, the more convinced she became that Scott Hartnett, her father's friend and personal physician, was administering the long-acting paralytic to keep Petros from communicating with her. The irony was painful. The poor man already had, quite possibly, the most horrible medical condition imaginable—locked-in syndrome. And his physician was doing all he could to make that condition worse.

Before leaving for the hospital, she had gone over to the carriage house and managed to intrude enough on Dimitri's video war to borrow one of his computers and look up the drug. If her brother was the least bit interested in what she was doing, he didn't show it, interrupting her research only to give a triumphant whoop at the destruction of one of his enemies.

Pancuronium was a powerful curare-like drug used primarily in the operating room to prepare a patient to have their trachea intubated. Onset of action one to two minutes. First cousin to the more rapidly acting but shorter-lasting sux—succinylcholine. Duration of action for pancuronium, two to three hours—quite a bit longer if the drug was administered along with opiates or barbiturates.

If someone wanted to continuously keep Petros Sperelakis from exchanging information with his physician daughter, an injection of Pavulon, the brand name of pancuronium, was the perfect way to do it. The antidote to reverse the effect of the drug, at least partially, was the class of pharmaceuticals known as anticholinesterases—edrophonium and neostigmine being the ones Thea had studied the most, and had even used clinically to reverse the effects of poisoning with certain insecticides and nerve gases.

"Dimitri, do you want to come in to the hospital and visit Dad?"

"Got 'im! Die, sucker, die!"

"Dimitri!"

"Would he know I was there?"

"He might."

"Well, I'll wait until I'm sure it's a worthwhile trip. Watch this. . . . See that guy sneaking up on me over there? The gnome . . . Well, I just take aim at his gnome belly and . . . pow! Splat! *Gnome*or gnome."

"How about the barbecue at Niko's tonight?"

"What barbecue?"

"Dimitri, I told you about it. More than once. Niko said he did, too."

"Count me out, little sister. Those twins are double trouble."

"What do you mean?"

"Greedy they are. Yaargh! Take money from poor Petros, they did. Double yaargh!"

"Why would they do something like that? They're both surgeons. They must have plenty of money."

"My dear naïve housemate. You need to begin playing video games. That's where you'll find real emotions. True human frailty."

Thea felt herself getting irritated.

"Dimitri, will you please stop this nonsense talk and say what you mean?"

Dimitri immediately took a monocle from a small box of props on his desk, inserted it over his left eye, and adopted a distinguished British accent.

"I assure you, madame, that both of our siblings are just as adept at losing money as they are at making it. One twin never invests without clearing it with the other twin, and neither twin knows the first thing about investing. Neither, for that matter, does their father. Talked the Lion into investing in some sort of Internet dot-com company they and a friend of theirs started. He went in big-time even though he doesn't know the first thing about the product they were marketing. Let's just say he didn't lose nearly as much as the Twinkies told him he lost."

He set the monocle back in the box and shot something on the screen in front of him.

"But how do you know that?"

Dimitri stayed focused on the screen as he talked.

"Let's just say that sometimes, when I'm bored, or even when I'm not, I find myself hacking into their e-mail. I know, I know. The shame of it. Don't worry. I follow the hackers' creed and never use my material for anything other than personal amusement. And the twins are nothing if not amusing. Anyhow, count me out of the barbecue. They never come to any of mine."

Thea left without even bothering to ask if her brother had ever had a barbecue.

Throughout the ride to the hospital, her mind had been in turmoil as to what to do about Scott Hartnett, Lydia Thibideau, and Hayley. The first thing she had decided to do was to draw blood on Petros to confirm her belief that he had been receiving pancuronium and perhaps secondary drugs to enhance its duration of action.

She considered and rejected the possibility of administering one of the antidotes to the paralytic agent. At this stage, even with her newly acquired staff privileges, it might be difficult getting a nurse to inject such an arcane medication, especially given her father's compromised physical state. Reputations in a hospital were quickly damaged and always difficult to repair.

Was it worth waiting until she had absolute proof before confronting Hartnett? It sounded as if the private-duty nurse was quite confident in what she had witnessed. No, there was no sense in delaying matters. If nothing else, she could put an end to Hartnett's machinations, whatever the purpose. It made sense to draw the blood, see if Dan could get it analyzed in the state crime lab, and call Hartnett.

As for Thibideau, hers was a hornets' nest best left undisturbed until the meaning behind her bogus MRIs became clearer. Was she in some way aligned with Hartnett? It certainly seemed that might be the case. Research grant money? Possibly. FDA approval of new, wildly profitable anticancer drugs? Even more likely. The constant, powerful pull of influence, fame, and fortune was difficult to resist, to say nothing of the basic need for continued employment. Thibideau certainly wouldn't be the first academic to cheat on his or her research. In their recent meeting, she had seemed aloof and even haughty, but there was nothing about her that suggested dishonesty or a lack of respect for medical science.

Thea's natural, Asperger's tendency to give people the benefit of the doubt was being stretched toward the breaking point.

She pulled into her father's spot at the institute wondering how to deal with Hayley. Her new friend was razor sharp and highly intuitive. There was no sense in trying to shield her from the truth. But what, exactly, was the truth? She was receiving an investigational medication doled out by the hospital research pharmacy, but a great deal of evidence pointed to the fact that she did not have cancer in her body, and in all likelihood, she never did. Was it too risky for her to stop her chemo? Was it too risky for her to continue?

Feeling increasing fatigue, Thea took the tunnels through the underbelly of the hospital to the step-down unit, wondering where Dan was and also when the last time was that she had eaten anything except for a few sips of tea.

Marlene was massaging lotion into Petros's foot, and adjusting the splints that were keeping his contractures at bay. Still, Thea knew, every muscle group was atrophying from disuse. It was inevitable, despite the splints and the lotion and the physical therapy, that the more powerful flexor muscles in his wrists, fingers, and ankles would begin permanently overcoming the weaker extensors. The image of what her father's body would look like before too much more time had passed was disheartening.

"How're things going, Marlene?" Thea asked, immediately pitching in and rubbing lotion into Petros's other foot. "Any more visitors?"

"Amy was here for a while," she said, referring to the nursing director. "She seemed a little upset that you would be hiring nurses to special your father. It's always her position that her nurses, whether it's in one of the units or on any of the med/surg floors, are perfectly capable of caring for their patients."

"I'll speak to her."

"Actually, she asked if you would do just that. She said something about having spoken to your sister, and that your sister didn't know anything about special-duty nurses being brought in."

That's because I never told her.

Thea stopped herself at the last instant from sharing her belief that Petros was in constant danger, and also her newest belief that Scott Hartnett was using paralytic agents to keep him from communicating. It had been a mistake for her to share the discovery of Petros's locked-in syndrome in the first place. She was learning to be less trustful and more careful, but her natural tendencies had already proved costly.

"Anyone else been here?"

"That hunk of a security guard, Daniel Cotton, was

here for a little while about an hour ago. It's his second visit that I've recorded. What a nice guy. I have a little bit of a back problem, and he lifted your father for me and moved him as if he was a rag doll. I've actually heard a few tidbits off the hospital grapevine that Daniel Cotton might be involved with a doctor on the staff—a new doctor recently arrived from South Africa."

"That's absolute nonsense," Thea said. "I'm recently arrived from *central* Africa, not South Africa. But I will agree that he's a hunk."

"Oh, your brother and sister were here right after him, too, but they only stayed for a couple of minutes."

"I guess they don't believe that the energy of their presence is enough to make a difference," Thea said.

"I've seen a number of miracles over the years," the seasoned nurse replied. "Maybe they haven't."

Maybe they have, but didn't realize what they were experiencing, Thea thought, with uncharacteristic cynicism. Dimitri's disclosure about the twins bilking their father out of money disturbed her greatly—even more than the notion that he was eavesdropping on their e-mail. She completed the last of the physical care on Petros, wishing that she could be snuggling in Dan's arms, with her face buried in his chest.

This is no fun, she thought, wondering if she might have actually said the words aloud.

"Could I please have a few minutes alone with my dad?" she asked.

The nurse smiled as if she approved, gathered some of her things, and left the room.

"Dad, it's me, Thea," she said in full voice from close to his ear. She removed the paper tape from his lids. "Can you move at all? Can you give me a sign that you hear me?"

There was no response. Thea peered at his pupils and tried to convince herself that they were slightly more constricted than they had been—a known effect of narcotics. If there were a change, it was minuscule.

"Dad, try. Try hard to move your eye. Just look up and I'll see it. Look up and I'll know."

"Know what?"

Thea shot upright and whirled to the voice. Scott Hartnett stood just three feet away, smiling at her benignly, looking urbane and confident. Behind him, through the open doorway, she could see Marlene shrugging impotently by way of apology for allowing him past her.

"Know if my father can hear me," she replied, quickly regaining her composure.

Hartnett moved to the bedside and peered down at his longtime friend.

"You still believe he's alert?"

There was something about the man—a smugness, perhaps—that may have been there over the many years Thea had known him, but that now was intensely irritating to her.

"*And* able to communicate," she said, with an unmistakable edge. "At least he was."

"What do you mean?"

Thea's internal debate lasted only a few seconds. It was time for some answers. Beyond Hartnett's shoulder, she could see Marlene trying not to look as if she were paying close attention to them. Thea crossed to the door and closed it.

"I mean," she said flatly, "that I believe someone is administering a narcotic plus a paralyzing agent like pancuronium to my father, to stop him from using the one set of muscles he has available."

"But why?"

Again, the smugness.

Thea felt herself beginning to simmer. It seemed as if she had lost her temper more in the brief time she had been home than in all her years in the DRC.

"*Why* is not nearly as important as *who*," she declared. "I believe that person is you."

"I see," Hartnett said, surprising her by not vehemently denying the accusation. "You know, I wondered about what Marlene might be thinking when she saw me administering my mixture to Petros."

"Your mixture?"

Hartnett reached into his clinic coat pocket, withdrew a loaded five cc syringe, and passed it over to her.

"It's a combination of vitamins mixed with a small amount of a variety of anticoagulants."

"Vitamins? Anticoagulants?"

"I learned about the mixture during a three-week seminar I took from Dr. Boris Adamov and his staff in the Moscow Institute of Coagulation last year. Plavix, persantine, fondaparinux, that's—"

"I know, I know, a pentasaccharide bound to heparin."

"Very good, Thea. That's not an everyday drug.

Well, the dose of each component is minuscule, but Adamov has had remarkable results in preventing clots in bedridden older patients. I didn't want to burden our pharmacists by making them formulate this, so I have it sent directly to me by Dr. Adamov, and I administer it myself. I am really sorry that you would be suspicious of me, Thea. Your father and I have been so close for so long. But I know how much strain you have been under since coming home to this."

He gestured toward the inert figure of his onetime mentor.

Thea felt utterly deflated.

"Could I have that?" was all she could think of to say.

"Of course, but why?"

"I want to have it analyzed."

"Suit yourself, Doctor," Hartnett said without rancor.

"You know, I think I will," Thea replied.

THIRTY-SIX

"The confusions in life are there to give us strength and teach us lessons."

Dr. Carpenter's words, dating back to Thea's earliest sessions with her, were reverberating in her head as she sat down by herself in the cafeteria. Because Carpenter was on vacation, the appointment Thea had made with her was still a week away. Now, she considered calling to see if her therapist had decided to come home early.

The mushroom omelet, OJ, and plain toasted bagel on her plate seemed like a good idea when she ordered them, but not so at the moment. It was doubtful she could even manage a bite. In less than twelve hours, she had made a total mess of situations that were already difficult and confusing for her.

She had botched the break-in at Lydia Thibideau's office, put Dan in danger for having to rescue her, unjustly accused Scott Hartnett of trying to harm his patient and dear friend, alerted him once again of her belief that her father had locked-in syndrome, and allowed Dimitri to share his outrageous behavior of eavesdropping on their brother and sister. And now she was faced with the ordeal of having to confront Hayley with the fact that she might not have cancer, but that on the other hand, maybe she did have it and was now disease-free because of the chemo she was receiving.

Thea had jumped to conclusions regarding the injections Hartnett had been giving to Petros, and she might very well be off base in her conclusions as to what was going on with Thibideau and the MRIs. The files she and Flowers had gone after were not the official records, so the gastroenterologist might be using them for anything. The official records were totally electronic, and were securely locked behind the complex access codes of the impenetrable Thor.

Thea's breakfast lay uneaten as she struggled to untangle the situations initiated by her father's arcane, single-word message. *Kalishar.* At the moment, only one thing seemed totally clear—she was in over her head.

Maybe she had missed something in her reasoning surrounding the Thibideau files. She had misinterpreted Hartnett's behavior, why not this? She tried a few sips of orange juice, then gave up and pushed her tray aside, forcing herself to do what she should have done before confronting Hartnett—to search for other logical explanations that would encompass the facts as she knew them.

Perhaps there was some sort of comparison study going on, which Thibideau had not mentioned to her. Perhaps there were pairings or groupings of MRIs in her files that had nothing to do with the individual nature of the cases.

If Thea had used her vaunted intelligence and, instead of jumping to conclusions, had tried to come up with alternative explanations for what the nurse, Marlene, had reported to her, she might not have fouled things up so badly.

She needed Dan—needed him to listen to her, to keep her from jumping to conclusions, to keep her Asperger's at bay, even to make love with her.

At that instant, as if by request, she felt the vibration of her cell phone through her jacket pocket. Dan's name and number were on the caller ID.

"I'm trying to reach someone who would be interested in a caper," he said, "where we steal the Hope Diamond and replace it with an Easter egg."

"Very funny."

"Hey, you sound glum. I had expected you would be on cloud nine."

"Do you know what that means—being on cloud nine?"

"No, but I suspect you do."

"Actually, I do. It's Buddhist. And yes, I am glum."

Thea reviewed the events since her return home from her rescue in Thibideau's office. Dan listened patiently.

"Well, I don't know," he said when she was done.

"Don't know what?"

"Don't know if you're wrong about Thibideau. There's a lot of money at stake for anyone coming up with a wonder drug for anything. Maybe she's developed a drug that didn't work and she's faking the results."

"Two hundred million dollars."

"What two hundred million dollars?"

"I think that's how much Jack Kalishar donated to the hospital after Thibideau's experimental drug that you're speculating might not have worked saved his life."

Dan whistled.

"So maybe it wasn't the drug."

"Or maybe the people who weren't saved by her drug were killed by it."

"You're getting way ahead of me. All I can tell you, hon, is to do the thing with Hayley that you do better than anyone else I've ever known—be honest. She's capable of helping you to sort things out and ultimately it's her choice. Now, what about this business with Hartnett? Do you believe him? No, wait, don't answer that. You believe everyone."

"I guess until they give me reason not to, I do. The way Scott explained why he was injecting my father was totally believable. I mean, he *is* Petros's doctor."

"Do you still have the syringe he gave you?"

"Yes, but I was going to discard it. Why?"

"Call it a character defect or my personal genetic quirk, but I'm just not quite as trusting as you. I want to have it run at the lab."

"I want to see you, Dan."

"I want to see you, too, babe, but Josh is here with a fever of one-oh-one and a bad throat and a bad cough. I've got an appointment with his pediatrician in a couple of hours. His mother's away until tomorrow afternoon. She'll take over after she gets back. Maybe you can come by later this afternoon."

"My brother Niko's having a barbecue for all our relatives to come by and see me."

"Sounds like fun."

Thea decided not to bring up Dimitri's accusations regarding the twins. She had already piled enough of her worries onto Dan's plate, and now there was his concern for Josh.

"Any more word on that man from Delaware?" she asked.

"Gerald Prevoir. Not yet, but I've got a guy on it—an excellent private detective from New York that I got to know at a forensics conference a couple of years ago."

"I'll cross my fingers."

"And I'll cross my fingers that things go well with Hayley."

"Make sure they check him for mono."

"Prevoir?"

"No, silly . . . Oh, nice one. Take advantage of the Asperger's girl."

"I didn't know you got a cough with mono."

"Seven percent of cases."

"I'll bring it up."

"Do you want the reference?"

"Somehow, I don't think there's much to be gained in this case by intimidating Josh's pediatrician."

"I feel better for talking with you, Dan Cotton."

"And I feel better for talking with you, Alethea Sperelakis."

"Sean is back home in Georgia. He enjoys it when he gets a chance to fly in one of the company planes."

"I was happy when I heard that he wasn't caught."

"He almost never gets caught. Call it his specialty. He says you were very brave."

"That just means I fooled him. Tell him he witnessed the beginning and end of my career as a cat burglar."

"Okay, I hereby accept your resignation from the ancient and revered order of professional pilferers. Now, tell me what you found."

In an instant, Hayley's expression had become all business. Her dark eyes were fierce and alive, ready to focus in on whatever Thea had to present to her—cobra's eyes, ready for battle.

Sitting in her easy chair, her fine hands motionless on a copy of *The Economist,* Hayley listened to the account of the ultimately abortive break-in at her oncologist's office. Only when Thea had finished did she speak, beginning with a series of questions, the answers to which Thea could only speculate.

"What if I choose to stop my treatments until the dust settles and we can confront Dr. Thibideau with our concerns? . . . Is it even remotely possible that my cancer could be so chemo-sensitive it could have melted away so quickly? . . . Do you think Thibideau would share details of the death of this Grigsby and some of the other patients in her SU990 studies? . . . Could your acupuncturist tell from my *Qi* if I had ever had cancer in my body at all? . . ."

Never did she ask the one question Thea was certain she would. What would Thea herself do at this moment if confronted with circumstances identical to these?

An hour passed, then most of another. After Thea had answered the last of her unanswerable questions, Hayley called her husband, David, in Atlanta. Thea twice asked silently if Hayley wanted her to leave the room. Each time, a wave encouraged her to sit back. The billionaire was insightful, patient, and analytical in synthesizing material for her husband, who was, Thea had been told, a successful and respected architect and yacht designer. By the time the conversation between the two of them was over, Thea suspected she knew what the woman's decision would be.

"If it's okay with you, my friend," Hayley said, "David and I have decided, as he just put it, to stay the course. He lost his first wife tragically to an aneurysm whose warning signs she had ignored; he doesn't want to lose this one. And frankly, I'm not ready to go just yet."

Thea crossed to her as Hayley stood, and the two women embraced with deep emotion.

"I'm not ready to have you go just yet either," Thea said.

THIRTY-SEVEN

From her childhood to her thirties, Thea had never done very well at parties and other social gatherings.

Early on it was the commotion and the noise, and the perceived lack of interest the other children had in doing what she wanted them to do. Later, in her school years, it was the social dynamics and intrigues, combined with the feeling that everybody was connected with everybody else in some way, except for her. By college, her therapy, individual and group, had begun to take hold, and she was able to use her intellect to reason through situations and to react to them in a more logical, sensible, and acceptable way. Friends began showing up in her life and staying around. Men began taking an interest in her. And most important of all, she began to accept herself and various aspects of her Asperger syndrome, as well as her gradual evolution as a person.

But she still felt edgy at parties.

Niko and his family lived in a staid, opulent area of Newton. Doctor Village, some called it. Their backyard was easily capable of handling the eighty or ninety who were there this night, milling about beneath Japanese lanterns, gushing about the food and about the beauty of the grounds. His wife, a stunning nurse, Greek on both her mother's and father's sides, had stopped working soon after their marriage, and now devoted herself to managing their nanny and housekeeper, as well as the various groundsmen necessary to maintain such a place. And although the couple seemed like devoted parents of their three bright, talented, and charming children, in what time she had spent around her brother and his wife, Thea had seldom seen the two of them touch or talk.

From all Thea could tell, there was a mix of medical and nonmedical guests, most of whom, aside from the relatives, she either did not remember well or had never met. She suspected that her arrival back in the country was just a small portion of the motivation for the gala.

"Hey there, sis."

Selene, elegant in a white pantsuit with gold lamé trim, cradled a glass of champagne in her left hand, and a dainty lobster salad sandwich in her right.

"Oh, hi, Selene. Nice party, huh?"

"Niko and Marie throw the best barbecues."

"Everyone seems to be having a great time."

Small talk. There was a time when Thea didn't have the vaguest idea of what it was or what purpose it served. Now she smiled inwardly whenever she heard herself use it seamlessly.

"See Petros today?"

No more small talk from Selene.

"Twice."

"He blink you any messages?"

Thea sought to comprehend the tone behind the words, then simply gave up.

"How'd you learn about that?" she asked.

"Everybody *knows* about it, Thea. But I must add that not so many, me included, believe it."

"That's okay."

"Knowing how he felt about you leaving the country the way you did, it's a little hard for me to see him choosing you as the one portal for his communication with the world."

"Maybe I'm just misinterpreting things."

Thea began casting about for someone else she might want to talk with. The combination of Selene's now clearly disparaging tone, and the information passed on about the woman by Dimitri, were more than she wanted to deal with at this moment.

"You know, Thea," Selene went on, "in this family we pride ourselves on not keeping secrets from one another. If you have something to tell us about Petros, we'd like to hear it."

"Like what?"

"Like whether he's really awake and alert, and whether he's found a way to tell you that he knows whether or not the driver of that car actually hit him on purpose."

Thea felt slightly ill at the notion of how much conversation had been going on about her throughout the hospital, first about her and Dan, now this.

"Do you believe that was the case?" she asked.

"I believe what the police believe after their thorough investigation."

"Selene, if I learn anything at all from Dad, you'll be the first one I tell."

"You should have just let him die, you know."

"What?"

"Not everything is as simple as you think. It was his time. He could have had a peaceful passing, but you just couldn't let it happen."

Thea felt an intense burn across the back of her neck.

"No, Selene," she said, "I just couldn't."

She reached out to a passing waiter and plucked a cucumber-and-something hors d'oeuvre from his tray, then followed him across the lawn, consciously refusing to look back. When she finally did, on the far side of the yard, she saw Selene huddled in animated, secretive conversation with her twin. Twice, she thought Selene actually gestured in her direction.

Half an hour of standing by herself, except for an occasional brief visit from one of her Aunt Marys or a cousin, had Thea thinking about going home, even though the jazz trio had just begun playing, and there was no sign yet of dessert. None of those at the party were friends of hers, or even acquaintances from her school years. Dimitri might have been fun to have along, but then again, he was just as likely to do something outrageous and disruptive. In fact, she found herself wondering if Niko had actually invited their brother at all, or if she had just assumed he had. If *she* were somewhat out of place here, Dimitri would have been positively extraterrestrial.

Thea was about to return to the buffet for seconds when she saw Amy Musgrave striding purposefully toward her. The legendary director of nursing at the Beaumont, a trim, intense fifty or so, was married to a doctor, and had some children, but at the moment her husband, a psychiatrist, Thea thought, was nowhere in evidence. Remembering that Marlene had warned her about Amy being irritated that Thea had hired special-duty nurses, she was on alert. Within seconds, she knew she had good reason to be.

"So, Thea, what do you think of your welcome-home party?"

"It's very beautiful here. So peaceful."

"Yes, peaceful. Niko and Marie certainly know how to throw a shindig."

"Listen, Amy, I want to explain why I decided to hire specials for my father."

"No need," she replied coolly.

"My brother Dimitri has a theory regarding the hit-and-run. He thinks it was deliberate."

"Excuse me for saying it, Thea, but I've met Dimitri a number of times. He doesn't seem too, how should I put it, reliable."

"But he is very bright. You'll have to give him that."

"Actually, since you brought it up, it seems as if he goes out of his way to rile people up and upset them."

"Perhaps. But I've seen him be right any number of times."

"If you say so."

"Then, remember the fake orderly who assaulted the guard outside of the unit?"

"Of course."

"Well, I believe he was sent into the hospital to silence my father."

"The motive?"

"Well, Dimitri feels that Petros learned something that someone didn't want to have made public."

"About what?"

Musgrave suddenly seemed interested.

"I don't know."

"But you agree with him?"

"I do. That's why I decided to have Father watched around the clock—not because I thought he needed more or better nursing care, just to keep a closer eye on the many visitors to his room, and to stay on the lookout for anyone who wasn't there as a friend."

Musgrave sighed and gazed out across the crowd.

"Thea, someone needs to tell you," she said finally.

"Tell me what?"

"Tell you that in all likelihood, your father's accident was just that, an accident. But if it wasn't, if somebody had intentionally tried to harm him, it wouldn't have come as a surprise to a lot of people."

... *wouldn't have come as a surprise to a lot of people.*

Thea was stunned. She struggled to make sense of the words coming from a woman she respected—a woman whom she had thought was a staunch supporter of her father's.

"I don't understand," she managed.

The jazz trio had been joined by a singer—a stocky woman with a powerful voice, who was bemoaning the man who got away. Thea found herself unable to maintain even the slightest eye contact with Musgrave, and instead focused on the lantern light sparking off the singer's skintight sequined gown.

"Do you know," Musgrave said, "that the National Hospital Association is locked in a war with the nursing services from all over the country as to whether or not there should be legislation setting minimum standards for RN staffing?"

"Not really. I—"

"The nursing associations are battling bravely to see those standards implemented, but we're up against big, big money—insurance company money, managed care money, hospital corporation money. And the truth is we're going to lose. As things stand, the only hospital of our size in this country that meets the standards right now is the Beaumont."

"So that's good."

"Good for us, but we are fighting for other hospitals and their patients as well. The correlation between a sufficient number of RNs and hospital morbidity and mortality has been well established."

"I think I might be missing something. What has this got to do with Petros Sperelakis?"

"Your father has been fighting against the fundraising philosophy that has enabled our main hospital and its satellites to win award after award for our nursing service. If your father had his way, the Beaumont would not be in a position to lead the way in nurse staffing or any other area."

"Knowing my father as I do, Amy, excuse me for saying so, but I just don't believe it."

"Suit yourself."

"Exactly what do you mean by fundraising philosophy anyway?"

The figure written beside Scott Hartnett's thank-you in Jack Kalishar's chart flashed across her mind.

Two hundred million dollars.

"Your father was made a department chief in the Beaumont because of his name and reputation, and in that regard, he has also brought in a good deal of revenue—but certainly not nearly the sort of revenue we need to run and expand an institution of the stature of the Beaumont. The truth is, Thea, the man has been a thorn in the side of almost everyone responsible for raising the sort of money we need to keep our hospital at the top of the heap. There are a lot of us who feel Petros had been throwing his weight around just because he liked the sound when someone got hit."

Thea pulled her gaze from the singer and was finally able to level it steadily at Musgrave.

"Is Scott Hartnett one of those people?" she asked.

"I think I've said enough for now. I hear that you have decided to take over your father's practice. I hope you have allegiance to hospitals like ours and the lengths they have to go to in order to keep saving lives."

"I asked you if Scott was one of those who feels my father has been an impediment to raising funds at the Beaumont."

"That's not for me to say, but I just want you to know

that your father is not always the icon you might think he is. And you are beginning to make some enemies around here—very powerful enemies."

Without waiting for a response, the nursing director turned on her heel and was gone.

Utterly stunned by Musgrave's words and the vehemence behind them, Thea followed her with her eyes until the woman had disappeared around a corner of the house. Then she decided that she had heard as much as she wanted to hear about her deficiencies and those of her father, and had met as many people who were there to honor her as she was going to meet. Dessert or no dessert, she was leaving.

THIRTY-EIGHT

From her twenties until the day she was diagnosed with cancer, Hayley was seldom aware of having dreams or of having dreamed. Now, she was awakening from nearly every sleep—even short naps—to vivid, frightening scenarios. The recurring themes of her nightmares were helplessness and enclosure: being buried alive in a coffin, being staked out on sunbaked ground, running from an unseen pursuer through a structure with no doors and no windows. A fourth, recurrent theme, so realistic that she inevitably woke up gasping and in an icy sweat, was being eaten alive by vermin or insects.

She was invariably wearing a dress in those dreams—a yellow housedress with a matching belt. The ants or rats or more exotic bugs would climb her naked legs and begin to gnaw their way inside her, first through flesh and then muscle, until they had devoured her bright crimson tissues and eaten down to white bone.

So realistic were the images that she wondered if they were a side effect of the chemotherapy, or even of the death of the cancer cells in her body. She mentioned the dreams to Lydia Thibideau, but got only a somewhat bemused "don't know" shrug.

Hayley's mother, Belle, had been career Army and the center of her world. The nightmares began with Belle's death in a truck rollover when Hayley was nine. Invariably, the terrifying dreams centered on soldiers, explosions, and death. Her father, also military, though never married to her mother, took over her upbringing, and did the best he could between benders.

Throughout her early years, in housing units on military bases around the country, and indeed the world, Hayley had been a tomboy—resilient, stubborn, and determined to succeed. She earned her first hundred dollars at age ten, cashing in empty bottles and cans. Five years ago, when her Wildwood Enterprises acquired Harmon Electronics in a bitterly contested hostile takeover, her net worth passed three billion—placing her firmly among the wealthiest women in the country.

Still, she described herself as having enlightened toughness, and was routinely included on lists of the most active and broad-based philanthropists.

Now, though, all of her money and all her enlightened toughness were not enough to keep the cancer cells from eating away at her core, or the nightmares from attacking her spirit. If she ever made it past this chemo, she vowed, people would benefit. Many people. Curing cancer on an individual and global basis would be her cause, and the reason for her to continue making money. But first, she needed to survive.

"Ms. Hayley Long?"

Hayley had been asleep in her reading chair when the orderly awakened her. The dream this time had been even sharper than usual—a wooden coffin, seen from the inside, buried deep beneath the earth. She was on her back within it, her nose just inches from the lid, suffocating as she pushed and pounded against the wood, helpless to force her way out, and unable to keep sand from falling between cracks and into her eyes and mouth.

"That's me," she heard herself say hoarsely.

She mopped her face and under her arms with a hand towel kept on her lap for just that purpose.

The orderly, tall and slender, was wearing a surgical mask and standing behind a wheelchair.

"Chest X-ray, then an MRI," he said, checking the instructions he was holding.

"I didn't know I was scheduled for X-rays. It seems awfully late."

"I have no idea. They send me, I go."

"Well, can I at least see your face?"

"Oh, I'm sorry. I've got a wicked chest cold. I would have stayed home, but they couldn't get anyone else."

The man lowered his mask, revealing a lean, well-tanned face that many would have felt was good-looking, but that didn't hold much appeal for Hayley. She felt excited to be getting the MRI done, and wondered if Thea might have said something to her oncologist about Master Fang's findings. She transferred herself and her blanket from chair to wheelchair, and paused to inspect the orderly's ID.

"Okay, Mr. Elliot Smolensky," she said, "put up your mask and let's ride."

The orderly was well-spoken and amusing. He said he was in his last few weeks at the Beaumont before starting his second year as a nursing student at Emmanuel College—a career transformation from working as a salvage diver. Too bad, she told him as he backed her into the elevator. She had constant use for industrial divers, but not so much for nurses.

"That's very kind of you just the same," Gerald Prevoir said.

Those were the last words Hayley heard from the man.

In what seemed like a single motion, he stopped the elevator long enough to clamp a hand over her mouth and bury a needle deep into the muscle at the base of her neck. Then he depressed the plunger and waited for the thirty seconds it took the drug to work.

Hayley was slumped back in the wheelchair, no longer conscious, when the doors opened on the main tunnel. Prevoir held her head erect and turned off into a side passageway. Traffic was light, and no one seemed to notice them.

Moments later, Hayley was covered with sheets, in a fetal position at the bottom of a laundry hamper. Soon after that, Prevoir calmly wheeled her out of a service entrance and hoisted her limp form into the back of a waiting van.

Hayley regained consciousness slowly, accompanied by a headache slamming against the back of her eyes like storm waves against a breakwater. She was in a small, windowless room, no more than eight by eight. The floor was plywood, and the walls packed dirt. A single bare lightbulb, no more than forty watts, illuminated the space from a sconce on the wall. Air from some sort of compressor blew in gently from a vent set in the ceiling. Along the walls were an apartment-sized refrigerator, a small microwave, and a pile of perhaps twenty paperbacks—half fiction. In addition, there was a five-gallon bottle of spring water, some microwaveable food, and three pairs of pajamas.

WELCOME TO YOUR FORTRESS OF SOLITUDE, a computer-printed note on the wall read. PREPARE YOUR-SELF FOR A LENGTHY STAY.

Her mind unwilling to acknowledge her situation, Hayley sank down on the edge of a metal-framed cot with a mattress that smelled of mildew. Then she scanned the damp, unadorned walls and the crude floor, and she began to scream.

THIRTY-NINE

Thea knew that extricating herself from Niko and Marie's barbecue had become critical for her peace of mind, but she also knew it was not going to be easy—at least not without lying again. She stopped at the pod of guests clustered about her brother, mentally ticking off a list of excuses—most of them acute medical conditions—that she might use. In the end, she decided that lying about anything was not an option. There was no excuse with which she felt comfortable other than the truth—or at least the part of the truth that didn't involve her sister's unpleasant behavior, or that of the Beaumont director of nursing.

"Hey there, sis," Niko called out as she approached, "come over and meet some people."

In an instant seven guests, all beaming, swung from her brother to her, hands extended, titles and names and connections to her father or Selene, or Niko and Marie, flying at her like darts. With the onslaught, Thea began feeling shaky and confined. Still, she managed to pump each hand in the group. She had never passed out—never even came close that she recalled, but now, sensitized by Selene and Musgrave, and enclosed in a ring of Niko's friends, she wondered if it might possibly happen.

"Niko, could I talk to you for a minute?" she managed.

"Sure, sis. Hold the fort, everyone. That bartender looks like he's about to die of boredom. Why don't you all go and give him something to do? . . . You okay, Thea?"

"Actually—" Thea stopped herself again from taking the easy way out with a lie, the pounding headache one that she had selected as most believable. "I'm worn out, and I need to go home."

"But this is your party. Have you seen Aunt Mary? She came all the way from Springfield to see you."

"I'm sure I haven't missed *any* Aunt Marys. I've just had enough crowd and steak for one night. The party's been wonderful, Niko. Really, it has."

Niko tried to look hurt, but Thea thought that he missed. At that moment, she noticed Lydia Thibideau halfway across the lawn, deeply enmeshed in conversation with Sharon Karsten. Lydia, the specialist called in by Petros to care for Jack Kalishar and Hayley Long, and probably a number of other patients as well, and Sharon, Petros's paramour and possibly one of his heirs. Thea wished that she could be close enough to hear.

". . . Thea, tell me something before you go," Niko was saying.

"Yes?"

"Both Selene and I feel as if you've been acting rather distant toward us for a while now. Is it because we advocated for Petros to be let go?"

"I hadn't really realized that I've been distant. If I have, then I'm sorry. You know how I feel about him, and I know how you feel. For now, that's the way it is."

"Yes," Niko said, "that's the way it is. . . . Well, if you've gotta go, you've gotta go. Marie's upstairs making sure the kids are tucked in. I'll convey your regrets that you couldn't stay longer. Want me to have someone put a dessert plate together for you?"

"No, no. I'll be fine."

"Have you been talking to Dimitri much? Is that it?"

"I'm fine, Niko. I'm sorry you guys think I've been acting distant, but I'm fine—really. Besides, whatever Dimitri says I tend to take with a grain of salt, just like you probably do."

"You'd best do that, Thea. Our big brother has nothing to do cooped up in that carriage house of his except to make trouble. And he's extremely adept at doing that."

"Thank you again," Thea said.

She felt more anxious than ever to get away, but not home to Wellesley, she decided. At that moment, she wanted no more of Dimitri than she did of the twins. It was still early enough to go back into the hospital for a final check of Petros and some time with Hayley. Terrible things were going on at the Beaumont. She felt almost certain of it. The problem was that without her father's help, there seemed little she could do about them. Her allies were in precious short supply.

Like a servant taking her leave from a potentate, Thea backed away from her brother for several steps before finally turning and heading toward her car. Of all the unpleasant events since her return home, this party was the worst. She felt as if she had somehow swum into a whirlpool, and was being sucked helplessly into its vortex.

Her assault on Lydia Thibideau's office had provided nothing tangible. Hartnett was a dead end. Musgrave and Selene, and apparently any number of others, were annoyed or even furious with her. She could handle failures, but there had to be something she could do to increase the pressure on whoever was responsible for her father's condition, without putting him in even greater danger than he was already.

"Thea, wait!"

She was crossing the broad, arcing driveway, heading toward the spot on the street where she had parked, when Scott Hartnett called to her from behind.

"Oh, hi, Scott."

As done wanting to speak with any of her brother's guests as she could possibly be, she considered simply ignoring the man and dashing away to her car, but instead turned and took a step back toward him. Trim and dapper in a white suit and shirt, with a crimson handkerchief folded perfectly in his jacket pocket, Hartnett looked a little unsteady on his feet and, as he drew closer, somewhat glassy-eyed as well.

"I . . . just wanted to officially welcome you to the hospital fraternity—I mean sorority, I mean, well, you know what I mean—and . . . and to touch base with you after . . . what happened earlier today."

"Thank you, Scott. I'm certainly . . . honored to be a member of the club—even with the lingering restrictions that have been imposed on me."

"Yes, well . . . I heard about those from Sharon. We'll see what we can do about them."

He moved closer, listed to the right, and was forced to brace himself, full palm, against the highly polished hood of a black BMW.

"I'd appreciate that," Thea said.

"I . . . um . . . was certainly startled and upset by what you were thinking about me . . . doing anything to harm your father. He was . . . *is* my friend."

Thea felt uncomfortable talking to the man, who seemed barely in control of his speech. His eyes were bloodshot, and close up, through the evening gloom, his urbane good looks seemed worn and haggard.

"Well," she said, "with all that has happened, you understand why I might have been a little concerned."

"I was worried about that, yes. . . . So I brought this to show you. It's the description of the course I lectured at with Boris Adamov at the Moscow Institute of Co-agulation."

He fumbled for a folded paper in his right front pants pocket, opened it, made a largely unsuccessful attempt to smooth the longitudinal crease, and passed it over. Despite the location of the course, the program was in English. One of the talks, "Recent Advances in Platelet Medicine," was given by Hartnett himself. Several others, including "Use of Low-Dose Mixed Anticoagulants in Posttraumatic Patients," were presented by Boris Adamov, whom Thea had heard of.

"This is very interesting, Scott," she said, handing it back. "But it really wasn't necessary to bring this here tonight. I believed you. In fact, I believed you to the extent that I had decided just to dispose of the syringe you gave me, and not even to bother having the contents analyzed."

Hartnett was nodding, his lips pulled back in something of a smile, as he shakily replaced the course program in his pocket.

"As I said, your father means a great deal to me," he said deliberately, pronouncing *said* as *shed*. "I am glad you saw fit to trust me as far as analyzing the contents of the syringe goes, but either way would have been fine."

"That's great you feel that way."

"What . . . do you mean?"

"Well, I have a friend who's a former Boston policeman with connections in the state lab. Even though I completely trust that you were giving my father exactly what you said you were, he doesn't know you as I do, and he's not as trusting as I am. I've got the syringe you gave me packed away in ice. Tomorrow I'm going to give the mixture to him, and he's going to have it analyzed. That'll remove any question, right?"

There was a silence lasting several seconds.

"Right you are, Doctor," Hartnett said finally. "Let's get this business put behind us."

"I knew you'd feel that way, too. Listen, Scott, I want to stop by the hospital and see my father before it gets too late, and you have dessert to take care of. I'll see you tomorrow, okay?"

"Yeah," Hartnett replied, his eyes narrow, the muscles in his face tense. "Tomorrow."

Petros emerged from darkness slowly. He knew his eyes were closed, and that he could not open them, but light from above him was filtering through his lids. He had been having hallucinations—vivid, mostly pleasant hallucinations—although he had no sense of why they had been happening or how long they had lasted. He also knew that so long as he was hallucinating, he was virtually without pain. The nurses had to be giving him something, some sort of powerful narcotic.

He knew now. He knew that he had locked-in syndrome. He knew that the chances for any useful improvement were small. But according to studies, according to the experts in the field, the chances did exist. He knew that his older son didn't care. He knew that his twins, his pride for so many years, wished, for selfish reasons, to see him just die.

God knows I did right by them. I sent them to the best schools, guided them into medicine, provided for Niko's children during the lean years. Okay, so they had chosen to become surgeons, not internists; mechanics, not thinkers. I forgave them for that—I've said so any number of times to anyone who would listen. How could they care so little about me now?

Have I done something wrong?

My dear kouklitsa, *my Thea. She wants to help. She wants to communicate with me. She should never have left her place here to go off to the jungle, but she's back now. So intelligent. Such a fine doctor. Together we'll get to the bottom of whatever it is Hartnett is doing. Together we'll figure things out.*

FORTY

It was after eleven when Thea, using her electronic pass, pulled into the parking lot outside the Petros Sperelakis Institute for Diagnostic Medicine. Seeing her father's name on the façade of such an elegant building and such a renowned center of medicine brought a small jet of energy to what had otherwise been an absolutely discouraging and exhausting evening. Her brother's and sister's angry words, Scott Hartnett's alcohol-driven anxiety, and Amy Musgrave's allegations about a man incapable of defending himself were simply more than she wanted to deal with.

If only she had come away from Lydia Thibideau's office with the two different films with Hayley's name on them. With Dan's help, she might have chanced taking them to the police, and turning the investigation over to them. Maybe now she should consider going to a lawyer—seeing if there could be some sort of charges brought against Thibideau or even trying for a court order allowing a specialist to have access to the MRIs of Samuel Blackman and the late Warren Grigsby. But what would that accomplish? There would always be a logical explanation, and the whole matter could take months or even years to sort out.

Was Thibideau responsible for the hit-and-run accident? Was her cheating on her clinical research the secret Petros had uncovered—the secret that seemed to have cost him so much of his life?

Thea used the pass to open the door to a largely deserted lobby, and headed directly down to the tunnels and across to the building housing the step-down unit. The gleaming passageways were largely deserted, save for laundry trains, a janitor rhythmically swinging his massive buffer from side to side, and some haggard house officers. Thea flashed back to her own residency. It was a period of amazing growth for her, and one that established her ability to look beyond what others thought was best for her to what she herself thought was best.

At the moment, what was best was to put Niko's party behind her and spend some time with their father, and after that, a visit and maybe some tea with Hayley. Someone knew, she kept thinking. Someone knew what had happened to the Lion, and why. She just had to keep the pressure on without putting the poor guy in anyone's crosshairs.

The nurses working in the step-down unit weren't the least bit surprised to see Thea at such an hour. One of them had quipped that she was like a ghost who haunted the hospital at night. The private-duty nurse, a young grad named Tiffany, seemed superfluous given the lack of activity in the unit and the paucity of visitors, probably due to the barbecue. She was working on Petros's legs when Thea arrived.

"Anything?" Thea asked, moving in across from the nurse and massaging her father's quadriceps muscle.

"Not really. A little while ago, I was cleaning the corners of his eyes with a Q-tip and I could swear his lid twitched. But he didn't do it again."

Thea felt herself react to the nurse's words, but forced a calm response.

"If it's significant, it'll happen again."

She sent Tiffany on a break, then wiped the lotion from her hands and did a quick exam, talking softly to the man as she did.

"Hang in there. . . . Your skin looks great. . . . The nurses are doing a terrific job. . . . Niko had a barbecue tonight for about a zillion people. . . . They all asked about you. . . . Terrific food. . . . The kids send their love."

His joints seemed stiffer, especially at the wrists and ankles—not such a good sign.

Gag reflex: none.

Extremity reflexes: all absent.

Belly: soft.

Cardiovascular system: stable.

Lungs: scattered wheezes, pops, and other indicators of alveolar sac fluid. Not such a good finding, but not surprising, either.

Thea made a mental note to have his bronchial tubes suctioned out more frequently. When he was awake, the procedure had to be very unpleasant for him, but it was a vital, lifesaving maneuver, and besides, unless Tiffany's observation was legitimate, he wasn't awake anymore. Anticipating another nonresponse, she removed the paper tape from each of his lids and lubricated the inside of the lower ones.

"Dad, give me a sign. Give me a sign you can hear me. Come on, Dad. I love you. Show me you can hear me."

With agonizing slowness, Petros's left eye flicked upward, then returned to neutral.

"Yes!" Thea whispered, pumping her fist below the bed. "You're back!"

Intensely, she tried sorting out what might have happened to cause this improvement, and what Petros might be capable of in terms of communication. Looking upward, even a millimeter, seemed like such a consummate effort for him—quite a bit more difficult, it seemed, than the movement described by locked-in victim Bauby in his memoir.

There had been no arrivals recorded by Tiffany or her predecessor since Sharon Karsten's visit from three to three thirty. The last appearance by Hartnett was for ten minutes at two thirty. If he had been administering regular doses of a tranquillizer and a long-acting muscle relaxant like pancuronium, he might have assumed that with Niko's party, Thea would not be returning to the hospital this night, so he could wait until morning to give the next dose.

His mistake.

"I need to find a way to communicate with you without tiring you out. Look up if you understand me. . . . Excellent!"

The movement was faint, little more than an upward flicker, but it was definite. Thea added a tiny bit of lubricant. She felt determined this night to push to the limit Petros could handle. She needed to know what to do next, and with her father and Dimitri both convinced the accident had really been attempted murder, and with the grisly warning from the man in the parking lot, she needed to know quickly.

"Dad, I know this is difficult for you," she said to the motionless figure below her, his chest rising and falling eerily in response to the mechanical demands of his ventilator; the overhead monitor validating that within the shell of his body, his heartbeat was strong and regular. "I'm going to ask you some questions. All you have to do is look upward if the answer to my question is yes. Otherwise, don't move at all and I'll figure things out. Do you understand? . . . Please, do you understand?"

A flicker of movement.

"Oh, thank God . . . Okay. You figured out that Jack Kalishar never had cancer of the pancreas. That's why you gave me his name."

The upward movement of Petros's eye was tenuous but definite.

"Wonderful."

Through the glass door, Thea saw the nurse, Tiffany, asking silently if she was needed, and waved her away.

"Okay, let's try again. Is Lydia Thibideau behind all this? . . . Come on, Dad. Is she? . . . I take that as a no."

How could she not be involved? Thea wondered. *How could she not know?*

"Have many patients in the Beaumont been cured of illness that they don't actually have?"

Again, a positive response.

"Patients with diseases other than just pancreatic cancer?"

More slight movement.

"That's it. Good. Keep at it, Dad. Keep trying. Scott Hartnett is involved, isn't he? . . . Yes! I knew he was. He has some way of convincing patients and their physicians that the patients have a serious illness. They get treated and cured, and then they donate large amounts of money to the Beaumont out of gratitude. That's right, isn't it?"

Petros's eye movement this time was barely detectable. He had tried valiantly. Now it seemed as if he was running down.

But how? Thea's mind was screaming. *How could Hartnett work such deception?*

"One more. Just one more question. Do you know who is responsible for hurting you?"

Nothing.

"Dad, does that mean no? Move your eye if you mean no."

Again, nothing. Whether he was answering her question or not, the Lion was done—at least for the moment.

"You did great, Dad. You did terrific." Thea kissed him on the forehead. *"S'agapo, Mpampa,"* she said. "I love you very much."

FORTY-ONE

One issue clarified, many more to deal with.

Thea left the step-down unit well after midnight, feeling at once saddened and buoyed. There could be no doubt that Scott Hartnett, brilliant internist and a family friend for many years, was at the center of a medical scam that had added hundreds of millions of dollars to the treasure trove that was the massive endowment of the Beaumont Clinic. Nearly every building at the hospital, and most of the floors within those buildings, were named for someone, to say nothing of the individual rooms and pieces of equipment—even some of the individual furnishings.

Brass Plaques Are Us, she thought, smiling savagely to herself.

Creating, then subsequently curing illness, where none existed.

Remarkable.

Thea headed back into the tunnel on her way to Hayley's room, wondering just how many patients were involved. Certainly, Hayley Long was one of them. She and Jack Kalishar had to be among the wealthiest patients of the hospital. How many others were there? How many different illnesses?

Then, there were the doctors.

Assuming a complex, pervasive medical scam was going on at the Beaumont, how many others besides Hartnett were part of it? Were the primary care docs and oncologists and various specialists aware of what they were dealing with? The answer, for the vast majority of them, had to be no. If the scheme had been going on for as long as it seemed, someone almost certainly would have caved in and spoken up as Petros had apparently done.

As she entered the elevator in the basement of the building named for her father, Thea couldn't help but wonder if he was part of the deception. She found it nearly impossible to believe so principled a man, with more money than he was likely able to spend over the rest of his lifetime, and a worldwide reputation, would risk his legacy—risk everything that mattered—to pile up donations and add brass plaques to the walls of his hospital. Had he been involved and finally decided that enough was enough? Would he ever tell her if he were?

"Your father has been fighting against the fundraising philosophy that has enabled our main hospital and its satellites to win award after award for our nursing service."

Musgrave's exact words. She had sounded so sure of herself—so passionate. It was time for Thea to sit with Hayley, and later with Dan, and get their opinions. At this point, what she needed more than anything were allies—allies and ideas. One thing seemed certain: At the moment, Petros was as vulnerable to Hartnett and whoever else was involved as he was to the ravages of his injuries.

Hayley was not in her room.

The books were there, and her clothes, and a pile of papers on her bedside table, and a half-empty pitcher of water. Apparently, she had gone off wandering the hospital as she sometimes did. Perhaps she had even gone to see Petros, as she had in the past. Thea's revelations about the MRIs in Thibideau's files had to have been unsettling for the woman. A walk made perfect sense.

Feeling vaguely uneasy, Thea sat down in Hayley's reading chair and flipped through the pages of a dry business magazine without actually digesting the words. Five minutes later, her unease had intensified, and after ten minutes, she was at the nurses' station. There were four women—two aides and two RNs—on the night shift on PS-4, as the floor was known. None of them had seen Hayley leave, and it was their policy to have any patient departing the floor for any reason sign out. Thea checked the book. Nothing.

"Something's happened," she said, before even trying to reason out where her friend might have gone.

The charge nurse immediately called her supervisor.

"Page her," Thea insisted. "Page Hayley throughout the hospital."

"Can't," the shift supervisor said. "It's strictly against regs to broadcast any patient's name."

She called security.

At this point, although she was concerned, Thea did not believe that anything untoward had happened to

Hayley. Instead, she was becoming increasingly convinced that her friend had undergone a change of heart as a result of their conversation about the MRIs, and had used her vast resources to have herself simply removed from the Beaumont.

Thea couldn't help but recall a Sunday morning during her internship at the hardscrabble city hospital across town, when an angry suburban attorney stormed onto one of the busy, understaffed female medical floors. He was on his way in to see his mother, who was hospitalized there with some sort of progressive dementia, along with a myriad of other problems. A mile from the hospital, he had pulled his car over. There, wandering in no particular hurry down the other side of the street, wearing nothing but a Johnny, which was totally open in the back, was his mother. Livid, he bustled her into his car, brought her back to the hospital and to her bed, only to discover that no one on the floor knew she had left.

Instant legend.

It wasn't at all like the Beaumont to lose a patient with no one knowing where she had gone, but the place was gigantic, and those in the many private med/surg rooms had a great deal of freedom and autonomy. It was up to Amy Musgrave's nurses to know which patients could be trusted and which ones couldn't. Certainly there was no reason to anticipate that Hayley would be a problem.

By a quarter after one, the nursing staff and security people had come up empty. They had even bowed to Thea's insistence that they enlist housekeeping and any available nurses and aides to check every public bathroom stall—men's and women's—in case Hayley had experienced some sort of med reaction, and had gone into one of them before passing out.

"She's back home in Georgia," Thea said to the supervisor, when the last of the negative reports had come in. "We should call her husband."

"How would she get a flight at such a late hour?"

"It would be *her* plane. Or *her* limo. Or even *her* helicopter. Any helicopter takeoffs from here since she was last checked?"

"Not that I know of. And why would she leave everything in her room like this?"

"She's a multibillionaire. She's used to doing whatever she wants to. Can you give me her husband's number?"

"Sorry, it's—"

"I know. I know. Against regs. I'm pretty sure this isn't the circumstance the HIPAA people were protecting patients against when they drafted their laws. If I can't call her husband, then you call him."

The nurse was flustered and anxious.

"I think I'd better call Amy first. She might want the hospital lawyers brought in."

Thea could only groan. "Go ahead and get her in here."

One phone call to Atlanta and the whole matter could possibly be resolved.

But that one phone call, when it was finally made, only added to the confusion, and to Thea's concern. Hayley's husband had spoken to her twice that evening—

once when Thea was with her, and once an hour or so later. Initially, Hayley and he had decided that she would continue with her chemotherapy. But after some thought, she had completely reversed her stance and had decided to stop her treatment until a repeat MRI could be obtained. If the film showed no evidence of residual tumor, she intended to get a second opinion from a GI oncologist in Atlanta as to whether to resume her therapy. As to her whereabouts, her husband had nothing to add to the situation except his anxiety.

Musgrave, who had made the call, seemed appropriately alarmed. She spoke to *her* nurses as if they were the ones who had initiated the search, and more or less ignored Thea. She was about to order a second, even more in-depth search of the hospital, along with a policy-violating overhead page, when Thea had had enough.

She motioned Musgrave away from the group now clustered at the nurses' station.

"Call the police, Amy," she demanded in a harsh whisper, glaring at the fiery nurse. "Hayley's either gone into hiding someplace where we'll never find her, or she's been kidnapped."

"Why would she have gone into hiding?" Musgrave asked.

"You seem to be tuned in to most of what's going on around this hospital. I was hoping you might know something about the answer to that question."

"I don't know what you're talking about."

But she did.

Thea, who considered herself a weakling when it came to reading people's expressions and their tone of voice, could see fear and uncertainty etched across the nursing supervisor's face. It seemed for an instant as if she were going to blurt out something like *How did you find out?* But instead, Musgrave spun around and returned to the security officer in charge.

"Call in the police," she said. "I'll get ahold of Dr. Karsten. And I'll call in Dr. Thibideau as well. Perhaps she knows why Ms. Long decided to stop her treatments when they seemed to be working so well."

Good move, Amy, Thea silently cheered, praying that for whatever reason, Hayley had gone into hiding, but knowing in her heart that wasn't the case.

FORTY-TWO

Thea said nothing to the police about her father's condition or the information he had passed on to her earlier in the night. At this point there were no reasons to do so, and many reasons not to, most important among them, the constant, heightened jeopardy he would be in should word get out that he was awake and communicating what he knew. Dan would know what she should do, and whom she should trust.

He would know.

And after they talked, if he felt they could be of help to the police in their search for Hayley, and that heightening the threat to Petros was a price worth paying, they would pick a detective, maybe Dan's friend Lockwood, and tell him everything.

Lydia Thibideau had been as difficult to read as a sphinx. She seemed appropriately concerned about Hayley's sudden decision to stop her chemotherapy when she had been doing so well, but she also sounded like a seasoned clinician, who had encountered just about everything there was to experience from her patients, including many miracles.

Thea had listened closely for any hint of discomfort or guilt from the woman, but to the extent her Asperger's allowed her to make such a call, she found none. Still, whether or not Thibideau was involved, something deceitful, greedy, and potentially very dangerous was going on at the Beaumont.

Hartnett was a definite player in the scam, Thea reaffirmed as she left the hospital at almost three in the morning. And now, it seemed, Musgrave might be involved as well. But the real questions, at least for the moment, involved Hayley. Was there any way her disappearance could be connected with the questionable MRI that had brought her into the Beaumont in the first place? Doubtful, Thea decided. More likely, it was simply a matter of money. Hayley was worth a fortune. It had been a mistake to isolate her without protection in the Beaumont the way they had—a mistake for her not to have brought her own security people along with her. She was like a tapir in big cat country—nearly defenseless prey for any reasonably resourceful kidnappers.

Certainly, hostages had been taken for a lot less than might be demanded for her. In Africa, kidnapping was something of a sport, and might have actually been amusing had not so many of the episodes ended in bloodshed and death.

Eyes gritty with fatigue, and thoughts totally engrossed in her concern for Hayley and what might have happened, Thea left the parking lot headed, in no particular hurry, for Wellesley. Moments after she left, a pickup truck swung away from the curb and followed at a respectful distance. The truck was large and powerful—a Dodge Ram, black with a second set of doors and a full-sized cab in the rear. Attached in front of the grille was a thick steel and wood frame, the width of the truck and four feet high, used for attaching heavy-duty equipment. The driver of the truck had pulled a black ski mask down over his face.

Thea weaved through the back streets of the city until she reached Route 9. Then she slipped in one of Petros's albums of traditional Greek music and settled back, cruising west along with fairly light early-morning traffic. In addition to her concerns for Hayley, she found herself thinking about her experiences since her return to the United States.

At the Doctors Without Borders hospitals where she had worked, she had never once felt unaccepted or like an outsider. Back here in Boston, as it had been in her earlier life, she was an oddity—totally uncool in a world where cool was everything; more than two standard deviations from the mean in almost every measurement of fitting in. Yet in those weeks, she had managed to find a true friend in Hayley, and a lover who wore tight white underwear and kissed her like no man ever had before.

Not bad.

And now she was on the verge of helping her father gain some measure of vengeance against the killer who had harmed him more, perhaps, than could death itself. She just had to be patient—be patient and make sound decisions, searching her heart and mind, and incorporating the advice of those she trusted. Following that path, one day at a time, things would become clear to her. If she believed anything, she believed that.

Cruising into the Chestnut Hill section of Newton, with her father's favorite music enveloping her, Thea took down the evil eye—the *mati*—hanging from his mirror, and rubbed it. Then she made the sign of the cross three times, and spit into the air. It was as out of character for her to do so as it was absolutely in character for most of her many Aunt Marys. Fervently, she prayed that Hayley was safe and unharmed. Frustrating as it felt, there was simply nothing else she could do.

Just past the mall, traffic began to slow. WORKMEN AHEAD, a sign announced, ALL FINES DOUBLED. No surprise for Route 9. It seemed the busy thoroughfare was always under some sort of reconstruction, most of it done between midnight and dawn. At a rise in the road, Thea peered ahead. The double lanes of stationary brake lights seemed to extend to the horizon—far beyond Route 128. No detours that she could tell . . . no policemen directing the flow . . . just cars.

Thea was fine driving with her thoughts and the music for as long as it took to get home, but this traffic wasn't moving at all. Impulsively, she swung off onto a secondary road and turned left—toward Needham, she guessed, although it was a road she could never remember having been on. If her sense of direction didn't fail her, she could take the next right and be headed west again. Based on the complete lack of cars, it appeared that no one else had chosen this alternate route. Thea was pondering the significance of that fact when she felt the first contact from behind—a firm bump on her left side that snapped her head back and spun the steering wheel to the right, out of her hands.

Instinctively, she slammed on the brakes and looked up at the rearview. The truck that was forcing her off the road filled the mirror. Its windshield was so far above her that she could just see the bottom edge of it. An accident? A purposeful attack? A random thrill ride? All Thea could think of was the bone-breaking sensation her father must have experienced when a car sped out of the early-morning gloom and struck him.

Under the best of circumstances, Thea would never have been placed in anyone's driver's hall of fame. Her hand-eye coordination was below average, as were most of her other athletic abilities. She had waited until she was well past eighteen to go for her license, read every book she could get her hands on dealing with the dangers of driving and how to avoid or combat them, and then had barely managed to pass on the second try. On field trips from the hospital in the DRC, she seldom volunteered to drive one of the Toyotas or Land Rovers, and after experiencing the slow speeds that were comfortable for her, no one asked her to do so again. Now she couldn't begin to know what her response to this situation should be.

The truck accelerated, forcing her to skid to her right, over a low curb and across a grassy field, straight toward a massive tree—a gray ghost in the bouncing headlights of her Volvo. She managed to grip the wheel and swung it to the left as best she could. For a moment, some space opened up between her and her attacker, then the truck rammed her again.

This was no chance accident. The driver behind her

was either terribly drunk or completely committed to destroying her.

There was no way she was going to miss hitting the tree, which, she realized in an absurd moment of clarity, was a maple.

Pulling even harder to her left, fearing that her forearms were about to snap, Thea did all she could. The Volvo was lurching and skidding across the field, which was soaked from an earlier thunderstorm. At the last moment she managed to turn the wheel just enough to keep from a head-on crash with the maple. Instead, the jolting impact was against her right front, tearing off the headlight, fender, and mirror with a sickening crunch, and cracking much of the right third of the windshield. Instantly, the driver's and passenger's airbags snapped open. Then, as they were meant to do, they just as quickly emptied.

Actually, Thea thought, in another uncontrollable flash of knowledge, the bags didn't deploy instantly, but in one twenty-fifth of a second. She had read about the device and the subsequent chemical reaction when she was studying for her road test, and again, years later, when she bought her first car, an orange Volkswagen Beetle. As the airbags were unleashed from their containers inside the steering wheel on the driver's side and in the top of the dashboard on the passenger side, pellets of sodium azide combined with potassium nitrite and silicon dioxide to produce the nitrogen gas that inflated them, and also beads of common glass, which served to neutralize the highly toxic intermediate, sodium nitrite.

Smoke filled the car a moment after the bags deflated. Talc, Thea knew, used to keep the airbags pliable. While the talc was dissipating, she was virtually helpless, unable to see ahead or behind, skidding almost sideways across the field toward what she could vaguely tell was a forest of some sort. The passenger-side airbag had slammed upward against the windshield, as it was programmed to do, further dislodging it from the frame of the car. Meanwhile, the truck, its engine screeching like a monstrous bird of prey, was continuing its merciless onslaught.

To protect her arms and hands, Thea had taken them off the wheel. Now, worried about hitting another tree and not having airbags to protect her, she brought her hands up to her face and peered between her fingers. That was when the fog of talc cleared enough for her to see water ahead of her and maybe eight feet below—a pond of some sort, approaching fast through an opening in the woods.

An instant later, the Volvo was airborne. Parallel to the ground, it sailed through the opening in the trees and off the bank, turning upside down in what seemed to Thea to be excruciating slow motion.

Its wheels and chassis were pointing directly skyward when it slammed against the black mirror surface of the pond, jolting Thea forward and snapping her forehead against the steering wheel with numbing force.

For a time, she was barely conscious—unable to connect her thoughts in any useful order. Then, she became aware of an intense, unfathomable darkness, and of a dreadful pounding behind her eyes. Finally, her situation came into focus. The lights and all other electrical capabilities of the car had ceased to work. It was upside down, bobbing in some sort of murky pond, and steadily filling with water, which was pooling below her head and approaching her eyes. Her buckled seatbelt was holding her in place. There was still air to breathe.

Then, the Volvo began to sink.

FORTY-THREE

Thea's first thought as her consciousness returned was not that she was going to die—it was that she was going to find a way out. She fought the encroaching panic the way she had fought it during countless medical emergencies over her years as a doctor, by focusing on details and relying on system and logic. As a physician dealing with a life-and-death crisis, process was everything. In the eternal debate among docs about whether it was better to do the right thing for the wrong reason, or the reverse, she was nearly always on the side of process over gut instinct . . . except when she wasn't.

As her thoughts cleared, despite the need for action, she found it difficult to keep from wondering who had done this to her. How had he (she envisioned the driver as a he) known that she would be at the hospital at such an hour? Finally, like moving a giant boulder from her path, she was able to shove the speculation aside and concentrate on the situation.

Working in her favor, she wasn't badly injured, she was limber and reasonably strong, and she was smart. The loose sundress and light cardigan she had carefully chosen for the barbecue would in no way hinder her mobility, although she would take the sweater off as soon as she could. Operating against those advantages were the fact that the Volvo was now completely submerged, and settled on its roof on the bottom, tilted on an angle to her right; the darkness surrounding her was total; and the probable concussion from the blow she had taken to her forehead might be making her thought processes less agile than usual. The car's descent had taken only a few seconds—seven feet of water, she guessed, if that.

She could do this.

Her first step seemed simple: Get out of the seatbelt and try opening the driver's-side door. As she had countless times, she reached below her for the belt release.

No, the other way! . . . The other way!

Her confidence slipped a notch.

She calmed herself with a breath, and keeping her eyes closed against the rising pond water, reached above her, toward her feet. The seatbelt release opened easily, and she allowed herself to tumble onto the roof over the passenger seat. The space was much more cramped than she would have expected. The water accumulating there was at least six inches deep and seemed to be flowing in rapidly. Then she remembered the front windshield first cracking from the collision with the tree, then being blown loose from a corner of its frame by the explosive force of the passenger-side airbag. That had to be the source of much of the water.

It took an endless minute to locate the driver's-side door handle. She pulled it and pushed against the door with all her strength, but there was no movement at all.

Her leverage was poor. It took an exhausting amount of energy to swing around to use her feet.

What remained of her bravado vanished. With the auto tipped fifteen or twenty degrees toward the right, there was no way the doors on that side would open.

Twice her face became submerged, and she pulled up sputtering warm, stale water through her mouth and nose.

Eyes shut tight, she forced herself to slow down and think things through before expending time and energy getting into the rear seat. Her chest was beginning to feel tight and hungry for air. Without working through the logic, she began taking shallower breaths. In spite of herself, fears and doubts began filling her mind, turning logic to panic. How much time did she have? How fast was the water coming in? Every breath was putting more carbon dioxide into the small chamber. How much useful air was left? What did it feel like to die like this? Would she lose consciousness before the water entered her lungs?

The darkness had become a force pressing in on her from all sides. And now, disorientation was becoming a factor as well. Up and down, forward and back, right and left had fused into one. Each time she failed to account for the water rapidly pooling above her, she inhaled enough to send her into prolonged spasms of racking cough. More carbon dioxide . . . less air.

In spite of her decision not to try it, she fumbled for the passenger-side handle, then gave up. It had to be the windows. Somehow, it had to be the windows. Front? Side? Where could she get the most leverage? She remembered from her reading that there was no way anyone but a very powerful man—yes, *a very powerful man,* they had written—could kick out a car window under water. A tool. Everyone was supposed to carry a glass-breaking tool in the glove compartment. Did Petros know to do that?

Jesus, I really am going to die!

Unable to believe her father would have paid attention to such a detail, Thea huddled head-down on the passenger seat and managed to open first the storage box between the front seats, then the glove compartment. Nothing. The chamber seemed to have filled at least a third. There was no room left to move. No room at all.

And very little time.

She tried the door once more, then braced herself and lashed at the windshield with both her feet.

. . . only a very powerful man . . .

So what do you mean by that? . . . What am I supposed to do? . . . Just sit here and die? . . . I don't want to die. . . .

Half the cab was filled now. The headrest and at least six or eight inches of the seat back were submerged. Thea could breathe only by curling herself into a ball on the passenger seat. She was wearing Mary Jane flats with leather soles. That should have been good for something, she thought, as she flailed out in the overpowering blackness like a child in a tantrum.

I can't believe this. . . . I can't believe I'm going to drown. . . .

She took a deep breath, pushed her head down into

the water, and slammed her feet again and again against the windshield, until she was forced to duck back down, gasping and sputtering, to suck in what little air remained.

... Dan Cotton, I love you.... Come and help me.... Kiss me and then use your man-strength and kick this window out for me.... I need to get out.... I need to get out so I won't drown....

It was only then that she realized the windshield had moved. With one of the blows from her feet, the glass had moved—right in the lower corner—precisely where the tree branch and the airbag had separated it from the automobile's frame.

Time had run out.

Thea took as deep a breath as she could manage. Then, slouched on the seat, the water now over her mouth and nose, she braced herself against the backrest and pushed with all the strength she had left. What had been a small slit between the windshield and the frame became a gap. Water poured in and filled what had remained of her airspace. One push. That was all she had left. One last push and she would have to breathe. One last push and she was going to drown. Even if the space opened enough, she didn't have the strength or lung power to go out headfirst, and feetfirst would almost certainly leave her wedged between the windshield and the frame.

Hold it!

Hold on to your breath and try!

Push! Once more, push as hard as you can!

Dan, I'm sorry.... I'm sorry.... I really tried....

FORTY-FOUR

The first sensation to pierce the nothingness was the smell of wet dirt. Thea was lying facedown on the muddy ground, her head pressed against the exposed root of a tree. Her chest was gurgling with each breath, but she could not muster the strength to cough. The realization that she was alive was almost incomprehensible.

For several minutes she lay there, laboring for each breath and trying with no success to re-create the final minutes of what she thought was the end of her life. Finally, she was able to sputter out a feeble cough. Pond water and surface scum sprayed from her nose and throat. A minute later she was able to cough again.

She blinked open her eyes and allowed them to focus. It was lighter than it had been when she was attacked. Four, she guessed, maybe a bit after that. The throbbing behind her eyes had begun once more, monitoring each heartbeat with a shell burst. Her arms were stinging, as were her hips and knees. A flash in her memory bank momentarily lit the scene of her struggle to get out of the Volvo. She was desperately wriggling her way forward as she pulled herself headfirst through the smallest of openings along the right-hand edge of the windshield.

Again and again she became wedged or her clothing became caught. Again and again she kicked and flailed and freed herself for another inch or two. At some point she was forced to take a breath. Her lungs filled with water, but still, driven by adrenaline, and nearly beyond fear, she clawed ahead. Her flesh tore at every point that dragged across the metal and the glass. No matter, she thought now. They were wounds that would heal. She was battered, but she wasn't dead.

Get that, whoever you are? I'm not dead!

Slowly, Thea lifted her head. She was on the edge of a dense wood, no more than ten feet deep, that bordered the grassy field where her Volvo had struck a tree. That fierce collision, by cracking the windshield, was what had saved her life. To her left, at an opening in the trees, the sodden ground was gouged by the tires of the Volvo, and behind those marks were the deep trenches made by the much more powerful pickup. The memory of the screeching engine made her shudder.

She pushed herself to her forearms. The left sleeve of her sweater was torn nearly off, and a large patch of skin by her elbow was deeply abraded and oozing blood. By her left hip, her dress was torn through to the skin, and soaked with a mix of pond water, filth, and more blood. But no bones were broken, and none of the wounds seemed crippling.

Through the opening in the trees, she could see the pond itself, its placid surface reflecting the first light of the new morning, its banks waiting perhaps for a pair of lovers to stop by and snuggle together in the warmth of the day. Farther to the right, a narrow spillway emptied water from beneath a broad mat of algae and scum, adorned with several empty bottles. Nowhere was there any sign of the Volvo.

It was only then that Thea opened her tightly clenched left hand. Nestled there, having created a bloodless indentation in her palm, was her father's *mati*—his evil eye.

In the distance, Thea could hear the noise of moving traffic. Route 9. Someone driving into the city would stop for her and at least use their cell phone to call a cab, or Dimitri, or better still, Dan, who lived not that far away. No calls to the police, though—at least not yet. Police would mean endless questions, and probably a trip to some emergency room. And at the moment, those were the last things she wanted.

In the cool early-morning air, her thoughts had sharpened, and pieces of the past few days had fallen into place, cemented there by the scene in the street outside of Niko's home. How had the driver of the truck known she would be at the hospital? He knew because she had told him.

The man who had come so close to killing her had to be either Scott Hartnett or someone working for him. What she needed now was proof, starting with the plastic bag in her freezer containing the syringe of Hartnett's that she had come so close to throwing away.

FORTY-FIVE

"Ouch!"

"You're not supposed to be saying ouch. I'm the one who's injured."

"Yeah, but you're too tough to say it even though I can tell you feel this, so I'm saying it for you."

"Okay, ouch."

"That's better."

Thea, showered and toweled off, lay on Dan's king-sized bed, naked beneath his flannel bathrobe. Her wounds were nasty, but shallow, and given that none of them were on her face, and the bleeding was stopped with reasonable ease, stitches were not called for. Piled in the corner on the floor were her decimated party sundress, her shredded sweater, her sodden underwear, and the Mary Jane flats that in all likelihood had helped her get free, enabling her to kick out the windshield of her father's Volvo.

In spite of looking like she had just escaped from a car submerged in a nearby pond, or perhaps because of it, she had no problem getting a businesswoman heading into the city for a breakfast meeting to stop and lend her a cell phone. Thea glibly told the woman her husband was a policeman and that she was fine to wait by the side of the road for Dan, but the Samaritan insisted she wait in the car, wrapped her in a blanket, and to her credit, asked few questions.

After stopping at an all-night pharmacy to stock up on bandages and antibiotic cream, Dan took her to his place, the second floor of a neat, well-maintained duplex in West Roxbury. His downstairs neighbor and landlady was a woman in her seventies who clearly looked on the father and son as family. After Dan woke her following Thea's call, he had brought Josh down to her place and put him back to bed. Later in the morning, Dan's ex, Valerie, would pick him up there.

In addition to ignoring much of the discomfort from her wounds and contusions, Thea felt a warm, reassuring comfort being among Dan's things. His kindness, manliness, and spirit were in evidence throughout the modest flat, in addition to his scent. And in spite of her situation, Thea found herself wondering what it would be like to live there with him.

"I still can't believe you got out of that mess alive," he said, finishing up applying antibiotic cream, nonstick pads, and an Ace bandage to a nasty gouge on her left knee.

"Good thing I hardly remember doing that," she said as he gingerly applied the wrap.

"And you feel certain that Dr. Hartnett was responsible? He seems like, I don't know, not exactly the run-you-over-with-a-truck type. More like a hit-you-with-his-Vespa."

"He's the only one who knew I was going back to the hospital from Niko's party. And don't forget that my father told me he was involved. We need to find out where he lives and drive out to see if he owns a black pickup."

"I might be able to get his address from our records at the hospital. We might even have the makes and license numbers of his cars. If need be, my friends on the force can do this for us."

"Just be careful. Don't do anything that will get you in trouble. We can try WhitePages.com first. Then we've got to get out to Wellesley and pick up that syringe."

"My pal at the state lab will get it analyzed."

"It's going to be positive for a muscle paralyzer and some powerful tranquilizer. I promise you."

"What are you going to do for a car?"

"Maybe rent one."

"You need a license for that."

"Let me check with Dimitri. He's very resourceful. He once promised to get me a foolproof State Department visa if I needed it."

"I don't think I want to know."

"You probably don't."

Dan knelt beside her and kissed her long and gently.

"Mouth-to-mouth resuscitation," he whispered, holding her.

"Do it again. I think there's still a few drops of pond water in my lungs."

"You know," he said as the second kiss slowly faded, "I don't think I've ever kissed a beautiful woman who looked like she just finished fighting a no-holds-barred steel-cage death match with, like, an eight-hundred-pound gorilla."

"There's a first time for everything. You know, Dan, I've been trying to figure out how Hartnett *couldn't* be the one responsible for this."

"And?"

"And I'm wondering if maybe someone could have been following me all the time, looking for just the right chance to . . ."

Her voice trailed away as some of the true horror of the attack returned.

"I suppose it's possible someone had been following you continuously. But who?"

Thea shrugged and shook her head.

"I don't know. Maybe it's that guy who came after my dad in the unit and probably me in the parking lot—the guy who . . . what was his name?"

"Prevoir. Gerald. It's okay, you can say his name. And you can say what he did to me, too. You know, I'm going to get him. I promise you I'm going to get him. I've hired that private eye from Manhattan and—say, listen. I want to check on if he's made any progress and I want you to hear his secretary in New York, or more probably it's his answering service. She's like sort of a cartoon of what we Boston people think New Yorkers are supposed to sound like. Mendez—that's the guy's name—is a bit of a cartoon himself. But he's a pro, and tough. I can tell those things. Let's call. I'll put the phone on speaker."

Before Thea could tell him that she would much rather kiss some more than listen to cartoons on the speakerphone, he got a number from the pad on a small desk under his window, and dialed. The secretary spoke precisely as Thea anticipated from what he had said.

"Downtown Detective Agency. May I help you?"

"Hi, this is Dan Cotton from Boston calling. I recently hired Mr. Mendez to do a job, and I'm wondering if he's available to give me a progress report."

There was a long, uncomfortable pause.

"Who did you say this was?"

"Cotton. Dan Cotton. Albert and I met when—"

"Mr. Cotton, I'm afraid I have some bad news for you. . . . Mr. Mendez is dead. Some children found him floating beneath a pier in—"

"—Delaware."

Dan muttered the word in unison with the woman.

Ignoring the increasing aches in a dozen parts of her body, Thea sat upright and tightened the robe around her. Her expression was grim.

"Do the police know what happened to him?" Dan asked the woman.

"Not that I heard, but his girlfriend Rochelle—do you know Rochelle?"

"No."

"Oh. Well, Rochelle told me that he was badly beaten, and that two of his fingers had apparently been . . . you know, cut off."

"God, that's awful," Thea said after Dan had given the woman his number and got her promise to call him if there were any further developments.

Ashen, he set the phone down.

"Prevoir knows I'm after him," he said. "For two fingers I'm sure he knows exactly who and where I am. I'm going to call Valerie and get Josh to her place right now. Then I'll call Dennis Lockwood and tell him what's been going on. I hope he's on today."

"Good idea. Do you think this Prevoir could be working for Hartnett?"

"Do you?"

"I think we should go and get that syringe and then find out if Hartnett owns a black pickup the size of a tank."

FORTY-SIX

The syringe was gone.

Thea stood in front of the open freezer, having emptied its contents entirely onto the kitchen table. When she returned home from confronting Scott Hartnett at her father's bedside, she had put the syringe into a plastic bag and set it at the back of the bottom shelf. Now, it clearly had been taken.

"At the party, did you tell Hartnett what you had done with it?" Dan asked.

"I . . . I don't remember. Yes. Yes, I suppose I did. He brought the course program from Moscow describing the anticoagulant combination he said he was giving my father. Why would anyone go to that kind of trouble if they weren't telling the truth?"

"Better not to ask that question. He must have come over here after he waited by the pond and you didn't come up. Or else after whoever was driving that truck called to tell him you were history and it was time to pay up. I wonder how he got in."

"Remember how you got in? I don't always think to lock the doors."

"And you told him that, too?"

"No." She grinned. "At least I don't think so. Anyway, if the doors were locked, he could have broken a window."

"You know what you are, Dr. Thea?"

"What? What am I?"

There was uncharacteristic tension in her voice. Dan had never challenged her like this before.

"You're . . . the best. That's what you are."

He put his arms around her and kicked the freezer door closed.

"But just a little gullible. Go ahead, you can say it."

"I would rather have you trusting and gullible any day, than cynical and mistrustful of everyone. Besides, you said he had had too much to drink. Who would have expected him to remember such details?"

"Dan, I'm starting to feel like the walls are closing in. First this business with the truck, then your detective. And I don't even know what to make of Hayley's disappearance."

"I'm not so thrilled with any of those things, either. Mendez getting killed may be the worst of all. I felt like Prevoir was at a disadvantage as long as he didn't know I was after him. Mendez was full of himself, but he was tough. He didn't seem like the kind that would let himself get taken like this."

"I think after we take a drive past Hartnett's place and stop to see Petros, we should go to the police. Clearly Hartnett and whoever is in this scam with him appreciate that my father's a threat. Maybe we could hire an off-duty policeman to stay with the nurse. In act, maybe we could get an injunction to keep Hartnett away."

"If you say so, we'll do it."

"First I want to get a driver's license."

"First, maybe you ought to change. I love the way your behind looks in Josh's sweatpants, but some of the people at the hospital might take a more conservative stance. Can you make it up the stairs to your room?"

"I can. Over the years I've spent in the bush, I've had insect bites that were worse than what I've got here."

"Okay, Dr. Tough. I'm impressed. I have to be on duty at three, anyhow. If we get to the hospital early, I'll just clock in. You can use my car if you need to until you can rent one. This yours?"

He held up the cell phone that had been lying on the counter.

"It is. I thought I had put it in my purse when I went to Niko and Marie's, but I guess I didn't."

"Lucky for it, unless it can swim. Do you have another purse to put this in just in case we need to talk?"

"I think I can find one."

"I'll give you some cash if you need it. At some point after we speak to the police, you should notify your father's insurance company. Wish you had a credit card. You can't rent a car without one."

"We'll see what Dimitri can do about that, too."

Dan groaned.

"I'm glad I'm not on the force anymore," he said.

Dimitri took no small amount of pride in being able to produce an impressive replica of a laminated Massachusetts driver's license with Thea's photo on it in less than five minutes.

"It's not perfect," Dimitri said, passing the license over, "but neither are the good people who usually look at them while they're wondering how they're going to pay their electric bills. It won't stand up to a really close examination because of OVGs—the optically variable graphics. They're like digital watermarks that seem as if they're moving as the license is tipped one way or another. But I'm getting closer and closer, and if I really cared to get it just right, and I were willing to slow down my march to the absolute top of the heap in WOW—that's *World of Warcraft* for you uninitiateds—I could reach perfection. Ever play WOW, Dan?"

"I have a ten-year-old son whom I hope never discovers the game."

"If he's ten and if he has Internet access, and if he talks to the kids at school, I'm sure he already has, whether he's playing it or not."

"How can I keep him from getting addicted to it? I know of kids who have had to be hospitalized to be weaned from the game."

"You really want to know?"

"I do."

"From me?"

Dimitri looked genuinely affected by the request.

"Yes, from you."

Thea cringed at the prospect of what might come out of her brother's mouth, but at the same time, she was anxious to hear.

"Well, let's see," he said. "My advice is to tell your boy that you have no problem at all with him playing WOW so long as he promises to tell you if he thinks it might be getting out of hand. Oh, and when you tell him it's okay to play, don't forget to tell him you love him."

Thea stared at her brother, genuinely impressed with his advice. She knew as well as he did that none of the Sperelakis children ever heard those words from their father, although their mother did her best to make up for that—at least with Thea she did. If Dimitri picked up on the look, he gave no sign of it.

"That sounds like good advice," Dan said, apparently oblivious to Thea's expression as well. "Besides, telling Josh it's okay to do something is often the best way to make him lose interest. Thanks."

Perhaps unable to handle the compliment, Dimitri turned his back on the two of them and chopped off several virtual heads with a weapon that looked like a combination battle-axe and scythe.

"Now," he said, still looking at the screen, "I'll need about an hour to come up with a decent credit card, although it'll be one you shouldn't use too often—just for like renting a car. In the meantime, tell me what you make of this truck business. We Sperelakis kids tend to protect our own when it comes to attempted homicide against one of us. How sure are we that the guy in the truck and the guy trying to keep Father from talking, er, blinking, are both Scott Hartnett?"

"Or someone working for him," Thea amended.

"We're not certain," Dan said. "Actually, we have no hard evidence at all. But at the moment, Hartnett is the only possibility that makes sense."

"As soon as I have taken care of the credit card, I'll

spend a little time with my electronic friends at the Registry of Motor Vehicles, checking on what they've got registered to Dr. Scott Hartnett. Then we've just got to find a way to get him to trip himself up." Dimitri put his feet up on the counter, and rubbed his chin thoughtfully. "Give me some time. You got a cell phone, right?"

Thea and Dan exchanged smiles.

"Right here," she said, holding it up. "It's Dad's."

"One hour. I'll call you."

He had just said the words when the phone began vibrating, startling Thea so that she almost dropped it.

"It says 'private call,'" she said, setting it against her ear. "This is Thea Sperelakis."

"Thea, this is Scott Hartnett." His voice sounded urgent and strained. "Can you talk?"

"It's Hartnett," she whispered to Dan and her brother. "I can talk," she said icily. "What do you want?"

"Thea, I can explain everything. I need to talk and to show you something."

"Go on."

"Meet me tonight. One A.M. in the MRI suite. Bring your friend, the hospital guard, if you wish, but please, no one else."

"Was it you who tried to kill me this morning?"

"One A.M. in the MRI suite. I'll explain everything."

"Hartnett?"

The director of hospital development had hung up.

FORTY-SEVEN

For Thea, the rest of the day, with the minutes and hours creeping toward their 1 A.M. meeting with Scott Hartnett, seemed nearly interminable. A good deal of her time was spent explaining to people the origin of the huge bruise on her forehead, the black-and-blue under both eyes, and the limp. It made matters easier that the explanation she chose, an automobile accident, was close enough to the truth for her to deliver it smoothly.

From all she could tell, there had been no further developments regarding Hayley. Hospital lawyers were involved now, clearly expecting some sort of legal action from her camp. Detectives from the BPD were still questioning hospital employees in a luxury suite provided by the Beaumont. Thea had been called in for a second go-round, but had still withheld what information she had regarding Lydia Thibideau and Scott Hartnett, as well as her belief that certain patients of the Beaumont Clinic were being cured of serious medical conditions that they never actually had, except in their electronic records.

There was no note of Hartnett visiting his patient in the step-down unit, although both Niko and Selene had spent twenty minutes there earlier in the day. According to the nurse's log, the twins had made some efforts to communicate with Petros, and had actually removed the paper tape from his lids. Given what Thea knew of their father's obstinacy, it was going to take a lot of undoing of their bedside remarks before they got any response from the man.

Thea herself did much more talking with the Lion than she did questioning. Even though his responses were sluggish, and she was not always certain he understood her, she brought him up to date on the developments with both Hayley and Hartnett. One of the questions she did ask was whether he felt Amy Musgrave might have been involved along with Hartnett. Petros's answer seemed equivocal.

There had to be a more efficient, reliable method of exchanging information, Thea thought desperately. He just seemed so slow, so worn down.

The highlight of the difficult day was dinner with Dan. Clearly, Hartnett had invited him along to the meeting with him to put her mind at ease. What was a little hard to understand was how he knew about their relationship in the first place. The best Thea could do at tracing the hospital grapevine was that she had mentioned Dan to both Selene and Niko, and had been with him in the cafeteria for several meals as well as in the ER. Then she remembered the nurse, Marlene, in the step-down unit remarking that the two of them had become the topic of hospital gossip.

No matter. He was committed to meeting her outside the MRI suite, which occupied an expansive area off the main tunnel, and to accompany her to hear what

Hartnett had to say, whether it was inside the unit or someplace else.

After dinner, with hours still to spare, Thea wandered down into the tunnels to reconnoiter the MRI suite. She couldn't help but notice the large bronze plaque beside the entrance. The Grigsby Magnetic Resonance Imaging Center, almost certainly built in memory of Warren Grigsby, the late patient of Lydia Thibideau who had died while receiving SU990 in one of her investigational studies.

All but one of the techs had gone home for the day. The one closing up, a cheerful, attractive woman in her thirties named Stephanie, said she was happy to answer any questions Thea might have. She walked her down the corridor, and gestured through the control-room window at the massive electromagnet—a chunky open-ended tube, whose business end faced the control room from ten feet away.

"This is a superconducting magnet," Stephanie said proudly. "Three teslas of magnetic power, although there is a self-screening system built in that keeps the truly powerful magnetism contained to the immediate area surrounding the machine. Believe it or not, the patients inside that tube are surrounded by magnetic coils that are cooled by liquid nitrogen to a temperature of four hundred and fifty degrees below zero."

Four hundred and fifty-two, Thea thought automatically, having just reviewed the system in the library.

"That's amazing," she said.

"A layer of vacuum keeps the cold from reaching them. It's like a giant thermos bottle. It would be impractical and very expensive to shut our magnets down, so we keep them turned on full strength all the time. Ready and waiting."

"That's amazing," Thea said again.

And it was, although the information wasn't at all new to her.

"Well, welcome to the staff, Dr. Sperelakis," the tech said, concluding the brief tour. "Come visit us anytime."

She led Thea out and locked the door behind them.

Thea stayed behind near the Grigsby plaque, and watched as the tech merged with the others in the main tunnel. Her mind was engrossed in wondering why Hartnett had chosen this particular place for their meeting.

It didn't matter, though, she decided, so long as Dan was there with her. Together, they would insist on definitive answers from Hartnett to some very difficult questions—questions that could and should land the chief development officer in prison.

FORTY-EIGHT

At nine thirty, Thea caved in to a crushing fatigue, and after setting the clock radio in her father's office, went to sleep on the leather couch. It would be all over soon, she told herself as she settled in.

All over soon . . .

At twelve thirty she was up and washing her face in the small lavatory off Petros's examining room, feeling refreshed and anxious. She toweled off and swept a brush through her hair. Then she went back to the bookshelves in his office and took down a wonderful photo of her father and mother taken when they were sixty during a visit to the Greek island of Kefalonia, where he was born. The love between them was almost palpable, as was the characteristic arrogance in Petros's stance and the tilt of his head.

That was then. Now . . .

Thea tried without success to blot out intrusive images of the gorgeous man in the photo as he was at this moment, tethered to machines, with nurses tending to his bodily functions, and splints keeping his hands and feet from curling up.

You never know, she found herself thinking. *You never know where it's all going to come to rest.*

Alongside that thought came a mental picture of Petros's Volvo, lying on its roof embedded in the murky bottom of a pond somewhere in Newton.

You never know.

Thea grabbed her bag and hurried down the stairs to the tunnel. Again, the hospital was in deep night mode, with only light foot traffic headed from one building to another, and one maintenance man silently cruising past her on a Segway. It was ten minutes of one when she arrived at the door to the MRI suite. No Dan. No Hartnett. At five of, she was still by herself and getting concerned. She called Dan on his cell and got only a recording. The security office knew only that he was on rounds. Thea turned down their offer to call him on his radio. At two minutes past one, she called both numbers again. This time she got two recordings.

Exactly what had Hartnett said?

Thea's strength was in memorizing the written word. She was surprisingly inept at recalling the details of things that were said to her. Meet me at the MRI suite? . . . Meet me in the MRI suite? . . . Meet me outside the MRI suite? She checked her watch again. Four minutes after.

Where was Dan?

Thea peered through the glass in the hallway door and realized that the light in the outer waiting room was on. She distinctly remembered Stephanie, the MRI tech, turning it off as she left. Tentatively, she tried the door. It was open. Inside, the doorway connecting the waiting room with the inner sanctum of the unit had a small panel of glass at eye level. Through it she could just make out the repetitive flashing of a white light—a strobe of some sort, she thought. Had that been in evidence before? Had Stephanie turned it on before she left? What purpose could it serve?

One-oh-eight.

Thea's pulse was beginning to race. She crossed the waiting room, opened the door with the small glass window, and stepped into the corridor leading past the receptionist's cubicle and changing areas to the control room. Beyond that was the magnet itself. The flashing light intensified, pulsating off the walls of the hallway.

"Dan?"

She said his name out loud, but knew there would be no response.

"Dan?"

Something had happened in the hospital, she thought, an emergency of some sort. He was held up, maybe helping with an out-of-control patient in the ER, someone acutely intoxicated or having a psychotic break. Those sorts of things happened all the time—especially at this hour.

Aside from the eerie, repetitive flash, the carpeted corridor was dark. On highest alert, Thea walked slowly, carefully toward the light, which she now knew for certain was a strobe—a strobe coming from the imaging room itself. A few more steps and she was clear of the corridor and facing the solid door and two observation windows of the magnet chamber.

She gasped at what she saw inside, and raced across to one of the windows.

The massive superconducting magnet, seven or eight feet tall, looked like a spaceship in the rhythmic, silver-white light. The opening of the enormous cylinder—the powerful magnetic epicenter of the device—was directly facing her.

And held in place across the opening, fixed to the magnet by lengths of steel chain that were held in place by enormous magnetic force across his arms, was Scott Hartnett.

The sled used to transport patients into and out of the cylinder had been pushed aside. The development director's shirt had been torn away. His legs were tied together at the ankles, dangling straight down. He was thrashing his head about. His face, illuminated by the disturbing, almost supernatural strobe, was distorted in some way. It took a number of flashes before Thea realized why: there was a broad swatch of tape—silver duct tape, she thought—pulled tightly across his mouth. His eyes were eerily wide as he continued to thrash his head from side to side.

The scene was absolutely terrifying, and all Thea could think of at that moment was getting at the emergency Stop button on the wall, quenching the magnet, and getting Hartnett down. But after reviewing the process earlier in the day, she also feared doing so. Hitting the button would cause the rapid release of supercooled helium gas, which required immediate emergency ventilation to release the gas out of the building. If prepared for insufficiently, profound frostbite, asphyxiation, and death were possibilities. Still, most MRI setups were geared to clear the chamber of all cryogenic gas the moment the Stop button was hit. It was a gamble, but one she was willing to take to free Hartnett.

Halfway between Hartnett and the door, facing away from Thea, was a standard vinyl and metal wheelchair, clearly nonferromagnetic, with the letters MRI painted in white across the backrest.

"Scott, can you hear me?" Thea shouted. "Can you hear me?" There was no change in the man that she could see. It seemed as if he was violently shaking his head no.

No to what? Thea wondered.

The powerful strobe and the scene before her were hypnotic and unsettling, and were making Thea dizzy and slightly queasy. Her thinking felt pressured and unfocused. Was Hartnett hurt? Who had done this to him? With help, would it be possible for him to slip his arms out from under the chains? No, she decided. They actually seemed to be cutting into his skin. The best way, regardless of the cost and inconvenience, was to hit the Stop button.

"Scott!" she called again.

Hartnett's wild thrashing persisted, as did a continuous opening and closing of his hands.

In the control-room window, crisscrossed by fine, metallic wires to block interfering radio waves, Thea could see her own reflection, illuminated repetitively by the strobe like some macabre Times Square advertisement.

All she could think about now was getting Hartnett loose and getting to the bottom of things, including tending to her mounting fears that something might have happened to Dan. She set her watch aside and removed her earrings. Then she quickly scanned herself for anything else metallic, and located the Stop button up on the wall to the right of the magnet. Through the unsettling light, Hartnett could see her. She felt certain of that. His eyes, if anything, were wider.

Comfortable that she had nothing further on that was ferromagnetic, Thea cautiously eased open the door. Something on the floor caught her eye—a pole of some sort from a broom or mop, reaching from the base of the door to the frame at the base of the wheelchair. Slowly, impelled by the inward-opening door and the pole, the chair began rolling toward the magnet. Six feet . . . five feet . . . it began to accelerate . . . four feet . . .

Suddenly, Thea realized that the seat of the chair was not empty, but piled with sharps—all manner of them. At the moment the situation became clear, the chair rolled past the protection of the self-screening apparatus and into the full three-tesla magnetic zone. As one, in a fraction of a second, the dozens of blades and other metallic sharps, including several hatchets, breached the gap from the chair to the magnet, drawn at ferocious speed.

Scott Hartnett's death was instantaneous.

The objects piercing and passing through his body included countless nails, scalpels, needles, razors, knives of different sizes, pins, darts, and several knitting needles. Thea saw the projectiles in frightening detail as they shot through the strobe like missiles, summoned by the gargantuan electromagnet. The blade of one hatchet embedded itself dead center in Hartnett's chest. Blood, spurting from gashes in his neck, arms, and face, was frozen in stop-action by the strobe.

Thea cried out and raced across to the magnet, but there was nothing she could do. Needles and nails and dozens of pins were embedded in Hartnett's face. One of the sharps had cut through almost half of his neck. His head flopped impotently to the left. Blood continued to spurt out briskly from a severed carotid artery, forcing Thea to back away from the magnet.

The strobe, which she could now see was taped below one of the observation windows, was still pulsating, giving the scene a surreal cast that neutralized some of the hideous gore for Thea. The steel chains would be there in place until the magnet was quenched. Despite the horrible evidence before her that the maneuver was futile, she felt she had to turn off the machine.

Unable to take her gaze from the lurid scene, and unaware of the slowly opening chamber door, Thea took a single step toward the Stop button, primed to run if there was a failure in the helium evacuation system. Suddenly, a gloved hand shot out of the darkness behind her, and clamped tightly across her mouth.

FORTY-NINE

"Nicely done, Doctor," the man said. His voice, low-pitched and gravelly, was one she had heard before, in the parking lot of the Sperelakis Institute. "We knew you had it in you. Serves that nasty man right for messing with you. Now, come along quietly. We're headed out the back way."

Thea could tell he was tall, though not as tall as Dan, and strong. She struggled and tried to bite his palm, but his hand easily controlled her as he pulled her through the MRI unit and out an emergency exit. The main entrance to the unit—the Grigsby entrance—was on a spur off the central tunnel. This emergency exit brought them out into an older, less well-maintained, less well-lit portion of that same offshoot.

Thea remembered this area of the tunnels. They were still on B-1, the uppermost underground level, but there was a stone staircase straight ahead, screened off by a padlocked metal accordion gate, that led down to a series of narrower tunnels on the B-2 level, and below that, the true subterranean passageways of B-3. On the B-2 level on either side were storage areas used primarily for older equipment—rolling carts, tray tables, bed frames, and gurneys—all on standby in case of a mass disaster. Farther down the B-2 corridor was a freight elevator made partially of wood, and probably dating back to the time of the father of the modern elevator, Otis, in the 1800s.

Thea shook her head violently, and the man loosened his grip. She had little doubt that he was Gerald Prevoir, who had surprised Dan outside the ICU, and whom Dan had been able to track to a seaside town in Delaware. If she was right, then he was also likely the man who had killed Albert Mendez, Dan's street-smart private eye.

Prevoir was dressed as he had been when Dan stopped him in front of the ICU—in orderly whites. The difference this time was that, from what she could see, his hospital ID seemed to be in perfect order, including the photo and the name Elliot Smolensky.

"No screaming," the man said.

A deep breath, a plea with herself to stay alert and focused, and Thea felt her pulse begin to drop. She was allowed to take a step back. Prevoir was, in fact, tall. He was in his thirties and looked and felt absolutely solid. His jet-black hair was carefully trimmed, and his dark brown eyes were soulless. He wore a diamond ring of several carats on the little finger of his right hand.

"Why did you do that to him?" Thea asked, motioning back toward the MRI suite.

"What else does one do with a liability but get rid of it? That's the very essence of the insurance industry. Liability? Cancel the policy. The simplest rule in all of business—two words that pave the way to riches.

Liability? Cancel. That was Hartnett behind the wheel of that truck, you know."

"I wasn't sure."

"And when he called you about meeting him at the MRI unit, he thought he was baiting a trap for you. Instead, it was us—*we*—who were baiting the trap for him."

"Bravo for you. Who's *we*?"

"Besides, the real question to be asked after such a magnificently imaginative piece of work is not why, but how?"

"I don't care," Thea said. "That was a terrible way to die."

"So would drowning in that car have been."

"I wouldn't know. It didn't happen. Boasting about killing is small and insecure. I watched teenagers do it all the time in Africa."

Prevoir ignored her.

"You see," he went on, "the magnet has very little pull beyond six feet or so, but very intense pull inside four. Make that very, very intense. Hartnett was unconscious with a surgical mask on, and tied to that wheelchair when I brought him down to the MRI room. First I lashed his wrists to the machine with rope, and then I just flipped the chain over his arms from three feet or so, and voila. The magnet did the rest. You should have seen it—a perfect toss. If nobody turns off that magnet, he'll be there for all eternity."

"Where's Dan? You've got him, don't you."

"He's a pretty sharp guy, but I think he was distracted

thinking about hooking up with you at one. That was his undoing."

"I want to see him."

"All in good time, Doctor. All in good time."

"Now!"

"Setting up the wheelchair to roll toward the magnet when you opened the door was sheer genius, don't you agree? All it took was a mop handle—and of course, you."

"If it was genius, you must not have been the one who figured it out."

Without a hint of warning, Prevoir grabbed her hand and twisted it until her wrist was close to snapping. Thea cried out despite her determination not to.

"Watch your mouth!" he snapped, releasing her only after an additional twist.

She glared at him and shook the circulation back into her hand. In that moment, she knew that there was no way in the world that this man was going to let her live. Silently, she prayed that Dan was still alive. It had been foolish of her to set foot inside the MRI suite when he didn't show up at one. She should have known better, although with Prevoir just a few feet away in the darkness, it really wouldn't have made any difference.

Prevoir removed the padlock, which he had apparently left unlocked in the closed position. Then he slid the gate aside, closed it again behind them, replaced the lock from inside, and guided her down the stairs clutching the back of her blouse. The hundred feet leading to the elevator featured a well-worn cement floor and unpainted stone-and-brick walls, heavily caulked over many decades with concrete, and illuminated from overhead by incandescent bulbs. To their right, labeled with a hand-painted white *B*, was a storage hall full to the ceiling with rusting stretchers, and looking as if it might not have been visited in months, if not years.

"The strobe was pure theater, wouldn't you say?" Prevoir was rambling on. "Scary, distracting, hypnotic. Made you curious, huh? Made you not think about that pole."

Thea cursed herself for being sucked in as she had been. *Gullible.* Dan had said he was glad she was gullible.

Nonsense!

She began concentrating on the situation and the man, searching for a way, any way, to get an advantage—to hurt him or, even better, disable him. His arrogance and confidence were her biggest allies. They had almost gotten him caught by Dan outside the ICU. He wore a snub-nosed revolver in a holster beneath his left arm. If she could only get at that. . . .

The narrow corridor was damp and cool, with a distinct odor of mold. Twenty feet or so before the elevator was a second storage area, not nearly as full as the previous one. A white *A* was crudely painted on the wall outside the entrance. Suddenly, from somewhere inside that space, she heard Dan.

"Hello? Anyone out there? Help. Help me. I'm in here."

Thea broke free of Prevoir and rushed into the century-old space. Dan was on his back on a rusting metal gurney, tied in place with clothesline across his chest and ankles. He was naked except for his underwear, and had been badly beaten—especially across the face and the chest. His eyes were swollen, and drying rivulets of blood coursed from both nostrils. His lower lip was split down the center, and both his nipples were macerated and discolored. A pair of pliers resting on the gurney suggested how that was accomplished.

Thea held his face in her hands and kissed the bruises enveloping his eyes.

"Why'd you do this?" she screamed at Prevoir. "Why?"

"Many reasons," Prevoir said calmly. "I needed to know how our friend learned about me, for one."

"Because you were stupid, that's how!" Dan cried hoarsely.

Prevoir, with his hands still gloved, punched him in the face, snapping his head to one side and creating a dense spray of blood and saliva that traveled several feet.

Thea recoiled from the viciousness of the killer's assault. Dan seemed to lose consciousness temporarily, then was exceedingly groggy. In that moment, Thea spied something that impacted her own consciousness, and stuck. It was the opening to a narrow staircase that ran from this level down to B-3, the deepest bowels of the old hospital, three stories below the ground. A prison? An armory? A place of torture? A hiding place for treasure? She could only guess. The stairway was dark and narrow, and from what she could tell, steep. The walls were sheer stone. No railings. If she could

somehow start the killer falling, there would be no
easy way for him to stop.

"I'm losing my patience with both of you. I have
questions that need answers. I either get them from you
or you each get to watch while the other gets hurt. As
you can see, not only am I adept at inflicting pain, I
enjoy it."

Thea cast about Storage Area A for a weapon of
some sort, but saw nothing except the pliers, and Dan's
belt, which was lying on the floor with the rest of his
uniform. He had a heavy flashlight and a nightstick,
but there was no way she could see to get at them.

What about one of the gurneys? Could she shove
one against Prevoir hard enough to do damage or send
him down the stairs? There would certainly be some
irony to that given the way Hartnett had been mur-
dered, but it was doubtful she could get Prevoir in the
right position, and loosen one of the rusty stretchers
without making him aware.

It had to be the pliers.

In the time it would take a neurotypical person to
remember facts in a book she had read a short while
ago, Thea's mind flashed through dozens of varied vol-
umes, looking for some sort of idea, some sort of plan.
What she found herself focusing on was a book called
simply *Rape,* written by a karate man named Jeff De-
Lott. Thea had read it for a women's self-defense course
some years ago.

> The situation may not present itself often,
> but one of the most vulnerable areas of a

person is the backs of their knees. If you can somehow get behind a potential attacker, directly or at an angle, an unexpected block or kick to that area will cause the quadriceps muscles on the other side of the leg reflexively to relax, and the man will go down like a stone, long enough for you to turn if you are still standing, or to scramble to your feet, and run. If the blow is solid enough, count on dropping your attacker a hundred percent of the time. BUT HALF MEASURES WILL AVAIL YOU NOTHING! Your strike must be fearless, powerful, and precise.

Thea saw the words and the accompanying photograph as if they were etched on her mind. She bent over Dan and kissed him again, slipping the pliers into the pocket of her slacks, and testing the ropes that held him, which were not that tight. Dan moaned at her touch, and she thought he nodded, but otherwise he showed little reaction.

Burning for revenge, she approached Gerald Prevoir. The image in her mind was of the coquettes and charmers she had seen in the movies. Although roleplaying had never been one of her strengths, she felt her best chance was to get him off guard and distracted—to say something that would shock him, something seductive. If she tried taking a line from a movie, he might recognize it. Her best chance was just to open her mind and improvise.

"Mr. Prevoir, could I talk to you over here for just a minute?" she asked in a kittenish voice, pulling her shoulders back the way she had done in front of her bedroom mirror before her first evening with Dan.

"I'm running out of patience," he replied, following her to a spot right in front of the stairs. "I want cooperation from you or he's in for an enormous amount of pain."

"Please! Don't hurt him again. I'll tell you what. If you promise not to hurt him anymore, I promise you can have anything you want from me."

"What?"

"I said if you want to, you can have it all. Everything."

She gestured the length of her body for emphasis.

"I heard what you said. I'm just not at all sure I know where you're coming from."

"I'm coming from right here, and you can have me. Right on one of those gurneys if you want. I mean it. Let me just talk with him and I'll answer any questions you have and do anything you want."

She turned toward Dan and glanced back just as the killer looked away from her.

Fearless . . . Powerful . . . Precise.

Thea withdrew the pliers and with all her strength threw them over her shoulder and down the stairway. The clatter echoed off the stone like a Gatling gun. Prevoir whirled to the sound, and was instinctively reaching for his shoulder holster at the moment Thea dove at the backs of his knees like a football blocker. His legs collapsed just as the DeLott book promised they would, and he pitched face-first onto the steeply angled stairs, tumbling down into the darkness like a puppet. The sound of his head hitting the concrete below reverberated up the stairwell.

Then there was silence.

FIFTY

Thea scrambled to her feet, ready to fight, ready to run. The narrow stone stairway was so steep, and the base so enfolded in darkness, that she could see nothing of the man she had just sent tumbling to the bottom. For a few moments, she held her breath and listened. The only sound she could hear was Dan's sonorous breathing coming from behind her. She hurried over to him, ecstatic to share her news.

"Hey, you, big guy, can you hear me? It's over. It's over."

She kissed him softly on the lips and gently took his hand. His body was even more battered than she had first appreciated—especially his nipples—but none of his wounds seemed mortal.

"Dan, it's over, let's get you up and get out of here."

She untied the knots holding him to the gurney and cradled his head, searching for any signs of neurological injury.

"Thea . . ."

The sandpaper word was accompanied by what might have been a grin.

She kissed him on the lips again.

"Oh, I'm so glad you're not dead," she said, as excited

as she could ever remember being. "I would have really missed playing with you. Let's get out of here. This is a very bad place. I'll explain everything on the way to the ER or . . . on the way to get an ice cream if you want. You look like you could use an ice cream."

Dan blinked up at her.

"Where's Prevoir?"

"He had an accident when I pushed him down the stairs over there."

Dan gritted his teeth and tried to pull himself up.

"I want to see."

Thea tested the strength in his hands, then checked his neck for tenderness and, finding nothing of concern, helped him to sit.

"We can come back after someone has had the chance to look you over. After being injured people have a lot of extra adrenaline shooting around that can mask some pretty serious—"

"Thea, he came up behind me and threatened to kill the first three people we saw if I didn't come quietly. Then, down here, he forced his gun inside my mouth and made me strip and lie down here. I need to see for myself what happened to him."

"It's very dark down there."

"I have a flashlight in my belt. Grab it and, just in case, my nightstick, too."

"Promise to let me bandage you up and kiss you where you're hurt?"

"I promise."

Thea retrieved the heavy flashlight and the short,

stubby nightstick, and guided him to the head of the
stairs.

Behind them, in the darkest corner of the storage
area, the figure who had been crouching behind several
carefully placed gurneys lowered his gun, but otherwise remained motionless. He had been there watching
and listening since Prevoir arrived with Dan.

Dan fought to support his weight without help.

"I can't believe I let the bastard do this to me," he
said.

"You had no choice. There were lives at stake."

"Just the same . . ."

At the top of the stairs, there was still no sound from
the darkness below. For the first time, Thea wondered
if perhaps Prevoir had gotten to his feet and continued
along level B-3 to wherever the tunnel went. The passageway down to B-2 had been blocked by a padlocked
gate that the killer had managed to open, just as he had
the doors to the MRI unit. Could he have done the
same to a gate down there in the darkness?

Dan switched on the flashlight, and in seconds they
knew the answer. Gerald Prevoir, his orderly's whites
bright within the gloom, lay motionless on his back at
the base of the stairs, one leg folded awkwardly beneath the other, his arms spread out to each side much
as Scott Hartnett's had been.

Following Dan carefully down the stairs, Thea was
a third of the way down when she noticed the odd
angle of Prevoir's head. They were another third of the
way down when she saw him take a breath, and almost

at the bottom when she realized his eyes were open. Dan shined the light directly into the face of his nemesis. The killer's breathing was labored and shallow, but it was steady. A grunt accompanied each exhale. Aside from the rise and fall of his chest, he displayed no movement whatsoever.

Fracture or dislocation of the fourth cervical vertebra, Thea guessed. *Possibly the fifth.*

Before she could do anything, Dan had reached down and, making no attempt to keep from jostling the man, snatched Prevoir's pistol from its holster and stuffed it into his pants pocket.

"Just in case," he said.

He took a step back and allowed Thea to take his place.

"Can you move at all?" she asked, kneeling beside Prevoir, but careful not to jostle him.

"No," he replied suddenly, his voice weak and rasping. "Can't move . . . at all . . . Neck hurts."

"Don't try to turn your head. It looks like your spinal cord may be damaged. Trying to move your head could just make things worse."

"Kill me."

"What?"

"Don't . . . leave me . . . like this. . . . Shoot me."

Every breath was an effort.

"Who paid you to do this to us?"

"Don't know . . . name. . . . Just met for . . . first time."

"What did you have to do with all this?"

"Can't move . . . Pain . . . Hard to breathe . . . Kill me, please."

"Tell me how you were involved and we'll consider it."

"Negotiated contract . . . with enemies of patients."

Thea stared at the man in disbelief.

"You mean a contract like a Mafia contract? Someone paid to make sure the patients didn't survive their chemotherapy?"

"Yes. . . . Please."

"Dan, these people came into the hospital for diseases they didn't have, and some of them were killed for money in what looked like a reaction to their experimental chemotherapy or to their nonexistent disease. They were all on borrowed time anyway, so no one was that surprised when they died."

"And those who survived gave bunches of money to the Beaumont out of gratitude."

"Exactly," Thea said. "Prevoir, was Hayley Long one of those contracts? Was she supposed to die?"

"Yes. . . . I can't move. . . . Kill me. . . . Kill me. . . ."

"Prevoir, where is she? Where is Hayley Long?"

"Don't know. Van took her away."

"So, which do you think would be worse," Dan asked Thea, "killing him or leaving him?"

Thea didn't answer. She was absorbed in examining the man's laminated hospital ID. It included an employee number that was close to her own and a photograph that looked as if it were taken just hours ago. Something must have been wrong with the ID he had worn the last time he and Dan crossed paths, otherwise Prevoir would have trusted it. Had it been this ID, Prevoir would have had no problem allowing Dan to check it over, and in all likelihood, Petros would be dead.

"Dan, look at this ID," she said. "It's just about perfect—as perfect as my driver's license. You know, I hate what I'm thinking, but I wonder if—"

"You know what?" a familiar man's voice boomed from the stairs above, reverberating down the stairwell. "You were always too smart for your own good, that's what."

Dimitri leaned casually against the ancient wall, a heavy pistol dangling at his side. He was absolutely dashing in a tweed sports coat, slacks, polished shoes, and a dress shirt, and looked like a corporate executive on a holiday. Thea recalled that he hadn't been this neatly dressed at their mother's funeral.

"You know," Thea said, standing and turning to face her brother, "a couple of times I thought briefly that you might have been involved in this business. But each time I decided no. You know why?"

"That cartoon," Dimitri said simply. "The one I made showing why Father's accident couldn't have been accidental. You think you're the only one in this family with an off-the-chart IQ?"

"No, Dimitri, I never ever thought for a moment that I was as smart as you."

"I sent you guys in the right direction by suggesting that the hit-and-run was premeditated. By right direction, I meant away from me, of course. The police say accident, I say murder. How clever is that?"

"He thought he was clever, too," Thea said, gesturing down at Prevoir.

"You were too much for him, sis. Outfoxed him, you did. That you-can-have-anything-you-want bit was magnificent. All he was thinking about was what it might be like making the beast with two backs with you. I swear, he didn't know if he had lost a horse or found a rope. Then *boom*, right behind the knees. Brilliant and tough. A true Sperelakis."

"Dimitri," she said, "I've always been on your side. Please don't hurt us."

"Oh, you don't have to worry about me hurting you—at least not for the moment. I need your help, sis. Yours and the big guy, here. And you know who else needs your help? Your sweet, cancer-free friend, Hayley Long, that's who. Do everything I say and she lives. Cross me and she'll learn what it's like to die—not of cancer, but of dehydration and starvation. First, though, I believe we have a bit of unfinished business. Too bad my little company doesn't have any workman's comp."

Without moving a step, Dimitri raised his pistol to his hip in a line that would take its bullet inches from Thea's cheek, and from twenty feet put a single shot into Gerald Prevoir's forehead, just above the eye.

FIFTY-ONE

"This is never going to work, Dimitri," Dan said.

"That's what they told Columbus, and look at all the places he's got named after him."

It was two thirty, and the trio was headed west to Wellesley on Route 9. Less than a mile away from where they were at that moment, at the bottom of an algae-covered pond, was the Volvo that had so nearly become Thea's tomb.

The three of them had left the hospital through the Sperelakis Institute entrance, and had taken Dan's car. To counter the fact that whatever exit they chose would be monitored, Dan called the security office and got permission to take his sudden migraine headache home to bed.

"Sure, go ahead," the woman covering the office said. "Seems quiet enough around here anyway."

Dimitri had shared very little with them, but he did make it clear that Gerald Prevoir had taken Hayley from the hospital with no problem and had turned her over to him. She was deep underground someplace, he reported now, in a cell with enough food and water to last a week or more, and enough air to keep her going as well, provided Dimitri was of a mind to keep her ventilation system running. The timer controlling the electricity would shut off in precisely ten days. She was to be an insurance policy against Thea or Dan turning on him.

"If anything happens to me," Dimitri had explained, "Ms. Long is worm food. You know I'm willful enough to do it, don't you, sister?"

"Dimitri, please, you need help and I can get it for you," she had replied.

"Aw, isn't that sweet. Let me help you, says the woman who is the reason everything has gotten so flummoxed up—the reason a perfectly decent thief like Scott Hartnett had be dispatched, and a perfectly decent killer like Gerald Prevoir had to beg for his life to be taken. Let me help, indeed. Well, dear sister, you shall get your wish. You will be helping me all the way to my new home."

"What's that supposed to mean?"

"All in good time, sweet Thea. All in good time."

Abutting the wooded land that made up the Sperelakis family estate was a dense forest of some hundred acres, willed to the town many years before as a land preserve. Dimitri directed Dan to take the gravel road cutting through the preserve, and then the dirt drive that ended in the small parking area behind the carriage house. During the trip, Dan twice took Thea's hand and brushed it against the pistol he had taken from Gerald Prevoir.

Thea prayed the moment would never come when he might have to use it. For one thing, as long as Hayley's life was at stake, this was Dimitri's game. And of the many things her eccentric brother did well, playing games of all kinds was what he did best. For another, as far as she knew, the first time Dan had even held a gun since his resignation from the force was when he took Prevoir's. She didn't know him well enough to be able to predict the consequences should he ever be forced to fire one again.

"Okay, everybody out," Dimitri ordered. "We've got flights to check on, money to move, and packing to do. Up the stairs to the loft. After I'm done, you, dear sister, can get packed. If no one causes me problems, I promise to return you to Bostontown safe and sound in time to rescue the fair lady, who will, by then, have become a true damsel in distress."

On the surface, Dimitri was his usual singsong, take-nothing-seriously self, but Thea could tell he was tense. He had to be. His plan seemed to involve travel—perhaps even travel out of the country. To the best of her knowledge, he had rarely been outside of the carriage house, let alone the state of Massachusetts.

Meanwhile, there were many frustrating holes in what she had uncovered regarding the massive scam at the Beaumont—many questions she wanted him to answer, starting with the biggest one.

"Dimitri, was Gerald Prevoir the one who ran Dad down?" she asked as they trudged up the stairs to the carriage house loft.

"You two sit down over there in my conversation pit. No touching."

"Was he?" she asked again.

"No answers so long as your boyfriend keeps looking at me as if I were crazy."

"Are you?" Dan asked.

"Ask my late employee, Mr. Prevoir, how he feels about that subject, or my bankers in Zurich and Grand Cayman."

"I guess that answers my question," Dan said, with venom.

"Please, Dan. Enough! There's nothing to be gained by baiting him."

"Aha," Dimitri said, making some sort of bank transfer on one of his computers. "Nothing like a rousing game of good cop, bad cop. Let me tell you guys something. If you're looking for one of those sessions like in the movies where the bad guy has the drop on the good guy, and then tells all because he's really an egomaniac and is desperate for the good guy's acknowledgment of how inventive and resourceful he is, you're just going to have to wait. But in the interest of sibling solidarity, and getting you to stop playing good cop, bad cop, it was your friend from the MRI suite."

"Hartnett?"

"Himself. He was a clumsy, nervous twit, and worse than that, he was greedy."

"And Dad was figuring out what he was doing."

"Hartnett should have steered clear of the Lion's patients altogether, but he kept going to the well and choosing them, because that's where lots of the money is. Then your father made the same mistake as his lovely daughter did—saying too much to Hartnett. And out of the barn on his gentleman's farm, the same barn where I keep my van and my Ferrari, I might add, comes the truck. Hartnett was always a hands-off kind of guy."

Thea was shaking at her brother's coldness. In all the years she had been around him, she had never seen him so lacking in emotion.

"Why would you do this, Dimitri?" she managed to ask. "Who else is involved?"

"Sit still and stop asking questions, or I'll wind down the timer on Ms. Long's light to fifteen minutes a day. That'd turn her into a bat relying strictly on sonar by the time you return to save her."

"Dimitri, please. Let me get you some help. Wherever you're going will be very hard for you. Any change is hard for you. Why do you think you're so comfortable here?"

Dimitri completed another prolonged set of instant message exchanges, then stalked over to his bureau and threw, more than placed, clothes into a well-worn suitcase that Thea felt certain belonged to their father. Her feeling intensified that her brother was under explosive strain. He was operating without input or support from anyone, and with the knowledge that there would be no returning from wherever he was headed. Whether he admitted it or was even aware of it, he had to be terrified.

But he was also a grenade with the pin halfway out.

"Okay, lady, I think we can head over to the great house and pack a small bag. Just the basics. Subequatorial. We'll have plenty of money to buy whatever we need when we get to where we're going. Plenty. Cotton, I'll send her back with pictures of my new digs and the names of all the servants, so you can look at that measly duplex of yours in West Roxbury and ask who's really the crazy one. That's right, I know about your place and your kid and your resignation from the force and why. Ask my sweet, compliant children here questions"—he gestured to his bank of computers— "get answers. Just be grateful for my sister, because my late employee, Mr. Prevoir, hated that you had been causing him difficulty and compromising his identity, and he was prepared to make things rough for that boy of yours. Very rough."

Thea saw Dan stiffen, and thought he might go for the gun in his pocket then and there.

"Let's go to the house," she said, cutting through the tension as best she could. "I won't take long. There's not very much in there for me to pack anyway."

"We'll come," Dimitri said, motioning them down the broad staircase to the heavy front door. "I know I hold all the cards here, but you, dear sister, head the very short list of the people in the world who are too smart for me to trust."

Dawn had broken in filmy pink streaks as the three walked across to the main house and up to Thea's room at the head of the stairs.

Dimitri was right, she was thinking. As long as he had Hayley, he held all the chips—well, almost all the chips. He wanted to talk. She sensed it in her gut. There were things he desperately wanted to tell her. It was her job to keep him talking, in any way she could. The pot of gold at the end of that rainbow was a hint of any kind as to where Hayley might be imprisoned. Then and only then might their other chip—the gun concealed in Dan's pocket—be of any use.

While Dan and her brother waited outside her bedroom door, she filled the small suitcase she had carried from the Congo, and then took a final look around. With no idea how unstable Dimitri really was, or what he had in store for her, she knew there was a good chance she would not be seeing the room again.

"Okay," she said. "I'm ready. I've got all the shots I need. You all set with shots?"

"Clever," Dimitri said. "Very clever. It so happens I have been preparing for this eventuality for years. The Hayley Long wrinkle I added when I heard you and she had become chums. Like I said, I've never trusted that you wouldn't be trouble. Too many brains tucked up in that little head of yours."

Thea allowed Dan to take her bag, and they stepped outside into what was to be a perfect, cloudless day. Her mind was spinning rapidly through every possibility she could imagine as to where Hayley might be when Dimitri motioned them to a rustic Adirondack love seat in the wooded backyard, and took a single matched chair across from them.

"So, we have a bit of business to attend to," he said, slipping out the pistol with which he had killed Gerald Prevoir. "You, Mr. Cotton, have something in your right pants pocket that it is no longer convenient to me for you to have. Take out that gun you have so lovingly been toting, and toss it over there at the base of that tree."

FIFTY-TWO

"What time do we have to leave?" Thea asked.

"We have a little while."

She was sensing once again that her brother wanted to talk.

Dimitri, his pistol resting in his lap, rubbed at his eyes.

Sitting next to Dan, across from Dimitri, she wondered when he had last had any real sleep. It might have been fatigue, or what she had said to him about his being vulnerable to the stress of leaving home, but it seemed as if some of his trademark flippancy—some of his bravado—had dissipated. As ordered, Dan had tossed his gun against the base of a massive oak tree about ten feet away, but still Dimitri seemed tense.

"You know," Dan said, "except for your man Prevoir, you haven't directly killed anyone as far as I know, and Prevoir was severely damaged goods. Besides, it could just as easily have been one of us shooting in self-defense. I have friends on the force. And—"

"Enough! The one inexcusable sin you can commit around here is to talk to me as if I were some kind of dolt. On my very worst day, my brain could wrap itself around yours and wring it dry. You know, Thea, it's none of my business, but I really think you could do a lot better than this guy here."

"Actually, I think he's pretty terrific." She squeezed Dan's hand and gave her brother time for a rebuttal, but he simply sat in the chair that was their father's favorite, nudging at an acorn with his foot and looking amazingly like the man. "How did this happen, Dimitri?" she asked finally. "How did you get involved with Hartnett in this scheme?"

There was clearly less arrogance in Dimitri's tone when he replied. In fact, he sounded more direct, more human, than she could remember—except for his remark to Dan about needing to tell his son he loved him before putting limits on the boy's use of certain computer games. It was as if he had something to say, and wanted to ensure he was taken seriously.

"Actually, I wasn't involved with Hartnett," he began. "Hartnett was involved with me. When they were developing Thor, that's the Beaumont's system of electronic medical records, Hartnett knew me and put me on a retainer as a troubleshooter. And believe me, there was plenty of trouble. Before long several of the IT people had told him that the whole program would have crashed had it not been for me. He increased my hours and took me around to see some of the private doctors in action. What an education that was."

"I think I can see what's coming," Thea said.

"What I saw, watching doctor after doctor sitting glued to their computer screens and making almost no eye-to-eye contact with their patients, gave me an idea."

"Go on, please. In addition to making little eye contact with their patients, the doctors only communicated with one another through their computers, right?"

"Consultations, pathology reports, surgical notes, lab results. Because of the pressure put on them by the managed care and insurance companies, nobody had the time to communicate person-to-person with anyone. Not exactly your old horse-and-buggy house calls."

"And with your skill, everything that's written in a computer database is—"

"Like a palette of paints to an artiste, or raw chicken to a gourmet chef. You got it."

"Hartnett provided the medicine, you provided the IT."

"Actually, sister, not to belittle your profession, but it really ain't that hard. I read Harrison's internal medicine text and did some other studying. Most of medicine is pretty routine."

"I'll agree with you there. Of course, it does help to have, like, a hundred and eighty IQ."

"Aw, you flatter me. Hear that, Cotton? A hundred and eighty. What's your number?"

"No idea. I always thought it was as high as it needed to be. I know my football jersey number, though, eighty-nine. You ever play football, Dimitri?"

"Don't goad me. I warned you once about doing that. Twice is my limit. The third time, I blow. Ask your friend Thea, there, what happens when I blow."

"Leave him alone, Dan. I was always scared to death of him when he lost his temper. Then again, there were a lot of people who were pretty scared when I lost mine, too. Dimitri, Prevoir told us about the other patients—ones that you got paid to—"

"You know, I thought when I got to the head of the stairs back there in the hospital, that was what he was talking about, but I wasn't close enough to hear. Bad Gerald. I suppose you believe him."

"I do, yes. Are there reasons I shouldn't?"

"Well, probably not. Hartnett and I were each taking a finder's fee off the donations that people like Jack Kalishar made to the hospital, but as I said, Hartnett was greedy. Okay, okay, I'm greedy, too. When I presented my little variation on a theme to him, he jumped at it, so we hired Prevoir to be our middleman."

At her brother's admission, Thea felt a deep sadness wash over her. During their time growing up in this home, there was a distance between the twins and her that widened as the years passed. In school they had popularity just for being attractive and being twins. That they were bright and able only heightened their celebrity and increased their annoyance with their odd little sister. They were successful, but they were uninteresting. They were skilled, yet totally self-centered. They always won, but they were terrible winners.

Dimitri was different.

All his life that she could remember, he had been zany and unpredictable, obstinate and incorrigible. But he was also approachable and funny, self-deprecating and egomaniacal. And despite the nearly twelve-year difference in their ages, he taught her things and shared secrets with her at almost every level of her life.

"Why would you do that, Dimitri?" she asked, knowing the answer, perhaps, even more clearly than did the man himself. "How could you?"

"Boredom," Dimitri replied lightly. "It's like the age-old question: Why does a dog lick his genitals? Answer: Because he can. It was a challenge to research our subjects and to choose enemies who might be willing to part with a large sum of money in exchange for jealousy, or revenge, or more power, or pure greed, or . . . or because they could. If I had lasted in that community college longer than the month or so I did, I would have made a hell of a psychologist. I'm proud to say that almost one hundred percent of those I researched and ultimately approached said yes to making a deal with us. Two million, three, five—we operated on a sliding scale."

"How did you manage to switch the MRIs around?"

"I didn't say our little operation didn't take some work and some patience. We mostly got our patients from the Executive Health Program at the Beaumont. They think they're doing their clients a favor with their detailed history and all those tests. The one they're doing a favor for is me. Information. In my world, it's all about information. Then it was just a matter of monitoring their physician's electronic medical records and making the switch when I saw a useful test result coming. Anything that pops up on a doctor's screen is gospel. It's like, look at that cute little computer. Would it ever lie to me?"

"But what about Hayley?" Thea felt pleased at seamlessly working the woman into their exchange. The more they talked about her, the more chance there was that Dimitri might slip. "She had her test done in Atlanta."

"She could have had it done in South Africa or Bora Bora. The Internet is the Internet. Dr. Stephen Bibby, Rhoads Terrace Professional Building, Atlanta. I hacked his system—it was a piece of cake, incidentally—and monitored every test he ordered on Lady Long, waiting for one that fit with what we had in the library. It actually took most of a year before I learned that an abdominal MRI was ordered and moved to intercept it. Forty-eight-year-old woman, one hundred thirty to one hundred sixty pounds, no prior surgery, no fractures. Finding a match in my rather extensive library of films wasn't that hard. MRIs are like looking at an anatomy text. I've actually become quite good at reading them."

"So you showed me. The woman you chose to replace Hayley had calcifications in some of her abdominal lymph nodes, though, that Hayley didn't have."

"Nice pickup. I won't miss those next time."

"I can't believe no one caught on to this."

"We see what we wish to see, dear sister. Lydia Thibideau is spread way too thin building her pancreatic-cancer empire. She sees the cancer and ho-hum, enrolls the patient in one of her studies, and then pads back to her stately office to apply for another research grant."

Thea shook her head in utter amazement. This wasn't her quirky, outrageous, unfocused brother speaking. This was a violin virtuoso, a batter capable of hitting a home run almost every time at bat. This was a man who could have changed the world. If only . . .

"You are the master, Dimitri," Dan said. "I am genuinely impressed."

There was no hint of cynicism in his voice.

"Thanks," Dimitri replied. "I'm pretty impressed myself."

"Dimitri," Thea said, "boredom may have been a factor in what you did, but I think I know now what was really driving you, and I don't think you're being completely honest about what your real intention was."

For nearly a minute the only sounds were the songs of morning birds in the dense New England woods.

"I hated him," Dimitri said suddenly.

FIFTY-THREE

"I hated him more than anyone could ever imagine."

Aching for him—for all of Petros's children—Thea stared across at her brother, then stood and took several tentative steps toward him. He stopped her with a flick of his gun barrel, then rose and backed away, his arms extended, hands warning her.

"Dimitri—"

"I don't need your pity or your understanding or your sympathy."

"Dimitri, Petros didn't know the first thing about parenting, let alone parenting children with special needs."

"The things he said to me. The pain he caused me not by violence, not by hitting me, but by ignoring me. He gave up on me. From the very beginning because I was different, he gave up on me."

Thea made no attempt to stem her tears.

"Dimitri, all he knew was what he got from his parents. He raised us the way he was raised. That was the best he could do. Think of how bad it would have been for us without Mom."

"It was bad *with* her, at least for me it was. Listen, people came from all over the world to get a second opinion from your father," he went on, marginally calmer. "They named an institute after him. The Petros Sperelakis Fucking Institute of Fucking Diagnostic Medicine. Maybe I didn't have Asperger syndrome like you did, but then again, maybe I did. Your father never made any effort to find out."

"Dimitri, he's an internist, not a psychiatrist."

"He was a doctor, just like you are. He could tell when someone wasn't right—when they needed a diagnosis, when they needed help. He knew enough to understand that something exists from a person's neck on up."

"I'm . . . I'm sorry, Dimitri."

"The great Dr. Second Opinion never made any effort to get me diagnosed and treated. And by the time I understood what had happened, it was way, way too late. I hate him more than anyone could ever imagine. It gave me joy every time I did something to disrupt his little empire. The worst thing that ever happened to me was when he started asking questions about why so many patients were being cured so easily. That's why I had to . . ."

His voice trailed away and he stared down at the gun in his hand.

"Oh, no, Dimitri," Thea groaned. "No! You're the one who ran Petros down, not Hartnett."

"And I was thrilled he ended up the way he did—at least until you came home I was."

Dimitri's gun hand had begun to shake. His lips were tight and bloodless.

"You didn't hate him," Thea said. "You were afraid of him. All of us were."

"Don't psychoanalyze me! I hated him. He deserved everything he's gotten."

"Were you the one who tried to kill me, too?"

"No. Hartnett never told me he was going to do that or I would have stopped him—at least I think I would have. Now, let's get going. We have a plane to catch."

"No! I'm not going."

"The hell you're not. You mess with me and she's dead, Thea. Surely you've heard enough to know I'll go through with that. What do I have to lose?"

"So tell me the truth, Dimitri, if you can. You have a deal with someone about Hayley, don't you?"

Dimitri shrugged matter-of-factly.

"There's a fellow named Gregory Rose who's willing to part with a good deal of money—although not to him, it isn't—to keep her from causing him trouble anymore. Is that what you mean?"

"You know that's exactly what I mean."

"Yeah? Then why did you screw that arrangement up, too, by talking her out of continuing her treatment? Too bad. According to her medical record, which I happen to have on file up there"—he gestured to the carriage house—"she has a wicked penicillin allergy, and I was about to arrange for her next chemo treatment to contain enough penicillin to cure every case of strep throat on the East Coast. Whammo! Can you imagine it? The mother of all anaphylactic reactions. Lydia Thibideau's chemo agent would have gotten all the blame, and I would have gotten all the cash."

"Oh, Dimitri. You never did plan to let her live, did you?"

"You'll just have to trust that I have decided to re-turn the down payment and let her live. Disrupting Petros's world just isn't as much fun anymore. Besides, no one would ever be able to find sweet Ms. Long to validate the kill."

"I don't trust anything you say. Dimitri, I love you. You're my big brother. But you've done some bad things—some very bad things. You're not well and you need help. Just put the gun down and tell me where Hayley is. Please don't let anything happen to her. She's a very good person. There are people who can help you—meds you can take. Please."

"I don't need your kind of help. I-I'm upright and leaving the country, and he's a vegetable. Don't tell me I need help. Now, if you want your friend to live, you'll come with me. So long as you cooperate, you have my word that Ms. Long will stay alive and well in her for-tress of solitude."

Fortress of solitude.

The words resonated in Thea's mind. Superman had referred to his secret arctic ice palace by that name, but there was something else. . . . *Something else.*

"Shit!" Dimitri exclaimed at the instant Thea con-nected with the significance of the phrase.

"I know, Dan!" she cried out. "I know where she is!"

Muttering more obscenities, Dimitri grabbed her by the hair and pulled her toward the carriage house.

At the same instant, through the corner of her eye, Thea saw Dan dive from the love seat and roll toward the gun he had tossed aside.

She went absolutely limp and dropped to the ground,

but Dimitri grasped the collar of her blouse and continued dragging her toward the door.

"Don't hurt him, Dan!" she screamed. "Please don't hurt him!"

Dimitri kept his grip on her and turned long enough to fire off two shots at Dan. Both missed badly, sending up jets of dirt and pine needles.

By the time Dan reached his gun, Dimitri had shoved Thea into the carriage house and closed the massive door with his foot.

"Dimitri, please," Thea begged. "It's senseless now. I know where Hayley is. I remember about the fortress of solitude. Please let me help you."

"Up!" Dimitri snarled, dragging her up the stairs.

"No!"

Halfway up to his loft, Thea pulled free of his grip and rolled over against the ornate balustrade. Dimitri looked down at her, and for a moment she felt certain he was going to shoot her point-blank. He was wild-eyed—confused and absolutely frantic. This was not a puzzle he could reason out. This was not a malfunctioning computer, or a predictable video game. The variables in this scenario were changing too fast, and Thea knew that his lack of flexibility was being strained past the breaking point as he struggled to keep up.

"Dimitri, stop!" she cried as he reached the top of the staircase.

At that instant, the massive front door burst open, and Dan dove in and rolled, coming to rest in a prone shooting position, his gun pointing up the staircase.

Dimitri fired twice, splintering the floor a foot from Dan's face.

Dan scrambled behind the door. He was now shielded and his line of fire was well clear of Thea.

"Put down the gun, Dimitri," Dan called out. "Let us get you some help."

"You should have just stayed with me, Thea," Dimitri said, tears streaming down both cheeks. "You should have just come to Brazil with me and helped me get settled in a new place. I would have told you. I would have told you where she was."

It was the first time Thea had ever seen him cry. She pulled herself to her feet and reached a hand out to him. Below her, Dan had moved to the base of the stairs. He had no cover, and his gun was fixed on Dimitri's chest, but still he didn't fire.

"Dimitri, it's over," Thea said softly. "It's over."

"You're right about that," he managed. "You could have helped me, Thea. It wouldn't have been so hard. You could have gone with me and helped me get set up. New places can be scary, you know."

With that he whirled and sprinted to his right, into his sleeping area. A moment later, before Thea could reach the top of the stairs, there was a single gunshot.

She cried out and ran to him. Dimitri was on his back, his head turned to one side, the pistol still in his mouth. The back of his skull had blown open. On the pillow beneath him was an expanding disc of blood. His eyes were peacefully closed. Beside him, resting beneath his hand, was a ragged, filthy stuffed animal—a lion no more than eight inches high, with most of its mane and the tuft at the end of its tail still largely intact. From her earliest memories, Thea had associated the animal—Rex, she clearly remembered—with her brother, but she had no memory of seeing it with him since he began living in the carriage house, maybe twenty years ago.

A lion.

Thea knelt beside him and gently moved the gun aside.

"Oh, Dimitri," she said, making no attempt to wipe her own tears, "oh, baby, I am so sorry."

Dan moved behind her and set his hands on her shoulders.

"He missed me on purpose, Thea," he said. "He was a terrific marksman. You saw the shot he made in the hospital. He could have put me away with every shot he made. He wanted me to kill him. He wanted me to end it."

"But you didn't."

"I could have, but I could see in his eyes that he wasn't going to shoot me. I knew it in my heart. That look wasn't there in Patrick Suggs's eyes, Thea. I know now I would have seen it if it was."

Thea stood and buried her face against his chest.

"She's right below us, Dan," she said. "Right down there. I couldn't have been more than six or seven when Dimitri told me about a tunnel he was digging in the basement of the carriage house with a secret door. He said no one knew about it, and no one would ever find it, and that it was going to go way underground to a room he would call his fortress of solitude, just like Superman. He kept the basement locked. I never saw the door or the tunnel or the room, and he never mentioned it again. But the moment he said the words just now, we both knew I remembered."

"Well, let's go get her," Dan said. "I suspect she'll know how to deal with the man who took out a contract on her, and I also think she'll be happy to learn that her cancer is cured."

EPILOGUE

At 10 A.M. on the first day of summer, Thea eased her three-year-old Volvo sedan to a stop in front of the elegant Point of Pines chronic care facility. She left her bouquet of wildflowers on the seat and entered the spacious, comfortable foyer. For her wedding, she was wearing a surprise gift from Dan—a bright red and brown African kente skirt and a white peasant blouse, both bought in an import store in Cambridge. Dan, headed with his son, Josh, toward the ocean-side park where the small ceremony would take place, had looked beyond handsome in his white morning coat and trousers, with a heavy necklace of Mauritanian amber beads replacing a tie.

Petros was essentially as he had been for the ten months since awakening from the hit-and-run. He had gotten back movement in his right eye, and strengthened the movement in his left, but in all other respects, he remained totally locked-in. Private nurses and regular physical therapy had kept him in as good physical shape as possible, but Thea had now reluctantly joined her brother and sister in believing there would be little in the way of further recovery.

They had not told Petros about Dimitri's responsibil-

ity for the hit-and-run accident, or his subsequent tragic
end, and as far as they knew, the Lion still believed his
oldest child was alive.

Thea greeted her father with a kiss on the forehead,
while making the now customary survey of his status
and the settings on his ventilator. His pulse felt marginally less forceful than it had been three days ago, although his heart rate was up from sixty to seventy-six.
She used the nurse's stethoscope and thought she heard
some slight evidence of fluid in his lungs—early pneumonia versus increasing heart failure. She would stop
back later in the evening to check things over again.
Returning the stethoscope, she sent the nurse out of
the room. Then she moved to a spot in Petros's line of
sight.

"Dad, today's the wedding. Two blinks if you
understand. . . . Good. I'm very excited. We're getting
married at World's End in Hingham, on a little hill
overlooking the ocean. Remember when you took us
for walks there? That's why we chose the place. There'll
be about twenty or twenty-five friends and family there,
that's all. Then, next Saturday, my friend Hayley—the
one I told you about whose life you helped save—is
sending us away for a week on her boat. It has a captain
and crew, including a chef. I wonder if he'll be willing
to make me macaroni and cheese.

"So, I just wanted to stop by to tell you how happy I
am to have found Dan, and to thank you for everything
you've done for me over the years. I know with Mom
passing when she did, it hasn't been so easy for you.

Two blinks if you got all that. . . . Good. Oh, I almost forgot. This blue scarf I'm wearing was hers. That's my something blue. And this ring belonged to Dan's mother. That's my something old, and this African dress from Dan is something new. . . . Well, it's time. Keep checking the clock up there. At precisely two o'clock you'll know your kid is married. *S'agapo, Mpampa.* I love you, Dad."

Thea kissed her father, then returned to the Volvo. On the passenger seat, beside her corsage of wildflowers, was a white velvet purse. Inside the purse was her something borrowed—a small tattered stuffed lion with the mane and tail tip almost intact.

At 3 P.M. that afternoon, in Room 110 of the Point of Pines, the chest pain Petros Sperelakis had been experiencing on and off all day intensified beneath his breastbone and began radiating up into his jaw and down his left arm. He had been experiencing the crushing sensation on and off all day, since an hour before Thea's arrival. Now, it had gone from a five out of ten in severity to an eight, maybe a nine.

It didn't matter.

I'm ready, he thought. *My child says she loves me, and I know she does. She's a good doctor. No, a great doctor. S'agapo, Alethea. I love you. Your father loves you.*

For several seconds, the pain intensified to a ten. Then, suddenly, there was none.

AUTHOR'S NOTE

Fourteen years ago, my wife and I sat numbly in the office of a child development specialist and listened to him tell us that our beautiful four-year-old son had Asperger syndrome, a form of autism. He said much, much more, but as you might suspect, the only word we really heard that day was *autism*.

We did not know it at the time, but we were on the edge of what was about to be an explosion in the field of so-called autism spectrum disorders, as well as an alphabet soup of related diagnoses such as ADD (attention deficit disorder), ADHD (attention deficit hyperactivity disorder), PDD (pervasive developmental disorder), PDD-NOS (not otherwise specified), NVLD (non-verbal learning disabilities), and others.

Now, after years of groups, therapies too numerous to mention here, specialists, and intense parental involvement, Luke is a witty, creative, sensitive, kind, insightful, and utterly interesting young man who has been a joy to be around and who has a boundless future. There are and always will be situations that are challenging for him, but the same is true for all of us.

Having raised the issue of adult Asperger syndrome in this novel, I want to answer some questions for those who are interested in learning more. To that end I have enlisted the help of the wonderful Dania Jekel, executive director of the Asperger's Association of New England, and the talented, dedicated Nomi Kaim, also from that office.

The brief answers presented here are just the tip of the iceberg of our knowledge, but hopefully they are a door to further discussion.

1. Is there really an epidemic increase in Asperger's cases and other forms of autism?

Although Asperger syndrome was first written about in the 1940s, it did not gain widespread recognition until the mid-1990s. Since then, diagnoses of AS have been rapidly on the rise. However, as of 2008, not enough data exists to reliably determine whether the incidence of AS itself is increasing or the diagnosis is being given to people who were formerly left undiagnosed or were misdiagnosed with psychiatric, behavioral, or emotional problems.

2. What are the core traits of people with AS?

The unusual neurological profile of the AS individual can afford him or her unique perspective on the world. Many have extreme talents and skills strengthened by intense, focused interests in such diverse areas as mathematics, literature, music, engineering, astronomy, or meteorology. Most people with AS score in the normal-to-high IQ range and are very systematic and attentive to detail. Unfortunately, some of the challenges faced by people with this condition are vital to modern-day society. These areas of challenge include social communication (the appropriate use of language in social situations), social conventions (understanding others' intent), executive functioning (ability to anticipate outcomes and adapt to changing situations), sensory sensitivities, and frequent anxiety and depression. As a result, many people with AS feel alienated from peers and have difficulty connecting with others.

3. Why is the condition "lumped" in with autism?

Because AS shares some of the core traits of autism (although they may be expressed differently), and because the two may occur within the same extended family, AS is generally considered to lie on the "autism spectrum."

Both AS and autism involve a neurobiological difference in how sensory information is processed and integrated.

4. Why do people with AS differ so much from one another?

People with AS are all very different from one another. Some, like Thea, are very successful in their careers and friendships, and use their special interests and strong memories to their advantage. For others, like Dimitri, getting through each day (or even out of the house) is a significant struggle. AS, like autism, exists along a continuum or spectrum. Moreover, each of the many traits that characterize AS has its own spectrum. So, a person with AS may have more or less social difficulty, more or less sensory sensitivity, more or less rigidity or organizational trouble, and so forth. The manifestations of AS are always layered upon the underlying genetics and personalities of the affected individual.

5. What does it mean that AS is a developmental disability?

Every person with AS is developmentally delayed—not intellectually, but on the social-emotional level. This delay can be significant. For example, a twenty-one-year-old may be socially and emotionally more like a fourteen-year-old. In childhood, the delay becomes particularly conspicuous during middle school and high school, when clear social expectations and friendship groups arise among children, and children with AS become more and more likely to be excluded and not fit in. Adults, however, have greater ability to choose their own social groups and lifestyles and are thus freer to find the place where they belong. Adults with AS often continue to grow and develop throughout their lifetime.

6. What causes AS?

The etiology of AS is not yet completely understood. Many believe that environmental factors, toxic exposures, and vaccinations are causative, although to date results of scientifically designed studies have not supported these hypotheses. We do know that there is a significant genetic component: AS and AS traits are seen within many immediate and extended family members of AS individuals. Also, studies of identical twins raised together—one with AS and one without—

suggest some additional factor or factors as yet unidentified.

7. Is AS manifested differently in women?

Many women with AS appear to have greater success than men in blending in socially and generally managing their social environments. The reason for this common dichotomy is unclear. It could be related to biological or cultural differences in the roles of women as compared to men. Their greater social competence may cause some women to "pass under the radar" and not get diagnosed when their male counterparts do, and this in turn may account for why four times as many men as women are diagnosed with AS.

8. People with AS are so verbal, what is their problem with language?

Many people with AS have complex vocabularies and sophisticated speech, but using language to communicate, also called pragmatics, is a different matter. The rules of everyday conversation that come intuitively to most people have to be actively learned by individuals with AS. Difficulties arise in two spheres. First, people with AS generally do not notice—or notice but misinterpret—the nonverbal aspects of what other people are communicating to them, including facial and vocal expression, body language, gestures, volume, pauses, and so forth. Instead, those with AS miss the context and hear only the words that are spoken. The second sphere includes difficulties in areas of expressive communication such as filtering thoughts before they are spoken and socializing for the sake of inter-personal connection rather than for conveying infor-mation. Making "small talk" and talking on the phone are often a challenge to individuals with AS.

9. To what extent do sensory issues impact daily functioning of someone with AS?

A percentage of people with AS are either hyper- or hypo-sensitive to such stimuli as touch, sound, taste, and visual cues (like bright light). There is significant variation among individuals for this trait, often called sensory defensiveness. Some with AS are affected only a little, while for others seemingly normal sensory stimuli can throw up significant barriers to living in the world. Sensory defensiveness tends to be most severe in young children and often lessens over time; some individuals are much improved by adulthood. Thus, a child who cuts tags out of his clothing or re-fuses to eat certain foods may have a much easier time as he grows older.

10. Can AS be cured?

There is no cure for Asperger syndrome. However, over time, the profile of a person with AS may change. Like Thea, the individual often acquires social skills that before were elusive. With time and practice, other troubling traits can be compensated for as well. People with AS can use their many strengths to their advan-tage as they seek out, and often find, the most construc-tive environment to match their strengths and interests, and also one where their vulnerabilities are considered acceptable.

11. Is everyone with Asperger's a genius with data or information?

No. Most, but not all, individuals with AS do have some area of exceptional talent or ability, but that area is not always information. People with AS can excel in ideas, in creative, artistic, or technological abilities, or even in intuitive abilities. Some, like Dimitri, have multiple areas of talent (Dimitri excels in information, technology, visual/spatial ability, and intuitive ability). The IQs of individuals with AS can range from 70 to genius.

12. Are all people with AS avid readers with outstanding rote or verbatim memories for what they read?

No. Some read everything they can get their hands on; others do not. Verbal memory is generally strong in the Asperger's population, but only a minority have the ability to recall verbatim what they have read.

13. Do all people with AS have superior visualization powers or photographic memories?

No. A percentage of people with AS possess the ability to recall visual scenes in great detail, often after seeing them only once, and a considerable time after seeing them. Moreover, some recall specific episodes from their lives in early childhood or even infancy. The

Asperger's tendency to notice and focus on details no doubt contributes to this ability. On the other hand, it is common for AS individuals—even those with superior visualization powers—to have difficulty remembering faces.

14. Do people with Asperger's have feelings or not? How do they differ from those of people without AS?
People with AS do absolutely have feelings, although they may have difficulty identifying and discussing them. In fact, many feelings, such as fear, anger, and joy, seem to be experienced more intensely by those with AS than by average people. In addition, some individuals with AS report that they can incorporate others' feelings, so that if someone else is upset, they themselves will quickly become upset as well. This intriguing empathy appears to happen more with AS than in the general population. People with AS may not show their feelings in the same way, or to the same extent, as others. There may be less outward manifestation of feelings, or facial expressions might not match what the individual is feeling inside.

Like many traits among individuals with AS, the capacity to experience empathy lies on a continuum; some have it more than others. There is also variation in the way empathy is felt and expressed. Some people come to empathy through an intellectual process, using logic and reasoning to arrive at the feeling. For unknown reasons, it is particularly common for people with AS to feel a deep concern for global humanity.

Thea's comfort in her choice to work for Doctors Without Borders is an example of this trait.

15. Why does Thea sometimes insult people or say the wrong thing, but so often says the right thing and act very intelligently?

Like many people with AS, Thea has certain interpersonal vulnerabilities that rise to the surface when things get most stressful. She has difficulty with theory of mind—anticipating what other people are thinking and feeling and how they will react to her. She is quite literal and misinterprets language quite a bit. She sometimes doesn't understand unwritten social conventions and expectations, such as when she declines to see her father alone because he'd "still be in a coma." She also has gaps in her cognitive filter, sometimes saying things that should have been kept in check.

All of these things are harder for Thea to manage when she is stressed, such as when she is around the twins or certain hospital personnel. On the other hand, when Thea is calm and comfortable, such as when she is with Dan, her weaknesses diminish significantly and her intellect, wit, and encyclopedic knowledge serve to her advantage.

16. Is Thea and Dan's relationship typical for AS?

The relationship is not particularly typical. Except in the stylized, telescoped world of the novel, it is quite rare for individuals with AS to fall in love so quickly and easily. However, love, dating, long-term relationships, and marriage do certainly play a role in the lives of many with AS. While dating presents challenges, and some may decide that intimate relationships are too much for them, other individuals with AS simply take on the relationship challenge later in life (in their thirties, or even later). Sexual orientation is as varied in people with AS as in the general population, although there may be a higher incidence of asexuality, homosexuality, and sexual role confusion among those with AS. The overall success of an Asperger's partnership depends in part on the choice of partner. The most compatible partnerships are often between two people with AS or an individual with AS and one with AS traits.

—M.S.P.

Read on for an excerpt from
Michael Palmer's next book

THE LAST SURGEON

Coming soon in hardcover from St. Martin's Press

"I know you can't believe this is happening, Ms. Coates, but I assure you it is. I have been paid and paid very well to kill you."

Belle Coates looked up at the intruder through a glaze of tears.

"Please. Just tell me what you want," she said. "Just tell me what you want and you can have it. Anything. Anything at all."

The man sighed.

"You're not paying attention, Ms. Coates," he said with the accentuated patience of a third-grade teacher. "I am not here to bargain. I told you that. I'm here because this is what I get paid to do."

"But why? Why me?"

Belle made yet another futile attempt to stand. Her wrists and ankles were lashed to her kitchen chair by the sort of Velcro restraints she and other hospital nurses used so often on difficult patients.

"Those restraints look amazingly simple," the intruder said, "but I tell you they are a marvel of engineering and ergonomics. No pain, no marks. None at all. That's why I have a dozen or so sets of them in the drawer at home."

The man, six feet tall and wiry, had been hidden inside Belle's apartment, probably behind the couch in the living room, when she arrived home at nearly midnight. Her nursing shift—three-to-eleven in the cardiac surgery ICU at the Central Charlotte Medical Center— had been a tough one, and she had relished every stair of the trudge that brought her closer to her apartment, a cup of tea, and a steamy shower.

She was just choosing a tea when he appeared in the doorway of her kitchen, an apparition in sky-blue surgical hair and feet covers, latex gloves, black jeans, and a black long-sleeved T-shirt. She was so fixated on his appearance that it was several seconds before she noticed the huge, gleaming knife dangling at his side. Her hesitation was more than enough. In two quick strides he was beside her, seizing a handful of her hair, snapping her head back, and pressing the blade against her throat. With just enough restraint to keep from drawing blood, he forced her down onto one of the oak chairs she had recently refinished, and in moments, the restraints were on her. It had happened that fast.

A dozen or so sets in my drawer.

The statement was as terrifying as the knife.

Was he a serial rapist? A psychotic killer? Desperately, searching for even the smallest inroad to understand the intruder, Belle tried to remain calm and remember if she had read about such a man in the papers, or heard about him on the news.

"What do you want?" she said. "My fiancé will be home any minute."

He fixed her with pale, translucent blue eyes that were devoid of even the slightest spark of humanity.

"I don't think so. We both know about your failed engagement. 'Celebrate Belle and Doug's love.' I'm very sorry about that."

Belle froze at the words, quoted from her wedding invitation.

"Who are you?" she managed again. "What do you want from me?"

"Now we're getting someplace." The man produced a vial from his pocket and set it on the table. "I want you to swallow these sleeping pills I found in your medicine cabinet the last time I was here. I have augmented what was there with some that I brought with me tonight, so there will be more than enough to achieve our goal. But before you take these pills, I want you to copy and sign a brief note I have composed explaining your despondency and your desire not to live anymore. And finally, I want you to undress, step into your tub, and go to sleep. See? Simple and absolutely painless."

Belle felt her breathing stop. This couldn't be happening. She wouldn't do it. He wouldn't be able to pry her jaws apart with a crowbar. She began to hyperventilate and shake, grabbing and releasing the arms of her chair.

"I won't do it."

"You will."

"I won't!" she began screaming. "I won't! I won't! Help! Someone help m—!"

Her words were cut off by exquisite pressure around

her throat. A hard rubber ball was forced expertly between her teeth and into her mouth. The killer remained absolutely calm during the insertion.

"That was stupid, Ms. Coates. Do anything stupid again, and you will be responsible for causing both yourself and your sister a great deal of pain."

Belle stared up at him, wide-eyed. The mention of her sister was a dagger. Hyperventilating through her nose, she still could not seem to get in enough air.

"That's right," the man said. "I know all about Jillian. Just like I know all about you. Now, refuse to do exactly as I say, try anything stupid again, and I promise, both you and Jillian will die prolonged and painful deaths. Understand? I said, do you understand?" Belle nodded vigorously. "I'm still not certain you do. Now, listen, Ms. Coates, and for your sister's sake, believe me. I have no contract to kill Jillian—only you. And with very rare exceptions, those I am not paid to kill, I don't kill."

He took out his mobile phone, made a gentle tap on the screen's touch display, and held it up for Belle to see.

"I assume you recognize your sister's condo in Virginia—Arlington, to be exact, four-eighty-nine Bristol Court to be even more exact. Nod if you agree that is the case. Good. I know how close you two are. You see, I read your journal, or diary, including entries from the trip to Nassau that Jillian took you on after you learned about Doug's, how shall I say, dalliance with your friend Margo. Surgeons. They are just so full of themselves, aren't they? I see you are having a little trouble breathing. Okay, here's the deal: I'll remove

hat ball if I get your assurance you will stay quiet and
till."

Belle grunted her agreement and again nodded. The
man pulled the ball out, keeping his fingers clear of her
eeth, and dropped it into his pocket.

"Now," he said, "what you are about to watch is a
ive video feed—live, as in it's happening in four-eighty-
ine Bristol Court right this very instant."

Belle stared in disbelief at the full-color projection.
The footage was unquestionably taken from her sister's
astefully and lovingly decorated condominium. She
was certain that the woman sleeping alone in the queen-
ize bed, was Jillian, also a nurse, and one of the main
easons Belle herself had chosen the profession. Upon
he automobile deaths of their parents, Jillian had
tepped in to raise her fourteen-year-old sister, often
naking major sacrifices in her personal life. Belle con-
idered her to be the kindest, brightest, most centered
erson she had ever known. The camera had been
laced above the valance in the bedroom. At the sight
of Jillian, rolling languidly from her left side to her
ack, Belle began to hyperventilate again.

"Easy," the man warned. "Slow down. That's it. . . .
That's it."

"Please. Please don't hurt her."

The apparition holding the phone leaned forward.
Belle cringed as his empty eyes came level with her
wn. His pale white skin was tinted blue, a ghoulish illu-
ion cast by her ecologically friendly halogen lights.

"You must calm down your breathing and listen,
Ms. Coates. To save your sister's life, and yourself from

a great deal of pain, it is essential that you believe I will do as I say."

"I believe. I believe. Turn it off. Turn that camera off and leave her alone."

"I'm going to make you a promise, Ms. Coates," he whispered, his lips brushing her ear. "I promise that if you fail to follow my instructions, Jillian will die, and die quite horribly. Do as I say and she lives. Want proof? Look here."

He held the phone at eye-level.

"Enough," Belle pleaded. "Don't hurt her."

"I've placed small canisters of a potent nerve gas above the door frame inside the closet. From this phone I can control how much of the gas is released simply by tapping my finger. Incredible, yes? I am a virtuoso operating this set-up. I put another camera in Jillian's bathroom because I want you to see what happens when just a smidge of this gas is inhaled."

"No, please. Please stop this. I believe you."

The intruder paid no attention. It was as if he had planned this demonstration all along. Belle's brain was spinning. How could she believe him? How could she not? What choice did she have? Would he really spare Jillian as he promised? Why would he? Why wouldn't he? The unanswerable questions roiled on and on.

"If I wanted to," he said as if reading her thoughts, "I could kill your sister—I could kill *anyone*—any time, any place, and in any way I wish. But the point is I don't have to. I don't even want to. She seems like a nice woman. And as I said, there is nothing in her death for me."

He made two gentle taps on the phone's display, and

Jillian's quaint bathroom came into focus, illuminated by a night light beside the sink, and a small diamond-shaped window above the tub.

"There are four levels of gas I can administer. The first three will cause increasing pain and the symptoms you are about to see. The fourth will kill . . . slowly. This is level one."

Within seconds, Jillian, wearing flannel pajamas Belle had bought for her, burst into the frame, fell onto her knees, and began retching violently into the toilet. Between bouts, she lay clenched in a fetal position on the tiled floor, shivering uncontrollably.

"Can you believe that's only level one?" the man asked. "I think I should patent this delivery system."

"Stop it! Stop doing this to her," Belle cried.

"Keep it down or I'll cut your larynx out and set it on the table. I'm sensing you need a bit more motivation, Ms. Coates. Allow me to oblige by upping Jillian's misery to level two. I'll keep it on level two until you start copying this note. Audio is really a must to get the full effect."

He tapped his phone's display again, and now Belle could hear Jillian's grunting, labored breathing, interrupted by fits of gut-wrenching vomiting and sobs of pain.

"Please . . . stop . . . I believe you. I believe you."

He loosened her left hand and pushed the note she was to copy in front of her.

"Start writing your farewell letter, Ms. Coates. When you do, I'll stop killing your sister," he said.

Belle's face contorted in agony at the sound of Jillian's unrelenting anguish.

"Please . . ."

"Do you need more volume? Write the damn note!" the monster barked, pounding the table with each word. "You're dead regardless. But you can still save your sister's life; that is, if you have the courage to do the right thing."

The man shut off the gas as soon as Belle began to write. In just a minute, Jillian's moaning stopped. Belle managed to pen the first four words before she began to sob.

"Finish," he said, "or I'll fire it up again."

"Why me? I haven't done anything wrong. I don't even know you. Why do you want me to die?"

"Not my call. Somebody in this great big world of ours has decided you have to go. And that somebody is paying me to make it happen. I can do it to you alone or to both of you."

"This is insane," she said, as much to herself as to the man who was about to murder her. "This is absolutely insane."

"I guess you enjoy listening to your sister scream. Allow me to show you level three."

The tormented retching Belle heard could scarcely be described as human. On the tiny video display, Jillian's body convulsed more violently than before. As soon as Belle lifted up the pen again, the man pressed a button on his phone and her sister's screaming stopped. Belle found the strength to finish copying the note.

"I'm a man of my word, Ms. Coates. I'm also very good with handwriting and I have a large sample of yours from your journal. Mess with this and I'll dismember you joint by joint with that ball stuck back in your mouth. You'll still be alive to watch when I finally jack up the gas in Jillian's pad to level four."

"I did as you asked. Let her go."

"Sign it." The man studied the note with great care. "Okay, now the pills."

He shook the pills onto the table, motioning her to take one.

"Please," Belle begged, still trying to make inroads into the utter helplessness she was feeling. "Who's paying you? Why do they want to kill me?"

"I'm running out of time and patience."

The man pressed a button on his phone like a puppet master pulling on invisible strings. Jillian's body again twitched with violent spasms.

"No! You promised!" Belle cried.

"You have the power to make this easier on Jillian. Think of all your sister has done for you. You owe it to her, don't you? Make me stop. I want you to stop me, Ms. Coates."

She could not listen to her sister's cries anymore. Her only thought was of the man's chilling proclamation.

You're dead regardless.

As though in a trance, her hand shakily reached out. Jillian's moaning abated as soon as Belle swallowed the first pill.

"Please . . . don't. No more."

"Keep swallowing and that's the last time you have to hear that nasty sound, Ms. Coates.

Belle tightened her jaw and nodded that she understood.

"Promise?" Her voice sounded like a child's. "I said do you promise?"

"Ms. Coates, I might be a killer, but I'm a professional. You have my word. But I'm going to resume torturing your beloved sister unless all these pills are down the hatch."

It was too much to take. Belle raced to swallow the pills.

What else can I do? her mind kept asking. *What else can I do? . . . What else can I do?*

The action, in a way, was liberating. Her heart rate slowed and her tears stopped. In minutes, she no longer felt agitated or even frightened. The man's eyes, once haunting, now made her feel nothing at all.

"Good girl. You are simply going to close your eyes and go to sleep."

Her tongue already felt heavy. "You promised," Belle managed.

"You have my word."

After a while, he filled the tub, then undid her restraints.

"Clothes," he said.

Feeling the wooziness of the drug take further hold, Belle stepped out of her scrubs and dropped her bra and panties onto the floor.

Then she stepped into the tub.

"I love you, Jillian," she murmured. "I love you."